"*Midnight's Budding Morrow* is a moving portrayal of God's grace in the midst of tragedy and sorrow. Sarah and James's relationship is forged in fire, but it is all the stronger for it. This second installment in the Regency Wallflowers series has a message of redemption and forgiveness which is sure to resonate with readers of inspirational romance."
—ALISSA BAXTER, author of *The Earl's Lady Geologist*

"What a rich, lovely atmosphere! A crumbling estate that shelters a crumbling family is the backdrop to this story of unlikely love. A reserved yet resourceful young woman slips quietly into a muddled household, hoping desperately to one day belong—especially where it concerns her roguish husband, who isn't such a rogue anymore. For all the darkness and shadowy corridors in this novel, hope and surprising tenderness grace the pages. Fans of Julie Klassen and Abigail Wilson will delight in this newest offering from Regency favorite Carolyn Miller."
—JOANNA DAVIDSON POLITANO, author of *A Midnight Dance*

"Miller takes the reader on a journey of poignancy and hope as she weaves Sarah and James's story, making *Midnight's Budding Morrow* difficult to put down. I loved it."
—JENNIE GOUTET, author of the Clavering Chronicles series

"So wonderful! Sarah and James, from their disastrous first meeting, through their worsening misunderstandings, to their ultimate happily ever after, captured my heart and brought tears to my eyes. What more can I say about this amazing book? What more can I say except more! More!"
—JULIANNA DEERING, author of the Drew Farthering Mystery series

"What a delightful read! Peppered with charming characters and the best sort of rogue, Miller's latest captivating romance is rooted beautifully by the threads of redemption and hope. This marriage of convenience story simply drew me in and wouldn't let me ~   ire to recommend!"
—ABIGAIL WILSON, au   ss

Midnight's
Budding Morrow

REGENCY BRIDES:
A LEGACY OF GRACE

◇◇◇◇◇◇◇◇◇◇◇◇◇◇◇◇◇◇◇◇◇

The Elusive Miss Ellison
The Captivating Lady Charlotte
The Dishonorable Miss DeLancey

REGENCY BRIDES:
A PROMISE OF HOPE

◇◇◇◇◇◇◇◇◇◇◇◇◇◇◇◇◇◇◇◇◇

Winning Miss Winthrop
Miss Serena's Secret
The Making of Mrs. Hale

REGENCY BRIDES:
DAUGHTERS OF AYNSLEY

◇◇◇◇◇◇◇◇◇◇◇◇◇◇◇◇◇◇◇◇◇

A Hero for Miss Hatherleigh
Underestimating Miss Cecilia
Misleading Miss Verity

REGENCY WALLFLOWERS

◇◇◇◇◇◇◇◇◇◇◇◇◇◇◇◇◇◇◇◇◇

Dusk's Darkest Shores
Midnight's Budding Morrow
Dawn's Untrodden Green

REGENCY WALLFLOWERS

Midnight's Budding Morrow

CAROLYN MILLER

Midnight's Budding Morrow
© 2022 by Carolyn Miller

Published by Kregel Publications, a division of Kregel Inc., 2450 Oak Industrial Dr. NE, Grand Rapids, MI 49505. www.kregel.com.

The persons and events portrayed in this work are the creations of the author, and any resemblance to persons living or dead is purely coincidental.

Scripture quotations are from the King James Version.

Cataloging-in-Publication Data is available from the Library of Congress.

ISBN 978-0-8254-4654-2, print
ISBN 978-0-8254-7684-6, epub
ISBN 978-0-8254-6850-6, Kindle

Printed in the United States of America
22 23 24 25 26 27 28 29 30 31 / 5 4 3 2 1

To all those who dare to forgive

. . . on the shores of darkness there is light,
And precipices show untrodden green,
There is a budding morrow in midnight,
There is a triple sight in blindness keen.

John Keats, "To Homer"

Chapter 1

"Oh, Sarah, please. Please? What would it take for you to reconsider?"

"But I am needed here." Sarah Drayton smiled to ease her friend's disappointment. Well, her presence was not needed here exactly—a thousand balls could take place and she would not be missed—but at her aunt and uncle's in nearby Hartsdale.

"But *I* need you more," Beatrice Langley complained. "And really, why would you not want to come visit me? Am I not your oldest and best friend?" Her bottom lip protruded in a childlike pout.

"You are certainly my oldest friend, and you must know such an invitation holds a degree of interest. To be sure, I would enjoy the chance to finally see the sea," she teased.

"I see. I'm merely a degree of interest, am I?" Beatrice asked, eyebrows aloft, before pleading further. "You simply must come. Langley is a little shabby these days, but it *is* interesting. And I know you would enjoy seeing a place which has hosted many important people over the years."

Sarah laughed. "You are incorrigible, that's what you are."

"Runs in the family, so I'm told." Beatrice's lips curved with wryness.

A flicker of interest pulsed. No, she would *not* indulge in common curiosity and ask about her former school friend's older brother. But incorrigibility and James Langley seemed to go hand in hand, or so the rumors said.

"*Dearest* Sarah, you have no idea just how lonesome it can be living at Langley."

"Yes, with all that family, and all those servants, and all those parties you write about in your letters. I imagine it must be terribly hard, Bea."

Beatrice's blue eyes shadowed. "There is only Father and James now, and there have been far fewer parties of late. I'm afraid the place is falling into decay, so it seems overwhelming at times." She smoothed the pale-rose skirt of her silk gown. "Which is why I was ever so glad to learn you would be here tonight, so I could speak to you in person about such things."

Sarah's heart twisted. Perhaps Aunt Patricia and Uncle Loftus would be sympathetic for her to leave them to spend some time with a friend whose situation somewhat resembled Sarah's own.

"I will ask my aunt and uncle and see if they can spare me."

"Sarah, you are the truest of friends."

Sarah smiled as anticipation surged through her veins. To exchange the drear of duty to live in a castle by the sea? Who else would hesitate? Had she not prayed just this morning for God to direct her paths? Was this of His leading?

An older gentleman moved into view, his attention fixed on Beatrice, as had been the case all evening.

Not that Sarah minded. Fading into the background was her wont, after all.

"Ah, Miss Langley. We are honored with your presence tonight."

"Good evening, Sir John. May I introduce you to my dear friend, Miss Drayton? Sarah, this is Sir John Willoughby, one of our neighbors."

He barely spared Sarah a glance, the merest nod, a brief word.

Beatrice narrowed her eyes and drew Sarah's arm into her own. "I don't think you understand, Sir John. Miss Drayton is one of my oldest friends—we have known each other from the schoolroom—have we not, Sarah?—and she has promised to come and pay me a lengthy visit in the not-very-distant future. Isn't that quite marvelous?"

"Why, ahem, quite, er, marvelous, I am sure." His lips turned up in the semblance of a smile. "Anyone who is a friend of my dear Miss Langley is sure to be a friend of mine."

Sarah bowed her head, hiding her amusement at the man's pomposity, even as she struggled to discern the nature of their friendship. That the man was enamored of Beatrice was plain, but did her bright-eyed friend return his regard? It did not appear so. She would have to wait for a gap in this post-dinner conversation to make polite enquiry.

The two moved to the side in conversation, but Sarah remained by the pillar. With her unadorned cream gown and plain pale features, she would almost blend into the wall. Her attire was several years out-of-date, and she had been made acutely aware of this by the dismissive glances cast her way from Durham's fashionable and rich. Normally she did not mind, but tonight . . .

Something astringent seemed to have entered the room. Something that tipped her heart toward unease, toward a vague sense of fear. She shook her head, lifted her chin higher. How foolish. She wasn't normally one taken in by such fancies.

She glanced around the rest of the room, noting the titled, the wealthy and assured. There was Lord Danver, a peer in his late forties said to be abominably wealthy, his politeness to all evident in the way he patiently listened, even as his dark eyes seemed tinged with weary sorrow. There was Miss Georgiana Barnstaple, a fussily dressed blonde whom Beatrice had said was one of her blackguard brother's greatest admirers, "but he never has any time for her." There were other notables too, most of whom treated Sarah with indifference, unless it involved a raised-nose sneer at her clothes. Ah, well. It was a good thing she would but rarely meet with such people.

Sarah accepted a glass of punch from a passing servant as the couples assembled for the first dance. The music began, but her mind wandered from the melody. How best to approach her aunt about the proposed visit? It was not as if her mother's sister actually ever had any meaningful work for her to do, save acting as an unpaid housekeeper of sorts. And at Sarah's advanced age, she was certainly not bound by any duty save that of the familial, which Aunt Patricia had exploited to such an extent that none of the warmer feelings of family connections remained. Perhaps an appeal to her aunt's well-developed sense of economies might work: one less mouth to feed, one less person constantly in the way.

Ears pricking at the name of Langley, she grew aware of voices speaking behind her.

"Such a temper I've never seen!"

"Gets it from the old man, if you ask me."

"Aye, that's for sure and for certain. How that lass ever got her sweetness I'll never know."

"They say—" Here the voices dipped in volume to make the words indiscernible.

Sarah's ears strained, wishing to hear more, even as she despised herself to be so low as to want to know gossip about her friend and her relations. She wrinkled her nose at her transgression and inched away from temptation, closer to the window.

A gush of new arrivals brought another man into view, brimming with vitality and good looks. He glanced around the room, features narrowing when he saw Beatrice and her admirer, and hurried down the steps to speak to her.

"Bea." He clutched her arm, drawing her a few steps away from Sir John and across to the window without apology. "I've come at last."

"Oh, thank goodness!" Beatrice's previously bored features now lit with an internal glow. She caught Sarah's gaze and motioned her forward, body angling in such a way that Sir John was excluded. "Peter, I want you to meet my dear friend, Sarah Drayton."

The man's green eyes sparkled. "Ah, the famous Miss Drayton. At last we meet."

"Indeed we do, Mister . . . ?"

"Oh, forgive me," Beatrice said. "This is Peter Grayling, a . . . a friend."

"A friend?" His quick glance at Beatrice seemed to hold a degree of disappointment. "Is that all?" he added in an undertone.

"All for now," Beatrice murmured.

Sarah curtsied to his short bow, heart alive with interest. Now *this* was more the sort of man she could envisage her vivacious friend having as a suitor. She peeked over her shoulder at the rumpled brow of Sir John.

He seemed to notice her noticing him and hurried away to speak to Beatrice's elderly father situated across the room. Urgent whispers and gesticulations made it apparent that neither man was enamored with

Beatrice's choice of beau, but Beatrice and Mr. Grayling remained caught in their bubble of mutual admiration.

Sarah sighed. The dance had concluded and couples were re-forming lines to prepare for the next. Near the door, Mr. Langley and Sir John continued their discussion, ignoring the two new guests stumbling their way down the steps, even as the shorter one shot the older men a scowl.

Who were these gentlemen? A few years older than Beatrice, of a similar vintage to Bea's beau, they appeared cavalier in their presentation, careless of their lurching movements that suggested they had imbibed rather too heavily before their attendance tonight. The taller one with blond hair seemed oblivious to the whispers behind raised hands, while the shorter, dark-haired man almost reveled in it, eyes taking in the room as if glorying in the attention.

He paused, focus fixing on Beatrice and her suitor, and he moved through the twirling couples without care for how his movements impeded theirs. "Beatrice," he pronounced loudly.

Definitely drunk. Sarah eyed him with disfavor. Who dared speak to a young lady so?

"Whatever are you doing with thish puppy?" he slurred, gesturing to Mr. Grayling.

Beatrice blanched, while Mr. Grayling's slackened jaw suggested he was dumbstruck. A glance across the room revealed Mr. Langley and Sir John had absented themselves, perhaps to find food. Or to avoid such shameful scenes.

As if sensing Sarah's disapproval, the newcomer turned to her. "Something to say, Miss Prim?"

"Prim?" Beatrice protested. "No, no, this is Miss Drayton, my friend."

His eyes narrowed. "Looking down her nose at me as though she thinks I'm spoony drunk." He lurched closer, a gold chain glinting at his throat, his beery breath igniting a spark of fear.

"Forgive me, sir," Sarah murmured. "I did not mean to give offense."

"Leave her," Beatrice implored. "Go talk to Papa instead."

"Father?" The man uttered a curse word. "Barely looked at me when I walked in. Too busy talking to Sir Pompous Jack O'Dandy."

Papa? Father? Did this mean this man was—?

"Sarah, allow me to introduce my brother, Captain James Langley."

The captain gave a mock bow, the movement tipping him to his knees, where he gave a great shout of laughter, unmindful of the humiliation of his sister.

Around them the music paused, the dancing stilled, the atmosphere grew thick with shame and ignominy.

"Cap'n Blackwood, get us another pot of Sir John Barleycorn," he cried. "And a shovel of port for Miss Soursides here. She looks as if she could do with a good drink."

Sarah blinked, took a step back, as his taller friend grinned and enquired loudly for two large strong drinks.

"Afraid of me, are you?" With surprising quickness Captain Langley rose and drew close, his dark-green eyes fixed on her, mouth a twisted sneer. "I'll give you something to remember me by." And in one swift movement he closed the space between them, his hands jerking her to himself as his alcohol-soaked mouth pressed down on hers.

She struggled for air, pushed away, slapping his cheek with a *thwack* that echoed off the walls, then wiped a hand across her contaminated lips as she stumbled back. "How dare you?"

"Sarah, I'm so sorry!" Beatrice hurried forward and grasped her arm, then hurried her up the stairs and into an anteroom, away from the shocked whispers and stares. "Oh, forgive me, forgive him. James is so lost he barely knows what he does anymore."

"Has . . . had he done that before?" Sarah's heart still thumped wildly. If only she could scrub away the scent of his breath, the feel of his arms, the shocking violence of her first kiss.

"He's not well," Beatrice murmured, evading Sarah's gaze. "I only ask you don't let this stop your visit."

She shook her head. "I cannot stay at Langley House if he is there. I *will* not visit if he is there."

"He shan't be, I assure you. James is returning to the army, which is probably why he's here for one last merriment before he ships abroad. How I wish I could make this up to you. You have no idea how sorry I am." Shame and sorrow shone in her friend's eyes.

Beatrice could not be blamed for her unfortunate brother. "You are sure he will not come?"

"He won't. He and Papa do not get on."

"Really?" The sarcasm was thick.

"I beg of you, do not hold his behavior against me."

Sarah exhaled and slumped into a round-backed wooden chair. "You promise I need never see him again?"

"I give you my word." Beatrice placed her hand on her chest. "If he does happen to visit, I'll see you are locked inside the tower."

"How reassuring," she said dryly, even as her heart prickled. Beatrice's castle had a tower?

"Please, Sarah?"

She sighed. "Oh, very well."

She would not permit Captain James Langley to impede her one chance to grasp a new life. She would go as Beatrice's friend, and pray she'd never see the scoundrel again.

The smell of alcohol and cigars scented the air, and a distant grumbling sound permeated his dream. James cracked open an eye. Sunlight stabbed, piercing the relentless thumping of his brain. He closed his eyelid, willed himself back to sleep. He needed rest, just as he'd needed to extract every last ounce of pleasure from these remaining few days.

The past nights of carousing seemed to have soaked into his bones, the nights of drinking until the dice turned against him leaving him headsore and out of sorts. Drinking deeply didn't mend the ache. Women didn't meet his need. Reckless play might give a thrill of anticipation, but soon the guilt washed in. He was weary, unutterably weary, a broken stick washed in on the shore, useless, waiting, wishing for purpose, wanting futilely to be more.

James groaned, the pounding in his head drowning out the last wisps of a dreamed life he occasionally doubted had ever really happened. Some days he wished he need not wake. Some days he couldn't believe he'd once been happy. That he had known a softer world. Until life had shown that even the softest of people could not be trusted. Those days of happiness had been an illusion, a zephyr of his existence, a place he could never find again.

Nausea from last night's imbibing rose, and he swallowed, forced his thoughts away from the mistakes of the past and focused on deep breathing to gain control over far more recent ones. Why he had allowed Blackwood to convince him to visit that seedy club in Newcastle, he had no recollection. Or perhaps he had convinced Blackwood. Regardless, his body was protesting the excesses of the night, even as the sounds from the laneway outside insisted he face the day.

"Blackwood?"

A grunted sound stole into his ears, but still he did not open his eyes. He rolled to his other side, hoping it might convince the sloshing feeling in his stomach to settle.

Some days he hated himself. Loathed, despised, grew sick at himself. Like today. Two days after that insipid ball and despite the ocean of alcohol he'd consumed, it had only blurred the edges of his memory. He had still not forgotten that kiss. Her shock. That slap.

His lips lifted. Call him a scoundrel—join the long queue—but he'd been surprised by the forceful slap. Who'd have thought Miss Prim had it in her?

He supposed he shouldn't have done it. She was Bea's friend, after all. But he was never one to let conventions get in the way of the inspiration of the moment. When he'd succumbed to the temptation of his baser self, he'd expected to meet lips as lemonish as the sour expression she wore. But they hadn't been, and if it hadn't been for that slap he might've been further tempted—

No. James coughed. He must be coming down with something. He was starting to imagine all sorts of bizarre things. He was obviously suffering from a condition that could only be remedied by more of the liquid he liked to pour down his throat.

Another cough, but none of the wretched fire in his lungs that signaled a return of the fever, his reward for serving King and country. Only the fire of wretchedness that pulsed through his veins since that day near two decades ago, the day he'd never forgive himself for.

A pounding at the door matched the one inside his head. "Langley?" a deep voice called. "Langley? You in there?"

Lethargic eyelids now flew open as a hammering deepened in his veins. He knew that voice. Knew what that man wanted. The vagueness of last night's drunken exploits sharpened into awful clarity and he muttered a curse. "Blackwood," he hissed, pushing to a seated position.

The great lump of a man didn't stir.

Head reeling, James staggered upright, tugged on his breeches, moved to his friend, and shook his arm.

"Whatsa matter?" Blackwood slurred.

"Tell Carter I've returned to London."

"What?"

James gathered his few possessions, stuffing them into his pockets.

The pounding came at the door again. "Langley?" The voice cut like a sword between honor and self-preservation.

Blackwood was an army man; he could take care of himself. Besides, it was James from whom Carter wished to extract his pound of flesh. James hastened to the opened window, quickly calculating the drop to the ground as the great thumps at the door suggested Carter was heaving into it with his shoulder. He had but a matter of mere seconds now.

"See you in London, Blackwood," he said, shifting his legs over the windowsill.

"London?"

"London," James affirmed. "Until then." He offered a sardonic smile and grasped firm hold of the window frame, pausing for a moment as the excesses of past nights blurred his vision and made his head swim.

But there was not a moment to waste. This was neither the first time he'd found cause to escape from his creditors, nor the first time he'd resorted to bending the truth in order to ensure his safety.

For to London he would go, just not immediately.

Instead he'd go and attempt to scrounge money from the old tyrant at the place he'd sworn he'd never return to. The place which haunted his dreams. The place which had destroyed his life.

For everyone knew there was no cause to seek for him there.

Not at the crumbling ruin known as Langley House.

Chapter 2

"Not long to go now, miss," the driver shouted from the bench next to her as they jostled down the lane.

Sarah nodded at Jem, the creaks and groans of the ancient cart permitting little more than loud exclamations to be heard. Never mind. She was busy getting her fill of the autumn-ripened scenery. The last of the common pink heather of the moors had given way to burnished grasses, and it was all so beautiful, so wildly fascinating. Her eyes soaked in all the glory now that they had left the rush and hustle of the city.

When the Mail had arrived at the Newcastle Inn, she had climbed from the carriage expecting to be met by a servant dressed in the Langley livery as per their arrangement, but instead she had been met with a hastily scrawled note from Beatrice. In it, Beatrice apologized for the lack of personal transport, assuring Sarah that the driver who would meet her was reliable, and all would be explained upon her arrival. Such a put-off only seemed on par for Sarah's situation so far. Her aunt and uncle had been nonplussed at her desire to leave, unable to understand why she might wish to have an adventure and see something of the world rather than continue as unpaid labor in the dullness and drear of the cold manse in a tiny village at the junction of Yorkshire's most northerly dales.

Now, anticipation mixed with a strain of trepidation. Would she be so unfortunate as to encounter Beatrice's brother again? She hoped—she prayed—she would not. She had barely been able to forget his actions that had left her feeling violated and soiled. Anger churned within anew. How dared he treat a woman unknown to him—his sister's friend, no less!—in such a despicable, degrading manner? The man certainly lived up to his deplorable reputation as a wicked rakehell.

The cart dipped into a deep rut and wedged, throwing Sarah against Jem's homespun-clothed shoulder. She murmured an apology and straightened, pushing her bonnet back from her eyes as a fine curricle approached. The features of the occupants—a young man and younger woman—were soon distinguished, and it was with a sinking heart she recognized the young blonde as Miss Barnstaple, her haughtiness as apparent as it had been at the assembly a week earlier.

Sarah affixed a smile. Would they afford her acknowledgment?

The curricle moved on, the gentleman driving seemingly oblivious to Jem's pleas for them to stop and help.

"Well!" Sarah peered over her shoulder at the retreating couple, whose laughter floated upon the air. A groan summoned her attention to the poor cart driver below. "Oh, Mr. Jem, forgive me! I should assist you."

She jumped down, and, ignoring his protests, removed her pelisse, flung off her foolish bonnet, and assisted him in pushing the cart's wheel from the muddy groove in the road.

"Oh, thank ye, miss," Jem gasped, his face red with exertion. "I shouldna be surprised young Barnstaple didnae want to stop, so I'm right glad for your help. But I'm verra sorry that you've spoiled your fine dress."

She glanced down. The hem of her third best gown was coated in at least five inches of thick dark mud, a spatter of which now spotted her bodice. So much for wishing to make a good first impression. "Ah, well. It will clean." She hoped. "Is the cart able to be driven now?"

"Aye. Hop on up, and we'll be there in two shakes of a lamb's tail."

She inwardly smiled at the expression as she resumed her seat. At least she had a chance to compose herself in these upcoming minutes, as well as attempt to mend her appearance. The cart eased around a corner, through a thicket of elms, and she caught a glimpse of shining water.

"That be the North Sea."

Breath suspended. "How beautiful!" Diamond glints twinkled grey and green and blue as far as the eye could see. She was used to the vast openness of the dales, of waving grass and stray sheep across barren fells and tors. But this . . . this was something quite different, so wild, so endless, so free. "I have never seen the sea before."

"You get used to it after a while, it be always there. There be some folks who can't stand the sound of the waves, nor the storms we see here."

"I don't imagine that ever being a problem for me."

"Now, as we go down this hill, take a look just beyond that tree."

She followed his pointing finger. All the air escaped her lungs, as a heart-deep tug accompanied the strangest sense of recognition, almost as if her destiny lay beyond the high stone walls.

"That be Langley House, or as folks like to call it around here, *the castle.*"

She studied the great structure greedily, the round grey towers jutting into the sky against a backdrop of silver-blue sea, dominating the landscape, its authority and power undeniable. Tall walls topped with battlements led to rectangular towers closer to the shoreline, one of which seemed partly ruined, while another overlooked a small harbor.

"That further one be Lilith Tower, the other Egyncleugh. That means 'eagle's ravine' in the local dialect."

Egyncleugh. She sounded the word on her tongue. Ee-gan-cluff. This was a different world indeed. They reached the top of another rise, and Jem pulled the horse to a standstill. From here she could see the castle's reflection in the long stretches of still water: tall, imposing, grand. "Is it on an island?"

"Near enough. They be man-made lakes, *meres* we call 'em, with a causeway built between 'em. But on very high tides, the water covers the causeway, and it be island enough."

A tremor of excitement rippled up her spine as she studied the broken tower. "It seems perfectly gothic."

"They say there be ghosts that haunt the place."

"Truly?" Why had Beatrice never mentioned this?

"Aye. A chambermaid caught in the sea, and a long-ago relative of the current Langleys thought to have been lost in the tunnels underneath whilst searching for treasure."

"Treasure? You jest, surely."

"The castle has been here far longer than you or I, miss. I wouldn't be too quick to scoff if I were you."

The churning inside increased. While she would continue to scoff at apparitions and the like, perhaps this wasn't a wise idea after all. And why, oh why, had Beatrice never mentioned the grand magnitude of her home, instead describing it as a little run-down?

She shivered and drew her pelisse tight around her throat.

They commenced their descent, as Jem pointed out other landmarks: the nearby village of Langburgh, tucked beside the tiny harbor, with its small church complete with tall spire. The magnificent iron gates that led down a long drive to another grand residence, Knaresborough Hall, that was occupied by the Barnstaple family—the son and daughter of which had passed them on the road, Jem said. In the distance a silhouette of a tower was pointed out as the residence belonging to Sir John Willoughby, the baronet and local magistrate she'd met at the party, whose family had often accounted themselves as the most important in the district, according to Jem.

But it's always been the Langley family who the village looked up to, he continued. They might not have a title, but they always had the money and the heart to care for the village. "Well, they did," he finished uncertainly.

They did? What had changed? "And the Barnstaples?"

"Nowt but new folk," he sniffed. "Been here for less than thirty years. Like to think they can mix with the old, but they dinna yet know it's how you treat others that shows whether you are truly worth respectin'."

She nodded, eyes widening as the cart veered from the road through a large fortress-like gate, with lichen covered stone walls stretching for what seemed like miles. Beyond a few scraggy trees outlining the drive, the road lowered to a causeway, stretching in a straight line between the two lakes, the meres half filled with water. Stones clattered beneath the wheels as momentum sped their journey, then they were on the causeway proper, as the castle entrance loomed ever larger.

Her insides tightened, as if bracing for what awaited. "It's awe-inspiring."

"Aye."

What a dramatic and intimidating way of entry, with its carved stone gargoyles and crenellations. Two imposing drum-shaped towers stood on either side of the gatehouse, the slitted windows like narrowed eyes peering out to see who dared come this way. A figure appeared in the second-story tower, and Sarah leaned forward to gain a better view, but the person retreated.

"I hope you'll be happy here, miss."

"I do too," she acknowledged. "Miss Langley has assured me of a warm welcome."

He cast her a swift glance but said nothing, and they passed the thick stone walls under the raised portcullis and moved into the shadows of the curved entranceway. Ahead, inside the great courtyard, an imposing square tower three stories high was flanked either side by long mullioned glass windows and Medusa-like tentacles of ivy. A scattering of other buildings, no doubt once used for all sorts of medieval purposes, surrounded the weed-infested cobblestoned square. Beyond, lay a number of other buildings in various stages of disrepair.

She bit her lip. Just what had she got herself into?

Ahead, a massive oak door studded with nails opened, and Beatrice appeared, followed by several servants, her obvious joy chasing away trepidation. "Oh, you are finally here!"

Sarah descended to give her friend a hug. "I'm ever so glad to see you. That was a long journey."

Beatrice's eyes shadowed. "I'm so sorry we could not meet you ourselves. Things have been a little topsy-turvy here."

"Mr. Jem has been very kind." Sarah smiled up at him.

He tipped his hat and advised a servant which of the items in the back were to be removed.

"Thank you, Jem," Beatrice called.

He tipped his hat again, and offered Sarah a friendly nod before steering his humble equipage out through the great gatehouse once more.

"Put Miss Drayton's trunk in the Blue Room, please, Robert."

A wizened male servant nodded and hefted Sarah's small trunk on his shoulders.

Sarah watched with concern. "Is he strong enough?"

"How many books did you pack?" Beatrice teased. "I told you it was not necessary. Our library may be old and dusty, but it has many volumes you can enjoy."

Sarah's lips lifted as she looked up at the commanding walls, eyes skipping over the gargoyles that scowled down with such ferocity. "This is . . . there are simply no words, Bea. I never realized your home would be quite so, quite so . . ." She shrugged helplessly.

"It is rather spectacular, I'll grant you that. But I sometimes wish I could live in a small abode somewhere, where we weren't always worried whether the roof will leak or if a tower shall crumble during a storm."

"Oh, to have the problems of the rich," Sarah teased.

Beatrice's look of amusement faded. "I am very sorry we did not meet you. It felt the height of rudeness, when you were coming at my invitation, but Father, and, oh—" She bit her lip.

"What is it?"

"You will despise me."

"Never," Sarah said promptly. "Nothing you could say could impair my good opinion of you. Now, what is it?"

"It's James," Bea whispered, casting a look around, as if she feared being overheard.

Sarah's heart froze. "What about him?" she asked slowly.

"He's here. He arrived without warning, gave us all the greatest shock, I assure you. Oh my dear"—she clasped Sarah's arm—"I understand you may not wish to stay now, and I cannot fault you for desiring to leave, but I assure you that if you do decide to stay, then the castle is big enough you need scarcely see him. He is out today and must return soon to the army anyway. He and Father have never got on, and already have quarreled about the usual—money and Mama . . ." Bea's eyes sheened.

At the sight of her friend's tears, Sarah's first instinct to leave immediately thawed. As disheartening as this turn of events was, something deeper urged her to selflessness and to stay.

What trouble could a man cause whom she would barely see?

Sarah patted her arm. "It is of no matter. I am here, ready to ease your boredom, is that not right?"

"Yes." Beatrice clutched her arm. "Truly, you are sure you do not mind?"

No. But she sensed this was the right thing to do. "I have no wish to let the unpleasantness of the past intrude upon my delight in spending time with my dearest friend."

"I am so *very* glad you've come." Beatrice enfolded her in a swift hug. "Now"—she led her inside—"I must take you to see Father, then I'll show you to your room. It has the most splendid view of the sea, which I know you'll enjoy. Then there are a few servants I will make you known to."

The stone-floored antechamber opened into a huge dark-timbered hall, the high walls stretching to soaring rafters and a wooden ceiling carved into a multitude of medieval designs. High above, small leaden-paned windows permitted some light to alleviate the sense of gloom and highlighted a series of giant pictures positioned as if to guard the space.

The men and women were attired in clothes revealing the past ages, but in the final portrait a man and woman were dressed in more contemporary style. The young man resembled Beatrice's father, which meant the beautiful woman wearing a lovely pearl necklace must be her mother.

"This is the Great Hall," Beatrice explained, leading her past the stone fireplace, the dimensions suggesting one could easily roast a large pig. "Father is in the library, so we shall go there."

Sarah's insides tensed. From all Beatrice had said in the past, and Sarah's very brief meeting with him a week ago, Beatrice's father was not particularly genial or warmhearted. A retired military man—what might he ever have to say to her?

Beatrice pushed open a door to a red-and-gold-stripe wallpapered room, one lined with dusty bookshelves and cobwebs. A fire sputtered in the hearth, before which sat Mr. Langley.

She eyed him curiously. He seemed older, his face more lined, the thick dark brows and square chin the only evidence of his kinship with Bea. She smoothed down her pelisse, wishing it was less wrinkled and longer, and thus would hide the brown stains marring her gown's hem. Would he notice, or be oblivious, as her uncle often seemed to be?

"Father, Miss Drayton has arrived."

He grunted and glanced up from the book he'd been perusing.

Her mouth dried.

His gaze was piercing and not kind. And most certainly *did* seem to notice she was not as precisely trim as she'd wish to be.

She curtsied. "Good afternoon, sir."

He grunted again.

Was that his chief form of communication? No wonder Beatrice had been so keen to have her here.

"I am going to take Sarah up to settle in now. I thought we'd put her in the Blue Room. It has such a lovely outlook after all."

He nodded, his attention returning to his book, leaving Sarah to feel as if she had been summarily dismissed.

"Don't mind him," Beatrice assured in a hushed voice, as they exited the room toward a grand central staircase. "He has not been well since . . . oh, never mind."

Sarah followed her up the stairs, and along a hall whose carpet was worn and thin. A sense of gentle decrepitude floated on the musty air. How many servants did they have? Were they all as aged as this house seemed to be?

"I wish Mrs. Copley would see to this," Beatrice muttered, lifting a dark-smudged finger from the banister.

"Is she the housekeeper?"

"Supposedly. More of a glorified maid really, but Father has always been reluctant to let the old staff go. Not when they are willing to work here for pride more than wages." Beatrice stopped, faced Sarah with wide eyes. "I don't mean to sound disloyal, but oh, if you only knew what it is to finally be able to speak of these things."

Sarah held her tongue. Having lived with an aunt inclined to cantankerous and frugal ways, she knew only too well the challenges associated with showing deference to one who seemed to scarcely notice such courtesy.

"Enough of such misery." Beatrice reached the second-to-last door. "Look, here we are." She flung open the door, revealing a light-filled bedchamber decorated in blues and cream.

"Oh my." The room would easily be thrice the size of her bedchamber at the manse, with its large four-poster tester bed and dresser. The rugs on the parquet floor possessed a similar hue to the blue brocade that lined the walls, and likely had been there for years, for both were slightly faded in places. Above hung a modest chandelier, which might not often be used, given the wall sconces held candles.

But the most wonderful part was the view. She hurried to the partly opened window and gazed out. Something within eased, soothed at the sight of the endless blue, the sun shimmering light and promise in contrast to the castle's dim interiors. Waves echoed, both on the rocks directly below the castle walls and on the small sandy beach a little farther on, their ceaseless susurration a sound not unlike the constant winds over the dales. She closed her eyes and breathed in the salt-tinged air.

"Sarah?"

"This is lovely, Bea." She turned, grasped her friend's hands. "Thank you for asking me here."

"I'm so glad you came." Beatrice's eyes seemed to hold a desperate kind of relief. "I've been so worried, so confused . . ."

"About what? Bea, what is it?"

Beatrice simply shook her head. "I cannot say right now. Soon perhaps."

What mystery lay here? But any chance for further speculation was cut short by the arrival of the elderly servant with Sarah's trunk.

"Oh, thank you, Robert." Beatrice motioned to the corner. "Put it down there." She waited until he left the room, then studied Sarah's attire with a small frown. "We shall need to find you a gown more appropriate for dinner. What on earth happened to you?"

"The cart had some trouble."

"Did you get out and push?"

"It wasn't going anywhere with me sitting in it." She refrained from telling Beatrice about the passers-by who ignored Jem's plea for help. She had no wish to be uncharitable. Perhaps they had an appointment they were rushing to.

"It might be autumn, but with you here it shall be like a breath of spring, and we can certainly do with some new life to blow through this gloomy old place."

"I cannot wait to explore," Sarah admitted, with a return to her earlier anticipation. This castle might be ancient and enormous, but it was also Beatrice's home. Even with the presence of James, Sarah would trust no harm would come to her here, no matter what those gargoyles might imply.

"There is much to see. But first, a new gown. Father may seem as though he doesn't care, but he can be quite scathing of those he thinks do not give him what he considers his due."

"You need to tell me what I should do to keep on his good side. I would not do anything that would cause trouble for you or give him reason to want me gone a moment sooner than you wish."

"Well, if it were my wishes that were taken into consideration, I'm afraid you would simply never leave!" Beatrice said gaily.

But something in her eyes made Sarah shiver in the cold breeze.

He was going to have to find another way. James dealt the cards and took a large swig from the tankard, carefully eyeing the men crowded in the small chamber in the back of the hostelry. If his luck did not improve, he would have to speak to his father again, see if he could perhaps unknot the man's miserly ways and convince him to part with some funds. It wouldn't take much, just enough to cover the three-hundred-mile journey south to London, with a little extra to alleviate the drear. If he could win tonight, he'd make some progress toward clearing his debts. And if he didn't . . .

James ignored the hulking figure of Falcott, Longhoughton's innkeeper, a man whose size and temper James was loath to cross. Fortunately, his absence from the area for the past dozen years meant he had been able to pass himself off as a mere soldier, not as the son and heir of a well-known local landowner, especially since he'd used Blackwood's name.

His lips twisted without amusement. *Blackguard* would be a more fitting title. Wasn't that how people—his father and sister included—regarded him?

His arrival several days ago had put the house in uproar, even if some of the more obsequious servants pretended to differ. Servants like Dawkins,

Dawson, whatever his name was, who had met him with effusive insistence that he had been missed, and old Copley, the woman whose airs of self-importance had always sickened, who had greeted him with flattery he suspected as false. It hadn't taken long before the old invisible chains of reproach and condemnation had led him to escape outside, to seek freedom from the perpetual game of blame his father always played.

"You playing or what?"

James inclined his chin and threw out a card. His heart sank. *No.* He swallowed a curse. *No.*

Years of experience helped preserve his countenance, as he struggled to maintain an illusion of care-for-nothing, which was perhaps not such an illusion after all. He might be known in the regiment for his hard heart and careless ways, but such were mere means to survival. For what was life but a mere precursor to death? No, he could not afford to care, when life had proved that caring was just another word for heartbreak.

Another round, and he was forced to admit defeat. But this man was not one he could easily gull into believing he had the readies at home. He'd need to come up with another plan. "I'm afraid, gentlemen, that I have just remembered I have left my funds elsewhere."

"Whaddya mean? Have you no blunt?" Falcott staggered to his feet.

"I mean—" His mind blanked. Where were his quick wits and silver tongue now? Alcohol be—

Thwack.

He reeled back from the force of the blow, which had set his teeth to rattling.

"What's this?" Falcott snatched at the chain James wore around his neck, the piece he'd sworn never to remove, a memento to both his reverence and his shame.

"Don't," he pleaded. "It belonged to my mother."

"Belongs to me now." Falcott broke the thin golden loops from its dolphin head clasp and ripped it from James's neck. "Until you pay."

Until he paid—with what?

"Now get out of here," Falcott snarled. "And don't show your face 'ere again until you show the coin."

"But—"

Further protest died at the application of such force to his torso that he was left outside on the dirt wheezing, and conscious of two things. That the loss of his mother's chain proved yet again how careless he was with important things. And that the sharp teeth of regret proved perhaps he wasn't as careless as he'd liked to appear.

Not when he'd do anything to get that necklace back.

Chapter 3

After an evening meal that made Sarah wonder at the strained relationship between father, daughter, and the still-absent son, and the cavalier manner in which the servants seemed to treat their mistress, Sarah fell asleep to the sound of the waves crashing on the rocks below. She dreamt strange dreams populated by wizened men and gargoyle sneers and hidden passages, as snatches of conversations blended with memories of what Beatrice had shared over nearly two decades of friendship.

Upon waking, Sarah met Beatrice downstairs in the breakfast room—a room she'd needed to ask a servant for direction to, given the many corridors and winding passages and galleries and stairs. Inside this pleasant morning chamber, she found Beatrice and her father, who rose and nodded to Sarah before muttering his excuses and taking his leave.

Beatrice dismissed a waiting servant, then murmured, "Please excuse Father. He did not sleep well last night, and sometimes his gout pains him. He does not mean to be rude."

"It is of no matter." Perhaps it was just his way. The older gentlemen in her uncle's congregation were ofttimes gruff and terse, and hardly examples of gallant courtesy. She'd learned over many years that it did not pay to be thin-skinned.

"James has not come down yet," Beatrice said. "Dawson said he didn't return until the wee hours, so he's unlikely to make an appearance until noon."

By which stage Sarah would ensure she was elsewhere.

Beatrice instructed Sarah to help herself from the covered serving dishes on the sideboard. "You were able to find your way all right? Did Daisy wake you late?"

"Remind me, who is Daisy?" Sarah took her plate of eggs to the table and resumed her seat.

"The young girl who helped you unpack last night. Was she not with you this morning?"

"I'm afraid not."

"Oh dear." Beatrice's brow creased. "I thought I'd told her . . ."

She had. Sarah swallowed her eggs, wincing at the flavorlessness. If one judged by last night's meal and this dish, it seemed the Langley's cook cared as little for her duties as young Daisy did.

"I'm sorry. The servants are such a trial at times."

Sarah sipped her tea, which was most fortunately hot. "I imagine a place as grand as this must require scores of workers."

"Yes." Beatrice's mouth pulled down on both sides. "But what we require is not what we can afford, so we make do with under a dozen."

"And Mrs. Copley runs the household servants?"

"When she feels like it," Beatrice said wryly. "Dawson is supposed to assist. He performs the functions of Father's steward and agent, and acts as butler, seeing as the estate doesn't bring in nearly what it used to. I'm afraid that previous generations of Langleys have preserved the castle at the expense of the lands, so the farms don't yield as much as in years gone past, or so I'm led to understand. You must excuse my bluntness, but my father has little love for anything other than his books, and James has been forever focused on the army."

"My uncle is not dissimilar. If it is not the Bible or books of sermons, then he's devouring texts concerning Greek or Roman history, with no care for anything else."

"Father does love the house, is indeed most proud of it. You would think that Langleys had lived here for many hundreds of years when, in fact, it is not even two hundred."

"Scarcely any time at all," Sarah teased.

Beatrice laughed, and after enquiring whether Sarah was finished with her meal, took her on yesterday's promised walk around the house and gardens.

She learned something of the castle's history, how it was believed to have been built on the site of an Iron Age fort later occupied by Romans, and constructed by a distant, untitled cousin of King Edward II, who had later seen said cousin executed. The ownership of the castle had fallen through various hands until the seventeenth century, when the extremely wealthy Langley family had taken possession, and retained their control ever since.

"Of course, we're scarcely wealthy now," Beatrice said, with a wry twist of her lips. "Father hates to admit it, but it's obvious everywhere one looks."

"I imagine a house of this size and age requires a great deal of upkeep."

"We barely use a quarter of the rooms." Beatrice led Sarah up one staircase, then down another, along corridors of faded carpets and dusty paintings, under carved archways, and past aged tapestries and chambers named for every color of the rainbow. "My mother used to sleep in that room." Beatrice pointed to a door in the corner of one of the galleries. "It has the most wonderful view of the North Sea. You can see for miles down the coastline on a clear day."

"Are we to see her chambers?"

Beatrice stilled. "I can show you her private sitting room, but ever since my mother's death, Father has insisted the main bedchambers be closed. At least until the day that James finds a wife. Poor woman. I do not envy her at all."

Sarah held her tongue, but privately agreed.

An enquiry about the supposed treasure brought a laugh and an explanation as Beatrice led the way down to the tunnels. "Oh, if only that was true, then all our money worries would be solved. But alas, it's only rumors."

"Is it also a rumor that someone went missing down here?"

"Wherever did you hear that?" At Sarah's report of Jem's tale, Beatrice chuckled. "Truly, I think that as tall a tale as the idea there might be treasure. But you are most welcome to see if you can find anything to aid our coffers."

"I shall see what I can do," Sarah promised, to Bea's peal of laughter.

Beatrice summoned Robert and the aged servant led the way from the cellars into the musty darkness beyond a well-bolstered door. The lit lanterns cast eerie shadows as Beatrice explained how the castle hosted several tunnels and dungeons, and regaled Sarah with such terrible stories of child prisoners and the like that she breathed more deeply when Beatrice suggested they leave the darkness and ascend the stone steps to the gardens above.

Outside Beatrice showed her a walled kitchen garden, which, given its weeds, had clearly seen better days.

"Yet it still produces," insisted Meeks, the castle's only gardener—save for a young apprentice named Joseph—as he fingered a plant.

"Are they potatoes?" Sarah asked.

"Very good, miss," Meeks said, brows lifted as if surprised.

"My uncle is quite partial to potatoes, so my aunt insisted on growing them." She didn't mention her aunt had also insisted Sarah do the lion's share of garden cultivation and harvest.

"For how else is a girl of your age to earn her keep?" Aunt Patricia would say, seemingly forgetting all the housework and domestic management duties Sarah already carried out.

"We don't need that much, seeing as it's just Father and myself these days," Bea said. "And the servants, of course."

Sarah nodded and surveyed the garden, noting the glass-covered hotbeds of fresh manure, which would encourage vegetable seedlings to grow, and the upturned pots protecting small plants against the harsh elements of this northerly seaside site. It seemed to be a relatively straightforward matter to reinvigorate the garden to productivity again. "The walls are quite high."

"Aye, miss. The wind can be that strong the only way we grow anything is to try to keep it out as much as possible."

Beatrice released Meeks back to his duties and then led the way through a door into another small enclosed garden, where a pair of benches were centered by a dried pond. "The fountain stopped working years ago, and Father never saw the point in replacing it."

Sarah nodded. Paying for a roof or servants' wages was likely far better economy. Still, this would be a charming location with its exotic trees and small shrubs and roses that no doubt would still bloom magnificently in spring. How sad that neglect and a lack of money had stolen so many of the castle's lovely things.

Beyond a stone archway lay a vast open space covered in knee-high grass, with only a few stubby yews, which looked as though they had been growing there for centuries. "This is the outer bailey, which has been used for cultivation at various times, but now is left as sward." Beatrice took her to some of the stone structures in the distance, including "Lilith Tower, which overlooks the Rumble Churn."

"The Rumble Churn?"

"It's a narrow channel where water pushes through. Some days it's so loud one can hear it from inside the house."

Beatrice led the way back via the stables and other outbuildings. "I knew you'd enjoy the history of the place," Beatrice said with satisfaction as they reentered the house, where the vaulted ceiling of the Great Hall once more stole Sarah's breath as she noted further details she'd missed on her first survey. What a magnificent room, so medieval with its giant fireplace and oak paneling, a suit of armor standing guard against a lime-washed wall. But here, too, were signs of decrepitude. The wooden seats' cushions were threadbare and frayed. Dust-laden cobwebs hung heavy from the ceiling, proof that the servants either did not notice or did not care, which made her question what else Beatrice and her father might not recognize. Perhaps if she was to stay long enough, she might ask Beatrice if she could be permitted to employ her one useful accomplishment and embroider new cushions.

They passed through to the main staircase, and Sarah almost ran into Beatrice, who had come to a sudden halt.

Dawson was coming down the main stairs, a sight that seemed to surprise Beatrice.

"Dawson? What are you doing up in the family rooms?"

He lifted his chin, and seemed loathe to answer for a moment, before finally replying, "Your father asked me to find something for him."

"Where is my father?"

"In the library, miss."

Sarah's stomach tensed. The words might be innocuous enough, but the way he spoke, all ingratiation and smirked deference, drew indignation on Bea's behalf. She exhaled, narrowing her gaze at the man, before following her friend to the library.

Inside, Mr. Langley was again reading, and looked up as they entered.

Her footsteps stumbled at the lounging figure of the other man. Oh heavens. It was—

"James."

James sketched a mock bow to his sister, ignoring the ache in his shoulder courtesy of last night's incident. "Beatrice," he echoed her with a singsong voice, before his gaze alighted on the woman beside her. "And who do we have here?"

The woman dressed in grey met his gaze squarely. Her cheeks were pale, her hair faded to a shade neither blonde nor brown, she was not in the first blush of youth. But for some reason her eyes were ablaze. She gave a stiff curtsy.

He nodded.

"This is Miss Drayton."

Drayton? Why did that name ring the faintest bell? It mattered not. "It seems strange to me that Father here has once again assured me that there are no spare funds available, and yet here you have employed a companion."

Beatrice gasped. "A what?"

He ignored his sister's outburst, studying the woman whose cheeks had flamed to a rosy pink, a sight which rendered her looks slightly more appealing. "You. I have seen you somewhere before."

He half expected her to deny it—he'd met many women over the years, and they had all started to blur after a time—but that flash appeared in her eyes again. *Had* he met her before?

"Yes."

Her voice was lower than he'd expected, but maybe that was because he was used to the simpering high-pitched tones of the ladies of the *ton*, some of whom were so silly as to adopt a babyish lisp, as if they thought it rendered them sweet and appealing. Fools. It wasn't their voice he was interested in.

He blinked, conscious of a sense of shame at such a thought, and studied her from under lowered brows. "Well?" Where would he have met a domestic?

"At an assembly in Durham, sir."

"A servant at an assembly attended by lords and ladies? I think not." His gaze tapered. "I'd remember such a social travesty."

Her chin lifted to a militant angle. "I'm surprised you don't remember, sir. Seeing as you had the audacity to kiss this particular travesty."

"What?"

James echoed his father's question a half-second later, adding, "You must be suffering from some kind of delusion. Perhaps you should be in Bedlam, not harping around here."

"You kissed this young lady, James?" His father looked appalled.

"Of course not," he scoffed, mind casting back through the blurriness of time to recall that particular event. He'd kissed a lot of women since then. "The only person I may have kissed was one of Beatrice's friends."

He stared at the woman, as a horrifying suspicion gained purchase. No. "You?"

She bobbed a curtsy, eyes narrowed with dislike. "Miss Drayton, at your service, sir."

Breath hitched. Fire and brimstone, she was the very woman. "Beatrice's friend? Then what are you doing here?"

"I invited her," Beatrice said impatiently. "This is my school friend, Miss Sarah Drayton. I told you this before, but once again, it seems you have no care to remember."

He sank back into his seat, eyeing the whiskey bottle waiting to be poured. Was it too early? Or would a drink help clear his brain? How had he not remembered?

He was still puzzling it over as Bea complained about Dawson being upstairs, which Father dismissed in his usual disinterested manner, before asking this plain creature what she thought about the house.

"I think Langley House is very fine." Her face animated once more. "I have always enjoyed learning about the past, and this castle is certainly brimming with history."

"History, eh? Neither of my children can stand it."

So true. James exchanged a look with Beatrice. Who could enjoy history when one's history forbade enjoyment?

"I'm sure it's different when one is surrounded by it all the time," Miss Drayton continued, with a small smile. "My uncle is rather fond of Roman antiquities, and would often insist on my taking notes and writing his correspondence concerning such things."

"We have some Roman pieces found here. Beatrice? Get the urn and the fish."

The fish?

Beatrice moved to a side table and drew out a small box and brought it to her father. He gestured for Miss Drayton to look at it.

Inside, a reddish stone urn decorated with flowers, gladiators, and mythical beasts lay next to a tiny stone amulet shaped like a long-bodied fish.

"So striking," she murmured. "I'm sure this urn is just like one from one of my uncle's books. You say this was found here?"

"In the cellars, by one of my ancestors."

"How absolutely marvelous." She glanced at Bea. "Don't you think it wonderful that people who lived so long ago once held these in their hands?"

"*So* wonderful."

Miss Drayton smiled, and James's resentment toward someone who seemed determined to win his father's approval eased a smidgen. She couldn't be all bad if she shared the family's propensity for dry humor.

"The castle certainly has a unique history. You are most fortunate to live here, Mr. Langley."

"It's not quite what it could be," Father admitted with a sigh. "A shame one can't get good servants these days."

"This castle is the most magnificent building I've ever been in." She gestured around the room as if encompassing the whole house.

James was tempted to roll his eyes. Please. Another flatterer.

"And I truly don't think many of those things that require attention would be hard to manage."

What? "Oh, you don't, do you?" James said, affronted.

She turned to him. "I meant no offense. I simply cannot but think it is a shame to see these wonderful rooms filled with history going to ruin because of dust and neglect, from servants who seem to demonstrate little respect and even less skill."

"Is that so?" Father peered at her.

She returned a firm nod.

James exchanged another look with his sister. When was the last time anyone had spoken to Father so fearlessly? He was reluctantly impressed.

Father studied her intently a moment longer, then turned to Bea. "Well, Beatrice, I hope you have planned something nice for dinner tonight. I'm expecting Sir John to join us for the evening meal."

The sudden subject change seemed to take the wind from Miss Drayton's sails, and bring a dampener to Bea's expression too. Not that he blamed her. Sir John was little better than the silly pup Beatrice had been talking to at the ball. Why Father might think Bea and their neighbor could be well suited, he had no idea. But then, the only thing he really knew of his father's thoughts was how far James fell below the expectation of a dutiful son. He moved to grasp his mother's chain, regret kneading his chest anew at its absence.

Bea's answer was all politeness. "Of course, Father."

Their discussion of the meal took a few moments, then Father returned to his book, a clear sign that he had lost interest in the conversation.

Beatrice returned the box to the side table and gestured for Miss Drayton to follow her from the room. James's gaze followed, returning when his father cleared his throat. "Well?"

"Well what?"

"She's an interesting thing."

"Who? Beatrice?"

"Clodpole," his father muttered. "The friend."

"You cannot be serious."

His father eyed him with a bushy-browed intensity that wrought misgiving within.

"What is it, Father?" Perhaps he'd reconsidered, and had thought of a way to secure James's financial future.

His father shook his head. "When do you leave for the Continent?"

He blinked at the abrupt turn of conversation. "I'm due to return to London in a week or two." Or sooner, if the debt collectors came knocking.

"A week or two. How good of you to come visit your old father before you depart for heaven knows how long."

"I have never been assured of my welcome," he said stiffly.

"Only because you engage in activities that would make a lecher blush."

His insides tensed, and James lifted his gaze to a dark cabinet crammed with books. "I don't pretend to have been a saint."

"No." Father's voice held a wealth of pain and disappointment. Disappointment that said little good would come of staying and hoping Father would change his mind. Perhaps James would need to travel further afield to find the readies. He had acquaintances up near Coldstream who didn't mind a flutter. Perhaps he could regain the chain that way.

Regrets churned with guilt-laden frustration. As far as his father was concerned, it was too late now. They both knew when he had first embarked on this road to debauchery. They both knew why. And nothing could ever bring her back.

Chapter 4

The next morning Beatrice proposed an excursion to the village, which Sarah was most happy to oblige. For as fascinating as the castle was, its dark dim halls and walls seemed designed to oppress one's spirits. The chance to explore beyond—and escape the speculative gazes of Beatrice's father and brother, and the insolence of the servants—was all too enticing.

She had apologized to Beatrice about her forthright words yesterday, for that strange moment when something within—likely that same thing her aunt had always taken exception to—had made Sarah meet Mr. Langley's gaze and speak with honesty.

Bea had laughed it off, declaring Sarah had said nothing that wasn't true. "I am sure that Dawson and Copley still see me as being the age I was when Mama passed. Whenever I have tried to speak to Father about it, I always end up looking and feeling like a fool. They have this way of twisting things so Father believes them and not me. You heard my father simply dismiss it. He cares little about the state of things here, but more about his books and his stomach. It was far more interesting that James felt he had a right to be upset."

James. Sarah's chest cinched. She had managed to avoid James fairly well. Despite being seated nearby at last night's dinner, he'd barely spoken a word, although his scowls and frequent refilling of his glass said plenty. Unfortunately, that left Sarah free to observe with sinking heart the obvious attentions Sir John lavished upon Beatrice, and the fact that Mr. Langley seemed to promote conversation between the pair.

If only Beatrice possessed a female relative to advise on those more tender matters of the heart. Or even housekeeping. The lack of a living mother had proved one of the bonds that had drawn them together at school, Sarah's long-standing status as an orphan engendering sympathy for Beatrice's newly motherless one.

Apart from the young man at the assembly, Beatrice seemed to have no young men wishing to pay their attentions, which reminded Sarah to enquire about whom he was to Bea.

She put such a question to Beatrice when they had escaped the castle, walked across the small drawbridge from the Egyncleugh tower and across the narrow moat, then down to the small harbor bounded by the village of Langburgh below.

"Mr. Grayling?" Beatrice gave a careless laugh. "He is a friend. That is all."

"Truly all?" Sarah persisted. "You seemed very friendly at the assembly."

Beatrice was silent for a moment as they picked their way down the steep slope to the low stretch of grassed-over sand between the mere and the sea. "Sarah, can I trust you?"

"You know you can."

"Has it seemed that Father is keen to promote my acquaintanceship with Sir John?"

Sir John Willoughby. The only visitor to the castle these past days. "He has been warmly welcomed by your father," she said cautiously.

"I believe Father wishes me to encourage him. He likely thinks Sir John's funds will be useful for the castle, and Sir John has always had an eye for me, even though he's nearly twice my age." She shuddered.

"Are you sure? I cannot think a loving father would wish his only daughter away."

Beatrice nodded, blue eyes large and scared. "I have heard them talk about the need to unite, that it will help the village and our futures. I dare not speak with Father lest it encourages him to pursue the matter further."

"I think it would be better to talk with him. Surely you cannot think your father will ignore your wishes."

"Sarah, you cannot know what it's like to fear one's father."

Her heart caught. Poor Beatrice. No, Sarah could not relate, because she could scarcely remember her father at all.

"And Mr. Grayling?"

"Mr. Grayling wishes to marry me, but he is without funds or much in the way to provide."

"Where did you meet?"

"At an assembly in Newcastle. He wasn't even supposed to be there, and I'd only agreed to go to keep my cousin company, but as soon as we met it was as though the heavens aligned, the stars shone brighter, and I had found someone from whom I could never part."

A throbbing sensation filled Sarah's heart. Oh, to have someone express such things about her.

"I visit the vicar, Mr. Edwards, as an excuse to collect the correspondence Mr. Grayling sends to me. He is a friend of Mr. Edwards and has known him for years."

Sarah's brows rose. A clandestine relationship?

"Don't look at me like that, Sarah. It is simply letters, that is all."

Letters from a single gentleman to an unmarried lady were scarcely considered respectable. But perhaps, in circumstances like these, such a thing could scarcely be considered reprehensible.

"But you do not want it to be all, do you?"

"I wish more than anything that I could be his wife," Beatrice said fiercely.

"Have you spoken of Mr. Grayling to your father?"

"He would not countenance such a match. He would say it was degrading."

"They know each other, then?"

"They have met once or twice, but Father will have nothing to do with him. Did you not see his manner with Peter at the ball?"

Sarah chewed her lip. "Then could you enlist the support of your brother?"

"James? He thinks of no one but himself. Besides, he left for the north this morning, with no goodbye."

He had? Thank heavens. She couldn't pretend to be sorry. "You have no other family who might aid you?"

"I have a cousin, Frankston. He lives in London and is something of a dandy. James is sure Frankston is jealous of him, as he's the heir should James not wed and have a son."

"Is that likely?"

"Who knows? Perhaps there is someone out there who finds his roguish ways appealing."

She had no real interest in Bea's brother's matrimonial interests save in how it affected her friend. And Sarah's heart hurt for her. *Lord? What should she do?* She blinked. "You are of age," she said slowly. Eight and twenty, same as she.

Beatrice laughed without humor. "You cannot think I could speak to Mr. Edwards and have the banns read, can you?"

God forgive her, but . . . "I wasn't thinking that, no."

Beatrice turned with widened eyes. "Do you suggest I travel to the border?"

"It is not far, is it?"

"It is at least forty miles."

"And forty miles of reasonable road could be traveled in a day, could it not?"

"I . . . I cannot believe you would suggest such a thing."

"I cannot believe you have not contemplated it. Bea, if you love him, then why allow yourself to be held prisoner here?" Sarah gestured to the castle. "You and I are of a similar age, and neither of us are getting younger."

They had traversed the fields of barley and were approaching the church with its high steeple. Beatrice wore a frown, as if thinking very deeply. "I would be cast away."

"But you would have Mr. Grayling to comfort you. A family too, one day."

"I do not know where we would live."

"That is something you should perhaps ask him to consider, if indeed he wishes to marry you."

They stopped at the moss-laden stone wall surrounding the churchyard. "I do not know what to say."

"What to say about what?" a deeper voice asked.

Beatrice murmured introductions, and Sarah met the enquiring gaze of the vicar, Mr. Edwards, his cherubic features shining in the morning sun. She dipped a curtsy. "Good morning, sir."

"Miss Drayton, Miss Langley. How are you both today?"

Beatrice replied in a distracted manner, then moved to a gated section of the cemetery to stand before a well-tended grave. Mr. Edwards cast Sarah a curious look. She shrugged. Such things were Beatrice's to share. Instead, she asked, "I wonder, Mr. Edwards, are there any persons of significance buried in your churchyard here?"

He led her on a short tour, pointing out the headstones of the notable and notorious, such as a widow with fourteen children, and just beyond the sacred grounds, the field where it was rumored lay buried the hung, drawn, and quartered remains of a highwayman "who had the temerity to attempt to rob the king."

"Well, he was certainly bold."

"Aye, and a wee bit foolhardy."

She glanced at him, wondering whether he'd consider her suggestion to Beatrice the same. But surely he must have some sympathy for the couple's situation, given his role with their correspondence.

"Tell me, Miss Drayton, how goes your stay at Langley House?"

"It has been very pleasant. Certainly different from my usual environs."

"Miss Langley has mentioned previously that you are from upper Yorkshire."

"Yes, a small village called Hartsdale."

"I don't believe I've been there."

"Not many people have," she allowed. She glanced across to where Beatrice stood distractedly in front of what Mr. Edwards had indicated as her mother's final resting place, the carved-stone angel atop the headstone casting a shadow across her furrowed brow.

"Miss Langley does not seem in cheerful spirits," Mr. Edwards said in a lower voice.

Was this her opportunity? "I understand you are a friend of Mr. Grayling."

He nodded. "We have been friends for many a year. A capital fellow."

"I . . ." Should she dare? "I was saddened to hear of the challenges facing Miss Langley's future happiness."

He glanced quickly at her. "You are aware of what those challenges comprise?"

"Her father's opposition, and Mr. Grayling's lack of fortune."

"Oh, Peter does not lack the means to provide."

"No? Beatrice seems to think so."

"He has a snug establishment near Morpeth."

"Then what keeps him from proposing?"

"I suspect a sense of honor. One doesn't want to be the man who steals a young lady from her well-established family and possibly impair her chances with someone better connected."

"Like Sir John?" She raised her brows at him. "You cannot think that match is bound to succeed."

His lips flattened. "This may surprise you, Miss Drayton, but I agree with you."

He might say that, but would he agree with her outrageous idea? "I think they should elope," she confessed in a whisper.

"You surprise me," he said, with no apparent censure. "I did not suspect such a romantic heart."

"I cannot abide to see her hamstrung by her father's lack of care for her happiness. As for the insolence of the servants?" She shook her head.

"Your loyalty does you much credit, Miss Drayton."

"I would rather it do her some good," she murmured, as Beatrice approached.

"Perhaps it shall," he said. "Ah, Miss Langley. I trust your time of reflection has helped?"

Bea smoothed her skirts. "It did."

"It's always good to pause to allow the agitation of one's heart to be soothed by prayer. Now, I have a paper you may wish to see, if you care to wait here a moment."

"From Peter?" At his nod, Beatrice's eyes shone. "Oh, yes please."

They waited outside the vicarage, the passing pedestrians offering nods and touched forelocks to "Miss Langley."

How strange it was that everyone should know Bea, should appear to care for her, but be willing to do so little to assist to promote her happiness.

A gig approached, and Sarah heard Beatrice's faint sigh as it became apparent who the occupant was.

"Ah, Beatrice." Miss Barnstaple ignored Sarah. "Is it true that your brother has returned at last?"

Beatrice inclined her head, then motioned to Sarah. "I believe you have met my friend, Miss Drayton."

Miss Barnstaple's gaze flicked to Sarah and back. "Your companion, yes?"

"No," Beatrice said, with an edge to her voice Sarah had rarely heard before.

"Oh. I must have misunderstood." Her look that trickled the length of Sarah's attire gave reason for her misbelief. "Well, if you'll excuse me." She nodded, departing as another vehicle approached.

The second rig stopped before them also. "Good morning, ladies." Sir John's gaze skimmed over Sarah to land squarely on Beatrice. "You are looking fresh and lovely today, Miss Langley."

Beatrice bobbed a short curtsy, but returned no answer, her tension plain as Mr. Edwards returned and she spoke to him in a low voice.

Sir John now studied Sarah. "Miss Drayton. How long shall we have the pleasure of your company, I wonder?"

"As long as Miss Langley wills it, sir."

Silence filled the air, save for the hushed murmurs of the vicar and Beatrice and the ever-present shush of the sea.

"Well, I can see my company is not needed here. Good day."

Sarah nodded, chest easing with relief as he finally drove away.

"Oh, thank goodness." Beatrice exhaled. "I thought he'd never leave."

Mr. Edwards cleared his throat. "It may prove of interest to know that last Sunday Sir John was asking about the availability of the church for matrimonial purposes."

"Did he really?" Beatrice grabbed Sarah's arm. "What am I to do?"

Sarah glanced at Mr. Edwards, then back at her friend. "You are going to write to your Mr. Grayling and tell him he must marry you at once, and that if he is going to let some scruples stop him, then you will be forced to marry Sir John instead."

"But how could that even happen?"

She drew in a breath. "I am not completely certain, but I'm sure between us we can hatch a plan to see you wed."

Purpose hummed through her veins. Perhaps this was why she had been led to Langley House. At her age, she would likely never find romance of her own, but she would do all she could to promote the joy of others.

"Oh, excuse me." Sarah stumbled to a halt just inside the door. The room—which she had believed this past week to be the lady's morning room—had instead proved to be the servants' hall, or at least such was suggested by the lounging staff who looked at her with incredulous eyes. She met their gazes evenly—is this where they hid, ignoring their duties and the many bell-rope summons from Beatrice?

"Something we can help you with, miss?" Mrs. Copley had not moved from her slumped position in a chair beside a long wooden table littered with tea things.

Sarah may not have much experience with grand houses, but surely such a lack of deference was not acceptable. She cleared her throat. "It is something you can help Miss Langley with. She has been ringing the bell for the past half hour, yet no one has gone to her aid."

"The bells don't work none," said Dawson.

"Are they so difficult to fix?" she asked gently.

"Who are you to tell us what to do?" Dawson pushed to his feet, thickset features crumpled into a scowl. "You're nothing but a poor companion."

Her stomach clenched, but she refused to take a step back, instead taking a step forward as she strove to display pleasantness. "On the contrary, Miss Langley and her father consider me her guest."

"That's not what others say," he muttered.

"Which others?" she challenged.

But Dawson refused to meet her gaze, forcing her attention to the quasi-housekeeper.

"Mrs. Copley, I hope you can make the staff here understand that they should pay attention to those who pay their wages, and not those who speculate from afar and remain unnamed. Now, Miss Langley requires assistance in the green drawing room—"

"The Princess Room?"

Was it the Princess Room? She could scarce remember which was named which in the castle's vast labyrinth of rooms. "In the room beside the stairs."

"The main stairs or the side-wing stairs?"

"The main stairs."

"Aye, that's the Princess Room." Mrs. Copley nodded slowly, as the rest of the staff remained seated, arms crossed or with stares baleful.

Perhaps an overture of friendliness might assuage this animosity. "Do you know why it's called such? Did a princess once stay here? How wonderful if that was the case."

But no answer came other than shrugs and lifted brows, and she left the room deflated, feeling as though her efforts to alleviate Beatrice's worries had instead only made things worse.

She retreated through the dark corridors, relieved to see her memory had not been faulty and that Beatrice still remained in the green drawing room, wiping the dust from precious ornaments she'd said once belonged to her mother.

"I didn't know this was called the Princess Room," she said, hurrying to help her.

"That's because it's not." Turning, Beatrice revealed a dirt smudge on her cheek. "Whatever made you say so?"

"Mrs. Copley said so."

"Oh, you found her, then? Was she in the morning room?"

"She was having tea in the servants' hall."

"Really?"

Sarah nodded. How much was she supposed to say? Would it help

Beatrice's worries to know how lackadaisical the staff here were, or would it only increase the strain that had intensified in recent days? Ever since Beatrice had finally written to Mr. Grayling last week, tension had clung to her like a cloud, and it was all Sarah could do to distract her with suggestions of walks and questions about the castle's fascinating past. Still, ignoring the situation had scarcely worked well, had it? "She was there with the rest of the staff, from what I could see."

Beatrice's shoulders rounded, and Sarah's chest knotted with regret.

"Forgive me, but I truly do not understand why they are kept on. My Aunt Patricia would have packed the lot of them off years ago."

"Perhaps you should work here, Miss Drayton," a male voice said behind her.

She turned, surprised to see the older Mr. Langley had entered the room. "Oh, sir, I meant no disrespect."

He eyed her with that penetrating glare that quite unnerved her. "Do you think you would make a better housekeeper?"

What? Was this a test? Was she about to be turned out? But something within made her meet his gaze squarely. "I do, sir."

"Oh, Papa—"

"I know how to keep things in good order." Sarah ignored Beatrice's protest. "And I know how to ensure things are kept clean. I have never been afraid of hard work."

"Hmm."

Really, his gaze was most unsettling. What was going on behind those bland features?

"Sarah, I will not let you—Father, you should not goad—"

"Please forgive me if I have spoken out of turn, sir," Sarah said. "I do not wish to cause offense—"

"Don't be mealymouthed with me, girl, I cannot abide it." He crossed his arms. "Speak what you think, and the consequences be hanged."

Very well, then. "In that case, I will speak freely, and say that I think you should sack most of your staff and engage new servants immediately."

"Oh, you do, do you?" His perusal sharpened.

"Yes." She willed the stoutness of her legs to give strength to her voice and heart. "When I spoke to the servants just now, I was told that the bell ropes didn't work, yet there seemed no plan or even intention to mend them."

"Truly?" His voice held surprise.

"Yes, sir." She nodded. "Forgive my plain speaking, but from an outsider's perspective, it seems that many of the servants have little care for this place, which I cannot help but feel shows a shocking disregard for the Langley family and their important heritage. If I were you, I would employ servants from a larger center, say Newcastle or York."

"Is that so?"

She nodded, ignoring the return of his sardonic tone.

"Tell me, who is your family?" he asked, moving to the mantelpiece and studying the porcelain figures Beatrice had been dusting mere moments ago.

The swift change of topic left her reeling for a moment. "My parents are dead, sir." Unexpected sorrow clutched her chest. Her parents had been dead for many years, but sometimes the loss of her family seemed freshly real. Oh, how she yearned to feel like she belonged somewhere.

"You have no brother, no sisters?" He glanced back at her.

"I was not blessed with siblings who survived past infancy."

His brows rose.

"My father was a solicitor, my mother the daughter of a reverend in a rural parish in York, where my uncle is now the minister."

"An honest, pious background, to be sure."

She straightened. "I would like to think I continue their legacy and such qualities are mine as well."

He eyed her narrowly for a moment longer, then nodded. "You, Miss Drayton, are one of the most—"

But any further insight into his opinion was cut short by the knock and immediate entrance of Mrs. Copley. "Oh! Mr. Langley, I did not know you were here." She bobbed a curtsy. "Sir, there is a visitor for you. Mr. Edwards."

"Edwards?" He frowned. "I wonder what he wants?"

Beatrice glanced at Sarah, her brows lifting higher. They followed

Mr. Langley and Mrs. Copley to the Great Hall, where Mr. Edwards pushed to his feet.

"Ah, Mr. Langley, ladies." He nodded to Beatrice and Sarah. "I wondered, sir, if I might beg a few moments of your time."

"Of course."

Mr. Langley led the way to his library, and as he passed, the vicar was able to hand Sarah—standing nearest him—a sealed note.

She swiftly thrust it in her pocket, but not before Mrs. Copley eyed her askance. She raised her brows in a silent challenge, then looped Beatrice's arm in her own. "Let's go finish the work in the green drawing room, unless your father needs you."

He waved a hand of dismissal behind him, and they moved away, then Beatrice paused. "Mrs. Copley, why did you tell Miss Drayton that the green drawing room is called the Princess Room?"

"Forgive me, miss," she said, chin lifting, "but I did no such thing."

"I rather think you did," Beatrice countered.

"Perhaps the young lady is hard of hearing."

"Perhaps Mrs. Copley has a poor memory." Sarah tsk tsked. "That might account for why she forgot to send any helpers when I expressly asked her to."

"How dare you suggest such a thing?" Mrs. Copley blustered. "Can I help it if you don't know the way things be done around here?"

"Tell me, how long until the bells will be fixed, Mrs. Copley?"

"I don't answer to you—"

"That is enough!" Beatrice snapped, in a rare show of spirit. "Tell Dawson to fix the bells—in fact, why is it that I did not know they were even broken?"

Mrs. Copley said nothing.

"Better yet, tell Dawson to come see me in the green drawing room now. And if he is not there within ten minutes, you can be sure I will see your wages for next week are cut."

"But you can't do that!" Mrs. Copley's nostrils flared, cheeks flushing.

"Are you sure that I cannot?"

Beatrice hurried away and Sarah rushed to catch up.

A moment later the door to the drawing room was closed with a *thump*, and Beatrice sank on a seat, shaking. "Oh, how I hate confrontation."

Sarah placed a comforting arm around her. "You did very well. You even had me quaking in my boots."

Beatrice laughed, but quickly sobered. "She will take it out on me, I just know it."

"She might be less inclined to do so if she reaped the consequences of her defiance."

"You mean dismissing her?"

"Or at the very least, seeing her wages cut, as you mentioned."

Beatrice's expression took on the pensiveness Sarah had seen far too often of late.

She pulled out the letter Mr. Edwards had passed to her and handed it to Bea. "I hope this contains good news."

Eyes brightening, Beatrice quickly scanned the short epistle, breath hitching in a loud gasp.

"What is it?"

"He's agreed!" Rapture lit the blue eyes.

"He wishes to marry you?"

Beatrice nodded, clutching the note to her chest. "He wants me to—oh!"

"Bea?"

"I . . . oh, forgive me, my friend, but I cannot say. That is, Peter wishes to keep this a secret, and I would not have you get into trouble for anything."

The hurt cramping her chest at the earlier comment eased. "I am not afraid of a little trouble, Bea."

"As proved by your conversation with Papa before. How peculiar he was! And you, pretending you could be a housekeeper, when I know you've done nothing of the sort."

A cleared throat saw them jump, and glance at the just-opened door, where Dawson waited. "Mrs. Copley said you wanted to see me?"

"Yes, Dawson. I was hoping you could find time to fix the bells."

"Well, miss, I have been a mite busy with other tasks, there being such a lot to do."

"In that case—"

"What Miss Langley means to say is get the bells fixed today." Sarah said firmly. "If you cannot do it yourself, find someone who can."

Dawson bristled. "I don't need to be told what to do by you, miss."

"That's right, you shouldn't need it. But if you don't listen to Miss Langley here, or refuse to fulfill her requests, then perhaps you *do* need someone to remind you of your duty."

He stared at her, belligerence in his expression, which she stared down with her own constricted gaze. Finally, he muttered, "I'll get Robert to look at the things."

"Today, if you please," Beatrice said.

"Or even if you don't," Sarah murmured.

He shot her a most unpleasant scowl but nodded to Beatrice before leaving.

"You are so brave," Beatrice said, admiration in her eyes.

"It's funny that I am not so very brave, not when it comes to my own situation at least." How many times had Sarah let her aunt browbeat her? "But I simply cannot stand to see you mistreated. I don't know how you put up with them."

"I won't have to for much—" Beatrice broke off her comment, glanced at Sarah nervously, then moved to the cabinet of her mother's china. With her back to Sarah, she said, "Do you think my primrose gown will be laundered by now?"

"I can find out if you like."

"Would you? I . . . I think I'd like to wear it for dinner tonight. I won der if Mr. Edwards will be staying?"

"I could learn that too."

"Oh, yes please. It would make a difference to Cook's dinner preparations, and I'm sure she wouldn't like a last-minute addition to our meal."

"I'll be back shortly."

Beatrice nodded distractedly, lifting a figurine of a dancing lady with both hands.

It did not take long to learn from Daisy the whereabouts of the required gown, and garner a promise it would be delivered to Miss Langley's room immediately.

It took longer to summon her courage to knock on the door of the library, through which she heard words like "Sir John" and "banns read" and the like. Oh dear. Wasn't Mr. Edwards supposed to be on Beatrice's side?

At the call of "enter" she did just that, and found the men sitting opposite each other in front of the fire, the matching creases in their foreheads suggesting intense conversation.

"Excuse me, gentlemen, I did not mean to interrupt. Beatrice asked me to enquire whether we should expect any addition to the dinner table tonight."

Mr. Langley's brow lowered further as he looked between her and the vicar. "Well, Mr. Edwards?"

"Sir, I would be honored."

"Well, Miss Drayton, there is your answer. I hope you'll be satisfied."

She was tempted to ask his meaning, but simply nodded instead. "I'll let Cook know at once."

"Stop," he commanded.

Her feet jerked to a halt.

"Tell me, Miss Drayton, what do you think of matrimony?"

Her heart began beating hard. Oh, what did he know? What did he suspect? "I'm afraid I don't quite understand the question."

"Oh, don't become missish now. Tell me, what are your views on equality between prospective marriage partners?"

Her mouth dried. Oh, he must know! How could she save Beatrice and her fledgling romantic prospects? "Sir, I believe that there are many ways people can be unequal. I don't think one's station or rank or wealth is the only factor to consider. One's character, whether one shares interests with another, one's faith or lack thereof, these are also very important to consider."

"And what say you to age?"

Oh no! Was he talking about Sir John's vast years compared to Beatrice's? "I think it could be very challenging to have a great disparity in years, say, when a man of two score years wishes to marry a girl half his age."

There came a hissed-in breath as Mr. Langley's eyes tapered. "Exactly my case with my late wife."

Heat flooded her cheeks. "Oh, forgive me, sir. I did not know." That accounted for his great age now, she supposed.

"And how old are you, Miss Langley?"

"I will be nine and twenty next May, sir."

"Same age as Beatrice, then." Mr. Langley nodded, his attention turning to Mr. Edwards, who had kept a wide-eyed silence. "And you, sir? How old is our vicar?"

He coughed. "I am four and thirty, sir."

"Hmm." Mr. Langley's brows lowered. "Tell me, Miss Drayton, would you have any objection to marrying a man of Mr. Edwards's years?"

She gasped. "Sir, I cannot see how this pertains to anything."

"I take it that's a no, then?"

What had been the question? "I have no plans of matrimony at this time, sir. Now, if you'll please excuse me, I must tell Cook about the addition at table tonight."

"Go, then." He made a gesture as if shooing away an unwanted bird, and she fled.

Why had he asked such strange questions? Behaved so oddly? And just what were the contents of Beatrice's note?

Dinner passed uneventfully, Mr. Edwards's earlier embarrassment at his host's questions having been overcome as he talked about the gulls one could see near Lilith Tower.

"Perhaps you should take Miss Drayton for a walk," Mr. Langley suggested.

Her mouthful suddenly proved most difficult to swallow. Was Mr. Langley playing matchmaker?

"Thank you, sir, but I, er . . ." Mr. Edwards's round cheeks pinked as he shot her an apologetic glance.

"I have no wish to disturb Mr. Edwards from his duties," she eventually managed.

She was relieved when Beatrice soon pleaded a headache and a wish to retire, which saw a hug for her father—surprising for its warmth—and a nod for Mr. Edwards. Her exit provided Sarah with the means to escape too.

"I don't know what has come over Father," Beatrice said once they were safely ensconced in her room. "He has been most solicitous to you."

"I could not say, save this has been a very strange day."

"How glad I am you have come to help me. Truly, I could not have managed these past weeks without you."

Touched, Sarah wrapped her in an affectionate hug. "And I am so very glad you asked me. I won't deny that I have enjoyed my time here immeasurably."

"You will not leave soon?" Beatrice said, brow wrinkling. "I . . . I truly meant it when I said I hoped you might live here forever."

Her words held a sweet sting. How lovely it would be to put this house in order, to feel herself situated, cared for, and her future assured. But fairy stories were lovely too. "And what would I do when you married? No, I could not stay."

"Oh, don't be like that. Perhaps you might marry yourself. Father seemed keen to see you wed Mr. Edwards."

"I don't know why. He is pleasant enough I suppose, but one hopes for more than pleasantness when it comes to matrimony. And I certainly did not think Mr. Edwards was keen at all."

"Yes, it is very strange," Beatrice agreed, her brow smoothing. "Well, never mind. I will pray that your future will be as happy as mine."

Another close hug, and a renewed murmur of appreciation for their friendship, and Sarah returned to her own room, mulling the strange incidents over in her mind.

A restless sleep ensued—one populated by disturbing thoughts where she wondered if Mr. Edwards had kissed anyone before, and if so, would it hold the frightening elements she'd experienced with James—and she woke early to a bleak morn, the half-open curtains revealing the drear of the day.

And when Daisy finally made an appearance, it was to hurriedly share that Miss Beatrice Langley was nowhere to be found, and, it was suspected, had run away.

Chapter 5

James squared his shoulders. The past week's infernal trip north had only seen his financial straits grow in desperation. He *had* to secure something from his father, even a pittance. No matter what it would take. James might be able to outrun some creditors, but his journey to London and return to the armed forces in two days meant he needed to extract whatever funds possible to pay his debts, retrieve the chain, and make his departure south.

"Why, Mr. James, sir!" Dawson offered an obsequious bow.

"As you can see," he growled.

"It's wonderful to have you back." The man hurried to keep up with James's longer strides through the front entry. "Things have been in such an uproar since—"

"Where is my father?" he interrupted.

"In the library, sir."

James veered course to that direction, through the Great Hall, which seemed a tad cleaner and less depressing than normal—were those fresh flowers on the sideboard?—and strode into the room his father preferred as his domain.

"Father, I have returned." He mock-bowed.

"Not an apparition, then."

His lip curled. His father's caustic wit was one of his few qualities James claimed too.

"I don't suppose you have seen your foolish sister?"

"Beatrice? Is she not here?"

His father exhaled, and in that moment seemed very old.

"Father? What is it?"

"Your sister has run away. She fled to the border and married that young fool Grayling, can you believe."

He muttered a curse. "What a silly widgeon my sister is."

His father cleared his throat. "You should mind your manners in front of ladies, my boy."

Ladies? His heart sank. Was Miss Barnstaple and her grasping mother here? He turned. "Forgive me, I . . ."

But the woman dressed in grey rising from her position seated at a desk in the corner who met his gaze did not hold Miss Barnstaple's striking prettiness. He swallowed. "Miss . . ." Deuce take this confounded memory-numbing headache that only whiskey could remedy.

"Miss Drayton," his father supplied.

Why did she have in front of her a ledger he recognized as one of Father's? "What are you doing here?"

"Beatrice invited me to stay," she said in her soft voice, "then, when she left, I was without a home—"

"So I invited her to stay on as my secretary." Father's eyes held a glint of something that looked suspiciously like defiance.

"I don't understand." Was his father mad? James sank into a seat. "What happened to old Dibbins?"

"You may recall he died a few months ago."

Well, no. Obviously he didn't.

"Miss Drayton—unlike my own progeny—seems to hold both an interest in this grand pile, and a sense of forthrightness, duty, and responsibility that is sadly lacking elsewhere."

Judging from his hostile stare, James didn't need to wonder exactly who Father suspected as lacking in said things. But that didn't mean he would not protest. "Who has ever heard of a young woman—or any woman, for that matter—holding such a post?"

"I did not think you one who cared much for what others thought. You seem heedless of your own reputation."

James felt himself flush. "It appears the world is going mad."

"Besides," his father continued, as if James had not spoken, "I consider Miss Drayton's role as overseeing the household too."

"What about Mrs. Copley?"

"She has proved unsatisfactory for quite some time."

Well, yes, but that didn't mean Father ever noticed such things before. What had Miss Drayton done to bewitch Father so? James pushed to unsteady feet. Hound's teeth, but he was tired. He poured himself a drink and offered one to Father, but he declined.

The alcohol proved sweet momentary relief, numbing the questions racing around his head and heart. What—? Beatrice. That's right. "So, what are we to do about finding Bea? You don't seem too concerned seeing as you're sitting here. Who is looking for her?"

"No need. I have just received a letter from her."

"Then where is she?"

"She tells me they are now in Morpeth. Apparently Grayling has a cottage there."

"From a castle to a cottage? I can scarce believe it!" He placed the glass on the table with more force than necessary.

His father ignored his outburst and studied him with lowered brow, his gaze calculating.

"Well?" His gaze shifted from his father to Beatrice's friend. "Did you help her?"

"I beg your pardon?"

"My sister. You must have known what she was about."

"I knew she loved Mr. Grayling," she said, eyes steady on him, as pink o'erspread her face. "And I knew she wished to marry him."

"You are shameless! How dare you?"

"James!" His father's voice cut as a whip. "That is enough."

"And when I learned of your sister's absence, I immediately spoke of my suspicions to your father."

"What suspicions?"

"I, er . . ." The pink deepened to rose, before she said stoutly, "I mentioned that I believed she may have gone to the border."

His eyes narrowed. "And just why would you suspicion thus?"

A pause. "Because I advised her to."

What? "You cannot be serious."

"Oh, but she is," his father interposed. "I was not at all best pleased when I first learned this."

"I can imagine," he muttered, staring at the demure Miss Drayton with a mix of horror and awe. Who ever dared to admit such things to Father? "So you rewarded such appalling candor with employment, did you, Father?"

"That's about the sum of it, yes."

Mind awhirl, James sat down. Truly, the recent journey was playing havoc with his mind. Perhaps he was the one in need of Bedlam.

A knock came at the door, and at his father's invitation it opened, admitting Dawson and Mrs. Copley, who both sent narrow-eyed looks of disgust at Miss Drayton.

"Well? What is it?" his father demanded.

"Sir, I'm afraid there's a problem with the servants," Mrs. Copley huffed. "And I—"

"Then speak to Miss Drayton about it. Dawson?"

Mrs. Copley's cheeks reddened as Dawson spoke with his father about a farming matter. She turned to James and offered a bobbed curtsy. "Mr. James, I'm that pleased you're back."

"Why?" he asked coolly.

"Oh!" She blinked as if taken aback. "I, er, well . . ." She glanced at his father, then at the new housekeeper, her mien hardening. "It's that things have been quite in disarray in recent days, and"—her voice lowered—"I fear have gotten rather out of hand."

"I'm afraid I do not take your meaning." Nor did he have any desire to. He'd never liked her miserable, nipcheese, slack-mettled ways.

She glanced across to where her father was talking in quiet tones to Miss Drayton and Dawson. "It's your father, sir. I'm afraid he's been blinded by that young lady."

"In what way?" Surely she didn't suspect Father of holding a candle for the bran-faced woman sitting there.

"Here she is claiming to be a housekeeper," she sniffed, "when Mr. Dawson overheard Miss Beatrice say this one had never done such a thing before."

His brows rose.

"And *I* caught Mr. Edwards passing her a note just before Miss Beatrice left," Copley continued.

"Who?"

"The vicar," she hissed.

A disbelieving chuckle pushed out. "Do you suspect a man of the cloth of aiding and abetting my sister's elopement?"

"I can only speak what I saw with my own two eyes, sir," she said with another sniff. "And when I see how your father has been bamboozled by a young lady's face—"

"I should be very careful how you proceed, Mrs. Copley," he said softly.

She stiffened. Then, sidling a glance at Dawson, lifted her chin. "Mark my words, Mr. James. Things have come to a pretty pass if your dear sainted mother is to be forgotten, and a servant of many years standing is to be passed over, for the likes of a brazen hussy like *that* one."

Her voice wormed into his ears, prodding his headache to a greater severity. "That is enough, Mrs. Copley."

"But sir, you should hear how she speaks to the staff."

"I said that is enough!" he roared, jerking Father's and Miss Drayton's attention back to him.

"Is there a problem?" Father lifted a brow.

James glanced at Miss Drayton, her clear grey eyes meeting his coolly.

What hold did she have over his father? Was Father losing his wits? Or was James losing his? Oh, how his head ached. "I am tired," he snapped. "I wish to find my bed."

"Will you be requiring some food, sir?"

Miss Drayton's request, echoed limply a second later by a glaring Mrs. Copley, he met with a scowl. "Send it up to my room. I'll eat there. Dawson, I'll want heated water."

The man nodded and exited, followed quickly by Mrs. Copley and Miss Drayton. He nodded to his father and made his way up the great stairs.

What a bizarre set of circumstances. The world indeed seemed zany, almost as if he had sickened and was delirious.

Perhaps a good night's sleep might bring some order to his brain.

The afternoon's inexplicable events were not made any clearer the following morn. He made his way downstairs and met his father at the breakfast table, his grunt of acknowledgment equivalent to his father's standard morning greetings.

James's sleep had left him heavy-eyed, the questions of the previous day refusing to ease. What was happening here? The castle seemed the same yet strangely different, as if the air held renewed freshness. Not that the place was cold. Instead, he'd been pleasantly surprised to see the rooms dusted and more light-filled—was that the result of polished window glass?—like they were at long last cared for. But it was more than polished surfaces and fresh flowers. It was as if the old rooms seemed to vibrate with a sense of expectancy—or was that just the state of his befuddled heart?

At least the food was hot and as it ought be. He shoveled in an overlarge forkful of baked ham.

His father's newssheet lowered. "Didn't you get fed last night?"

He knew a moment's shame for behaving in such a schoolboy manner. "I did, thank you." And surprisingly delicious it had been.

"Don't thank me," his father said. "You can thank Miss Drayton."

Ah, yes, the ever-efficient Miss Drayton. She who, unlike his foolish sister, seemed to have wrought a mysterious change over this house and his father. Clearly she was suspect.

He tried for more decorum as he finished his meal, and obeyed his father's summons to the library, taking his freshly refilled glass with him. On the way they passed Miss Drayton, her nondescript gown making her seem mouselike indeed.

Father paused to speak to her, giving James ample time to study her Lilliputian figure, the plain features and dull ensemble she wore not his preferred style at all.

"Thank you, my dear."

His brows rose. My dear? Had his father ever used such an endearment before?

She inclined her head and moved away, her gaze meeting his for the briefest moment then shying away, leaving James with an unsettled feeling, as if those grey eyes perceived his very heart, a place so filled with chaotic ruin he rarely dared contemplate it himself.

Father gestured for James to shut the door and be seated, which he obeyed.

James cleared his throat. It was time to shake off such weird musings and learn precisely what kind of spell Miss Drayton had wrought over his father. "Exactly what is Miss Drayton's role here, Father?"

"I told you. She acts as my secretary and has taken on some of the household duties."

"Even after persuading your own daughter to run away?" He took a sip of beer from his breakfast glass. "I still cannot understand the sense of that."

"I trust her. And heaven knows there are few people who keep their word these days."

No need to wonder who Father meant with that comment. "What happened to your plans for Bea and Sir John?"

"What plans?"

"I could've sworn Beatrice believed that Sir John wished to marry her, and that you agreed."

"Good heavens, you don't think I ever wanted Beatrice to wed the man, do you?"

James felt his eyes widen. "You didn't?"

"Of course not. The only plans I ever had with Sir John were about the building of a new quay into the harbor." He wheezed out a sigh. "It grieves me to think my own children lack the fortitude to speak to me on such matters and feel instead that they must run away."

An uncomfortable knot enlarged within his chest.

"I suspect Beatrice has made a rod for her own back, but she has chosen to live so, and such an action cannot be undone. She has since written and asked for forgiveness, which is a little rich, don't you agree? Do as you please then ask forgiveness as if your actions don't really matter. I replied in no uncertain terms just what I thought of that."

No surprise there. "You are angry with her?"

"Disappointed more than angry. She has shamed the family name, running off in such a way. I thought I'd raised my children to be more courageous than that."

Well! Apparently wonders did happen. James leaned back in his seat, eyeing his father. Who *was* this man? What had changed him so? Was this yet more proof of the disturbing influence this Drayton woman had over him?

"I must say the entire episode has given me reason to consider."

Why did that thought fill him with trepidation? "Consider what, Father?"

"You." His eyes seemed to bore into James's own. "Tell me, what have you done to secure your future?"

"I'm afraid I don't quite know what you mean."

"Don't play coy with me. It is exactly this type of mendacity that I abhor."

His chest tightened. "If you're asking me what plans I have, then I must tell you I will soon return to fight Napoleon. We were unexpectedly delayed but—"

"I don't care about your playing at war."

He didn't? Then what was James doing trying to garner his approval—by taking a role in his father's own regiment, no less?

"I want to know your thoughts about securing the Langley line. About what you intend to do about all this." His father waved a hand at the library's walls.

Of course. Father's greatest love had always been this house and securing a successor. He sipped his beer again. "If you wish to know if I have found someone I could consider bringing here as a bride, then no, I have not."

"Too busy with all your light-skirts."

It was said more as a comment than as a question, which gave him to wonder just how much of his reputation had spread its poison to the north.

"I have come to a decision," Father said.

His heart lifted. Perhaps Father meant that James would be able to escape the dreary boredom of this place with funds at last. Hiding here in the north, trying in vain to think of ways of robbing Peter to pay

Paul—or at least to pay the innkeeper at Longhoughton and retrieve his mother's chain—had sent him into a head-pounding fever not unlike that he'd first experienced years ago at Walcheren. Fortunately, this fever could be assuaged by more liquor. He squared his shoulders. "What is it, Father?" Anything. He'd be willing to do anything.

"You're about to go to war, where there is every likelihood you will be killed, and I'll be left without an heir."

His insides roiled. "Do you wish me to marry, sir? Is that it?"

"That's it entirely," his father nodded.

Blast and rot it. He'd be willing to do anything but that. "Am I to suppose you have someone picked out?" He studied him over his emptied glass, calculating the distance from this seat to the sideboard. He had a feeling this conversation would require several more stiff drinks.

"That's correct."

Dear heavens, no. Obviously Father had lost his wits, which was why this Drayton creature had managed to slither her way into his good graces. Seemed he would need to humor the old man a little more. "Well, before you go palming me off to Miss Barnstaple or whoever the lucky lady may be, may I remind you that I have to leave for London in a day or so. There will be no time for banns to be read or any such thing." He pushed to his feet, relieved to see his steps had steadied.

"That doesn't matter. I have it all arranged."

His progress to the decanter stilled, and he glanced at his father. "Precisely what have you arranged?"

"You cannot think I'd ever let my son marry a greedy girl like Miss Barnstaple, can you? No, I have someone far better in mind."

Oh, fire and brimstone, no. "Who?"

His father's thin lips stretched in a catlike smile. "Why, Miss Sarah Drayton, that's who."

No. A thousand times, no. He returned his attention to pouring the drink, albeit with an unsteady hand. "I must confess the idea holds little appeal."

Marriage to a homely servant? He'd sooner die. He took a large swallow of his drink, relishing the burn. If only it might burn away this conversation to oblivion.

"Come, come. You cannot have thought it through clearly. Just what did you expect? For the daughter of an earl somewhere to overlook your tarnished reputation and accept your hand? Any lady of good family would turn up her nose at you."

"Thank you for your belief in me, Father," he muttered.

"It's not my belief that's at fault here. It's your years of selfish inclinations finally taking effect. That, and your drinking, and your propensity for gambling, which has been the bane of my existence."

"Something you could have mentioned in the past if you were truly concerned."

"I thought I had. Did you not get my correspondence about your allowance being cut off?"

Is that what old Dibbins had written about? "I confess I did not." He couldn't acknowledge something he hadn't opened, could he?

"Come, James, you must admit you have never liked correction."

"Who does?" Yes, another drink was definitely in order. Liquid sloshed onto the silver tray, droplets dotting the mahogany table.

"You have always been one to kick against the goads, and I, to my regret, have felt myself unable to bring you into check. Perhaps if your poor mother had lived . . ."

A thousand regrets needled his chest. "Leave her out of it," James rasped.

"The fact is you are my heir. You are about to leave again for war—though why I do not know."

Perhaps he should try this Drayton creature's version of honesty. "Believe it or not, I thought I might try to do something for once that would make you proud."

"Yes, well . . ."

A world of disappointment layered those words. What a fool he was to ever think his father would overlook his past as he tried to make amends.

Father eyed him, fingers tapping together. "Miss Drayton is the kind of young woman I think could prove an asset to this family."

"How? She encouraged your own daughter to run away!"

"She is here and would likely not say 'no' to a proposal from even someone like yourself."

"Recommendation indeed!" Was his father serious?

"Her parents are dead, and from all accounts her family is good honest stock who hail from the midst of Yorkshire."

"You wish me to marry good honest stock, as though she were a cow?" James asked, voice pitching higher. "Well, it scarcely matters, Father. I'm leaving, and there will be no time to marry regardless of whichever plain country maid at her last prayers you desire to see me leg-shackled to."

His father said nothing for a moment. Then, "You would rather see the castle go to your cousin Frankston?"

No. He despised the man. A foppish macaroni with even less wit than hair. James took a large swig of whiskey, unease tipping and tilting within. He supposed he would have to marry one day. And Father was right. No woman of good sense and family would have him.

James studied him, his alcohol-soaked brain honing in on his father's weathered, weary countenance. How much longer did the old man have? What if this was his last chance to somehow garner Father's approval and redeem the past? War was no man's friend, after all. And with any luck he might get killed . . .

"I have a special license that would permit you to marry Miss Drayton at once if you agree."

His jaw sagged. "But that requires our signatures."

His father shrugged. "Yours is still a chicken scrawl, is it not? It was not hard to feign."

For someone with a preference for honesty, his father certainly had an odd way of showing it. "You mean you lied?"

"It is an imperfect world, Son."

James blew out a breath of disbelief. "How on earth did you manage to procure such a thing?"

"Mr. Edwards, for his sins in assisting your sister, owed me a favor. And it just so happens his uncle is the Bishop of York. And I had ho— suspected you would not return to war without a final goodbye to your father."

Had his father been about to say he'd *hoped* for his goodbye? Regardless, this only confirmed what Copley had said earlier. Had Sarah hatched this scheme with Mr. Edwards? "Father, no. This is mad."

"I believe Sarah is quite capable—"

"Who wants a *capable* wife?"

"You need scarcely see her. Especially seeing as you'll be leaving so very soon."

"Just see her long enough to do the deed, as it were," he said sarcastically.

"There is no need to be crass," his father admonished.

"And just what does Miss Drayton have to say about all this? I hardly think from her reaction earlier that she's enamored with the idea of my being her husband."

"She will take some persuasion," Father admitted.

For a moment, irritation surged—what right did an unknown nobody from goodness-knew-where have to object to him, the heir to Langley House and its fine heritage and estates? He quashed it to concentrate on the matter at hand. "If she's so reluctant, then how did you get her signature?"

For the first time in James's life, his father looked a mite uncomfortable. "She, er, may not have known precisely what she was signing."

"Father! That is unscrupulous!"

"Thus saith the pot."

Was it any wonder he never came home, with Father's constant slings and arrows? He forced himself to sit upright, to speak as slowly as his brain allowed. "Even I have more honor than to allow some poor girl to marry a scoundrel she loathes."

"I'm glad to finally see it," his father said calmly.

"What?"

"The fact is Miss Drayton knows she was duped and has still agreed."

"I cannot believe you would stoop to do such a thing." He drained his glass, poured out another one. "I cannot believe it."

"Do you want me to release those funds?"

"Yes," he said through gritted teeth. As soon as Father did, he'd ride straight to Longhoughton and see Falcott and reclaim his mother's necklace.

"Then you best start trying to believe it," his father said, rising from the table. "The ceremony begins at five o'clock."

What a predicament to be in. Foolish Beatrice. Foolish Father. More fool him.

Chapter 6

Sarah stared at her reflection in the looking glass, unable to believe what was about to occur. No one had arrived to help her with her gown—the same one she'd worn at the assembly all those weeks ago. No one could give her advice on what to do with her hair—or more importantly, what to expect on the wedding night. Such things had hardly featured in her aunt's long list of advice and admonitions, especially as she'd long been considered past her last prayers.

Yet here she was. About to marry. About to wed a man she barely knew, yet all she *did* know of him was abhorrent. She had no one to advise whether what she was doing was even legal. She supposed it was. She had signed papers that the elder Mr. Langley insisted made it so. Mr. Edwards had apparently agreed to perform the ceremony, so it must be lawful, although she wondered what had been said to make him agree. She had a measure of trust in him, even if she lacked trust in everyone else around her.

However, she still couldn't believe Mr. Langley's machinations. How could she have ever thought him a kindly man? Obviously she had proved a bigger fool than she'd known in believing his act of charity when she'd admitted her role in Beatrice's disappearance. His act had proved exactly that, a charade, and he'd merely been waiting for the opportune moment before enacting his revenge. How could he have coerced her into agreeing to marry his son? She still struggled to recall which of the many documents she, as secretary, had placed her signature on where she unwittingly gave her life away. He'd tricked her by strategically placing another form over the top, that much she knew at least, for she would never have agreed to marry the drunkard of rakehell reputation and ungentlemanly behavior. Her horror and confusion at Bea's father's deception had been mitigated by the guilt at her own role in Bea's disappearance, which melded with a strange sense that had stifled further protest. Perhaps this was a way to secure her future. Perhaps God might still wish to use her in this place. She'd barely heard Mr. Langley's mumbled explanations and veiled threats to call the authorities for her involvement in encouraging his beloved daughter to run away, the sense of purpose weighing more and more heavily on her heart.

For if she did not marry James Langley, then the question of *what next* still plagued her. Her aunt and uncle had wiped their hands of her when she'd last written and explained her intention to stay at Langley House and work for Mr. Langley, dismissing her stab at independence as inconsiderate and most improper. Beatrice might receive her, but such a move would likely only further strain relations in the family. Apart from that, she had no other options. Run away? The servants who loathed her here would never help her.

"Lord," she whispered to the empty room, "is this really what I should do?"

She breathed in, her gown's bodice straining, then exhaled, her nerves pattering in her veins. Perhaps James Langley would object. How could he not, when this was forced upon him as much as on her? She did not fool herself to think the man had a whit of kindly feeling for her, much less affection. A hastily arranged marriage with someone he clearly deemed so far beneath him—there could be nothing he'd want less.

A *thud* came at the door. "Miss Drayton?" Dawson's voice. "Mr. Langley wants you downstairs."

Only the older one did, though she scarcely knew why. When she'd begged to know Mr. Langley's reasons for his deceit, he'd simply shrugged and murmured of her steadiness of character as "something my son could well learn from" and that she'd likely never see him beyond tonight.

Was that reason enough?

"Lord, help me," she whispered.

Perhaps an angel could spirit her out the window. Or whisk her through the locked door, blinding any servants out there. The God of the Bible remained the same today, didn't He?

"Miss Drayton," Dawson said. "Must I unlock this door and drag you downstairs?"

No. This couldn't be right. She would go downstairs, admit there had been a mistake, she could not go through with it, she was sorry—

"Now!" There came a scrabbling of keys at the door, and she moved to open it just as the steward-butler nearly fell in.

His eyes narrowed, and she braced inside. How dare this self-centered man condescend to her so? If she did indeed marry the Langley heir, she would quickly show Dawson to the door. Perhaps her presence here as part of the family could actually be of benefit, as the older Mr. Langley seemed to believe.

She moved to the great stairs, scanning the servants gathered below. Was there a kindly face who might be persuaded to help her? Robert seemed kinder than most. She forced her lips up in what must appear a garish attempt at a smile.

He ducked his head, moving forward to offer her a few of the last roses in what appeared to be a hastily made bouquet.

That someone should be so thoughtful tightened her chest, her throat, refusing words to escape. She nodded her appreciation, blinked away sudden tears.

Before her breath could reinflate her flattened lungs, she was escorted into the castle's bleak and gloomy chapel. Her heart fell.

Disheveled and drunk though he might appear, James stood there nonetheless, gaze rigidly fixed ahead. There was no time to beg for Mr. Edwards's assistance as Mr. Langley instructed the service to begin immediately. Surely God saw her predicament? Was this wrong?

But a strange tug inside insisted she stay. Would it be so bad to go through with it? To marry and finally find a place to belong? How many marriages were love matches after all? Perhaps God could do something extraordinary and redeem such inauspicious beginnings. Besides, as Mr. Langley senior had said, after tonight she would scarcely see James again.

But first she had to get through tonight.

So she stood in the cold chapel and her lips made promises she doubted her heart could determine to keep. How could she, when her bridegroom swayed and mumbled his responses with slurred speech, his breath reeking of the courage he had found in a bottle?

She was a fool to do this. A fool to agree. But even as Mr. Edwards eyed her with compassion—had he been blackmailed by the Langleys too?—she knew something else. Marriage into this strange family would give her roots. She could settle and perhaps one day feel as part of the fabric of this place as the ancient tapestry hanging on the wall. Perhaps one day she might even be afforded something of the respect that still clung faintly to the Langley name. Perhaps what felt so wrong could actually be made right.

A moment later and she herself was swaying on her feet, unable to believe the words as Mr. Edwards uttered "husband and wife."

There was no kiss—her husband seemed to loathe her presence as much as she did his—and besides, they had already shared that particular intimate embrace, albeit weeks ago and in front of scores of witnesses.

Bile rose and she touched her mouth, willing it to subside.

Oh, how wretched was she.

An hour later, having moved the remains of her wedding supper on her plate sufficiently to suggest she'd eaten something, she rose from the dining table and made her way back to her bedchamber. What happened now remained a mystery. She moved to the seat near the window and sat down, unable to shake this heavy vagueness, this lethargic sense that she was an observer, and this was not truly happening to her but to someone else.

A sound outside drew attention to a horseman, a horseman who looked awfully like her husband, riding as if the hounds of hell were on his heels. He was leaving? Already? She did not blame him, but still . . . A measure of hurt unfurled inside.

Loneliness pummeled anew, as thunderous and all-enveloping as the waves that crashed on the rocks outside. Tension stiffened her limbs, as images of the ceremony pecked through the mental fog. Mr. Langley, barely able to look at her—had that been guilt or shame? Mr. Edwards, eyes soft and sympathetic. James Langley, drunkenly standing, even as he somehow still managed to look handsome.

Could she ever learn to like this man who now was her husband? James unnerved her with his hard gaze and unsmiling countenance. But there had been times when she had thought she caught a glimpse of something softer, a wisp of sorrow in his features when he'd look at his father, there but for a second before it disappeared. Nonsensical, but enough to draw the slightest strain of pity, which didn't sit at all well when she wanted to despise him for his actions at the ball, for his willingness to be manipulated into wedding someone he despised.

A knock came at the door.

Her eyes flew open, fear clutched her insides. Was he back so soon? What would he expect from her tonight? Oh, why hadn't she thought this through more? She glanced at the window. Was there time to escape?

"Mrs. Langley?"

Breath escaped in a whoosh. Mrs. Copley. Oh, *dear* Mrs. Copley might be able to help. She hurried to the door and undid the latch. "Mrs. Copley, would you mind—?"

"I have nothing to say to you," she said with a sniff. "I should have known this was your scheme from the moment you first set foot in this house, and now you are here, I cannot like it, but I will do my duty."

"No, you have it wrong—"

"*Mrs. Langley,*" the servant said with a mock curtsy, "if you would be so good as to come this way. You are to be moved to the main bedchambers."

What? "No, no. I have no desire to do so. I quite like it here."

"I am obeying Mr. Langley's orders. Mr. Langley the elder. You are to have his wife's quarters, and young Mr. Langley will move to the master's."

"But I do not wish—"

"Your wishes are neither here nor there. Now, please come with me, *Mrs. Langley,* and I will have done my duty."

Further repudiation was pointless. As Daisy moved inside to pack her things, Sarah collected her most treasured items—a painted portrait of her parents, her mother's hairbrush, her Bible—then followed Mrs.

Copley down the hall, around the corner to where the larger family bed-chambers were located, feet dragging in dread. It seemed most of the household servants were there, their eyes widening when they saw her before lips curled in derisive mock bows and obsequious curtsies.

There was no way she could explain herself to them, for to attempt to explain the breadth of this bizarre situation was beyond her. Mrs. Copley's words held a grain of truth, she could not deny, as she *had* wanted to secure her future. She would simply have to act with a degree of dignity and civility and pretend their snubs did not sting.

Head high, she entered the room once forbidden her, then gasped. The room was twice the size of her previous accommodations and boasted an even more wonderful view of the sea and coastline from its two aspects. It was the corner room, and thus was designed to be one of the grand-est rooms in the entire house with its magnificently carved oak bed-stead with embroidered tester, and the matching padded seats in window embrasures.

Mrs. Copley gave a cursory summation of the various features of the room—the special closet where a hipbath was permanently located, the wardrobe she could walk into, the door connecting this to the master's chambers next door—features that only reinforced just how magnifi-cently appointed this room was, and just how inappropriate and unsuit-able she was for taking possession of such a space.

"I should not . . ." she faltered.

Mrs. Copley's eyes narrowed, as if she were only too willing to agree aloud with any protestations Sarah verbalized regarding her presumption at taking the mistress's room.

Sarah cleared her throat. "I should not like to sleep with closed windows."

"But, miss, the night air be bad for you."

Would insisting upon being addressed by her new title draw derision or respect? "I do not believe that to be the case. And you may call me 'ma'am' from now on."

"Very well, *Mrs. Langley*, ma'am."

Sarah met her bold gaze squarely, waiting until the older woman finally looked away. "That will be all, thank you, Mrs. Copley."

The servant's eyes flashed, and her lips pressed together as if she fought to contain whatever protest wished to erupt.

Sarah moved to the window, gazing unseeingly at the view as she waited to hear the servant leave and the door to close. Then she exhaled, shoulders slumping, as the enormity of what she'd agreed to buckled her knees. She sank onto the rose-pink plush window seat. *Dear God, what have I done?*

She was alone, virtually friendless, vulnerable to the manipulations of the Langley men. Had she sinned in agreeing to marry? But a persistent tug that this *was* right refused to abate. She would simply have to trust God directed her paths.

A clatter came at the door dividing this room from the apartment belonging to the master.

Fear traveled up her spine, freezing her limbs. *God, help me.* She had no desire for what was about to come next. The vows she'd uttered mere hours before had implied she would be willing to participate in something when she had only the vaguest notion of what to expect from the couplings she had seen of animals.

The dividing door rattled. "You in there, *wife?*" a deep voice slurred.

God help her! She braced internally. "Yes."

The door swung open, admitting alcohol fumes and the rumpled figure of her husband. She backed up against the wall as he advanced, the candlelight catching the glint of a chain at his neck. His eyes narrowed. "You."

She lifted her chin. He wouldn't hurt her. Would he?

He glanced around the room and shuddered. "I hate this room." His gaze swerved back to her. "And you, thinking you could take my mother's place. You'll never be her equal."

His words arrowed deep. She knew that. She'd never be beautiful. Never be revered. She was an imposter, someone of no great importance, trying to play a great lady's part. "I am—"

"Don't speak," he commanded, clutching her arm and dragging her to the bed, his intoxication evident in his slurred mutterings, in his stumbling over the carpet, and in his liquor-soaked hot breath.

And the way he passed out snoring on the bed.

Chapter 7

TEN MONTHS LATER

The crumple of paper being unfolded shouldn't strike fear into Sarah's heart. But these were not normal days; rather, ones of uncertainty, ones of fear. Such was the case for her situation, anyway.

Sitting opposite the faded sofa occupied by Mr. Langley, she waited, chest constricted, as the quiet of the room was punctuated by the older man's rasping breaths. A string of cobwebs high against the torn wallpaper of crimson and gold floated gently against a soundless draught. Her lips pressed together. She would need to speak to Mrs. Copley again. For all the good that would do.

James's father continued his perusal of the letter that had just been delivered, then sighed, and with a low hiss shifted forward on the sofa, his face creasing further with pain.

"Please, let me help you." She shot to her feet and hurried to draw his stiff limbs forward until he tipped into a hunched standing position.

He grunted—not in appreciation, she suspected, but in discomfort—and glanced at her. "He's coming back, y'know."

Her heart froze.

As if sensing her fear, he cackled loudly. "Sure to be a fine reunion, that one."

She pasted on indifference, willing her features to assume the nonchalance her heart could not feel, but said nothing. Anything she said was sure to be scoffed at, anyway.

"Three weeks, my dear. Three weeks. Then what do you think he's going to say, hmm?"

She met his gaze but held her tongue. In a room far away, a baby's cry prickled her skin.

What *would* James say? She dreaded to know the answer. So instead of following the teasing of a dozen anxious thoughts, she began to pray.

The baby's cry continued unabated.

If Sarah she did not move to appease her, then Mr. Langley would complain. She murmured a soft excuse, and exited the room and spoke to Evan, the new footman, in the hall. After requesting he keep an ear out for the old gentleman and to assist him if his gout prove troublesome, she ascended the stairs.

The staff had accepted her terminology to distinguish between Mr. Langley senior and her husband, James. *Husband.* The events of ten months ago still did not seem real. But if they had not taken place, that dear child would not be lying upstairs, proving a blessed ray of light within dark days.

The piercing sound grew louder, hurrying her steps to the nursery door. Nanny Broomhead glanced up with an air of relief. The older woman was a sweet-faced angel who had been another of Sarah's first appointments in her new role, and her staunchest ally against the likes of Mrs. Copley and Dawson, neither of whom had yet been persuaded to relinquish their animosity to Sarah, and both of whom seemed to think her actions in adopting poor Fanny Caflin's newborn as of one deranged.

After smiling at the nurse, Sarah swooped the crying infant from her arms. "Oh, sweetness, why are you carrying on in such a way? Never fear, your mama's here."

Her heart swelled with tenderness. Despite all the wretchedness of the beginning of her stay, despite all the pain associated with this child's birth and questions over her background, it was all worth it for the magnitude of pure love she had for this little girl.

"Bethy?" She snuggled the downy head close, pressed her lips against her hair. "Oh, how I love you."

The tiny girl gave a squawk of protest, before her whimpers eased into shuddery sighs. Warmth cascaded through Sarah's heart, swirling tenderness around and within.

"You love that little mite so much," Nanny Broomhead said fondly. "That lassie is very lucky to have you as a mother."

"You mean I'm very lucky to have her." Little Elizabeth had proved an oasis of loving calm and focus in an otherwise emotionally parched desert. Bethy had saved Sarah from despair.

"She's much calmer now," observed the servant.

"She's always been a good girl."

"And three months old soon. How big she is getting."

"Perhaps we should have a small celebration." Sarah gently adjusted the white bundle to delicately trace each of the baby's wool-shod toes.

But as Nanny Broomhead enthused over the idea, Sarah remembered the contents of her father-in-law's letter from downstairs. James would soon return, and she would need to offer an explanation for the child. She bit her lip. What should she do? How could she possibly explain?

"Mrs. Langley?"

"Pardon?" Sarah forced herself to attend. "Forgive me. I have just heard news that . . . my husband"—such a word still seemed so strange to say, even this many months later—"will return soon."

"Oh, how wonderful that will be!"

Would it? Sarah eyed the woman. Perhaps it would be all right, if he kept his distance. Perhaps she was worrying over nothing. Except she'd overheard some of the castle's servants talk about her "disgraceful conduct" concerning adopting an illegitimate baby. How much of such gossip might influence him?

"Now she is settled, I can put her down for a nice long nap." Nanny Broomhead held out expectant arms, thus forcing Sarah to release her sweet burden. "You look as though you could do with a nap too, if you don't mind me saying so, ma'am."

Sarah nodded. "I have been a little weary of late."

"And if your husband soon returns, well, you would no doubt wish to be all well and lively for him, now, wouldn't you?"

Sarah offered a small smile but said nothing, instead giving the now-sleeping infant girl a final caress. She nodded to the servant and made her way down a flight of stairs to her chambers, closed the door, and lay down on the large bed.

She closed her eyes but rest refused to come, her mind too busy ticking over the challenges presented with this morning's news. What *would* James say?

"Heavenly Father, help me." She drew in a breath. "Help me to trust You, help James to accept dear Bethy, help me to learn to like him, and"—she swallowed—"him to like me."

Memories of his last night here—his rejection, his desire to marry her simply to gain funds and reclaim the golden chain that must surely be a token from a woman he had loved, or so his father had informed her the next day—slowly faded in a kind of soothing peace, and her mind turned to other things. More pleasant things. Like the time she'd been walking along the beach only to encounter a lost seal pup, a stray from the nearby Farne Islands, or so Meeks had told her. The fluffy white-grey creature had mewed and lolled and brought a smile as she'd contemplated a bleak Christmas alone. Other pleasant things, such as the gradual ordering of some of the castle's rooms to what she imagined they should be. Then there were those times of getting to know the Langburgh villagers, doing her best to fulfill the role that her status as Mrs. Langley demanded, something that both humbled and brought joy. Time had led to a deepening of relationships with various villagers, a greater measure of trust, so much so that now she'd consider Mr. Edwards as one of her good friends.

The castle itself had seen quite a number of changes since James had left, apart from the unexpected arrival of Bethy to their lives. She hoped he might find things to appreciate in such improvements, in the house and grounds and beyond. But more importantly, she yearned to know what he would say about the one piece of sunshine in her world. Would he accept Bethy? Would he understand?

"Lord, let him show mercy," she breathed.

Then there were the servants. The older Mr. Langley had not countenanced the departure of the most troublesome of them but had offered no debate when she had said she wished to be responsible for the hire of new servants from York. He'd simply said he doubted anyone from such a big town would want to work in such an isolated location. However, her interviews had secured persons willing to work in a castle—and be happy with the basic remuneration Mr. Langley had provided.

That Mr. Langley senior entrusted such things to her was a sign of her role as chatelaine, this strange dual role of housekeeper and daughter-in-law—and as such, mistress of the house. Her time was largely her own, and she could trust most of the servants to carry out her wishes, although Mrs. Copley and Dawson both seemed inclined to argue. But whenever they had the temerity to suggest such things to the old gentleman, he'd simply dismissed their complaints and instructed them to follow their mistress's instructions. He, whether from guilt at his scheming or not, seemed to be on her side, and nowhere was that greater than his unexpected support concerning the manner of Bethy's arrival.

Thank God the man had proved to have a softer heart than what his gruffness suggested, with his assurance that given the circumstances, and the innocence of the child, they certainly were in a position to assist and provide.

But just what would his son—her husband—say?

Her eyes opened, and she studied the rose pattern of the canopy above. Pink- and blush-stitched blooms intertwined with embroidered leaves of green and silver, the pattern at once soothing and yet having inspired many hours counting roses when others may have counted sheep to attain sleep.

She'd stared at it through tears on the night her husband was supposed to make her his own, her heart a strange place of tumultuous emotions—fear, concern, relief, and, perhaps worse, rejection—which only eased in the normalcy of totting up the blooms, the simple addition creating a sense of control in an otherwise overwhelming, exhausting night.

Her skin prickled, her stomach tensed. Surely he would not grow so drunk again that he would fall asleep without taking advantage this time. Did the man own a tender side? And what on earth would his harsh tongue say when he discovered his wife had installed a tiny child into the castle, one he would know he could not have fathered?

The pace and hurry of London traffic seemed so odd to his ears. No more the sound of artillery or guns blazing, of men's groans or whimpers of pain. Well, his own whimpers might still exist, but he barely paid them heed. A ball to the shoulder had ensured his return to England far sooner than he'd wished, to this hospital room he'd shared with others rather less fortunate. At least he wasn't blind, like Lieutenant Edgerton, a hero from the Peninsular stripped of wholeness by the insidious sickness James had first encountered three years ago. And at least he had a home to go to, though he rather wondered whether his actions on his last visit there would see him truly welcomed. No, he might never be widely lauded as a hero as Lieutenant Edgerton or Captain Stamford had—although James's actions at Ciudad Rodrigo had ensured a promotion, at least— and it was little wonder.

Guilt washed across his stomach, a never-ceasing swirl of recrimination. If nothing else, his recent time in the armed forces had ensured he'd learned to live to a different code, one which made his awareness of his former life sicken him to the core. A lifetime would not be long enough for James to amend for his mistakes, to prove he was no longer a man of dishonor.

He took a moment to pray for his wife, to pray she might know mercy, that God would soften her heart—and that of his father—for his upcoming return. "Lord, help her to forgive me, just as You have pardoned my many flaws."

The prayer was constantly on his lips and in his heart, something he greeted each day and ended it with. Captain Daniel Balfour may have led him to an understanding of the Lord, and an awareness of the depth of God's forgiveness, but he suspected other members of his family might need heavenly persuasion.

"Langley," a voice spoke over him.

He turned, the padding over his cheekbone making it difficult to see the doctor.

"You're being released."

He nodded, the action eliciting a hiss of pain.

The doctor offered a wry smile. "How many times have I said you must protect your shoulder? You need to treat it gently, no heavy lifting at all, else you'll find yourself destined for a life of pain."

"No heavy lifting, understood."

"You have means of transport?"

"I have passage booked on the Mail."

"Good, good. Well, I'm sure your family will be pleased to see you."

How nice it must be to blithely offer such platitudes. There was nothing sure about his family's welcome. He could only pray that his letter had arrived and welcome there would be.

Thoughts and prayers concerning his reception accompanied him all the days-long journey from London, through Huntingdon, Grantham, Doncaster, York, Durham, and finally Newcastle. He barely noticed the other Mail passengers, although a lady with a screaming infant he could scarcely not attend to. She seemed exhausted, poor thing, as much by the child's ceaseless mewling as by the caustic remarks offered by less-than-charitable fellow travelers, and he'd done what he could by offering her his seat whilst he took refuge on the roof. Hang what the doctor might say; his ears could do with the respite. But when she'd noticed his awkward movements at the inn in Ferrybridge, and learned his strapped shoulder resulted from his involvement in the war, no amount of cajolery was enough to persuade her to accept his seat, and he was loath to relinquish it for the use of the overlarge cit from London, whose accent and barely disguised bulging purse spoke of a vulgar preoccupation with money.

He studied the passing countryside, the rolling hills green with late summer crisscrossed with aged stone walls. He wondered how the estate was faring, if the men had thought to plant barley—and then wondered at himself for wondering so.

How his old friends would have laughed, the old set whose debauched ways he'd once led and which now only made him sick. But no. Their opinion did not matter. He was most concerned with redeeming past mistakes and ensuring a better future.

The carriage dipped and rattled, and he clutched the loop of leather to stay upright. A gasp escaped, and he shook off his fellow travelers' enquired concern. "'Tis nothing."

He clenched his teeth, gaze feasting on the landscape. The moors had given way to the flatter sections of coastline, and every so often he glimpsed the North Sea shining beyond the rim of trees. A few minutes more and he'd finally see the Lilith Tower of Langley House silhouetted against the sky, always a sign he was nearly home.

The carriage gave another rackety judder, slamming his shoulder into the glass, and he swallowed an oath. Too many days of such travel had left him with a thumping in his head that only sleep would solve, although once he might have tried to cure it with rum. Those days were gone now. Captain Balfour had offered an alternative to drowning his sorrows, and while James still drank—what Englishman didn't?—he no longer drank to get drunk and drench his sorrows. He'd promised God to never get drunk again.

A bend in the road and he was finally permitted the best view of the castle, the long stretch of wall a sanctuary for centuries. He'd never found it such, but more like a prison before. Would it thus prove a safe shelter or more shackles today?

"One of the largest castles in this part of England," a man who had taken on the manner of a guide, offered to the passengers at large. "The Langley family still live there, so I'm told."

The awed murmurs of the other occupants suggested they did not yet know this was his home, and James had not advertised his name. When the carriage pulled into the village, there were some queries as to why there was a detour from the publicized schedule, and he was expecting their surprise when the ostler spoke his name.

"Captain Langley!"

He nodded to Mr. Wade, and exited with caution, taking care to guard his shoulder as the baggage rained from above. The expected arrival times barely allowed the coach to stop, let alone detour as it had, though the coachman had received handsome recompense.

A man dressed in faded livery pushed forward, hat doffed, and touched his forehead. "Major Langley, sir."

Ah. So word from other pens had reached his family of his new rank.

"Major?" Mr. Wade said, amid the surprise echoed in the murmurs of the coach passengers, many of whom pointed and stared.

"Hello, Robert," James said to the elderly servant, who joined him in gathering his bags. "How are things with you?"

The man blinked, as if shocked by the question, and James experienced a moment's shame. Perhaps it was the first time he'd enquired after the servant of many years' standing. "As well as can be expected. Thank you for asking, sir."

As the carriage trundled away, Robert put the bags into the gig and clambered up. James followed, as a sudden great weariness weighted his limbs. He'd known a renewal of the fever in the transports sailing home, a heated prickling along his neck that precluded the wearing of high neckcloths. Rest, and not fashionable entertainments for the county, was what he longed for.

"I trust my father is in good health."

"Mr. Langley is doing well, or so I'm led to believe."

"And, er," he swallowed—how was he supposed to enquire about this?—"the rest of the household? How are they?"

"Everyone is well," Robert said with an air of relief. "The mistress and the young lass too."

The young lass? What young lass? Oh well. Probably a companion that his wife—his wife!—had sought to employ. He felt himself frown, so made an effort to assume pleasantness. He could hardly blame her for seeking to have someone to talk to. He rather doubted his father provided much convivial companionship, and Mrs. Copley—if he recalled correctly—was never one to warm to newcomers, especially those whom others might consider to be perched above their proper station.

How should he negotiate his relationship with his wife? To his shame, he'd scarcely written, save the once for his departure home. He'd felt sure in those early days, when he'd had no care for his life, that he would not return. Then, later, when it seemed that despite his best efforts, God was determined to keep him alive, the campaign's movements and the like had kept him far too busy to write—even if he had known what to say.

Surely his father and his . . . wife would not have expected him home so soon. She, at the least, would be disappointed. He could scarcely blame her. Remorse twisted within. What must she think of him, knowing he'd agreed to wed simply to have money? Father must have shared that by now.

The gig had just passed the church when a curricle turned swiftly onto

the road. Judging from the light bright hair, that was Miss Barnstaple—
if she still was a miss—and her brother. The curricle slowed, the twin
expressions of astonishment perking amusement in his chest. Clearly
news of his return had not traveled far. A twist of discomfort as to just
why that might be was thrown in the shade by the Barnstaples' raptur-
ous welcome.

"Captain Langley! What a wonderful surprise to see you."

"Good afternoon, Miss Barnstaple, Barnstaple."

"Have you just returned?" She glanced at the luggage strapped to the
back of the gig.

"Of course he has." Her brother rolled his eyes as though his patience
with his sister was at naught.

"But why did we not know?"

"It was something of a surprise," James hedged. Not for anything
would he admit it was because his family was ashamed of him. Likely
why they had not shared about his promotion to the villagers.

"I'm surprised we did not receive an invitation to your homecoming,"
she said, pouting prettily.

"That is because there are no plans at this stage for such a thing. Not
that I am aware of, anyway."

"Oh, but you must have a dinner, at the very least." Her smile stretched.
"Do say you will have a dinner, Captain Langley?"

He wondered how many men had been able to resist that winsome
smile. "If plans for such a dinner are made, I will see you receive an
invitation."

"Oh, thank you, sir!"

He inclined his head. "Now, I trust you will please excuse me. It has
been a very long and trying few days."

"Of course," she murmured. "You must be anxious to return and see
your wife again."

He forced his lips up but made no comment, and before he knew it,
Robert snapped the reins, the gig was moving, and the curricle was lost
from view. The horse picked up pace, only slowing when they turned
at the gatehouse and traversed the causeway. A high tide had filled the
meres to their banks, up past the earthworks developed long ago as added

protection for the moat. Ahead, the great gatehouse loomed in perfect symmetry. He'd never loved his house, not like his father did, but he could appreciate the architectural audacity to design something so pretentious for an untitled man of means.

The gig passed through the entranceway, the deep shadows passing over him as if in reminder of his sins. His nerves tightened. He was not expecting any great welcome, but it would be nice not to see disappointment lining anyone's features.

They passed into the courtyard, and he at once noticed its improved state. Gone were the weeds and broken stone pots, and the main entranceway looked freshly painted. So, Father had finally got around to sprucing things up. How much blunt had that cost him?

The gig finally stopped, and several servants drew near, two whom he did not recognize, but one he most certainly did. "Dawson."

"Mr. James." The man's florid features widened in a gratuitous smile. "How wonderful to see you again, sir."

James simply nodded. Quite the excessive welcome from a man whose motives always seemed self-interested. He glanced at the other servants, unloading the bags. "And who are these?"

He'd asked Robert, but Dawson hastened to interrupt with, "This be Evan and Derry, sir. A footman and outside man, sir."

"And how long have they been employed here, Robert?" he asked pointedly.

"Not long after the new mistress became, er, the new mistress, sir," Robert answered with a measure of evasiveness.

Hmm. What else had his good wife managed to change in his absence? How much money had she spent in effecting such changes? It had to have cost a pretty penny. Had his father approved such things? Had his father even cleared all of James's infernal debts?

He eased his way down, refusing assistance as Dawson hurried forward with wide eyes and murmurs concerning his strapped arm. Then he was entering the cool entrance hall, before moving through the Great Hall to his father's preferred abode.

Heart tight with strain, he nodded acknowledgment of the servants'

bows and curtsies, then stopped, fingers grasping the library's door handle. *Heavenly Father, give me mercy.*

A quick twist, a push open, and he entered the room and saw his father
and his wife sitting cozily by the fire. And saw his wife was holding a baby.

Who—?

"Well, look who has returned." His father placed his book down, his
expression as hard to read as ever.

"Hello, Father." He turned to his wife and offered a small bow.
"Hello—" Oh, dear heaven! He'd forgotten her name. What was it?
Something plain and unpretentious . . . "Sarah," he finally said, despis-
ing himself, even as he could see her grey eyes narrow in an expression
of dislike. Not that he could blame her. What kind of man forgot his
wife's name?

"Good afternoon." Her voice was stiff, echoing the coldness in her eyes.

"You are looking very lovely," he said honestly. His memories of her
were rather dim, clouded as they'd been by alcohol and resentment, but
she was rather prettier than what he remembered, dressed as she was in
a round-necked gown of a flattering cut and rose color.

She said nothing, but her attention shifted to his cheek and shoulder.
Her lips pressed together, and she bowed her head.

"You are injured, Son," his father said, forehead creasing.

James lifted a hand to his cheek. "'Tis just a cut, and a ball to the
shoulder which the surgeons managed to dig out." And the strong suspicion that the legacy of illness from his previous time in the Netherlands
had flared again.

"It is good to have you back."

"Thank you, Father." Surprise at his father's genial welcome arresting
further words. He glanced around the room. The paintings appeared
brighter, as if they'd been cleaned at long last. "The house is looking well.
I did not recognize some of the servants."

"There are some new faces, that is true," his father said.

"One wonders how their wages are paid for."

"Your wife is a most capable and careful manager." His father glanced
at her with what looked like approval in his eyes.

James's heart twisted. Had Father ever regarded him so? "That capable and careful?"

"Indeed so," Father said with a decided nod.

"My wife is full of surprises," he drawled, his attention slipping guiltily from the look of dismayed hurt on his wife's face to the tiny sleeping girl she held. "Who is this?"

Not their child, surely. He barely remembered his wedding night, save for the shameful knowledge he'd drunk so much he'd not fulfilled his husbandly duty, such dishonor leading him to slink away the next morning at first light. He did the mathematical calculations. No. This child had to be several months old. There was no way she could be his. Unless . . .

His gaze narrowed, lifting to meet his wife's fast-blanching features. "Who is this child?" he asked more sternly.

"This . . . this is Bethy."

"Bethy?" What kind of ridiculous name was that? "And who, exactly, is Bethy?"

Sarah licked her bottom lip, and his attention snagged on it. It had been so long since he'd kissed a woman, since he'd—

He shook his head at himself, guts wrenching. Had his wife convinced his father that she was keen for this marriage of convenience because she'd needed a father for her baby? Had Mrs. Copley and Dawson been correct in attributing her with hidden motives? How had such a meek-seeming person fooled so many people?

Bile rose. His headache sharpened. "Whose child is this?"

"Mine," Sarah squeaked, fear—or was that defiance?—in her eyes.

How dare she taint the Langley name with her illegitimate child? How dare she look at him with pleading eyes?

"How dare you bring her into my home and pretend that she is mine?" He felt himself slipping back into his former tempestuousness, but the tiredness of a week's worth of travel and bone-deep pain in his body had loosened the bridle from his tongue. "You may have appeared meek, but this proves your true colors."

"James!" his father's voice cracked as a cat-o'-nine-tails, but James paid it no heed.

A kind of desperate fury propelled him on, a desire to prove himself in the right for once. "All this time I've been regretting my actions, been so remorseful for my sins, when really you have proved yourself no better than I!"

She swallowed, eyes wide as she appeared to shrink in her chair. The child stirred into whimpers, which saw his wife lift the girl to her shoulder, and murmur soothing words as she patted the girl's blanket-swathed back.

He found the action oddly touching, and his voice dropped in volume, but also triggered derision for his weakness. "I was a rake, and I'm not proud of what I have been, but I at least know myself to have been immoral and depraved, unlike you, madam, sitting there so shameless and debauched—"

"That is enough!" his father roared.

The baby cried, her little voice ascending into catlike shrieks which seemed to pierce his very marrow.

"Look what you've done." Sarah shushed the baby with such concentrated consideration, he wondered what it would be like if her attention turned to him. "How could you? This innocent child does not deserve your senseless anger."

James recoiled, gaze flickering between his father and this woman he'd all-too-foolishly agreed to make his wife. His father might be cantankerous, but he was not naïve. How had she hidden her deceit? Was his father blinded by this nurturing guise? "She does not belong here."

"You are mistaken," she whispered.

"You're not about to tell me that this is my child?"

"No." She swallowed again, met him bravely in the eye. "This is *my* baby, and I won't let you take her from me."

Chapter 8

Sarah trembled, fear shooting spikes of panic through her chest. He would *not* take her baby. He would not!

His eyes narrowed and the contours of his face sharpened as she remembered his harsh words of last year. He spoke, the words sounding like slush in her ears so she could barely discern what he was saying. ". . . Scandalous . . . improper . . . stain . . ."

She turned to her father-in-law, the man whose support for her circumstances she'd relied on thus far.

His gaze averted.

Her heart fell. Of course. He'd proved himself capable of duplicity before. How could she be so foolish as to think he might support her cause above his own son?

She staggered upright, clutching the now-calm child to her breast as James—she could barely think of him as her *husband*—continued speaking. She could not listen, she would *not* be made to feel an outsider in this place, the castle she had dared to hope she might finally call her home.

"Where are you going?" James demanded.

"I am tired. I have a headache." She was also rippling with anger and frustration and betrayal. But these last she could not say, so she hurried away before more could be asked of her.

She hastened up the stairs, mind ticking over what must be done. Surely Beatrice would understand if Sarah begged to visit. Bea's lack of a visit since her wedding was because of the awkwardness of being in the neighborhood after bringing disgrace to the family name, and not because her father had forbidden such a thing. From the handful of letters that Mr. Edwards had smuggled to her during services, Sarah knew that Beatrice held no animosity toward her, had indeed rejoiced in Sarah's finding favor with Beatrice's father. Surely that generosity of spirit would extend to a motherless mite Sarah had been raising?

But as soon as she contemplated all that would involve—how could she escape with a baby and not be seen?—she discarded it.

Perhaps Mr. Edwards might have an answer. Her faith in the young vicar had undergone some testing in the past year, even as she sat in the Langley box in church listening to his sermons espousing forgiveness. And although she still held him partly responsible for his involvement in her marriage, the gift of Elizabeth more than repaid any resentment. He had been the first to mention poor Fanny Caflin's predicament, wishing aloud when Sarah had been visiting the sick and the poor that a suitable home might be found for the dying mother's illegitimate newborn. When she had offered, he'd called it an answer to prayer, and when Mr. Langley agreed, it had seemed a miracle indeed.

For from that first moment of holding that precious child, Sarah had known a rush of deepest affection as pure and strong and vital as if she'd given birth herself. And nothing that man she had married, nothing anyone would do, would ever take Bethy away from her.

Perhaps God might release another miracle to her predicament soon.

She breathed in the warm sweet scent of Bethy, her head buried in the infant's neck, as she prayed that very thing.

"Mrs. Langley."

Sarah paused at the landing, glancing without fondness at Mrs. Copley below. "What is it?"

"Cook says we will dine at six tonight."

Didn't they every night? She nodded and continued her flight up the stairs, but the pause had proved long enough for James to quit the library and see her. His face darkened, and she knew her flight from the room had angered him all the more. Regret at not giving him full explanation fled in the face of fear, lending extra wings to her feet, and she hurried to the nursery to find Nanny Broomhead snoring in the rocking chair. "Nanny, wake up!"

Perhaps it was the agitation in her voice, or that which filled her heart, but the child grew restless and began to cry again.

Nanny roused with a jolt. "Oh, my goodness, Mrs. Langley, how you startled me!" Her face softened, and she held out her plump arms for Bethy. "The poor wee duckie. Come to Nanny."

Sarah gently placed the crying girl in the woman's arms, instantly feeling the loss of her snuggled comfort but relieved to see the motherly woman's soothing effect as Bethy's whimpers eased. She rubbed cold hands up her arms, trying vainly to warm them.

A creak at the door spun her around. Dread filled her heart at the commanding figure there.

"So this is where you have her."

Nanny Broomhead rose, glancing at Sarah, her arms holding the child as in a protective shield. "Who is this?"

Of course. Nanny had never met Sarah's husband. Sarah swallowed, her mouth suddenly very dry as she murmured, "This is . . . my husband, Mister"—Oh, was she supposed to address him with his armed forces title?—"Captain James Langley." Oh, she sounded like a fool!

He cleared his throat. "Major James Langley, actually."

Relief overspread Nanny Broomhead's wide features as she smiled and bobbed a curtsy. "Well, I am pleased to see you, sir. I am Nanny Broomhead. I hope this wee one has not been giving you any trouble."

He gave a smile Sarah recognized as grim. "I have barely had the chance to get acquainted, so . . ." He stepped forward and held out his arms.

Sarah's breath caught and she froze. Oh no. What was he going to do? He might have exchanged harsh words with her, but surely he possessed a measure of decency to not wish to harm a vulnerable child?

Nanny Broomhead placed the infant in his large hands.

Her husband looked up from the child and met Sarah's anxious gaze in a long, assessing look. Dark eyes still fixed on her, he said, "Excuse us, please."

Did he mean her? Sarah shifted anxiously. She would never leave!

"Not you, *wife*. You and I need to talk." He now looked at Nanny, whose dramatically widened eyes signaled she would have a juicy story to soon share downstairs in the servants' hall. "You may leave us."

The room filled with forbidding silence after Nanny's departure, giving Sarah time to study the man whose attention had returned to the child. Did he search Bethy's features to trace his own? How much did he remember of the failure of their wedding night? Even if he could not remember passing out, surely he knew the dates would be all wrong.

His earlier reaction made her wonder if his previous exploits had seen other women present him with potential issue. If so, no wonder he had been so irate.

"Please, James." His name tasted sour in her mouth, and she realized she'd only spoken his name a handful of times. "Please, I can explain."

"You can explain that scene downstairs?" He hooked a dark brow in a gesture so like his father's she felt a renewed sting of inadequacy.

She opened her mouth to explain. "I—"

"Please forgive me," he rushed to say. "I . . . I am not very good at all of this, but I am sorry my actions made you flee."

What? She took a step back. She had braced for his anger, not this . . . this sympathetic understanding.

"Your face tells me you do not believe me. I cannot blame you. My father was so good as to share the details, though why you could not tell me, I don't know." His gaze grew softer, thoughtful. "Or perhaps I do."

James glanced down at the child while Sarah's thoughts clattered and clashed to make sense of this all, and somehow find words to explain. In this room's soft afternoon light, he seemed more gaunt than what she remembered. Paler, too, his shoulders hunched as if a great weariness burdened him. Or perhaps that was the effect of his arm hooked up in a sling.

She shook her head at herself. She wasn't about to feel sorry for him. Not after how he'd treated her. Not after how he'd just spoken downstairs.

He gently stroked Bethy's pink cheek, showing a tenderness she'd never dared expect. "She is a pretty thing."

"So was her mother," she said in a low voice.

"An innkeeper's servant's child?" He winced as he shifted Bethy more firmly against his chest, as if easing the burden against his injured shoulder.

Sarah's offer to hold her died as Bethy held out a small hand, her eyes roaming his face. Sarah's chest panged. Bethy seemed quite content.

"Father told me you persuaded him to accept the child."

"Mr. Edwards said she had nowhere else to go. I was here, and . . ." *Desperately lonely, wanting some purpose, needing someone to love.* She ducked her head, escaping his probing gaze.

"And so she ended up here." He waited until her attention crept back to him again. "I must express my admiration that you managed to convince my father to agree. He's not exactly known for his largesse."

"I am in his debt."

"Yes, I imagine you are." The softness in his face dissipated, as if he recalled why she might be indebted to his father. "And he, remember, is in yours."

"I beg your pardon?"

"Perhaps you have forgotten the circumstances of our so-called marriage."

Her heart stung. *So-called?*

"You may ignore who exactly pulled those strings, but I certainly will not." His jaw clenched and a muscle throbbed in his cheek.

Fear for the child made her dare move closer, to draw Bethy slowly from his arms, to soothe her anxious whimpers and brush a hand over her tiny face as she tucked her into her cradle. "I had little choice," she whispered.

A long moment pregnant with unspoken recriminations filled the space between them. What would he say next? Would he annul this *so-called* marriage and drop her and Bethy in the streets? Indignation swirled, a sense of his injustices building within, begging for release.

"She is sweet. You have done a good thing."

What? That was it? Her belligerence crumpled. She peeked up, saw him rub a hand over his face, the lines of fatigue marked on the sheen of his forehead.

He was injured, and had been traveling for days, only to arrive home and discover his unwanted wife had an unexpected child. No wonder his first reaction had been one of anger and confusion.

"Dinner will be at six."

He shook his head. "I'm so weary I can barely keep upright." He glanced at Bethy, sucking on her fist, then back at Sarah, his expression not unkind. "I . . . we have much to talk about. But not today."

"Does that mean you will not send Bethy away?"

"Of course not."

She exhaled, shoulders dropping from near her ears, relief weakening her knees. "Thank you."

He studied her a moment longer, then gave a brief nod and walked away.

Leaving her to sag into the rocking chair and stretch out a soothing hand to quieten the restless stirring of the child, as relief magnified inside, only to escape in grateful tears.

Were the walls tilting? Why did he feel so achy and fatigued? His gaze flitted to the window, where the light drapes moved gently in the breeze. Why was it opened? Was it morning? Didn't they know he was cold?

His teeth chattered, and he burrowed deeper under the blankets as worry crept in. This must be yet another relapse of the flushing sickness that he had first experienced three years ago. His bout there had proved mild and had cleared sufficiently for his further transfer to see action in the Peninsular, and he had managed to stay relatively healthy until the ball to the shoulder put him in hospital again. But since then, the attacks had proved more frequent. Would the cooler climes of Northumberland help or hinder him as he healed?

He closed his eyes, his body continuing to shiver as if encased in ice. Memories surged of his time away, of when this insidious disease had first struck. Upon the army's disembarking on the nearby island of Walcheren, they'd been lulled into confidence due to the lack of French opposition; little had they known the French relied on weapons not of their own making. Their march to Flushing, on Walcheren's south coast, saw them later begin a siege and their optimism did not surrender. Even when the enemy tried to flood the dykes, they were only partly successful, and it did not dampen British enthusiasm, for Walcheren seemed a land of gardens, where flat fens had become rustic playgrounds, and the soldiers had leisure to feast under the shade of luxuriant fruiting trees.

And then it changed. In a matter of days, the pleasures of walled towns like Middelburg, with its ornate Renaissance-style buildings unlike those found in England, were swiftly exchanged for utter misery, as the putrefying contents of the canals released a markedly offensive effluvia, and mosquitos buzzed and bit, rendering sleep meaningless. Then the sickness struck. Water of tolerable quality proved hard to find, men's faces started swelling, and the first deaths began. Soon the sick outweighed the healthy; unsurprising, when the hospital conditions were appalling, and the sick were packed together in hovels, with sometimes only a blanket or two to be shared between twelve men. The noxious night airs and damp straw to lie on did not aid recovery, nor did the awful sounds accompanying the hundreds of burials conducted in utter blackness, candle preservation deemed higher than respect for men who'd fought in the king's service only to sink into the arms of death. Even now, the rasp and grunt of those employed to carry out such a gruesome task lingered in his brain.

He shuddered and rolled over, but the weight pressing against him made it difficult to move. How could anyone have thought the plan worthy of persisting? How could their commanding officer—accompanied by his pet turtles, so rumors said—have proved so heedless of their suffering? James had counted himself lucky to escape with but a mild bout of sickness, perhaps because he'd grown up near marshy lands, but so many of his colleagues had proved less fortunate. His luck had eventually seen him deployed with what able-bodied men remained to the battlefields of the Peninsular, where he'd conducted himself with enough credit that the failures of further north were deemed less important than giving honor for courage. But the Walcheren campaign had left an indelible legacy, one that returned in fits and starts, and made him vulnerable to whatever sickness lay in wait.

He coughed, the pang that traveled his shoulder at the jolt releasing in a moan. Had anyone noted his absence from downstairs? His arrival had been rather less than what he'd hoped for, but why, oh why, had he overreacted as in the old way when his wife presented the child?

His wife. He groaned. He was such a sinner. Such a failure. Such a hopeless man.

But a forgiven one, a faint voice whispered.

He sucked in a breath, hugging himself against the cold, against the weighty memories, and instead recalled the words of Captain Balfour, the man who had offered a lifeline of hope when he'd been in the pits of despair.

Thank You, Lord, that I'm forgiven.

It still seemed so presumptuous to assume this was the case. But he still dared believe, still dared trust the promises found in the Bible, still dared hope that God's wondrous grace extended to even such a man as he.

Experience had taught he needed to distract his mind, else he'd enter the ceaseless fretful wondering that led to despair. So he prayed for his healing, he prayed for his fellow suffering soldiers, he prayed for his father and sister, and he prayed for his wife.

Lord, help her to forgive me.

He must have dozed for a few minutes or a few hours, for he was next aware of a person moving in the shadowed room. He opened weary eyes and spied a servant dressed in the livery of a footman.

"Who are you?" he rasped.

"Evan, sir." The young man's brow furrowed. "Is there anything I can do for you, sir?"

Apart from leave? "No."

"Excuse me, sir, but are you quite well?"

What kind of fool question was that? The lad might be obliging, but he seemed none too bright.

"Should I ask for Mrs. Langley to visit?"

"Who?" His mother had died years ago.

"Your wife, sir."

His wife? When had he become leg-shackled?

"Perhaps your father, then."

"No." His father had always hated him, even more after the death of James's mother. Had called him a debased wastrel and far worse. His father had no time for him, and the feeling was entirely mutual.

Thoughts of his father had always caused a tremor in his limbs, with only one solution. He raised up to a slouch. "I need a drink."

"A drink of water? Tea? Coffee? Would you like food sent up as—"

"A real drink," he interrupted. "Wine, ale, whiskey. I don't care."

James slumped back against the pillows, head throbbing with the effort, as the need for alcohol subsided and his eyes closed as his body wracked with shivers again.

Chapter 9

The breakfast parlor door swung open, and Sarah glanced up from her meal. As the mistress of the house, she could take her breakfast in her room, but such an action seemed so decadent, especially when she preferred the company of the old gentleman. Even if sometimes he barely acknowledged her beyond a nod to her good morning.

Dawson entered, his gaze not meeting hers, and bent to murmur to Mr. Langley, who frowned and cast her a look.

She swallowed her mouthful of egg. "What is it?"

Dawson cleared his throat. "It appears the Major has taken ill but is refusing visitors."

She glanced at her father-in-law, then back at the servant. "Have you sent for the doctor?"

Dawson flushed, sent the old gentleman a look. "Well, not as yet."

"Why ever not? Please do so at once."

His eyes glittered with leashed resentment, and she pushed her brows up higher. He flushed at her unspoken challenge, and looked to Mr. Langley senior, as if requesting his permission.

"I have no use for the man, but my son may have," the older gentleman growled.

"Of course, sir. Right away, sir."

He scuttled from the room, leaving Sarah to eye her father-in-law with hesitation. Would he expect her to perform the role of a dutiful wife and go check on her husband? Or would he release her from such obligations, conscious theirs was not a normal marriage in any sense of the word?

"He does not like me," he finally said.

Her breath held. Of whom did he speak? Dawson or James? Mr. Langley rarely spoke of his feelings. Was she supposed to offer a protest? She settled for a noncommittal admission. "I am not sure he is fond of either of us at this moment."

He uttered a raspy chuckle, and she felt a rush of relief that her comment had not been taken in offense, followed by a stab of conviction. James's actions yesterday had not led her to assume he held her in the same degree of aversion as she did him. Rather, he had offered something of approval, at least regarding her actions with Bethy, something she'd prayed about but barely dared dream could happen. Her lips twisted. Oh, she of little faith.

A knock prefaced the entry of Dawson once again. "The doctor has been sent for, sir."

She knew a jab of pique at the way he ignored her again. Dawson and Mrs. Copley trod a very fine line of apparent deference when Mr. Langley was within earshot, and outspoken defiance to her face. She supposed it was her fault for choosing to overlook their manner in the beginning, not wishing to cause trouble for their somewhat-understandable resentment of one they believed had bettered her place. But now she wished she had conducted things differently. Perhaps when explaining things to the old gentleman, she might today receive a listening ear.

"Sir, I was wondering—"

"Stock markets." He slammed the paper on the table and pushed back his chair. "I'll be in the library." He met her gaze, expression inscrutable. "I expect he'll be happy enough to talk to you."

"Oh, but I—"

"You're his *wife*, after all."

Sometimes she was tempted to despise the man who had forced her into this ridiculous position. But, a quieter voice always protested, she had been just as much at fault as both Beatrice's father and Mr. Edwards. They were the three corners of the triangle of shame, equally culpable for the burden she now bore. A burden, it appeared, that would result in her adopting a veneer of care for the man she'd wed in the chapel five rooms away.

But she would not go see James now. She had other matters to attend to. Including seeking out exactly why Mrs. Copley had still not seen her way to attending to the torn wallpaper in the library.

Sarah left the remains of her breakfast and moved to the hall, where she collected the antique chatelaine and slipped it onto her belt. The impressive set of keys unlocked various cabinets of valuables throughout the house and had proved something of a challenge to wrest from Mrs. Copley when Sarah had first taken on the housekeeper role. But she loved the assurance they gave her, the sense of purpose such a responsibility bestowed, and this feeling that she was linked to the past, imposter though she might feel at times. She traced the ornate gilded decoration of birds and music, wondering again at the woman for whom they had been designed. Such beauty suggested it was for the mistress of the house, not merely a housekeeper, and possessing such a thing on her person made her yearn to fulfill the legacy of this grand and ancient house.

"Ah, Mrs. Langley, there you are."

"Mrs. Copley." Sarah returned no artificial smile. "I was just coming to find you. I wished to speak about the wallpaper and—"

"And I wished to speak to you about that new maid you insisted on hiring. Why, she does not know the first thing about how to beat a carpet! And then, when one has the audacity to berate her, she skulks off weeping, as though she's used to being treated with kid gloves. I certainly do not think she's fit for service, and simply must object to the manner of employment, when obviously you do not have the right understanding of such matters."

Sarah stared at her, throat closing. This constant battle for supremacy was so wearisome, as was trying to find the perfect blend of politeness that still demanded a level of respect. She had been sure little Maggie would be perfect for this role, she had worked for the Barnstaples, and Mr. Edwards had said she had been unfairly dismissed. In listening to Maggie's story, she had known a sense of righteous purpose, a sense of doing good in the world, just as she had when she had taken on the care for little Beth. But she had also known her continued involvement in employing servants would meet with Mrs. Copley's disapproval.

"I will speak with her," Sarah finally said. "Now about the wallpaper—"

Mrs. Copley instantly began a long list of excuses as to why she still could not attend to the matter first brought to her attention weeks ago.

Lord, give me patience and wisdom, Sarah breathed. "Then I will speak to Mr. Langley and arrange the purchase of new paper."

"But he does not like to be disturbed," Mrs. Copley protested. "I really think it best if such a matter can be postponed a little longer, until he is not distracted with the return of Mr. James."

Sarah studied her, suddenly realizing Mrs. Copley's intention. If the woman could distract Sarah by pointing out the myriad of tasks to be dealt with, then she would be let off the proverbial hook.

Or so Mrs. Copley thought.

"Your opinion does not play into the decision as to whether or not it should be done," Sarah said. "Is the wallpaper in the library torn?"

The servant finally muttered, "Yes."

"Does it need to be attended to?"

Another pause, and then, "Yes."

"Will you see that the room is cleaned and cleared appropriately so that fresh wallpaper can be hung on the affected wall?" She raised her brows, waiting. A negative here would result in Sarah's oft-repeated statement that if Mrs. Copley could not see her way fit to fulfilling her duties, then she was free to seek employment elsewhere.

"Why of course, Mrs. Langley," the servant said through what sounded like gritted teeth.

"Then see that it is cleaned by the close of the day, else I shall have to speak to Mr. Langley, and we will be forced to reconsider your future here."

"Yes, Mrs. Langley." And with a flounce worthy of a debutante, Mrs. Copley hurried away.

Sarah released a long sigh. Then made her way to the servants' hall.

The stone-flagged room next to the kitchen held only poor Maggie, seated in the corner, trying valiantly to polish a pair of boots Sarah thought she recognized as belonging to her husband.

"Hello, Maggie," she said softly.

The girl looked up with a start, before scrambling upright and offering a slightly unbalanced curtsy. "Oh, miss, I did nivver see you there."

Sarah motioned for her to sit and continue her duties. "How are you settling in?"

Maggie's brow puckered, and she studied the boot. "I, er, it is nice enough."

"Have you been asked to perform duties or tasks that you do not understand?"

"Copley—that is, Mrs. Copley, well, she's nice enough I s'pose."

She was?

"But I feel right foolish asking for help. She thinks I should know such things by now."

"Remind me, please, what were your previous duties?"

"I was asked to help in the kitchens, and make up the fires, and be a general maid of all work. Whatever they needed I did," Maggie added with a burst of pride.

"And what has Cook said? Can you help her in the kitchens?"

"She said she doesn't need another body in there getting under her feet."

"I see." Sarah might need to have a quiet word to Cook and see if she could persuade her otherwise. Given the size of the family was small and the number of servants not large, she had managed the kitchens these past years reasonably well, even if some of the meals were less than appetizing. But with the return of James Langley, the pressure on the kitchen might change, especially if he was to stay, and there was an expectation of parties and dinners and the like.

That thought led instantly to another: what if he determined not to stay? What if he wished to return to London? What would that mean for Sarah, and for Bethy? Would he ever be willing to publicly acknowledge Sarah as his wife, or would he prefer her to be kept tucked away? A moment of lightheadedness made her sway.

"Ma'am?" Maggie pushed upright. "Are you all right?"

"I am well, thank you. Please continue with your work. I shall speak to Cook and see what can be done. And if you find Mrs. Copley asks you to fulfill a task you do not know how to do, simply ask for instruction. If that does not prove sufficient, then ask one of the other maids for help." She smiled. "And I am always available to help bring clarity too, if you should need it."

"Oh, thank you, ma'am. I don't know what I'd do without you. I thinks the Barnstaples thought I was a bit simple, and that's why they let me go—"

That's what Mr. Edwards had said.

"—but I do try to understand things. It's just not easy to remember everything, especially when someone talks with enough tongue for two sets of teeth."

Sarah suppressed amusement at the expression, willing her countenance to appear kind. "I am very glad you are here, Maggie, and we'll do what we can to ensure your tasks are not challenging. But it will require concentration until you have the way of things."

"Yes, miss. Thank you, ma'am."

Sarah did smile at the interchanging nomenclature, and went to speak to the cook, who was adamant she most certainly did *not* want another person getting in her way.

"But just think how such a person could assist you," Sarah objected kindly. "You need not bother peeling potatoes or washing dishes anymore."

"I like peeling potatoes," Cook insisted, "and I have a kitchen maid to do the cleaning."

Perhaps a change of tack was needed. "Forgive me, for there has been much going on, and I'm afraid my memory is not what it could be. Did you work here when Mister James was a boy?"

"Aye." Her weathered face softened. "He was a handsome lad even then, though always getting up to mischief. Of course, he changed after his poor sainted mother died. Got quite wild."

Sarah didn't need reminding of just how wild he'd become. Nor did she want to feel any sympathy for the man. This was merely a means to an end. "Did he have a favorite meal? I wonder if we might have it soon, now that he is home."

Cook's face brightened. "Well, that be right thoughtful, ma'am. I know the very thing. A lemon syllabub. I'll have to see if we have any still in the storeroom." She gestured to the broth bubbling on the stove. "Except I'm in the middle of fixing this stew for luncheon."

"Perhaps you might see if Maggie could go look for you."

"Aye, she could. And perhaps while she's at it, she could collect some of this type of onions from the garden. The young master always did like my onion soup."

"I'll send her in."

Sarah didn't need to find Maggie; she'd been listening at the door, and, eyes shining, instantly went to Cook and listened to her instructions. "I just love the out-of-doors, and back home we'd always be digging up things in the garden."

Sarah smiled and left the room. A small victory at last. She passed Mrs. Copley and mentioned that Maggie now would be under Cook's tutelage, so she did not need to worry about her anymore.

"But who will do the boots and beat the carpets?"

"Who used to do it before?"

"I think it was Robert."

"Then Robert, or one of the other men, can do it again. I really did wonder why a young girl was being asked to deal with the boots of a gentleman."

Mrs. Copley sniffed and glanced away. "I really couldn't say."

Sarah was tempted to continue sparring, but a doorbell jangling drew her attention. "That must be the doctor."

She really should speak with him, as Mr. Langley senior would have little to say.

In the Great Hall, instead of the doctor, Dawson admitted three of the Barnstaples. A visit no doubt in deference to her husband's return, as they had certainly not called before now.

Lifting her shoulders, she affixed a smile and moved to greet them from under the portrait of her dead mother-in-law. "Good morning."

The curtsies returned by Mrs. and Miss Barnstaple were not as deep as Sarah's had been.

"We have come to see Mr. Langley," Georgiana's father said.

Sarah must have looked surprised for his daughter added, "My brother and I saw him in town yesterday—"

Oh, they meant James.

"—and he promised we could visit."

He had? She wouldn't have expected him to say such things. But then,

Sarah barely knew James or what he would say, and the Barnstaples were their closest neighbors. She invited them to sit by the great fireplace, in hard-backed chairs that implied their stay would not be long. "I'm afraid he is not well."

"Oh dear," Mrs. Barnstaple sympathized. "Have you sent for the doctor?"

"Dr. Watkins has been sent for, yes."

"Watkins? He's a treasure," cooed the Barnstaple matriarch. "He's been here for years and knows all the latest treatments from London."

Interesting how someone ensconced here for years could be considered conversant with innovative treatments and the like.

Mr. Barnstaple cleared his throat loudly. "We require a doctor rarely, but have found his knowledge sufficient for our needs. Just as well, as the only other physician moved to Edinburgh five years ago." Another raucous clearing of phlegm. "What's the matter with young James?"

She was saved from further questions by the door's jangling chime. "I am sorry, you must excuse me. Ah, Dawson, thank you." She inched her way to the door and greeted the doctor. "Hello, Dr. Watkins. Would you be so good as to come this way?"

He gave a short nod, eyes hard. "Pardon the delay. I had twins over at Lambton this morning."

For some reason—probably tiredness—that thought struck her as mildly funny and filled the smile she offered the Barnstaples with more amusement than was warranted. "Please, excuse me. As you can see, I must attend to matters here." She offered to fetch Mr. Langley senior to entertain them, a suggestion that was met with quick excuses of their need to be elsewhere.

She was moving to the stairs when Maggie crept out to speak, but her words were smothered by Miss Barnstaple's cry, "What is *she* doing here?"

Maggie gasped, and Sarah moved to screen her. "Go back to the servants' hall." She gently pushed her in that direction. "You may come back here presently."

Sarah waited until Maggie had disappeared before saying, "Please forgive me. I really must see how my husband's health fares." Was this the first time she'd been glad to have reason to call him her husband? "Dawson, perhaps you might inform Mr. Langley senior that he has guests."

Dawson moved to the library door, which seemed incentive enough for the Barnstaples to rise as one and quickly effect their departure.

Sarah exhaled, perhaps a trifle too loudly, as Dr. Watkins glanced at her. Fortunately, his lips remained sealed. She led the way upstairs.

The room was one she had not entered before, despite it adjoining hers, so she couldn't help the spark of curiosity as she finally glanced inside from her position at the door. Surprisingly, she possessed a trace of real interest in seeing how her husband fared.

James was lying on the bed—a much smaller one than the one in her room—and the chamber was dim, so her eyes took a moment to adjust.

"Excuse me, ma'am."

Evan. She gestured for the doctor to go inside while she resigned herself to attending to yet another household matter. "Yes, Evan, what is it?"

"It's about the wallpaper, ma'am. Mrs. Copley—"

Mrs. Copley! She clenched her hands.

"—insists that we'll need to strip the walls of the current paper—"

"What?"

"Exactly my thoughts, ma'am, if you don't mind me saying so. Back at my last house we did not strip all the paper, but only that from the section of affected wall."

"Which is precisely what I thought I'd communicated with her. Evan, I—"

"Mrs. Langley, you best come in here," the doctor called from the master's chamber.

Her pulse sped up. "Evan, please see she doesn't strip anything yet. A clean of the room should be sufficient for now."

"Mrs. Langley!"

She finally hurried inside the dark room and was shocked by the smell of sweat.

"He's shivering. Has he been like this long?"

Guilt panged. How to explain she hadn't seen him today until this moment?

She studied James more closely, noting the pale cheeks and chattering teeth. Her stomach twisted. "He . . . he seemed fine yesterday."

The doctor frowned, and she moved to open the windows to release the fetid air.

"Close them," he commanded. "He needs that fire built up, not cool air."

"But surely fresh air would benefit—"

"Please do not trouble yourself to tell me how to do my job, and I'll not trouble you to tell you how to do yours."

Sarah gulped. Then pulled the bell rope for assistance. While she waited for a servant to appear, she bent to attend to the fire, stirring it with the iron poker, and tossing in small twigs to build the flames.

"Wait."

She paused at the doctor's directive.

"His temperature seems to be rising." He had a hand on James's forehead. "I have never seen the like. See how he's now flushed? James?" Dr. Watkins gently slapped his uninjured cheek. "Wake up, please."

She watched as he continued his ministrations, seemingly to no avail.

James continued to lie still, too still, so still that for a terrible moment she wondered if his life might cease. Not once had she felt a pang of concern when he'd been away. Rather, the thought of being freed from her vows had at times provoked more wishful thinking than dread. But now, seeing his pitiable state, she couldn't help but pray he might recover.

"His pulse is speeding. His eyes are dilated. Quick, fetch me that glass of water."

She obeyed, a quiet terror streaking inside her veins. *Lord, please heal him with Your mighty hand*, she finally prayed.

The door opened, admitting Evan. "You rang, ma'am?"

At that moment another paroxysm wracked James, and the doctor placed a hand upon James's brow. "He's burning up. Quick, support him," he directed Evan, who hastened to lift him.

"I have not seen such a fast-moving fever before," the doctor muttered. "Where could he have picked this up?"

Sarah swallowed. "He has only just returned from the Peninsular."

"What unit?"

She told him, and he frowned. "Was his unit sent to Walcheren?"

"I couldn't say."

"Find out."

"I'll ask his father." She fled the room and found his father ensconced in the library, most fortuitously alone. Regret kneaded within that she hadn't informed him earlier. "Excuse me, sir, but James is not at all well, and the doctor wishes to know if he was sent to Walcheren."

"Walcheren?" The horizontal lines on his brow deepened. "I can't remember. Why?"

"He has a fever, and seems quite sick, and Dr. Watkins is most concerned. Perhaps you could come upstairs and see him."

"Watkins." His face tightened. "I don't trust the man."

Which perhaps explained why he'd never called for his help when suffering the ravages of gout.

"James is not that sick, surely."

She met his gaze evenly and with compassion. "I believe the doctor thinks he is."

Another look of tension. "Ah, very well, then."

And she slowly accompanied him up the stairs and tried not to give in to fear.

Chapter 10

She knew from the quick inhalation of breath that Mr. Langley was as shocked as she'd been at James's appearance.

"Is he . . . is he dying?"

She touched his arm gently. "He is suffering from a ravaging fever, but he should recover."

The doctor growled something.

"I'm so sorry, I missed what you said. Could you repeat it?"

He eyed her with an expression that looked awfully like contempt. "It's a fool who thinks they can determine the outcome of such conditions. Why, if I cannae say what is wrong with him, then you, a mere nobody, surely cannot diagnose his condition and say whether he'll recover or no."

"I just meant—"

"I am a plainspoken man. If I think something, I say it. And I won't go offering false hope when there is none."

She kept her lips closed, his words lashing against her soul. Yes, Mr. Langley might appreciate more forthright speech, but surely his look of shock demanded a compassionate desire to offer hope also?

Was her role here—as James's wife, no less—to be as passed over as seemed to be the way in so many other instances?

"What is to be done for him?" Mr. Langley finally asked.

"First, I wanted to learn if he's fought in Walcheren. There have been many deaths associated with disease there."

Where precisely had James fought? He'd never written a letter to her, and strained relations meant he'd likely written none to his father, save the one informing he was coming home.

"Did your son's regiment fight in the Netherlands in 1809?"

Mr. Langley scratched the back of his head. "Now I think upon it, perhaps he did."

Sarah's eyes widened. James Langley had been a soldier for that number of years? Granted, her conversations with Beatrice had never featured James strongly, but why had everyone implied that he was simply a wastrel rather than a man fulfilling a dangerous and important role? A sense of pride in him rose within.

"I recall he once mentioned a place called Flushing," the old gentleman offered.

The doctor made an impatient noise. "Flushing fever, Walcheren fever, it's the same. Well, that's something at least. Has he had bouts of this before?"

"Not that I was made aware."

Sarah offered a shrug to the doctor's steely-eyed gaze. She felt his estimation of her understanding drop several more notches, and tried to redeem herself by asking, "Have you treated such cases before?"

The doctor's eyes narrowed a fraction further. Was he wondering whether she was questioning his competency?

"I simply mean, do you know what is the treatment for such a condition?" Oh dear. Now he really would think she doubted his abilities. "That is—"

"The remedy involves a regimen designed to remove the impurities from the blood, and typically includes drugs such as laxatives and emetics combined with other treatments."

"What other treatments?" she dared ask.

He snorted. "I don't think I need to explain such things to you."

Heat rose within. "As James's wife, I rather think you do." Surely not all medical practitioners held their patients' families in such disdain?

He made another sound of dismissiveness. "Venesection, blistering, and dousing with cold water. Alcohol and tobacco are also regarded as panaceas."

"Please excuse my ignorance, but what is venesection?"

"The drawing of blood from a vein, often using a cupping bowl or leeches."

She gasped. "How dreadful."

He harrumphed. "Not dreadful. Quite the usual practice."

"But if he's already weak, then how can taking more blood help him regain his strength?"

He eyed her with a supercilious sneer. "As I said before, I shan't trouble to tell you how to do your role if you won't take it upon yourself to tell me how to do mine."

She stepped back as if slapped. "Is there anything you require from me?" she eventually managed.

"Send up a servant. He'd be of more use than a milk-and-sop maid."

What had she done to incur such a degree of rancor? But how to ask that felt impossible, and would surely lead to more churlish comments, so she nodded and exited the room.

Outside, she drew in a giant breath of somewhat fresher air, one hand on the wall for balance. Was she a fool? She wasn't used to people treating her so poorly. Perhaps the gruff manner of the doctor hid the fact that he was worried he might not have the wherewithal to manage James's illness. Although she could not imagine him ever admitting such a thing.

The door creaked open, and Mr. Langley senior exited, looking a paler, older version of his previous self. "Sarah."

She drew in her spine. She needed to consider him, and how such news might have impacted his frail heart. "I was just about to send for Evan," she hastened to explain.

He nodded, and she hurried to his side as he seemed to crumple.

"Evan! Robert! Dawson!" she called.

"Hush, girl. You don't want to waken James," he reprimanded her, hoarsely.

The back of her eyes moistened. She blinked it back, pressing her lips firmly to withhold her hurt. She only wished to have help to ensure the older Mr. Langley did not fall down the stairs. As for James, his mutterings suggested he barely slept anyway.

But his father's acknowledgment of his son's condition suggested he cared for James, which was something at least. Her heart softened.

Evan hurried up the stairs, and she sent him inside the room. "Please do whatever the doctor tells you."

He nodded and moved to go in.

"Is Dawson around?" she quickly added.

"He left for the village a few moments ago."

Robert took the stairs two at a time. "Is there something I can help you with?"

She inclined her head to Mr. Langley, and Robert's eyes brightened.

"Of course. Sir, may I escort you down to the library?"

Leaving her to rub her aching arm, and wonder what would be the cause of their next predicament.

His head pounded with pain, each beat of his heart sending a new aching throb through his chest. He didn't want to be here, didn't want to live. Everything hurt most excruciatingly.

The low rumble ceased, the higher-pitched noise had been chased away. Who was here? Who had left? Oh, he was cold.

His teeth chattered, and his anxious fingers plucked at the sheets. Too cold. Or too hot? Now he was too warm, his body slicking with heated moisture. He drew in a breath. Nearly gagged. Where was the fresh air he remembered? He wanted—needed—to draw in that fresh salted tang.

Memories rose: men on pallets, sickbeds, dying. Why? That cursed sickness never left, it seemed to fester in his bones, waiting, forever lurking, ready to pounce. It had knocked him about in the Netherlands and then France, before resurging again in Spain. He had been lucky to have escaped these past few months with no recurrence, when he'd known a degree of good health—save for his shoulder.

But not now. He felt dreadful. His head was heavy, his eyelids refused to open, his neck felt so stiff. It was all he could do to breathe, but he didn't like the smell of this place. He wanted that higher-pitched sound back. That sound that accompanied the scent of roses.

The days passed immeasurably slowly, her former household challenges reduced to caring for the invalid she was married to. After a week he still had not improved, and now, not for the first time, she wondered if the doctor's methods were the best at seeing her husband's health mend. Dr. Watkins had reluctantly agreed to her assistance—he had other patients to see, after all—and Evan had other duties to perform. So her days had been spent stitching by the fire in James's room, moving to assist when his movements or rasping breaths signaled aid was needed, feeding him as best she could given her patient's dislike of the broth the doctor had recommended, and sponging his body from the ravages of the fever. In doing so, she couldn't help but wonder whether the chain he wore around his neck was a gift from a lady he'd loved, or still loved. Neither could she help noticing—reluctantly—his muscular form. She had no memories of such things from the wedding night last year, he'd been too drunk to do anything more than pass out as soon as he reached the bed, before leaving without a word of farewell the following morning. The rejection of her as his wife had felt complete when she later learned from his father James's reason for marriage: that his father would clear his debts.

"Hand me the cupping glass," the doctor instructed, snapping impatient fingers.

She carefully passed him the heated glass, then watched in horrified fascination as the warmed air drew the skin up in a mound of reddening flesh. The vacuum was supposed to encourage the blood to the surface, enabling a lancet to draw blood, to which leeches would be attached to help remove the bad blood. She wasn't wholly convinced about the effectiveness of such a treatment, sure that each time James underwent bloodletting that he was weaker. But any time she raised an objection, she was immediately subjected to another lecture from the doctor, who repeated his opinion that she was a silly widgeon who should keep her nose out of other people's business. Except . . .

Sarah glanced at James, pale, forehead gleaming, ever restless. A pang of sympathy stirred deep within. She wrinkled her nose at the unwanted emotion. She did *not* want to feel sorry for him. She did not!

But something refused to be ignored, something soft, something unsettling. She would never love the man she had married, but seeing him like this, so helpless, like a baby, she could at least appreciate him as a specimen of humanity who might not be all bad. Perhaps when he was better—for she refused to believe he would succumb to this vile disease—and if he could manage to resume some of the more kindhearted manner he'd adopted with Bethy the one time he'd held her, then Sarah might even learn to like him. *Like* him. But never love him. That would require a miracle she did not believe possible at all.

A knock came at the door.

"Come," she called.

Evan appeared. "Pardon the intrusion, Mrs. Langley, but Nanny Broomhead was wondering if she might have a word."

"Of course." She glanced at the doctor but, tired of his orders and control, did not wait for permission. It was not as if she needed his permission anyway, she reminded herself crossly. If only she didn't always shrink into meekness and uncomplaining compliance around people of his nature. Why could she be strong on behalf of others, yet falter in her own defence?

"Did she say what the matter was?" she asked Evan, whose long strides seemed to eat up the hallway's length.

He shook his head. "I'm sorry, no."

"'Tis no matter," she assured. "I'm sure Bethy is fine."

But when she arrived in the nursery, it was to discover that Bethy was not fine, was in fact suffering a mildly heightened temperature, and was pale yet restless. For a moment Sarah thought how much the baby seemed like James, but instantly dismissed it. Bethy did not share his disease. How could she? He'd barely seen her but for a few brief moments, and Sarah herself was the only other person who had had contact with them both. She herself felt fine. A little weary perhaps, but healthy otherwise.

"Hello, my little darling," she whispered, holding the tiny child to her chest. "You are the sweetest part of my life, you know that, don't you?"

The little girl whimpered, her downy head tucked under Sarah's chin. "There, there, my love," she murmured. "No need to fret. You shall be feeling better in no time at all."

"Do you think we should fetch the doctor?" Nanny Broomhead asked.

"I don't know if it's entirely necessary, but he is here, so it could not hurt to ask him to take a look."

Nanny exhaled, a sound holding so much relief that each beat of Sarah's heart seemed weighted with a greater degree of fear. "Are you that concerned, Nanny?"

"It is not like the little lass to be so listless. I'm sure it's nothing, but I would like to make sure."

Despite her concern, Sarah smiled at the expression. Yet she knew exactly how the nurse felt. One liked to think things would improve, and naturally one hoped for the best, but it was only wise to ensure that one wasn't living in a place of foolish denial.

"I will request him to come up," she promised, cradling Bethy to her chest, smoothing a gentle hand over damp blonde curls.

"Oh, thank you, ma'am."

With a kiss to the tiny girl's brow, she placed her back in her cradle and returned to James's room.

The doctor was packing up his things, having drawn an amount of blood he evidently deemed sufficient.

"Excuse me, Doctor, but I was hoping you could pay a visit to the baby. Nanny Broomhead is sure she has a temperature, and—"

"The Caflin brat?"

She blinked, shocked at his derision. "My daughter," she insisted.

"Come now, she is hardly yours," he scoffed. "Don't go fooling yourself that anyone else thinks that either."

Her chest tightened. "How dare you?" She sucked in a deep breath. "Regardless of whether I have birthed her, I—and the Langley household—still consider her as part of this family."

"Do they?" he asked cynically. "Really?"

"Yes! And regardless of the circumstances of her birth, surely you should care about all people. Bethy is one of God's children, is she not?'

"Perhaps He shall need to tend to her, then. I'm a very busy man."

She gasped.

"Mrs. Langley, there is no need for your hysterics. That will do nobody any good, least of all your husband here."

She fought to calm herself, and said with dignity, "I wish you to see Baby Elizabeth."

He sighed. "You say she has a high temperature?"

Sarah nodded, clinging to the small pearl of hope his thawed attitude seemed to hold. "Yes. Nanny is concerned—"

"Well, children often have fluctuations in their temperatures. I'm sure it's nothing to worry about."

"But could you not come and see?"

He slid a look at her she could not quite interpret. Hostile? Impatient? "I'm afraid I have other patients to see. This household cannot occupy all my time."

"But, Doctor—"

"Good day, Mrs. Langley. I trust you know what to do with your husband here."

She glanced at James, his complexion almost as pale as the sheet, but at least he now seemed to be sleeping. "I, er, yes."

"I've given him a sleeping draught, with tincture of opium. He needs to rest."

"Yes, of course." And not be constantly poked at and prodded by a doctor, or having vile amounts of blood removed. "And little Elizabeth?" she prompted.

"Who?"

"The baby!" she exclaimed, shocked he had forgotten so quickly.

He shrugged. "Only summon me if things get much worse."

"Doctor, I—"

He shushed her impatiently, retrieved his bag of instruments, and left.

Chapter 11

Mad dreams. Bad dreams. Or were they once lived and real? He barely knew what was real, days blurring into a new kind of nothingness, separated only into days when the doctor came and blessed days when he did not.

He loved those days. Those were ones when there was little in the way of jabbing and pain, when instead he heard gentle soothing sounds, encouragements to eat, a comforting arm to lean on as he attempted to eat soup. He feared he splashed more on his covers than consumed. But there was no word of recrimination. None like what he remembered. How many years ago had that been? Nurse Jenkins, tight-faced, full of admonitions and the fear of God. Why had no one ever told her God was not a rancorous old man seeking simply to destroy? Why had it taken so long before anyone ever told *him*?

He lifted heavy eyelids, forced the whirl in his brain to steady, focus, still. Beyond the bed's end he could see the chamber's oak-paneled walls, the fireplace screen, and soft daylight drifting from the window. Soothing sights, a thousand times better than those dreams that had stolen true rest last night. Dreams of shivering sickness, of emaciated men, punctuated with moans and cries, gunshots and tears. To be here, in his home, with his family, felt like a guilt-plagued dream. Why was he so blessed when others faced such torture still?

He rolled to his side. His shoulder still ached, but not as much. He was slowly improving. *Thank You, God.*

A soft tap came at the door.

He tried to answer, but nothing but rasping air escaped.

Light entered the room, the subtle scent of roses. "Good morning." A soft voice. "How are you today?"

Better for your presence, he longed to say.

Who was she? He should know. But memories had a funny way of blending with the now, of lending weighty haze to this uncertain existence he endured.

He knew so little, save that when the doctor came he felt a brooding presence, as if malevolence itself had entered the room. Those visits always left him weaker in both body and spirit. But the doctor was not here. Thank goodness. He closed his eyes, felt the weight of sleep, of peace.

For he also knew that with this woman he felt safe.

Long days continued, filled with nursing, house management, and cheerless conversations. It seemed the household and surrounding neighbors held grave fears for James's health, or such was indicated by the hushed whispers of the visitors she was forced to entertain. Eventually, after one too many appearances from the Barnstaples, she was forced to instruct Dawson to say they were not receiving social calls. She had too much to do, worries weighed too heavily, and she was unable to pretend to care about the platitudes and pleasantries of those whom she suspected as false.

Bethy had not improved, but neither had she worsened, and on the visits the doctor had made to James, he still refused to see the child. Well, once he had condescended to stop by when she had insisted that if he did not, she would then carry Bethy down to see him. He'd given her a swift inspection, said she seemed fine to him, and dismissed Sarah's and Nanny's concerns with a derisive "you coddle the bairn too much."

She could barely take offense, so relieved was she to have him finally look at Bethy, and his indifference fueled a hope that perhaps she and Nanny had indeed been too quick to imagine the worst. Thus her prayers continued, and she trusted that between God and the doctor, and Nanny's care and Sarah's love, that the little girl would soon recover and be strong and hale again.

A murmur came from the bed, and she moved closer to James. His fever seemed to have receded, although on both the doctor's visits the horrible practice of leeching had still persisted. When she questioned why, the doctor had only looked at her with one of those looks that made her insides shrivel, so she had quickly ceased her protest. But she had said something to James's father, hoping he might be able to offer advice about the welfare of his son.

"Watkins has his faults, but he's the only medical practitioner for miles. He's been the family's doctor for years." Again that indecipherable expression crossed his features.

"But don't you think the bloodletting makes James weaker?"

"We're supposed to trust our medical professionals," he countered, eyes flashing, as if that put an end to the matter.

But why did they need to blindly accept the word of those who believed they knew best? Surely one could be erroneous and still think a pathway most appropriate. She rather doubted whether Dr. Watkins was the type of man to ever be inclined to admit a mistake. If he was correct about the treatments, why did James's health improve on days with no bloodletting, no leeches? She had brought this to God in prayer, but He seemed to offer no direction, so the fears pressed on.

Now she waited for the doctor's next visit, conscious of James lying in the bed, his restlessness resuming once more. His hand shook, and she eyed it, biting her lip. Then slowly covered it with her own.

Instantly her fingers were held in a tight grasp. "Mama, is that you?"

Oh! Her heart wrenched. Poor man. Still, she pulled her hand away. "This is Sarah."

His eyes opened then, his face shifting to study her. She could see the exhaustion lining his dark-green eyes, the violet shadows underneath only making the green more vivid. "Sarah?"

Had he forgotten whom she was? "Beatrice's friend. Your . . ." she almost choked, "your wife."

"Wife?" He blinked, as if in confusion. "Am I married?"

She nodded, feeling another twist of pity for the poor man in the bed.

He offered a faint echo of a smile, the effort producing a strange tug of new emotion within her chest. He was being brave, and such an action—smiling at her when he was almost certainly still in great pain—could almost be considered gallant.

"Is the doctor coming today?"

"Soon."

He grimaced, and she waited, wondering at that expression. "How . . . how do you feel?"

"Awful. But at least my headache has cleared enough that I can now think straight."

"That is something to be thankful for."

"You've been here often, haven't you?"

"I beg your pardon?"

He frowned. "Tending to me, nursing me?"

"Evan and I both have," she allowed.

He sank back onto the pillow, eyes closed, lips turned up slightly in an expression that seemed to hold a degree of smugness.

"So you are aware of us, then?"

"I can tell when you're here." He yawned.

Poor man. He must be so wearied. But his words had provoked her curiosity. "How can you tell?"

"Roses." He yawned again.

"I beg your pardon?"

"You smell like roses."

Oh. A fluttery kind of warmth filled her heart. Was this the first truly kind thing he'd ever said to her? He might've said something upon his return to the castle about her looking well, but she'd recognized that as a mere civil greeting, with little truth behind the politeness. Yet now, unfettered by expectations of courtesy, his words seemed to resonate with sincerity. Oh, what a fool she was to care so. But at least she was willing to believe that perhaps he no longer disliked her.

"Are you very weary?"

"Exhausted," he mumbled, eyes still closed. "And every time the doctor is here, I feel worse."

"What do you mean?"

His eyelids lifted, his gaze holding hers, his eyes fringed by thick lashes. "The doctors in London said this disease comes and goes, that leeching has no benefit. I . . . I don't want to be leeched anymore."

Concern inched her closer. "Does it cause pain?"

"No. Just leaves me so . . . weak, like a wee bairn."

"I . . . I have wondered about this. I have even spoken to your father, but he seems to think Dr. Watkins is beyond reproach."

"Beyond reproach? That's a laugh." His hand found hers. "Please. Don't let him do it again."

She gently squeezed, and in this new spirit of accord, said, "I will do my best to stop him."

"Thank you." He smiled again, more warmly this time, and she experienced another twinge high in her chest.

A knock came at the door, and she instantly sprang away. "Come in," she called, smoothing down her gown, hoping her cheeks weren't as red as the heat there suggested. Not that she had any reason to feel embarrassed. Surely smiling at her husband wasn't something of which to be ashamed?

Evan entered. "The doctor is here."

"Send him in." She glanced at James. He nodded wearily, which prompted her to add, "But please wait just outside the door."

Resolve strengthened to do all she could to protect him. She might never love James, but she no longer disliked him. And as he'd said, he was virtually helpless, and if he had no desire for bloodletting, then she would not permit it.

The doctor entered, his attire scruffier than normal. He too wore the ravages of strain in the lines and shadows of his face. His whiskers seemed to hold more silver these days too.

"How is the patient?" he asked.

"Fine." James's voice held more strength than before, as if he wanted to convince the doctor of his improved health.

"Fine?" The doctor glanced at Sarah. "He's speaking, at least."

She nodded. "He seems much better today."

"Yet still lies abed." The doctor moved to his bag, drew out his instruments. "Well, I'm pleased to hear you're finally on the mend. It's been touch and go for a while now, I don't mind admitting—"

What?

"—but your fever seems to have finally resolved, so I'm hopeful one more round should finish the job nicely."

Sarah stepped closer. "One more round of what?"

The doctor gave a sound of impatience. "One more go with the lancet, and we should see this disease knocked firmly on the head once and for all."

"No." Sarah took another step toward the doctor. "Please, I don't think he is strong enough."

His bushy brows rose in surprise. "But you just said—you both just said—he was fine. Another leeching will certainly make that so. Now, please move out of the way."

"No." Sarah put steel into her voice. "I do not want you to do this."

"Yes, but it's not what you want that concerns anyone here, is it? You are nothing but a—"

"Ask James," she interrupted desperately. She turned to the patient. "James? Do you wish to undergo more bloodletting?"

"You know I do not." The dark-green of his eyes shaded with fear and pleading.

"Doctor, I must insist you put that instrument down."

"You are irrational and overly emotional. You have no right to insist such things of me."

"I am his wife," she said, "so I have every right."

The doctor ignored her and readied the lancet.

"Evan!" she called. "Evan!" She inserted herself between James and the doctor, tugging his hand away from where he tried to insert the knife.

He batted her away like one might a nuisance cat.

"Evan!"

The door sprang open and Evan charged in, panting slightly. "Sorry, ma'am, I was—what?" His wide eyes seemed to take in the awful truth of the situation, and he rushed to the doctor, held his arm, and whisked the instrument of death away.

"Oh, thank you," she gasped. "Please remove him at once."

Evan pinned the doctor's arms behind his back and marched him to the door, away from James.

She glanced at her husband, whose fear-filled eyes gradually relaxed, his feeble hand reaching out to clasp hers.

"You will regret this," the doctor shouted, trying to twist away from Evan, his face like thunder.

"I do not think we will," she said. "You will not attend to my husband anymore. Your services are no longer required."

"We'll see about that," he said.

"My wife is correct," James said, his voice weak but still able to be heard. "I do not wish for you to come to this residence ever again."

The doctor slipped from Evan's grasp and headed toward his supplies. "I shall speak to your father about this impertinence," he said, packing away his instruments.

"And I shall inform him of your treatment and how it has weakened me."

"But you are better now."

"So much better you wished to cut me open once again?" James said, with a reversion to the sarcasm she first knew him for. "I sometimes wonder if the only reason I am still alive is due to my wife's faithful nursing, rather than any of your quackery."

"Goodbye, doctor," Sarah said, adding with firmness, "Evan, please escort the doctor out."

"Yes, ma'am."

The doctor shook off Evan's restraining hand. "I am not a dog." He smoothed down his wrinkled coat, collected his medical bag, and glanced at James, then at Sarah. "That child you are so fond of?"

"Bethy?" She followed him from the room. "What about her? Her condition has not worsened."

He snorted. "Don't be so sure of that. I'm near positive she has caught your husband's infernal fever, and her weakened state means she may possibly die."

What? No. No, no. No, *no!*

He gave a mocking bow. "Good day to you."

Chapter 12

Mournful autumn winds lamented beyond the stone walls, but inside James knew peace. One week since the doctor's last visit and he was sitting up, reading Psalms, feeling his spirit strengthen as his body further healed.

The words of truth struck deep within. How well he could relate.

Bless the LORD, O my soul: and all that is within me, bless his holy name.

Bless the LORD, O my soul, and forget not all his benefits:

Who forgiveth all thine iniquities; who healeth all thy diseases;

Who redeemeth thy life from destruction; who crowneth thee with loving-kindness and tender mercies;

Who satisfieth thy mouth with good things; so that thy youth is renewed like the eagle's.

Blessing. Healing. Promise.

"Thank You, Lord." James glanced up from the words, his heart full. Oh, how thankful he was for God's mercies, for His healing, for His forgiveness, that He had chosen in His great mercy to redeem James's life from destruction.

A shiver wracked his frame, not from illness but borne of memories. When he considered his past, he could see how often his choices had led to further destruction—destroying relationships, destroying futures, destroying lives. Some of these consequences would last forever. His father would never forgive James for his mother's death. But a small but stubborn hope—desperate hope, perhaps—clung to the belief that God's promise might one day even extend that far.

"You have been more than good to me," James murmured, his gaze falling on the page once more.

Further verses from the One Hundred and Third Psalm burned within.

The LORD is merciful and gracious, slow to anger, and plenteous in mercy. How true that had been. Thank God He had proved slow to anger, and not struck James down in the height of his self-centered arrogance.

He hath not dealt with us according to our sins; nor rewarded us according to our iniquities. Tears pricked his eyes, a legacy of illness—or perhaps the great emotion weighting his heart. He blinked them away and read on.

Verses eleven and twelve sang to his soul.

For as the heaven is high above the earth, so great is his mercy toward them that fear him. As far as the east is from the west, so far hath he removed our transgressions from us.

He glanced out the window, gaze fixed on the ever-changing skies as his heart toyed with the truth he'd discovered in a Spanish hospital. His transgressions, his many, many sins, his faults and immoralities and failings and wrongs, had all been dealt with.

Captain Balfour had shared these truths, and James in his most piti-ful, piteous state had believed them. God Almighty, in His great mercy, through Jesus Christ's death and resurrection, had removed all of James's stains of sin and washed him with grace and love so he was new. He was forgiven. He had been made right with God.

It still seemed so ridiculous that he, such a scapegrace of a son, such a glimflashy, angry, maggoty young man, should find peace, should find ease within his soul for the first time he could ever remember.

But so it was. Because he dared believe the words contained in the Holy Book. That even his vast and monstrous sins could be forgiven and removed as far as the east was from the west.

He'd wondered about that phrase. Was there a point where east became west? Maps might suggest so, but God Almighty said no. Rather, the very impossibility of finding a midpoint suggested God didn't even want him to go looking for his sins or to focus on them. This verse suggested that his transgressions were removed, erased, dealt with, done. Oh, how great the grace that overlooked his shameful past.

James swiped at his eyes—this illness had a lot to answer for—and shifted up against the bedhead a fraction more. From his position propped up by pillows, he could see the sea, its glinting waves dulled under heavy skies. He'd never particularly liked storms and, thanks to his soldiering life, had spent too many nights huddling under canvas, trudging through mud, shivering in a forlorn attempt to stay well in the midst of wind and rain. But now, here, feeling healthier than he had in a long time, knowing he and his were safe, he could look out on the approaching tempest and feel glad. Not glad for the storm itself—and pity those poor people caught in its grasp—but thankful for this second chance at security, stability. He almost dared to hope that all could be made right in his world.

The fire crackled, sending welcome warmth through the room, as the first of the raindrops pattered against the window. He was seated comfortably, his shoulder had ceased aching, and his Bible lay open nearby. A cup of coffee waited invitingly on the small table within arm's reach. And an arrangement of roses sent a top note of sweet fragrance through the room, and gave reminder of the woman who was responsible for these little blessings. His wife.

His wife.

He'd barely seen Sarah in recent days, not since his improvement after the last of the doctor's visits a week ago. He smiled, remembering her terrier-like persistence to protect James, the way she'd forbade the doctor's vile treatments. He had never been so grateful as when the doctor had left the room. Evan—his most faithful visitor since, though he be a servant—had mentioned she was busy caring for the child and all the other household responsibilities his illness had distracted her from.

Sarah. He appreciated her, he valued her kindness and forbearance toward him, especially because she did not like him overly. He did not find her especially attractive, though he liked her scent and voice and found her presence strangely soothing. He supposed he might find her more appealing should he get to know her.

Or perhaps he wouldn't. They were such strangers, after all. Two strangers brought together by his father's overhasty machinations and mischance.

But perhaps God, in His abundance of mercy, had sought to provide James with yet another undeserved and unexpected blessing. A woman who had—according to his father—proved to be a boon to this old house, and even his own family. He believed Beatrice to be happy, and no one, save old Mrs. Copley, and perhaps Dawson, could deny Sarah's involvement in the improvements to the castle.

Another thought speared his heart. Perhaps Sarah wasn't here to merely be a blessing for him. Perhaps he could return the favor, and somehow—despite his disgrace, and despite her aversion—he could prove a blessing to her also.

So he began to pray.

"Oh, Lord, help me."

Sarah huddled against the cold stone pillar in the corner of the little chapel, mere steps from where she had wed James Langley. Today marked one year, their first anniversary, usually a propitious occasion for any new bride. Not for her, of course. She rather doubted James remembered. She rather doubted James ever thought of her at all, save how she might minister to his comfort, or care for his father, or run this great house.

She dragged in a breath, thoughts toiling, turning, in a spinning loom of pain. She'd come here hoping for some solace from the never-ending pressures, the constant questions and complaints from staff, and her own ceaseless fears. How much longer would Bethy remain sick? Could she even get better? Sarah dared not think of the alternative.

A nameless dread seeped from the old stones through her limbs to penetrate her heart. She'd needed to escape the nursery and Nanny's doomsday prophecies for a few minutes. To pause, to be still, to try to feel the peace of God, as Mr. Edwards had preached about on Sunday.

But she still could not find peace.

"Help Bethy, please," she whispered. "Heal her, Lord, I pray."

The poor darling had worsened, her temperature fluctuating between highs and lows, wracking her tiny body as she shivered then perspired.

Sarah's heart ached with the agony of watching, of knowing there was so little she could do other than hold her and cover her and cool her by turns. Sarah's thoughts whirled and terror filled her veins.

She shivered in the cool dimness, gaze lifting to the stained glass she'd first noticed on her visit here with Beatrice all those months ago. The trio of slender windows held simple images of disciples and a picture of Jesus Christ in the middle window. The light was dim, allowing her to see the details more clearly, the wistful expression of the woman, the jubilant face of the man. She couldn't help but compare it to her own situation, in which she suspected James felt far more full of joy than she did right now.

Her gaze lowered to the French tapestries depicting scenes from well-known Bible tales. The woman with the issue of blood reaching to touch the hem of Jesus's garment. The angel standing beside the empty tomb and exultant disciples. The touch of Jesus that brought the ruler's small child back to life.

Moisture bled from her eyes. Desperation rose in her throat. She fell to her knees, and, hands clasped, prayed aloud. "Merciful Father, have pity on me. Bring Your healing touch to little Elizabeth. Please"—her eyes flicked open to where Jesus's touch seemed so lifelike—"please heal her, I pray."

Her "amen" was swallowed in a rasping gasp, the sobs weighing heavy on her chest making it challenging to breathe.

The scene of the empty tomb, which was behind the simple wooden altar, held a potency of doom. How could anyone rejoice in death? Her heart felt in danger of crumpling, her faith felt so very small and weak.

She closed her eyes, exhaustion sinking her to a puddle on the wooden pew. Oh, if she could only sleep. If only she could rest. But still her mind refused its ceaseless worries.

A sound came from without, and she hastily sat up, wiped at the moisture on her face, smoothed down her hair.

"Excuse me, ma'am," said Evan, his face a picture of worry, "but Nanny Broomhead was wondering if you could come."

Her mouth dried. She swallowed. Swallowed again. "Is Bethy worse?"

His gaze lowered. "She feels you should come soon."

"But we need the doctor!" She rubbed a hand over her face, hiding her tears even as her voice wobbled. What should she do?

Evan cleared his throat. "Perhaps if Mr. Langley was to summon him."

"The old gentleman?" He'd barely noticed anything amiss.

"I was thinking, perhaps, the younger one."

James. "You think he would?"

"I think he might be persuadable."

But that would mean she would need to speak with him. And now he was well she barely knew how he would receive the wife he had not wanted. Let alone agree to summon the doctor she had sent away. And who else could she ask? According to Mr. Barnstaple, there were no others to be found for miles.

His Adam's apple bobbed as he swallowed. "I could, er, speak to him, ma'am, if you would prefer to see the child. I could simply say you wished for his help."

"Oh, yes, please! And send for Mr. Edwards. I can't help but feel he . . ." Her voice wobbled dangerously. "He might be needed."

"At once, ma'am." And he hastened from the room.

Sarah rose unsteadily, placing a hand for balance on the back of the pew, and exited from the chapel's cool, blinking as she entered the dimness of the Great Hall.

To the side, Dawson paused, his brows pushed high as if shocked by her disheveled appearance.

She ignored him save to direct he send for Mr. Edwards immediately, which, for once, he seemed inclined to do. She hurried up the stairs, each footstep weighted with dread and desperate hope. She longed for her darling Bethy to be safe yet feared for her life and that she might be too late, such a thought momentous in her chest.

Passing the family bedrooms, she heard Evan pass on her request, but she did not linger to hear the response.

Urgency propelled her feet onward. Up the two steps to the hall that led to the nursery. Even from this distance she could hear the desperation lining Nanny Broomhead's voice.

"Come on, sweet girl. Breathe. Just breathe!"

Sarah rushed forward, hurrying to scoop the girl into her own arms. "What has happened? She was not like this half an hour ago."

"I don't know what it is," Nanny cried. "She just sickened, and now I can barely feel her heartbeat."

Sarah placed anxious fingers on Bethy's throat, but finding nothing of hope, reached inside the baby's cotton gown and placed two fingers on her chest.

A heartbeat was there, but worryingly slow and faint.

"She's burning up!"

Nanny sobbed. "I've done all I could."

"If only the doctor were here," Sarah cried. "Oh, Bethy, I'm so sorry. I love you, just hold on." Tears filled her eyes until she could scarcely see the pink-and-white figure drooping in her arms.

She rocked her slowly, crooning prayers and whispered hymns, all the while pleading for God to preserve her. He wouldn't be so cruel as to take this precious life, would He?

After what seemed an interminable age, Bethy's neck lolled, as if she were a rag doll, her eyes closed, and the faintest rasp served the only sound of life.

Terror filled Sarah's heart. "No, Bethy, no!"

There came a sound of rushing feet, and she lifted her tear-filled gaze to see Mr. Edwards enter the room. "Oh, sir! We need your prayers. She is so very weak."

"Of course." He laid a hand on the tiny girl's head and murmured pleas for God's help.

She barely heard his words, her pulse rushing in her ears. Where was the doctor? Why hadn't he come? Oh, she'd never forgive herself if the worst happened and the doctor had not come because of her earlier actions. But surely a doctor would not let pique get in the way of professional duty. Surely he possessed compassion enough to extend help to an innocent mite.

Time passed in a matter of slow heartbeats, one anxious heavy beat after another. After each struggling breath, she willed Bethy on. "Live, little one, please live."

To lose the baby would be like losing her heart, losing her purpose to live. Sarah's own chest grew tight, her arms clutched Bethy closer, as she rained kisses on her small downy head. "I will not lose you," she whispered fiercely. "I *cannot*. You are all that is good in my world."

"Mrs. Langley," Mr. Edwards began.

"No." She shook her head. "Don't speak. I want to hear Bethy's sweet cry. Just to know she still lives."

"Mrs. Langley, dear." Nanny Broomhead laid a hand on her arm. "Please, let me see the sweet pea."

One glance and Nanny gave a heartrending sob. She glanced at Sarah, then at Mr. Edwards, and gave the slightest shake of her head.

"No. She still lives," Sarah cried. "I know it. I can feel her heart beating still."

"Let me check." Nanny moved to take her, but as she did, reaching out with arms that could never love Bethy as much as Sarah did, could never need Bethy as much as Sarah did, an awful aching hollowness yawned in Sarah's chest.

"I'm sorry, Mrs. Langley, but—"

"Don't say it, Mr. Edwards! Don't you dare say it!"

"Mrs. Langley, I'm afraid . . ." Nanny Broomhead lifted the still form.

Sarah drew in a desperate breath, the crushing pain in her heart overwhelming in its intensity. She could not bear this. She could not stand this. This was her fault. She was to blame. She crumpled to the floor. Oh no. Oh no. Oh . . .

"No!"

Chapter 13

An agonized cry pierced the quiet.

James sat up in his bed, the shriek of sorrow lending strength to his otherwise useless limbs. He strained to hear more but could not, and slumped down against the pillows. From Evan's conversation when he'd brought his meal not an hour ago, he guessed it was to do with the child. Had the babe succumbed to her illness? *Dear Lord, help her now.*

He stretched out to tug the bell rope, and within a few minutes Evan appeared. One look at his pale, stricken features and James knew.

"The child?"

Evan licked nervous lips. "Has passed."

Sorrow kneaded his chest. Poor thing. Poor Sarah. That's right, Sarah. "How is Mrs. Langley?" It still felt so odd to say.

"She, er, she is not at all well, I'm afraid."

"That was her cry?"

Evan finally met his gaze, his youthful features seeming at odds with the sorrow haunting his eyes. "She collapsed, I'm afraid."

His heart stabbed. "The doctor?"

"Has not arrived. Mr. Edwards is here, the minister."

Of course he was. He should have expected his wife to seek him out. She seemed to regard him as her only friend in these parts. He frowned. Hadn't Mrs. Copley once insinuated secrets between the two of them, that Edwards had once passed Sarah a mysterious note? A twisted thought from his past made him wonder about the baby's true parentage—

No. *God, forgive me.* He shook his head at himself. Such thinking was perverse indeed.

"Was there something I could get for you, sir?"

"What? Oh. No, no, I need nothing." *But your wife may,* his conscience whispered.

He ignored it, watching as Evan moved to the door.

And forget not all his benefits.

He released a silent groan. What kind of selfish blackguard was he? "Evan, do whatever you can to help Mrs. Langley. I . . . I'm putting you at her disposal. Whatever she needs, you are to do at once. Regardless of what it is, or what it costs, just make it happen."

"Of course, sir. But—pardon me for asking—but what about you, sir?"

He shrugged, the movement eliciting a hiss of pain. "Dawson or another servant will suffice. Right now, Mrs. Langley is your only priority. Understand?"

"Yes, sir. I shall go there immediately."

James nodded, watching as the footman departed, hating himself for the reversion to his old ways, shamed that he'd been so quick to forget the words he'd read earlier.

"Lord, be with her, comfort her, help her in this time."

He suspected she would neither welcome nor believe his words of sympathy. His prayers and actions would have to do.

In all the times she'd comforted others suffering the ravages of loss, she'd never known grief could feel like this. Her heart was an aching abyss where once a degree of peace had dwelled. Now she felt broken, burdened yet so empty, never to be whole. The loneliness she'd always known had amplified in recent days. Nobody understood. Nobody shared her pain. Grief isolated her, walling her inside her pain, as if in losing Bethy she'd lost the sun, and now only rain and wind swept through her soul as they did across the dales.

Mr. Edwards cleared his throat, and she dragged her gaze to his again. Wind buffeted her cheek, scraping hair into her eyes, but she cared not what she looked like. The few mourners here had already seen Sarah at her worst, weeping, curled up on the nursery floor when her strength had failed her, heedless of who saw. Mr. Edwards and Nanny Broomhead had shown kindness, the doctor—when he'd finally deigned to come—had been less sympathetic, looking at her as though she was a lunatic who should be locked up in Bedlam, as if expecting her to adopt the cool civilities of the family she'd married into.

The old gentleman had barely said a word. He took such little notice of those around him, Sarah wondered if he was all right in the head.

As for her husband . . .

She clutched her shawl closer as the wind stole inside, causing her to shiver as though she weren't already made of ice, her gloved fingers forming fists. She loathed the man. Loathed this evil disease that had killed her child. Loathed the fact that her husband had not said one word of comfort, had offered no condolences. She had suspected he thought the baby an inconvenience, but hadn't realized until this moment how much he must despise Sarah herself. The absence of a single kind comment only proved this.

A glance up revealed Evan's drawn face, her one comfort in past days. He had barely left her side, constantly at hand to undertake whatever was her bidding. Or so Nanny Broomhead had said, adding that it was the young master who had given such instructions.

As if he could assuage his guilt by giving Evan such orders.

He *should* feel guilty. It was his illness that had caused Bethy's death. Still, she craved a jot of human kindness not connected to one's wages. Nanny Broomhead had barely ceased her sniffling, and Evan seemed too young to bear her burdens.

She was alone. She had no one left to love. What was the point of her life?

The vicar coughed. "We therefore commit this body to the ground, earth to earth, ashes to ashes, dust to dust; in sure and certain hope of the resurrection to eternal life. The Lord giveth, and the Lord taketh away. Blessed be the name of the Lord."

"Amen."

She mouthed the words but did not mean them. She could never bless

God's name again. How could He be so cruel as to snuff out the life of a wee child? How could He be so hard-hearted to hold poor Bethy's parents' sins against her? Isn't that what Mr. Edwards had spoken of earlier? Something about the sins of the father being visited upon the sons—or the daughters, as this case might be.

For Sarah knew herself to be as much cursed as Bethy had been. God was punishing her for agreeing to this sham of a marriage. There could be no other reason for God to smite her in this way. God did not love her, no matter what Mr. Edwards might say. There was no way to reconcile the two. God couldn't be loving and allow this to happen. Ergo, He did not care.

"Mrs. Langley?"

Oh, how she despised that name! "Yes?"

"I . . ." Mr. Edwards twisted his prayer book between his fingers. "I am very sorry for your loss."

She nodded. His sorrow she believed. She'd seen the tears in his eyes when Bethy had just breathed her last, and his dealings with her through all the funeral arrangements had proved him kind and gentle. Mrs. Copley had been shocked, repeatedly saying how unorthodox it was for a lady to insist on arranging such things, and that the previous Mrs. Langley would never have dreamed of doing so. Sarah hadn't cared. Bethy would know she was loved, would know her life was precious, right up to the very end.

And Sarah didn't have the heart to admit neither Langley father nor son had offered to organize any part of the funeral themselves. Not that she would have let them. But still, the offer would have made her feel less alone, and not as though they thought Bethy's death was nothing more than a relief, her life as worthless as a torn handkerchief.

Their absence at the funeral today only solidified their lack of care, as did their lack of offer to bury Bethy in the family plot in the cemetery. Instead, Bethy had been relegated to this windswept corner of the church's burial grounds. Once again, she was being pushed to the outermost margins of society, furthest away from the sacred church building, to be dumped in the dirt like a piece of refuse.

Stop it! This eddying of bitterness and pity would likely suck her down entirely. She needed to have a clear head to know what to do next. But misery was a weighty garment that seemed to have turned her legs to lead.

"Mrs. Langley?"

She turned, recognized the compassion in Nanny Broomhead's red-rimmed eyes. Thank God someone had loved the little girl almost as much as Sarah had.

"Are you ready?"

No. How could she ever be ready to see a tiny casket lowered into the ground? To know a sweet body would be forever beyond her reach? Nanny had virtually had to pry poor Bethy's cold form from Sarah's desperate grasp, as she willed life back into her, praying desperate prayers, even offering to exchange Bethy's life for Sarah's own.

And now she was expected to say her forever goodbye to the one person who'd offered love? She couldn't do this. She *couldn't*. It was simply too much.

A forceful gust of wind swayed her. How she wished she could just fly away, to leave this earthly realm for some place without pain. Would God accept her? After all her failures, hardly. But after the past few weeks, she wasn't sure that missing His presence would matter much anyway.

Mr. Edwards moved to the side of the prepared hole, the measurements far too small.

Evan carried the diminutive box cradling her child—*her* child, no matter what anyone else might say!—and moved to the side of the hollow.

A whimper escaped. No. This was wrong. So wrong. So very, very wrong.

Nanny Broomhead moved beside her, patting Sarah's arm uselessly. What good was a pat? She wanted, *needed*, to feel warm arms, breath in her neck, a gurgle of life-filled laughter, that precious smile of delighted recognition that said Sarah was loved, that she was wanted, that she belonged.

Coolness rushed past her ears. A scent of late-blooming heather reached her nose. She was so cold. So cold. So intensely cold she could scarcely feel.

The casket was passed to the dirty gravedigger—why couldn't Mr. Edwards have hired a reputable-looking man rather than this grubby fellow?—who stroked the wood reverently.

New tears sprang to her eyes. Perhaps the grubby man held an ounce of humanity, after all. More humanity than that displayed by her husband and father-in-law, at least. She watched, bottom lip trembling, as he gently lowered the wooden box into the ground, her heart picturing the teeny girl warmly wrapped in the blanket she had knitted a few weeks ago. At least Bethy would be warm in there. At least for a little time.

A sob erupted, and she drew in a breath, willing herself to calm as Nanny Broomhead clutched her arm. She could do this. Just a few minutes more. Then she would be freed.

Another gust of wind threatened to rip her veil away. She straightened it, forcing herself to pay attention as the ropes slid away and the gravedigger stepped back.

Mr. Edwards murmured a prayer she did not listen to. How could God comfort her wee child? Bethy needed a mother's arms, not the comfort of angels. Anger streaked through her. How dare God take her away?

"Mrs. Langley?"

Mr. Edwards looked to her. What did he want her to do?

Nanny Broomhead handed Sarah a pink rose, the most perfect one Sarah had found in the castle's neglected garden. She looked at the soft petals, the exact color and texture of Bethy's cheeks, and knew her resolve to be strong was crumbling again.

She pressed the bloom to her lips, glad for the chance to once more hide her tears, and then slowly, reluctantly, moved beside Mr. Edwards to the hole. She glanced down, and through tears, saw the tiny coffin that housed her precious Bethy. Her heart crumpled again. She couldn't. This was too much to ask. No.

She felt a slight warmth on her back as Mr. Edwards touched her. "You can do this."

"I don't want to," she whispered.

"I know."

Somehow she found the strength to lift the rose, kiss it a final time, then throw it gently to the casket. One last kiss for her baby girl, though she'd never birthed her.

I love you, her heart cried. *I wish you were still here with me.*

Another rose followed, tossed in by Nanny Broomhead, then another by Evan. Even Mr. Edwards dropped in a flower, so the tiny casket was sprinkled with blooms from the people who had known her and had loved her the best.

The words from earlier rushed through her head. *Ashes to ashes, dust to dust.*

Bethy wasn't dust. She was her baby. Her *baby*!

Clumps of dirt pelted the wood, echoing flatly in her ears, signaling the frailty, the finality, of Bethy's life and this ceremony.

Poor Bethy. Dear Bethy. How could God think this was fair?

Dirt now covered the rose blooms. Dirt now covered her baby girl. Her baby. Her *only* baby, for she had married a man who did not love her, who would never love her.

Dirt. Petals. Bethy. She would never be able to look at pink petals again.

Oh, the world was spinning.

She felt light-headed, fainthearted, weak. She had to leave, to go . . . Away.

Chapter 14

The knock at the door woke him from light slumber. His body sought repose often, as though trying to catch up on all the past year's missed rest. He knuckled sleep from his eyes, pushed himself upright against the bedhead. "Yes?"

Evan entered, his somber dark suit legacy of today's funeral. "Excuse me, sir, and sorry if I woke you, but I thought I'd best tell you as things went, as you requested."

"And? How did the ceremony go?"

"It was very sad, only the vicar and Mrs. Langley and the nanny and myself there. She—that is, Mrs. Langley—was quite calm. At least she was right up until the very end."

His chest tightened. "What happened?"

"She, er, collapsed."

"Is she all right?" Fear pattered within. "She is all right, is she not? I thought I told you to help her—"

"I have been. She *is* all right, just . . ." He glanced over his shoulder at the interconnecting door, voice dropping. "The vicar called for the doctor to attend, who then said she must be sedated. She's to spend the next few days in bed rest."

Emotion balled in his throat. "Thank you for telling me."

Evan nodded, turned to go.

"You will keep helping her," James instructed. "Anything she needs, anything at all." A thought struck him. "Ask Cook to prepare her favorite foods, ask the gardener what flowers she likes best."

"You don't know what they are, sir?"

James narrowed his gaze. "I'm prepared to overlook the impertinence of that remark as it has been a very trying day."

"Of course, sir. Thank you, sir." And Evan hastened away.

James sighed, once more ruing his quick temper. The lad was only right to assume a husband knew enough about his wife to know her interests. He'd bet the family castle that Evan knew the Langley marriage was hardly normal. It would behoove James to learn what would comfort his wife, and thus provide a measure of solace as she had generously given him. That's what his Savior would ask. That's what a gentleman of honor would do. That's what a husband should do.

He exhaled, then spent some minutes praying for his wife in the next room. He could hear soft sounds, as if people moved around. Was it the doctor treating her even now?

He frowned. That business of the doctor being banished by Sarah still seemed very strange. He remembered portions of that time, remembered fear at the doctor's methods and relief and pride in his wife when Sarah sent him away. But Watkins's comments, calling her an irrational woman, someone who had allowed emotions to cloud her reason, made James wonder just what course of treatment he offered now.

What *would* the doctor be doing now? Dr. Watkins certainly had no liking for Sarah. For some reason, that thought peppered James with fear. He tugged on the bell rope and breathed easier when Evan soon appeared.

"Send the doctor in," he instructed. "And I think a servant should remain in Mrs. Langley's room."

"Mrs. Copley, sir?"

"I think not," James said wryly, remembering a few clashes between his wife and the servant. Why did Watkins think Sarah so incapable? She'd impressed his father with her efficient management of the household. In selecting servants such as Evan, she'd proved to James that she was a good judge of character—save for agreeing to marry him.

Realizing Evan waited for an answer, James struggled to recall what they'd been speaking of before. That's right—who might be with Sarah. "Perhaps the child's nanny would be agreeable."

"Of course."

Evan departed, leaving James to ponder these concerns. He supposed the nanny would soon leave their household—there was certainly no need for a nanny in a household where a child would never be born. Of course, if he could somehow make amends with Sarah, perhaps one day she might be persuadable to give their marriage a proper go.

A knock prefaced the doctor's appearance.

James's stomach tightened, as he was brought to uncomfortable awareness of how this man had visited James in this room so many times.

"And how are you doing now, Major Langley?"

"Improving, thank you, doctor."

"As I rightly predicted." The doctor nodded in self-satisfaction. "Was there something you wished to speak to me about? I must admit I was surprised to receive the call to tend your wife. She and I have not always seen eye to eye."

James refrained from pointing out the limited medical options available. "How is Mrs. Langley?"

"She really is not well in her mind, I'm afraid, collapsing in the nursery, then again at the graveside."

"She is grieving."

The doctor sighed. "This is unlike most forms of grief I've witnessed. I'm afraid she was rather too greatly attached to the child. I've given her a tincture of opium to sedate her."

Opium? Memories flashed. His stomach tensed. James eased back a little, careful to protect his still-tender shoulder. "Did you ever discover what was wrong with the child?"

The doctor looked surprised. "Did no one ever tell you?"

"Tell me what?"

"I'm afraid that I rather suspect it was the fever."

"What fever?"

The doctor eyed him without sympathy. "The same fever that bound you to bed for those many weeks."

Horror curdled within. No. Oh no. "You mean I passed it to her? The baby died because of me?"

The doctor's gaze slid to the side. "I would not like to say it that way precisely."

"But how else could she have caught it?"

"Your wife perhaps?" The doctor shrugged.

"No. No, that would not be possible. She—my wife—has not been unwell."

"That doesn't mean one cannot still pass these kinds of diseases on."

"But what makes you think"—what was the child's name?—"Bethy had the same disease?"

"I noticed a similarity in fevers, the swift passage from hot to cool, a likeness in the rasping breathing."

James shook his head. "You can never let Mrs. Langley know it was the same disease." She'd never forgive him. "And you must be certain to *never* indicate you think it possible she passed the disease on. She'd never forgive herself."

"But it's not only possible, but highly likely," the doctor said, avoiding the request.

"Promise me."

The doctor inclined his head. "But of course. Now, if that be all?"

James watched him go, unease billowing inside. To think he might be responsible for the infant's death?

Heavenly Father, forgive me, he prayed. And God forbid his wife ever learn he—or she—might have passed on the cause of her child's death.

It was cold. Too cold. Too painful.

She was fragmenting into pieces, lonely broken pieces, like a shattered vase that could never be made whole again. Sorrow had burrowed within, nestling next to her heart, where hope and a future had once lived.

She wanted—needed—comfort. But from whom? No one was here. Nobody save Nanny Broomhead. And the sight of that good lady only pierced her heart afresh.

Sarah would have to go away. Far away. Or at least send Nanny Broomhead away. But every time she tried to speak to suggest such a thing, her mouth felt as if it were filled with cotton rags. She could barely speak, let alone be understood. Her head's constant ache did not make understanding things anyone else said any easier either. And she was so tired. So very tired. And far too cold, cold, cold.

Another shiver wracked her being, the chills penetrating to her very core. Is that what happened when a body froze to death? Except she doubted too many people froze in such surrounds, in a grand bed fit for a queen, with a roaring fire, and people waiting to tend to her needs. She found she didn't care. She would rather freeze to death, freeze her thoughts, freeze her heart so she didn't need to think and feel and *hurt* anymore.

Was Bethy cold in her wooden bed? Had Sarah knitted the blanket warmly enough? She dared not think she'd failed. She hated to think of Bethy's little plump limbs stiffening under all that nasty cold earth. She hated to think she might be crying, missing her mama, wishing to be held. Oh, how empty Sarah's arms felt, missing the snuggling warmth of the tiny body that just craved love. *I'm sorry, Bethy. I'm so sorry.*

Oh, would she ever forgive herself? If only she had not argued with the doctor over James's treatment. If only another doctor had been available to help. If only Sarah had noticed her sickness sooner, and sought help. If only. If only. If only . . .

A sob escaped, and tears slid down her cheek, clogging her nose. She was to blame. She was responsible. Regrets pummeled her chest afresh.

A creak of chair. Nanny Broomhead's wide face appeared. "Oh, dearest Mrs. Langley, you're awake."

Sarah closed her eyes. No, she wasn't. She was exhausted. So weary. So tired. She ached. Exhaustion dragged her down into a land of lonesome, too-cold dreams.

Rest never really comforted. It only suspended for all too short a time the reality that broke when she awoke. Her eyes felt swollen, her eyelids too heavy, her nose clogged; her body, her heart, ached. The rose and blush flowers of the bed-curtains taunted her, daring her to think of all those who'd slept here in happier times. She should see them exchanged for fabric more apropos for her mood. A color somber, dark, and sober. Black, or midnight blue.

"Mrs. Langley?"

"Don't call me that." She shooed away Nanny's fluttering hands. "Mr. Langley is a stranger. He hardly counts as my husband. You might as well call me Miss Drayton."

Miss Drayton. She'd known a form of happiness then.

"Very well, ma'am."

Ma'am, not Miss Drayton? She was too tired to fight the noncompliance. "What is it?" She heard the note of peevishness in her voice but couldn't bring herself to care about herself much less her waspish attitude toward Nanny.

"It is a lovely day," Nanny offered tentatively. "Would you like to get out of bed?"

"No." Nanny had obviously never lost anyone she truly cared about. Otherwise the woman wouldn't pester Sarah so.

"But if you remain as you are, you may get bedsores. They can be most uncomfortable, or so my late husband told me."

Nanny had been married? Why did Sarah not know this? Guilt panged at her earlier dismissive thought. She inched her way to a sitting position. "Tell me about him."

"You really want to know?" Nanny asked, her blue eyes glistening in her round dimpled face.

"Yes." Anything to stop the ceaseless dreams, the endless regrets. Anything so she could fix her attention on that which was new, that which she could imagine, that which would make her forget her own relentless problems, if only for a little while. "What was his name?"

"Gregory."

"Gregory," Sarah echoed. "What was he like? Was he kind? Was he handsome?"

"Oh, bless you for asking. Yes, my Gregory was handsome—well, not as handsome as your Mr. Langley, but he was handsome enough for me."

Nanny gave a girlish giggle, and the desperate desire Sarah had to inform her that Mr. Langley was most definitely *not* Sarah's Mr. Langley subsided in this surprising development.

"And he was kind, one of the kindest men I've ever known." Nanny Broomhead breathed a wistful sigh. "So thoughtful, so considerate. Why, when we first met and I was working as a nursery maid for Sir Oliphant's family in Buxton, my Gregory insisted I say nothing about our attachment so I could keep my post. In those days, dear, they would fire a lass should she be known to have had an admirer." Her wide cheeks pinked. "Then later, after we got married and learned we could not have children—"

Sarah's heart clenched. How could she not have known this? Oh, selfish, selfish person that she was!

"—my Gregory was so very kind in letting me resume the work that brought so much joy to my life."

Sarah shifted uneasily on the pillows. "Your working with children."

"Yes."

She exhaled. "I . . . I am very sorry I did not know. Your Gregory sounds like a very caring man."

"That he was." Nurse Broomhead's eyes grew shiny. "He has been gone these past eight years."

"I'm so very sorry." Sarah placed a hand on the older woman's arm. The touch of warmth, of life and humanity in the midst of loss, breathed a sense of kinship in Sarah's heart. Perhaps she did not hold a monopoly on grief and pain after all.

"Thank you, Mrs. Langley, for asking after him. It does my heart good to speak of him, and not just feel he has been relegated to the past."

Would she one day feel this way about Bethy? It still felt too unreal to think of her as dead. But perhaps time might help, even if eight years seemed impossibly long.

"Would you like to get out of bed now?"

Sarah nodded, and Nanny Broomhead gently helped her from the bed, clucking over her as she insisted on exchanging Sarah's old nightdress for something fresh.

A few minutes later Sarah was sitting in a comfortable armchair near the fire, positioned to best capture the bleak and wintry view. There had been no snow as yet, but recent icy winds promised they might see some snow soon. From here she could see the castle's broken stone tower positioned closest to the shore and smell the sea. What was it called? Lilith Tower. Where the gulls gathered over basaltic crags above the narrow sea-cleft passage that wound through the treacherous rocks of Rumble Churn. Perhaps she should visit there one day.

"I'll just go see about a nice cup of tea, all right, dear?"

"Thank you, Nanny." Really, she was going to have to stop this ridiculous nanny business. "Nanny?" She winced, oh how she sounded like a child. "Would you mind if I call you Mrs. Broomhead?"

"Not at all, my dear."

"I just find the term Nanny a little hard. It reminds me of . . . of . . ." Emotion choked her and she could not finish.

"Of course, I understand," the older lady soothed. "Now, just enjoy your nice sit-down, and I'll be back very soon."

Sarah nodded but her gaze had caught on a vase of flowers.

Roses. Pink ones. Just like Bethy's cheeks.

Her heart caught, mood sinking faster than a body lost at sea. "Mrs. Broomhead."

"Yes, my dear?"

She pointed. "Those flowers. Why are they in my room?"

"Flowers? This beautiful bouquet?" Mrs. Broomhead ruffled the petals.

"Yes," Sarah whispered, as awful horror stole within. Her eyes pricked. How thoughtless! How uncaring. Her chest grew tight. "Who could be so cruel as to place those roses here?"

"Cruel? My dear Mrs. Langley—"

"Miss Drayton, if you please!" she summoned strength to say.

Mrs. Broomhead looked stricken. "I do not believe any harm was meant. Quite the opposite, in fact. Are these not your favorite flowers?"

They had been. Now they just reminded her of Bethy.

She licked dry, cracked lips. "But why are they here?"

"I believe Mr. Langley wanted to know your favorite blooms in order to provide you with some cheer. He has been most concerned for you."

The tempest in Sarah's chest subsided a fraction. That *was* most surprising and considerate. "I never thought he'd think beyond his news-papers and books." Or think about wishing her cheer in any capacity.

"I do not mean the older gentleman. It was the younger one, his son. Your husband."

Bile soured her mouth at that last word. "Well, he is wrong."

"But I'm sure he was trying to be thoughtful, to be kind. Really, I thought it was a most touching gesture."

"It isn't."

"Did you not once admire these flowers?"

"I did, but now I never want to see these flowers again! Don't you realize?" Tears choked her voice. "These pinks are the same as Bethy's cheeks, the very flower I dropped into her grave, and it . . . it only makes"—she dragged in a rasping breath—"it only makes me . . . miss her all the more."

"Of course, my dear. We should have realized. Here, let me remove them at once." Mrs. Broomhead whisked open the door and handed the offending vase of blooms to a waiting servant.

Judging from the low tenor of the voice, it might be Evan. Was he still on guard here?

She turned away, clutching her shawl tight around her, chest writhing with a dozen different emotions. Regret, sorrow, resentment, anger, fear. How could Mrs. Broomhead not realize the significance of those roses? Was Sarah forever to feel like she was a prisoner, trapped in this room, trapped in this misery, trapped in this marriage with painful memories on every side? Where was someone who understood, who cared enough to want to help her?

Sarah pulled up her feet, twisting to curl in her seat, arms crossed over her front as if she could ward off the chilled bleakness from the open window. Outside a mist rose, and a lonely gull cawed a desperate cry to find its mate and find its true home.

Oh, how well she knew the feeling. She was alone. She might live here and be known as the castle's mistress, but that was in name only. In truth, she did not belong. She would never fit in. She'd been so wrong to dare believe otherwise. And now her one purpose for living was gone . . .

Tears seeped from her eyes, trickling down her cheeks, sliding past her nose, salting her mouth. "Oh Bethy." Her heart shuddered.

The gull curved high on an upward draft, looking forever destined to be alone.

"Oh, Bethy, I miss you so. Why can't I be with you?"

Why could Sarah not join her, and just die?

Chapter 15

On this, his first day out of his room in weeks, James was relieved to find his legs still worked, even though at times he felt a little shaky. But it was wonderful to be freed from his shoulder's sling, to see walls that weren't his bedchamber's, to smell scents fresh and invigorating, and feel a sense of renewed appreciation for this historical heritage he called home.

"James."

He turned, saw his father in the hallway. "Good morning, sir."

"Glad to see you are finally up."

James nodded. His father had visited his room several times, but relations had always seemed strained. He grasped the stairway's banister, trying not to look as though he was so weak that he actually needed to use it. As he descended, careful step after careful step, a number of the staff moved forward to offer their congratulations on his recovery with bows, nods, and bobbed curtsies, as Dawson drew his father to one side.

"Mr. James, how are you?" Mrs. Copley offered a smile.

"Better, thank you."

"You are breaking your fast this morning, yes?"

"Yes."

"I'll inform Cook that you are ready."

James moved slowly to the breakfast parlor, restraining a faint desire to question why she would need to tell someone whose job it was to do this anyway. But then, Mrs. Copley had always struck him as officious and presuming.

He took his seat, thankful to finally rest his legs. His lips twisted. Who would have believed he'd fought in fierce battles when now he could barely hold himself upright? Clearly he'd overestimated his strength this morning when he'd thought coming downstairs would be feasible.

Food, proper food, made him doubly thankful for what he'd gone through. For if he hadn't undergone such trying times, he'd never have realized just how many blessings he had. Like a roof over his head. Hot food to eat. A body that worked . . . mostly.

His father entered the breakfast room and took his seat, and Dawson soon appeared with a freshly pressed newssheet. The meal passed as most of those taken with his father: his father reading while James wondered if they'd ever be able to scrape up enough scraps of dialogue to engage in what others might consider conversation.

Had he ever really shared his heart with his father? His time before soldierly life had always been weighted with disappointment, and during war his exploits had scarcely been those designed to win his father's affection. But now, after yet another brush with death, perhaps here was an opportunity to forge a new relationship with his father, before it was too late.

"Father, I was wondering—"

"How is that wife of yours?"

Sarah? "I have not heard anything this morning."

His father eyed him over his coffee. "She has not been well."

"No."

"Have you spoken with her?"

"I have a feeling she has little wish to hear from me."

"Be that as it may, it would behoove you to speak with her soon."

"Yes, Father." His father, advising him on relationships? What a laugh. He kept such caustic comments behind his teeth. "What are your plans today?"

"I have plans to read in the library."

How unusual. "I thought I might take a walk outside. It seems a good chance to do so before the weather truly sets in."

"And speak to your wife?"

"And speak to my wife."

So help me, God.

Despite the appeal of fresh air and desire to re-familiarize himself with the grounds, his body's sheer lack of strength meant the only walk he took was back up the staircase. By the time he reached the top—having refused every offer of assistance—he was sweating from the effort of the climb. But his father's words—and the subtle voice deep within his heart—meant he could no longer put off what must be done.

He moved past his own door to his wife's room and knocked. What would it be like to have a proper marriage, one where he and his wife shared a bedchamber and a bed, where conversation was as easy as rolling over and saying hello, instead of this nonsense of door knocking and permission? He exhaled. His heavenly Father may have forgiven him, but James rather doubted Sarah would ever overlook his sins. Stealing away an innocent woman's future simply to pay off Falcott and the others?

Father, please soften her heart, and give me wisdom.

The door opened and revealed the fatigued features of Mrs. Broomhead. "Oh! Good morning, sir."

"Good morning. I wish to speak to my wife." He winced at the harshness of those words so bluntly spoken. Had his life as a bachelor dulled his manners to this?

"I shall see if she's awake." She smiled and hurried from her post, the partly opened door permitting a greater wedge of view of the room. From this position he could see the rose-colored drapes of the bed, and, near the window, a dresser with a mirror that reflected the servant's movements as she bent to check the figure lying in the bed.

His stomach twisted as he recalled—his memories vague shadows— the last time he'd entered this room. Drunken. Hostile. Hungry. No. He would never again dare trespass unless his wife invited him in.

In the mirror's reflection, the prone, pale figure stirred and blinked.

He internally braced. What should he say? *I am so sorry for your loss. I am so sorry for the hurt I've caused. Please forgive me.*

The mental rehearsal stopped as the servant moved back to the door, the pleasure that had lit her strained eyes now drained away. "I am sorry, sir," the woman whispered, "but she is not well enough for visitors."

He wasn't a chance caller but her husband. That gave him a legal right to talk to her, even to do whatever he wished with her. The spurt of frustration faded as disappointment stole across his chest. Everything within demanded he tread softly. "Very well. Please give her my regards."

"I will, sir."

She bobbed a curtsy, and he turned, then halted at the vase of flowers gracing a nearby hallway table.

He faced the servant, who had begun to close the door. "Did Mrs. Langley receive the flowers I sent?"

Her gaze flitted to the vase and back, in a manner reminiscent of a nervous bird. "Why yes, she did, thank you, sir. Most thoughtful and kind."

He glanced back at the vase.

Pink roses as he'd requested.

A look of guilt shadowed the older woman's face.

"Are these the flowers I sent her?"

"I, er, well, yes, sir. I'm afraid they are."

Perhaps the perfume was too strong, or perhaps . . . "She did not like them?"

"Oh." She bit her lip, eyes saying what she could not.

Hurt cramped his chest. He nodded, feeling the familiar wash of rejection. "You may reassure her I shall not be so hasty again."

"Oh, but sir—"

He shook his head and strode to his room, thankful for the chair when his knees gave way. He was still too physically weak for this, his emotional fortitude too thin. How long would his wife have no care for him?

A bitter wind kissed her cheeks as she hurried through the knee-high sward. She had to hurry, else someone might see her from the castle main and report her escape. And over the past fortnight she'd had enough of Mrs. Broomhead's fussing, had enough of feeling trapped by people cosseting her in care.

"Come away from the window, Mrs. Langley. You'll catch your death of cold."

No, she wouldn't. She'd already caught death, and it had turned her cold weeks ago.

"You should eat. You have scarcely eaten a thing in days."

Food held no interest. It simply kept people alive.

"You should rest, Mrs. Langley. No good comes of all this worry."

No good came of all this resting. She'd known an urge to do, do, do.

And nothing needed doing like visiting the tower that had long beckoned from the window. She'd felt the weirdest pull to climb inside, and with Mrs. Broomhead stepping out for a few minutes, Sarah had seized her chance in what remained of the wintry daylight. Now she could, at least for a few moments, be free.

The grass tips dampened her gown, but she pressed on regardless. This section of the castle grounds had obviously seen little attention in years. Her priority when managing the house before—who ran things now?— had been for those parts of the castle grounds considered far more useful, such as the kitchen garden and small orchard, and those which made an impact upon first appearance—the drive and courtyard and gardens around the house. The acres of unkempt lawn behind the castle walls had never been a priority. And clearly hadn't been anyone's priority for quite some time. Perhaps she could speak to Derry about keeping sheep . . .

A quick peek over her shoulder revealed that nobody followed. Ahead, the gulls cawed and wheeled, grey bodies ascending on powerful gusts. Over the past weeks flocks of birds had soared in patterns most marvelous as they climbed and then fell, climbed and fell, as they fled winter's icy approach for warmer climes. If only such flight might be possible for her too. Alas, it seemed her escape would be limited to seeking out the tower·today.

Lilith's Tower loomed above, one hundred feet high, its broken walls like skeletal fingers pointing to the grey skies. When Beatrice had first brought her here all those months ago, she'd been awed at the grim tower's history, the role it had played in protecting the castle, the hundreds of years she could see grooved into the weathered stones. Perhaps this trip to the tower could hold clues to her future.

A push saw the tower's wooden door creak open, and she stepped inside the dark, musty interior. The thinnest of windows, arrowslits, provided just enough afternoon light to reveal the dirt-encrusted floors, the legacy of damaged walls open to the tempestuous winds, waves, and weather. A fractured stool of indeterminable age lay near the broken bricks of what appeared to be a fireplace, the space filling with unearthly moans as air pushed through the crevices and cracks. From them it was easy to understand the superstitious reports of ghosts. No matter. This place of desolation was where she longed to be.

She glanced at the steps leading to the upper floors. Was it safe? She barely cared. At least in these next few moments she'd live once more. Her pulse thudded in anticipation as she moved up the narrow circular staircase and reached the landing she'd once visited with Bea. Up higher, Beatrice had said, was dangerous, so they'd not ventured there that day. But Bea wasn't here now.

Sarah pressed on, one hand on the stone wall for balance, steps slowing as she picked her way through the rubble. The wind was sharper here, howling like a banshee, a living, clawing thing threatening to topple her to her knees.

Another step. Another. She was nearly at the next landing. There!

She peered, most gingerly, hands clasping either side of the wider window, at the grey waves pounding far below. Slim basalt crags, twelve feet high, stood in the water like a row of giant guards. Waves growled ominously as water thrust through narrow channels forged between the cliffs and scattered rocks, the Rumble Churn with its perpetual dirge. The sound was fierce, much louder than on that calm day before when the turquoise and emerald transparent waters gently swept over pebbly depths. It had seemed so beautifully enticing then, not at all like this ever-increasing fury.

She closed her eyes, inhaling the salt, feeling the sprinkle of moisture on her skin. Beatrice had mentioned this tower being used as a lookout against long-ago pirates and marauding armies. In this lonely stone tower, she could imagine the courage needed to stand guard against such things, a courage she could admit she no longer owned.

How could she have ever thought she could start afresh, could belong at a place like Langley House? That woman who had so boldly taken on the duties of the mistress of the castle seemed a vastly different creature to the failure she was now. Every time she tried to make a difference, she floundered. The staff did not like her. Her own husband had avoided her. She couldn't even succeed as a mother.

Her heart clenched anew, moisture heated her eyes, and she drew in a loud gulping breath. She was so tired. So tired of failure. So tired of not knowing whom she was anymore. Now her burst of earlier boldness had faded, the emotions of the past weeks had left her drained. She had reveled in her escape, in that momentary feeling of life, but now she might as well not have bothered. She'd be better off not to be here.

Not to be here . . .

Her body swayed. Her eyes flew open, body jerking instinctively away from the narrow window as she battled to stay upright, hands clasped on cool stone. No. She dragged in a steadying breath, even as panic still pummeled her veins. No. She needed to leave this place that seemed a testament to fear and destruction.

A glance up revealed the gathering clouds had darkened. Perhaps it would be wise to venture homeward, to persuade Mrs. Broomhead to overlook her absence, if indeed that good-hearted lady had yet returned.

Sarah picked her way down the broken steps more carefully, conscious of a prickling of cold. How harsh such conditions must have been for the soldiers posted as sentries to protect the castle from marauding Scots or competing kings. A shiver wracked her body, reminding her she'd not stepped outside in such conditions for many days. Her ears ached, her nose felt raw, and the air she breathed now seemed too sharp. She tugged her shawl close. She'd be lucky to escape this adventure with but a cold.

Down the stairs, breaking free from the clutches of the dusky shadows, a thrust of the door, and she was outside. The wind here was much stronger, and she bent to hurry back to where the castle proper waited.

A sudden strong gust sent her almost to her knees, then the next moment she was showered with rain. Rain? No. The foam flecks suggested it was a wave propelled by the wind. A furious wave, as if the elements were warning her to flee. She needed to hurry, else she'd be soaked to the skin.

Another step and she tripped, felled by a rock hidden in the long grass.

Her booted foot throbbed, as she hobbled, crone-like, to the castle walls. She wouldn't mind if someone thought to seek her.

The darkness swelled and thickened, as it often did in this stretch of coast, and while she might enjoy watching the variations of moody weather from her window, it was quite another thing to stumble along like a wayward traveler lost in the depths of midnight.

But she was nearly there. Was nearly—

"Sarah?"

She stumbled to a stop, chest tight at the sight of her husband emerging in the gloom before her, near a door to a section of castle she'd rarely visited. What could she possibly say to him? She stepped back, mind whirling with nonsensical explanations.

"Sarah, whatever are you doing?" He hurried forward, grasped her arm. "You're wet."

And, it seemed, in trouble yet again. She tugged her arm free, opening her mouth to defend herself, when another sheet of water fell from above. She gasped at both the dousing of water, and at the exclamation he made.

His gaze caught hers, and with his wet hair and astonished expression that quickly smoothed into apology and a rueful smile, her heart gave a treacherous leap.

No. He was a rake. A bully. She had no desire to find the man appealing. "What are you doing here?" she asked quickly, to hide the tumult of emotion within.

"We were searching for you. Mrs. Broomhead was most concerned when she did not find you in bed. I thought to look out here, that the bracing wind might refresh you as it does me, and give some strength." He hurried her forward to the shut door, instead of taking her to the usual entry.

The door didn't budge at first try, but he wrested it open, drew her into the dark passage, and shut the door against the stormy elements of outside.

She exhaled, savoring the relative warmth and stillness, before her body trembled, and her teeth chattered.

"You're cold."

Through the gloom, she caught what looked like concern as he removed his cloak and wrapped it around her.

Despite her nerves at her forthcoming explanation, she relished the fact the garment still retained his warmth. "Thank you."

She could not meet his eyes. He must find her so tiresome, being forced to search for her on this cold and wet night. Especially when she'd spurned his attention, had avoided talking to him for weeks. She had not talked to him since Bethy—

Pain clutched her chest again. She ducked her head, blinked away the sting of tears.

"Sarah?" His voice held a caressing note. "Are you quite all right?"

No. She'd never be completely right again. Emotion clutched her chest, making it suddenly hard to breathe. She tried to pull away, but he retained his grip.

"Sarah?"

That tender rasp in his voice triggered silent tears, and she weakened.

He reached out strong arms and held her, drawing her close to his chest. The turmoil within escaped in quiet tears as he stroked her hair, the unforeseen sensitivity at once calming and confusing. What was she supposed to do with this man whose actions so perplexed her? Was he the callous rake of infamous reputation, or this kind man who murmured prayers?

The swell of sadness slowly eased, and she drew in another breath, conscious of the thump of his heart against her ear, the abrading of his chin in her hair, the fact her sobs had soaked his shirt. She pulled away, grateful when he offered his handkerchief, with which she wiped away the residue of her weeping.

"You are allowed your tears," he said softly. "I remember what it was like to lose my mother. I cannot imagine what it would be like to lose a child."

His understanding sliced through her former opinions, further turning them upside down. This man puzzled her so.

"I do not blame you for wishing to enjoy a walk either."

What? No condemnation? She lifted her head and finally met his gaze.

The faint light from outside revealed warmth in the dark-green depths. He touched her hair, smoothed the wet ringlets away from her face.

From this close distance she could feel his body's heat, could sense the scent of salt and leather and a pleasant masculine scent. Her breath suspended, her pulse rose.

"There, that's better."

She stepped back, feet tripping in his long cloak, and he reached to jerk her upright, which pulled her close to his chest once more.

"I'm sorry," he said in a low voice. "I didn't mean to make you stumble."

"It . . . it wasn't you. Just my own clumsiness. Here." She moved to unclasp his cloak.

He shook his head, placed his hands over her cold, trembling fingers. "Wear it a little longer. I want you to be warm."

She nodded and moved—more carefully this time—backward. "Th-thank you."

He heaved out a breath, rubbed a hand through his hair. "Well. I am glad that we have found you."

Guilt twisted. "I didn't mean to cause trouble. I just needed to . . ." Words failed her, as helplessness swamped her again. How could she hope he'd understand?

"Escape? I can well comprehend the feeling."

He could?

"I thank God for the well-meaning individuals who care for our health, but there comes a point when it feels as though one is trapped inside one's bedchamber. Wouldn't you agree?"

She nodded, unsure if he saw her in the dark. Was this the first time they'd agreed?

He gently grasped her hand and placed it on his arm. "I hope you'll permit me to escort you."

"Back to my bedchamber?"

He stilled. "Was there somewhere you'd prefer to go?"

"Anywhere," she muttered. Any place without the constant memories of her poor lost girl.

He eyed her for a moment, then drew her to a nearby room, one she vaguely remembered from Beatrice's tour as a long-abandoned withdrawing room. "No one will disturb us here."

Her chest tightened, her steps slowing. The dim light filtering through a nearby window showed that his expression and tone contained no threat. She relaxed and followed him inside. The darkened room contained several armchairs, upholstered in a style and fabric of times past, positioned in front of a fireplace. It was to this area he moved, encouraged her to sit, and reached for a box atop the mantelpiece. A few seconds later he struck a flint, then moved to light several candles before bending to make a fire.

She watched his ministrations, the careful, patient way he worked and waited, worked and waited, until the flames took greedy hold of the kindling and twigs and drew her focus to the mesmerizing blaze.

"I did not expect you to know how to do that."

"I learned in the army." He studied the burning wood before glancing up at her. "I expect there is much we need to learn about each other."

She swallowed and sank deeper in the chair within the fragrant folds of his cloak. Oh, there was much to learn. Much to explain. Much to admit, and even perhaps, much for which to ask forgiveness. But somehow being here with him in this space that seemed tucked away from everyone and everywhere else, she rested in a sense of safety, a sense of relief, as though the very walls encouraged her to release tension and be soothed and lulled into comfort and peace.

Comfort and peace were two things she certainly had not ever anticipated experiencing in her husband's company.

"Are you happy to stay here while I inform the others you are safe?"

Happy, no. She doubted that was an emotion she'd ever know again. But content, "Yes."

He bowed, and left holding one of the candles.

And in his wake came the oddest sensation that perhaps in his company she might finally learn to feel at ease.

Chapter 16

James hastened away, wonder filling his heart. Who knew if Sarah would still be there when he returned, but the fact she'd talked to him, and let him touch her, had let him help her, was the most she'd permitted in days. Or ever. Regardless, it was a most promising start.

The undusted passage—clearly this section of the castle had not been deemed worthy of attention—concluded in a locked door. Where . . . ? He scraped his fingers along the top of the doorframe and retrieved the key, unlocked the door, and hurried to the kitchen.

"Why, Mr. James!" Mrs. Copley slunk from the shadows, her smiling expression swiftly melding to approximate concern. "There has still been no word concerning Mrs. Langley. Your father wishes to send for the constable."

"Mrs. Langley is safe. Please ring the bell to alert the others she is found."

"Oh." Curiosity—or was it disappointment?—flickered in her eyes. "Should I send for the doctor?"

"I don't believe that will be necessary. You may tell Mrs. Broomhead that a hot bath should be drawn in Mrs. Langley's room."

"Of course, sir."

Having no desire to alert Mrs. Copley to his movements—or the precise whereabouts of his wife—he waited until she left before completing his journey to the kitchen, where he requested Cook to prepare tea and have Evan deliver it immediately to the yellow drawing room.

"The yellow drawing room, sir? That hasn't been used for years, not since your mother—" She halted, gaze dropping.

"I know," he said quietly. "But I have a feeling that it will be in use again. Quickly, now."

"Yes, sir."

"And I'd thank you not to tell the others."

"Of course, sir. I'll just give Evan directions."

She bobbed a flustered curtsy and he hurried back, her mention of his mother eliciting a troublesome mood. This wing containing the yellow drawing room had been his mother's private quarters, providing space for the lady of the house to quietly amuse herself and withdraw from the more public rooms where the entertaining of encroaching visitors was demanded. More than once he remembered Mama retreating to her quarters, giving the excuse that she was previously engaged and could not attend to uninvited visitors, like the busybodies of the village or gossips like the Barnstaples. In actual fact, she'd been happily reading from her own private collection of books, or painting or sketching in the adjoining room, or simply playing with her cats.

Tightness filled his chest, regrets knotting with grief. He missed her so. If only—

No. God had forgiven him. He needed to remember that. And God help him to protect the current Mrs. Langley, and somehow help her know he cared.

For he *did* care for Sarah. He appreciated her efforts with his father, with his family home. He might never love her, but he recognized her qualities enough to fuel his concern and action when the Broomhead woman had raised the alarm about her missing charge. Which now raised further concern about his wife, and regret that theirs was not a relationship where she could seek him out and talk. Not yet, anyway. Perhaps—God willing—that might be one day soon. If nothing else, he wished to protect her as a godly husband ought.

His steps lengthened as he hurried back to the room. Would Sarah even be there, or would she have stolen back to her bedchamber, forgoing a chance to perhaps talk and reconcile?

He twisted open the door. The chair was empty. She had gone. Disappointment squeezed his chest.

A slight noise pivoted his feet to the bookcase in the shadowed corner. Sarah held a book and a guilty expression. "I hope it is all right for me to examine them. There are many fine books here."

"Of course." He moved to her, unwilling to examine the tumult of emotions the last minute had evinced. "These were my mother's books."

"Then I should not touch them." She moved to put the volume back.

"She is not here to mind."

"But would Beatrice mind?"

"Bea?" He scratched his jaw. "I suppose she could be asked if she'd like them. I know she didn't come to this room often."

"She said it reminded her too much of your mother," Sarah said softly.

"She missed her very much. As do I," he added more quietly.

Sarah's gaze caught his, and he recognized the sympathy as she nodded. His heart grasped at her kindness, even as he wondered at the relationship that existed between his wife and his sister. Sarah seemed to know infinitely more about Beatrice than he.

"Would you tell me about her? I know your mother was very beautiful—the paintings make that clear. But what was she like? I get the impression from the way some of the servants talk that she was especially kind and gracious."

"She was." She had been. "I remember she used to take baskets to the poor in the village."

She nodded. "I'd heard that."

"She used to love reading. She enjoyed sewing." And then she'd changed. "She was not well the last few years"—or decade—"of her life."

"I'm sorry."

He nodded. He was sorry too.

"Thank you," she said, her eyes meeting his tentatively. "I . . . I never liked to ask Beatrice too much because it all seemed too raw for her."

It felt rather raw for him too, but that was something he'd share another day.

"I . . . I could write to Beatrice and ask her about the books, if you like."

"Would you?" he asked, rubbing the velvety spine of a volume he recalled as one of his mother's favorites.

"I should think any daughter would love something of her mother's, and she left with little chance to take any treasured possessions."

"She made her choice," he began, but cut off his words when Sarah bit her lip. "But enough. I don't wish to live with past regrets anymore." He reached to hold her hand, when a knock at the door caused her to flinch.

James gave a smile he hoped was reassuring, and hurried to the door, wrenching it open to reveal Evan, tea tray precariously in hand as he raised his hand to knock again.

"Thank you. Put it over there." James pointed to a small table of delicate spindly legs.

Evan obeyed. "Cook wants you to know the maids will have the bath ready soon."

James nodded a dismissal and the door closed again. He turned to see Sarah clutching the back of the sofa, her face pale, her expression wondering.

"Would you care for tea?" He gestured for her to be seated.

"I, er, yes, please."

For the next few moments, it seemed they had entered a strange dream world where he poured tea and they partook as if such a thing between them was indeed normal. Perhaps it was the coziness induced by the fireplace and the feeling of warmth as it rained outside. Perhaps it was the darkness—the candles here were few. Or perhaps it was the sense of accord, exacerbated by his relief when he'd found his missing wife outside that served to induce greater appreciation for something so familiar. Regardless, he was glad to have this sense of normalcy, to pretend for a moment that they were indeed a happily married couple.

He watched Sarah over the rim of his cup, glad to see her shoulders drop and some of the wariness fade from her face. Her grey eyes met his again, her lips curving into a shy smile. "Thank you."

"You're very welcome. The night has turned much cooler and wetter than was expected."

She nodded, gaze untangling from his as she bent her head. "I'm sorry for the trouble I caused. It just seemed I had lain in bed for ever so long, and I . . ."

"You do not need to apologize further. As I said earlier, it is necessary to escape sometimes." Which brought to mind the circumstances that once had forced him to forsake all he knew.

"Is that why you joined the army?"

He blinked, disconcerted by her uncanny insight. How was it possible he barely knew this woman, yet at times it seemed she could read his soul? "I suppose so. That, and I have always had something of a thirst for adventure."

"Because you grew up in a castle?"

"And was inspired to live like the knights of old? Perhaps." Was that why he'd agreed to join the war? Partly, yes. And partly because he wanted to escape the stain against his name, and instead make his soldier father proud, and finally live up to the legacy of the Langleys.

"Do you miss it?"

He shook his head. "Not at all." Not the deprivations, not the fear and terror, not the guilt and shame, and definitely not the pretense of acting as if he knew what he was doing. So many decisions had been simply instinctive in the great battle for survival, as he'd fought to save his life—and those of his men—at the expense of another poor soul.

"But you were promoted to major."

Admit his act of recklessness had somehow led to saving lives? Perhaps to gain her trust he needed to show her he knew and owned his faults. "I was in a battle where I felt I had nothing to lose, and my instinct to survive caused the inadvertent saving of men. People thought me brave and recommended me for a higher rank." He shrugged. "It proved a moment of good fortune and God's mercy." For it had ultimately led to the hospital and salvation.

"You believe in God?"

"I do now."

Her eyes held a diamond light enhanced by the fire flames. Her lips parted.

What would it be like to taste them? To kiss her properly this time? Tenderly, as a husband should, with a respect borne from real love?

Regret arrowed within, prodding more truth. "For the longest time I did not believe God could forgive my many sins. No one need tell me how many they are, I know that full well. But when I was in hospital, God used Captain Balfour to show me how extensive our heavenly Father's grace is. He forgives us all our failures, and gives us strength to change."

"I want to believe that again, but it's so hard."

"It is. But it doesn't make it less true," he said softly.

Her gaze dropped. The silence that stretched between them could have been filled with awkwardness, but instead, he was conscious of a sense of sympathetic understanding. They both were broken people, but hurt hearts could be healed. Healed by God. Together.

"I would not mind meeting with some of my comrades in arms again, those who understand what I have gone through, who helped me in the most challenging of times."

Like Daniel Balfour, the man whose wise words had challenged James to seek a genuine relationship with God. Captain Balfour was one of only a handful of men he now considered a friend, and someone he would quite like to see again. One day.

"Perhaps you could write to invite them here," she said.

"You would not mind?"

"This is your house. Your father's too."

"It is your house as well now."

Shadows flickered across her face, illuminating an expression of mistrust, something he felt compelled to alleviate. *I want you to think of this as your house, Sarah. I want you to be my real wife, to trust me, to want me—*

"I believe your father might benefit from seeing new faces, especially if they are those who would understand when he reminisces of his own soldiering days."

"You are most considerate."

She demurred and lowered her head.

"I know my father has appreciated you, and such thoughtfulness as this gives hope that we might get back to normal again."

"Normal?" Her features stiffened.

"Yes. Well, I'm sure things don't feel too normal for you as yet, but they will over time."

She stared at him as though he was mad. "How can anything be normal again?"

At once he remembered what had happened, and regret roiled through him. "I didn't mean to diminish your loss," he said quietly. "I know too well how long it can take for sorrow to heal." Her eyes entreated him to speak more, and he placed his cup on the table. "Not that I'm sure sorrow ever really heals. I think it is more that grief becomes a bruise that slowly fades."

"How comforting," she said wryly, but in her face was a kind of desperate longing for it to be true.

He shifted closer. "When my mother . . ." He swallowed. Was taken? Passed on? Sickened? "When she died, I . . . I knew sorrow unlike any other. I'm sure that part of my drinking to excess was to try to hide the pain." He glanced at her. "I know I have hurt you with my words and with my actions. I am so very sorry. I will not blame you if you can't forgive me."

She stilled, and the air grew thick between them, the seconds passing slowly, until she peeked at him, her glance swift up and down. "I forgive you," she whispered.

"Truly?" At her soft affirmation, his chest felt like firing a cannon salute. "Thank you. You cannot know what that means to me. I can promise you that I shan't ever hurt you like that again."

Her gaze seemed wary, but she nodded anyway.

He exhaled. He'd take that as a sign they could move forward, even if he'd always know regrets. Regrets about how he'd treated his wife, regrets about his mother. He touched his mother's chain. Did he have a right to feel such depths of sorrow when the blame could be laid squarely at his feet? He tamped down the guilt, distracting his heart to ask about her family. "You previously lived with your aunt and uncle, I believe?"

"Yes. They did their best, but they were not exactly nurturing."

"No relationships are perfect." He smiled wryly. "My father and I have scarcely been on cordial terms these past many years."

"Why is that?"

Should he answer? Did he dare admit his shame? But this moment of honest exchanges demanded one more. "He blames me for my mother's death."

Her brow creased. "You cannot know that for certain."

Oh yes, he could. His father's very words had branded his soul.

"I'm sure you should not blame yourself."

Her sweet loyalty eased the tension encasing his heart. He would never have expected this much sympathetic understanding from his wife. He studied her, the meek little thing, and realized afresh just how much she might be lonely.

Heaven knew he himself struggled enough without someone who understood him. Perhaps he should risk his father's rage and see if Beatrice would like to pay a visit—*sans* husband, of course, else Father might die of apoplexy. Or perhaps Sarah might enjoy a visit from the Barnstaples. Their daughter must be nearer to Sarah's age. At the very least, he'd make enquiries as to whether she'd like a small pet to keep her entertained. Someone, something, to keep her mind occupied, to help her see beyond her recent pain.

He cleared his throat. "I can appreciate that you may have little inclination for the Christmas season—"

"Christmas? Can it be so soon?"

"I know my father does not care much for festivities. I'm sure that will shock you."

Her lips rose at the corners.

"Given the challenges of past weeks, I'm very happy if you think we need not go to any trouble. I'm sure I do not need to tell my father's secretary that our finances being what they are means any celebration would have to be quite pared back."

"I confess the thought of celebrating is anathema to me."

He nodded, heart soft with compassion. "Is there anything I can do to make your time here easier?"

"No, thank you, sir."

He recognized that for the lie it was, but what precisely she would appreciate he would need to pray about to discern. "If so, please know you need only ask."

She inclined her head. "Thank you, sir."

He withheld his impatience at her continual use of "sir," gentling his tone. "Well, this has been very pleasant."

"Yes," she whispered, as her gaze dropped away, as if uncertain.

How long would it take before she trusted him? "Perhaps we should return. I am sure that bath of yours is ready now."

"A bath?"

"You are not cold still from your earlier adventure?"

She shook her head. "I have found the fire and the tea sufficiently warming, thank you, sir."

"James. Please call me James."

"Very well, James. You may call me Sarah."

"Thank you, Sarah." His lips eased into a smile. "These are promising beginnings, would you not agree?"

"Beginnings of what?"

"Beginnings of hope that our marriage may not be a complete failure, God willing."

Her fingers plucked nervously at his cloak. "I . . . I don't think God wills for any marriage to fail."

"I am trying to live differently now, of that you may be assured."

After a moment she nodded and he rose, satisfied with proceedings. "Come. Let me escort you upstairs so you can be protected from the shilly-shally of servants." He helped her stand. "Oh, and Sarah?"

She paused in her attempts to remove his cloak.

"As I said before, you are to consider this house yours too. If you would like to claim these rooms in this wing as your own, you may do so. Feel free to make whatever changes you deem necessary."

Her eyes brightened, but her words remained hesitant. "Would not your father object?"

James shrugged. "These days he pays little attention beyond the confines of his library. I am positive he has not stepped inside this room for many a year."

"Still, I should prefer to have his approval before I should attempt to clean it or alter anything."

"Clean it? My dear Sarah, you are not to clean things yourself. That is why we have servants."

Her head ducked, and he remembered that some might regard her as such still. He had, until quite recently. *God forgive him.* "Sarah." He waited until her gaze met his. "You're my wife. This house is yours to command as mistress, and this room is now your own."

A small nod. "Thank you. I hope you will forgive me, but I would rather not have someone like Mrs. Copley or Dawson visit here, not if I want the room to truly feel like my own."

He smiled and tucked her hand in his arm. "Now that I can entirely understand."

Chapter 17

Her husband's strange solicitude kept Sarah awake for half the night. What did this mean for their relationship? He had apologized! Such was enough to soften her heart further to him, to wonder if the wisp of tenderness could kindle into more. Not only had he overlooked the incivility of her running away and shown her kindness in protecting her from the overly curious concern of the servants, he had been thoughtful enough to see to her comfort by ensuring the provision of the tea and her bath. Such consideration had only been further displayed by his enquiry on the staircase as to whether she would like a pet, in order to assuage her loneliness. She'd known a desire to retort that a pet was hardly recompense for the loss of a child but was glad to have bitten back her words when he mentioned he had been concerned for her and knew such a large, isolated place might induce loneliness.

Such thoughtfulness surprised her, even more so when he asked whether she might like to invite some people over for a quiet dinner, to provide some company for her. She'd been so shocked she could not offer a ready answer, save to reply that she would be happy to do so if he wished it. His response was also one of politeness, which made her wonder how long such polite-yet-oh-so-careful exchanges would continue.

Theirs had become a relationship of politenesses, of civilities, but nothing more. Not that she wanted more. But what would a marriage of affection with James feel like? There had been that moment when he held her close, and her heart beat foolishly fast . . .

This man kept tipping her off-balance with his kindness and thoughtfulness, with his support and bolstering words, but could she trust that he had truly changed?

The following morning, despite mild admonitions from Mrs. Broomhead, she breakfasted downstairs. Yesterday's excursion had given her a taste for life beyond her bedchamber, and she had summoned pluck enough to reclaim the mantle of mistress that she'd discarded during the recent weeks of illness. She would soon enquire of Mrs. Copley the availability of servants in order to clean the yellow drawing room. To *clean* the drawing room, not necessarily claim it as her own. That would depend on what the old gentleman said, which would depend on when she secured enough nerve to ask him.

James's presence in the hall outside the breakfast room drew her to a pause.

"Good morning, Sarah." He offered a bow.

"G-good morning."

"I trust you slept well."

She nodded, glad that for the second half of her night she had indeed slept better than she had in months. Until the nightmares had woken her, and she'd been unable to rest again.

"Might I beg for a moment to speak with you?"

She dipped her head in agreement.

He drew her inside the green drawing room, its austere formality a contrast to the comfort of his mother's room from yesterday. "I hope you don't mind my borrowing you for a short time. I simply wished to converse without the prying ears of servants."

Her stomach fluttered. "I am at your leisure."

He sent her a shrewd glance, which set her heart to wondering. "Have you given any further thought as to whether you'd prefer a cat or a dog?"

"Oh!" He was serious about such a thing, then? "I regret but I have not yet had the chance to truly consider it."

"Would you take the opportunity to consider it now?" His countenance softened, and she was once more taken by the evenness of his features, marred only by that scar on his cheek. "I would even be so willing as to consider a monkey or some such beast, but I rather fear for the future of such a creature, given our cold temperatures here."

She smiled at that. "I can assure you I have absolutely no wish to possess a monkey."

"You relieve me." He inclined his head. "I can't help but feel that my father would be relieved as well."

A chuckle escaped. "I'm sure he would be."

"Of course, you need not have any companion animal, if you do not wish it. I would not have you be lonely, though, if I can help it."

Then perhaps he should seek her out to speak with her more often. The words tangled on her tongue, refusing to be said. She studied the faded Axminster carpet instead.

"Let me know when you come to any conclusion." He turned toward the gilt-inlaid door.

She quickly laid a hand on his arm. "I would prefer a dog. My aunt owned a cat that always seemed inclined to look down its nose at the humans who served him."

"One can't have supercilious cats in residence, that is certain," he agreed solemnly.

She knew a surprising inclination to laugh, but, unsure if he was being completely serious or not, suppressed it. How much easier it would be if she knew her husband enough to know if he was funning or simply had a droll turn of phrase.

"A dog, then?"

"Yes, please."

"Any particular breed or age?"

"I do not mind. Something sweet more so than playful, yet not so old that it would be unwilling to go on walks."

He bowed. "I will do my best."

"Thank you."

He smiled and again her insides knew a fluttery sensation. This man she could like. One day. Possibly. But again, the question of trust hovered near. Memories of his drunken, womanizing history ate into her wavering confidence, urging her to protect her heart.

He made his adieu, and she was still pondering this transformation and whether it truly could be believed when Mrs. Copley entered the room, pausing at the threshold. "Ah, Mrs. Langley, here you are. We were wondering where you had got to this time."

Sarah bit the inside of her bottom lip. Should she expect to have the events of yesterday forever thrown back in her face? Her husband's care and recent encouragement about her role here renewed inner fortitude for dealing with this woman.

"Thank you for your concern," she said with irony, not missing the flash in the older woman's eye that suggested hers was a comment most certainly *not* borne of concern. "I wish to have use of Daisy and Maggie today."

"Oh, but I intended to use them to deal with the wallpaper in the library."

"Do you mean to say that has still not been done?" Sarah raised her brows, glad to see the flush marring the other woman's cheeks.

"Well, we have been so busy you see, what with all the illness in the house, and then needing to be released from our duties in order to spend time looking for people. Are you sure you are well enough to be up and about, Mrs. Langley?"

"Perfectly sure," Sarah said, iron in her spine and steel in her voice. "Send them to me at once, if you please."

"But the library—"

"Will still be there to be dealt with tomorrow. Or the next day. In fact," she added, as inspiration struck, "how about you accompany me there now, and we can sort this out once and for all."

"Oh, but I'm terribly busy—"

"Then I won't keep you, save to ask again for the services of Daisy and Maggie. I expect to see them in the hall within the quarter hour."

"Very well, miss," Mrs. Copley said sullenly.

"I think you mean ma'am, or Mrs. Langley, don't you, Copley?" James said from the doorway.

Sarah's breath hitched. How much of that exchange had he heard? Her heart sank. Would he despise her for her weakness in allowing the servant to speak to her so? And just when she'd finally felt strong enough to combat the woman's awful insensitivity.

Mrs. Copley flushed, muttered an apology, and escaped the room, leaving Sarah to slowly walk to her husband, whose gaze remained on the retreating servant's figure.

"She's quite rude to you," he observed.

"I think she still resents me for having worked here and then moved up in standing, and not knowing precisely the way things ought to be."

"The way things ought to be should include respect for my wife."

Was his anger directed at Mrs. Copley, or was it pique at a perceived lack of esteem for himself?

He turned to her, and she fought for her legs to not tremble. She'd not anticipated the degree of effort such a confrontation would demand. "Was there something else you wanted, sir?"

"James. I want you to call me James." He exhaled. "I wonder if it's the little things like that that make the servants"—he jerked his chin to where Mrs. Copley had retreated—"think that you and I are estranged."

Perhaps. Or perhaps people thought they were estranged because it was indeed true.

"Hmm." He studied her with a critical eye. "Your clothes. Have you nothing better to wear?"

She gasped. "I beg your pardon?"

"Forgive me." His eyes now held contrition. "I did not mean to cause offense, only I am finally seeing how others—such as Mrs. Copley—might regard us. And it seems I have been most remiss in not providing you with an adequate allowance to be dressed appropriately for one in such a position. Not that an allowance is easy to attain, given the parlous state of our finances." He pursed his lips.

"I have no need for more clothes, sir."

His brow lifted.

"James," she corrected herself. "This is one of my older gowns. I am very well aware it's out of fashion, but I was hoping to attend to the yellow drawing room today and did not want to soil something newer."

"Ah. Well, that is different, then." His gaze grew curious. "You really wish to take possession of my mother's former rooms?"

"If you believe your father will agree, then yes. I would love to."

His face softened for a moment, and her heart eased. "I am glad," he said simply. "Come."

He pushed open the door and escorted her to the library, wherein they found the old gentleman—as ever—reading the newspaper.

"Father, I wished to speak to you about something."

His father lowered the paper two inches, his glance shifting between James and herself. "Are you here to tell me I am an expectant grandfather?"

"No!" she protested, feeling herself turn rosy red.

"I'm afraid that happy circumstance eludes us," James said in his far more polished way.

"That happy circumstance doesn't usually elude those who share a bed."

James coughed. "Thank you, Father, for your observation."

"Not observation, my boy. Advice."

Dear heavens. If only she could sink into the carpet.

"Am I ever to see you return to helping with things here, Sarah?" With complaint in his tone, Mr. Langley gestured to the desk where she used to manage his accounts and correspondence, and conduct some of his research.

"Very soon, sir," she promised.

"But not right now," James said. "I wish to ask you if you had any objection to Sarah using Mama's old rooms. The yellow drawing room and such."

The older man's expression shuttered. "And why would she wish to use them?"

"I do not need to—"

"Because she is my wife," James continued, "and should have the respect and services such a position should afford."

Mr. Langley senior eyed Sarah, any geniality she had known from him hard to ascertain in the cold expression in his eyes. "I cannot like it," he finally said.

Oh. Her heart sank.

"But Father—"

"I do not think so, no." The older Mr. Langley lifted his newssheet again.

Sarah stole a glance at her husband, recognized frustration, and quickly turned back to his father. What was it about his dead wife's rooms that he objected to their use again?

"Father, please. I do not know why you should have objection."

He lowered the paper. "Can you really not think why?"

Sarah glanced between them, the hardness in both men's miens saying that whatever had caused upset would not be solved today. "It does not matter, James," she whispered, plucking at his sleeve. "I have no wish to cause a problem."

"Have you seen inside my wife's rooms?" James's father asked, his gaze now directed at her.

Sarah straightened. "I saw it yesterday, when your son took me there." She judged it wisest to refrain from mentioning Beatrice's brief visit on a much earlier occasion.

"I do not want them touched," Mr. Langley senior said.

"Father, I really think—"

"May I have your permission to see that they are cleaned, sir?" Sarah asked quickly to avoid an escalation into argument. "I'm afraid I could not help but notice they were in an extremely dusty condition."

"Nobody has used them, not since . . ." He glanced—or was it glared?—at James. "Not since your mother passed away."

"Nothing need be touched," Sarah assured. "Save for the dust, of course. They are such lovely rooms I do not wonder at your wife spending many a happy hour in there."

"Mariah loved to read," Mr. Langley senior admitted. "She liked it there very much. Very well. See to it being cleaned, but that is all, mind."

"Yes sir," she acknowledged with a curtsy. She left the room, glad to escape the furor she could see fulminating in James's expression. He had not looked happy at having his will thwarted. Was that for her sake or his own?

And just why was the old gentleman so adamant nothing be moved? She'd had no sense yesterday of the rooms being a tomblike memorial to the previous Mrs. Langley. This skirting around her predecessor was a mystery indeed.

Daisy and Maggie waited in the hall, so Sarah issued swift instructions and sought out the corridor that led to the wing housing the previous Mrs. Langley's rooms. Mr. Langley's reluctance for her to claim the room was a baton of offense she had no wish to carry. Perhaps he'd change his mind at a later time. Regardless, she was very glad for something productive to do—and that she had the strength in this particular moment to do it.

An hour later she was carefully cleaning years of soot lodged in the crevices of the fire screen, as the maids wiped away years of dust from the intricate moldings around the fireplace. It was a funny thing, trying to balance on this thin line between attaining the respect afforded James Langley's wife and all she knew of the falseness of such an office, and conducting herself in a way that would encourage the servants to greater industry. She suspected her willingness to work like this did not accord with what the servants thought as proper for the mistress of the castle. Mrs. Copley's many sighs and exclamation of how the dear sainted former Mrs. Langley would never stoop so low as to perform such menial tasks echoed in Sarah's ears from earlier tasks.

Did James view her as his wife he might one day esteem or merely a satellite in his orbit? She had very few accomplishments, and certainly none of the airs and graces that surrounded the ladies that she had met before.

She was no beauty, she cared little for gowns, she did not sing or play the harp or paint or draw. Really, the only talent she had—apart from a certain deftness with embroidery—was for helping set Mr. Langley's accounts and correspondence aright and keeping house, a function that even then was thwarted by Mrs. Copley too many times. Sarah was no fine lady. Certainly not the person that either Mr. Langley had ever envisaged to be an appropriate lady of the house, and definitely not a worthy successor to the beautiful woman painted in oils who greeted every visitor to the castle from on high.

Really, Sarah could scarcely pretend to be more than a glorified companion-housekeeper. She might be a failure in so many ways, but she did enjoy managing the house and setting rooms such as these to rights.

But in taking pleasure in such menial tasks at the expense of seeking out her husband, *had* she then permitted the servants to take advantage of her and think of her more lowly than James wished? Had she unwittingly encouraged her father-in-law to think the same? Oh, if only she could learn her husband's true feelings, whether he merely tolerated her as the unfortunate consequence of a wrong decision he'd once made, or whether he regarded her with the slightest warmth of feeling.

She glanced across to where the maids had made a substantial improvement already in the rooms. If nothing else, she could claim some credit for Daisy's improved efforts this past year. Gone was the lackadaisical attitude that had characterized her first weeks here. Maggie, too, seemed to have settled into working well. Two things to be grateful for, at least.

"Mrs. Langley?" Daisy asked. "Would you like me to take this lamp down to be washed? I'm afraid it's that dusty that a mere polish won't do much."

"Certainly. It would be good to do all we can to make this room shine."

"It's such a pretty room." Daisy evidently took Sarah's comment as invitation to talk. "It's such a shame it's been closed up for so long."

"Don't you know why?" Maggie murmured. She glanced over her shoulder at Sarah, then sidled up to Daisy with her back to her mistress.

There followed a whispered conversation with enough overheard references to "ghosts" and "shame" and "death" that filled Sarah with alarm.

"Please do not gossip," she instructed, suppressing the shameful desire to enquire. She did not know what had happened, but whatever it was had caused a rift between the Langleys. She hoped—no, was determined—to one day see it put right.

Chapter 18

When Father called him into the library on Monday morning, James had every hope he could finally convince his father as to the merit of Sarah having Mama's own quarters. Instead, he'd met with Father's gross displeasure.

"What is this I hear of my orders being disobeyed?"

"Forgive me, Father, for I do not take your meaning."

"Your mother's rooms."

"What about them?"

"I said not to touch things."

"And I am sure they have not. Sarah said she would only see to the room's cleaning, and she is not someone to disobey you, now is she?" James lifted an ironical brow, thinking of her willingness to fall into his father's scheme of marriage. Not that he minded so much these days. Sarah was an oddly taking creature, once a man got to know her, with that intriguing blend of meekness and strength.

"You know not what of which you speak," his father said. "I have sent for her—"

At that moment the door opened, admitting a pale Sarah, who shot a questioning look at James, followed by a triumphant looking Mrs. Copley, whose appearance held a mild resemblance to a falcon about to feast.

"Good morning, sir." Sarah offered James's father a curtsy. "I trust you are keeping well."

"I most certainly am not."

"I am sorry to hear this. Is your gout troubling you again? Shall I send for the doctor?"

"I need no doctor, you fool!"

Sarah blanched.

James took two steps toward her. "Now, Father, that is quite unnecess—"

"May I ask what this is about?" Sarah's voice was quiet and strained.

"Did I not tell you nothing should be removed from my wife's room?"

"And we abided by that fully."

"Then what's this about a missing lamp?"

"A lamp?" The crease in her brow smoothed. "Oh, I assure you, sir, that it was only removed for cleaning."

"You say that now, but a moment before you said you'd removed nothing. Which is the truth?"

Sarah glanced at James, her expression one of confusion, before she faced him again. "Forgive me, sir, if I was not clear before. A lamp has been removed for cleaning, which will be returned once that is done. I believe that will be finished tomorrow."

"You 'believe,' you 'assure.'" He sniffed. "How can we trust you?"

Sarah straightened. "Mr. Langley, have my actions ever led you to doubt my veracity?"

Mrs. Copley coughed loudly.

Father's brow lowered, his gaze switching between both women.

James clenched his teeth. "Is this your doing, Copley?"

The housekeeper, whose expression of puckish glee at the proceedings gave James a very good idea as to who had informed on Sarah, instantly sobered. "I have no idea of what you mean."

"Do not go blaming a faithful servant for simply speaking the truth of what is going on around here." Father glared at James. "I should have known not to expect anything more from someone so quick to agree to marry you."

Anger rippled through James's veins. How could Father not see how unreasonable he was being to Sarah, that it was Father's own machinations that had led them here? His struggle to formulate an argument that would truly be heard by his father faded as Sarah stepped forward, her cheeks pale, her slight body swaying.

"I apologize for causing you upset, sir. I will see it is returned without delay." She removed from the room without a further glance at him.

Her exit was followed seconds later by Mrs. Copley's, whose glinting eyes suggested she was well pleased with how the interview had progressed.

"Father, you are being most unreasonable."

"I want her gone."

"Finally," James said. "A fork-tongued creature is Mrs. Copley."

"Copley? She's the only one who makes any sense around here."

"Father, you can't mean that you want to get rid of Sarah, can you? She's my wife. Your daughter-in-law. The woman you wanted me to marry, remember?"

Another sniff.

"Copley is the problem. Can't you see her scheme, pitting you against Sarah?"

His father ignored his protests. "I won't have Mariah's rooms disturbed."

"Father, forgive me, but I don't understand this sudden concern for Mama's rooms. I've never heard you talk this way before."

"That woman that you married has taken far too much upon herself, giving herself airs and graces."

"Sarah? She's always so very meek—"

"That's not what Dawson says. Called her trumped up and haughty-eyed—"

"That's ridiculous. Sarah is the last woman I'd describe as such."

"You've known so many women too," his father said, shooting him a narrow glare.

Yes. He had. "Which is why I can unequivocally say that Sarah is humble, not given to trickeries and deceit. She is trustworthy, Father, and has proved her worth here for many months." He countered his father's glare with one of his own.

Eventually his father looked away. "Mebbe Copley and Dawson exaggerated."

Or simply lied.

"Mebbe that woman you married is less of a fool than she appears."

"She's not a fool at all," James countered.

"She is because she married you."

Hurt cramped his chest. "You wanted me to marry her, Father. Do you not recall?"

His father harrumphed, his grey eyes as cold as ever, the stubborn Langley pride evident in the tilted chin, the fixed glare.

"If Mariah were alive, things would be very different."

That was true. Father wouldn't be so morose. James might not have had so many wild years. And Beatrice would most certainly not have felt she must run away in order to be happy.

"Father, please. Won't you reconsider letting Sarah have the use of Mama's rooms?"

His father hissed, his fingers clenching.

"Sarah does not deserve your rancor. And she certainly does not deserve being mistreated by the servants," James stated firmly.

"What do you know about anything?" His father's cheeks reddened. "*You* are to blame for my wife's death."

So they were back to this. Would his father never stop picking at the carcass of regret? "You know that was an accident."

"You've always ruined things."

James swallowed, unable to deny truth.

"You even wrecked this marriage. You do not love her, and she does not love you. Am I to never see a grandchild?"

Perhaps it was prudent to forgo mentioning any children Beatrice might bear.

"This marriage was a mistake. You are husband and wife in name only. Edwards would've made her happy—"

Edwards? His chest constricted.

"—whereas you, you would've been better off marrying the Barnstaple girl after all."

And whose fault was that? He bit his tongue, prayed for patience. "I had no liking for her."

"You have no liking for Sarah either!" his father shouted.

"But I wish to mend things between us," James admitted gently.

"What?" His father studied James from his slumped posture. "Go. Just go. Leave me. I'm tired."

James left, a disquieting thought about his father's mental health making him wonder if he should send for the doctor. But first he needed to see how Sarah fared. He hurried up the stairs, heart hurting for her.

He knocked on the door.

Mrs. Broomhead opened the door and shook her head. "I'm sorry, sir, but Madam is unwell with a headache."

Previous encounters with other females suggested to James this was likely a subterfuge, yet he hesitated. Sarah might really not wish to see him. Heaven help him if she'd heard his father's rampaging and accusations of James's dislike. He could hardly blame her for not wanting to have anything more to do with Langley men, although she'd always seemed to find time for Mr. Edwards . . .

He acquiesced and let Sarah be, escaping the house not to see the doctor, but to see if he could somehow make amends to his wife by finally getting her that dog. A creature to distract her and provide comfort, a gift that said he cared about her, even if he would never really be able to love her or offer real comfort himself.

James strode to the village, the walk necessary to relieve the tension pumping through his body from the earlier argument. He sucked in a salt-tinged breath, the freshness of the air doing much to clear his head. Ahead he could see the spire of the church, a reminder of what he should be doing rather than allowing the darkness of his emotions to swell and pull him under. *Lord, forgive me for becoming angry. Give me wisdom on how to deal with Father, and with Sarah. Soften Father's heart to see truth and help him love Sarah again.* After a moment, he added, *And help me to love her too.*

The thigh-high grass either side of the steep path soon gave way to the shorter gorse and grass of the marsh and meadow, recent rain meaning he needed to watch his step to avoid mud spatters. Perhaps it would have been wiser to have taken the curricle, but this walk had proved effective, allowing time to ruminate, to reflect on what had been, to consider what could be. He was beginning to now feel much more the thing.

Robert had assured him the blacksmith had some whelps needing homes, so James steered a course to the building on the village outskirts. Along the way various villagers stared, most acknowledging him with nods or bobbed curtsies.

His appearance in the family box during yesterday's church service had been swift, as not to prolong the experience, especially as he was alone, his wife and father both claiming illness. He'd managed to escape the encounters with the villagers then. He wouldn't do so now.

"Good to see you, sir," Jed Collins said, the old fisherman had known James since he was a child. "It's been a long time."

"It's good to be back," James said, surprised that the conventional response was true. For even despite the difficulties with his father, being back in Langburgh felt right, as if life were as it ought to be.

There were some questions about his war experiences, which he answered as best he could.

"And how is Mrs. Langley?"

"Mrs. L—oh, you mean my wife. She is well." James dissembled with a smile. "Although a little tired."

"Haven't seen her in these parts recently." The old man rambled on. "Used to see her here in the village visiting the sick like my Tom, or taking baskets to the poor, just like your mother used to do long ago."

Really? Sarah had done so? Why had he not known? "She is kindhearted."

"Aye, you have the right of things there. Terrible sad when she lost the baby."

Guilt strummed his chest. "Yes." The word nearly strangled him. Were it not for the illness he had brought to the castle, the baby would yet live.

From the way the man puffed on his pipe, his keen eyes missing nothing, it seemed he was prepared to settle in for a long conversation, one sure to contain more impertinent comments and questions. "I imagine that would have been a shock for you, coming back to find a wee one up inside the castle walls. Caused quite a stir in the town at first. People thought Mrs. Langley was quite zany. But it kept the lass off the parish coffers, so Mr. Edwards thought it a fine thing."

Mr. Edwards. "I know my wife was very sad about"—heaven help him, but what was the child's name?—"the, er, child's passing."

"Never mind. You'll have your own one day."

Not if matters remained as they currently did.

James eventually extracted himself from the conversation, heart clanging at the revelation that Mr. Edwards had once more exerted his influence over Sarah. It seemed the man held more sway over Sarah than her own husband. He frowned, which seemed to repel further overfamiliar comments from villagers, and he soon attained both the blacksmith's and his goal.

The smithy assured he would have the mildest pup delivered to the castle in two days.

Satisfied, James calmed as he began his return journey, so that he was happy to oblige a few other curious villagers with his accounts of war. To his amazement they seemed rather proud of him, as if they did not hold his previous sins against him. Or perhaps the knowledge of such London doings hadn't yet reached their provincial ears. Still, it was nice to not have his every conversation tainted with regret and shame, or have the ghosts from the past resurrected in every encounter as with his father.

A gig drew nigh, its speed sending villagers scattering to the sides.

James's heart dipped. Mr. Barnstaple and his daughter. He nodded courteously as the gig slowed, its occupants staring at him with surprise.

"Langley! Whatever are you doing here? And on foot?"

"Good morning, sir, Miss Barnstaple."

"We were just on our way to visit you," Miss Barnstaple said, eyelashes fluttering.

Georgiana was a pretty thing, although far too young to attempt a flirtation, especially with a married man.

He frowned. He could not see Sarah ever doing such a thing. The honesty she'd claimed earlier flowed through all her actions. He knew another tug of admiration.

"You must forgive us. My *wife*"—he emphasized the word—"has not been well of late. We are not up to callers." And after this morning's episode, the mistress's mood would hardly be conducive to entertaining such neighbors.

"Oh, we know. Which is why we thought we would invite you to dinner. It must be so dreary having nobody to talk to, especially in this festive season. And we would so enjoy hearing about your times on the front."

But his heart had caught on her previous sentence. Truth was he had enjoyed talking with Sarah three days ago, had found the strange encounter in his mother's drawing room far more enlivening than he'd imagined. Her questions had proved gently probing, and he'd enjoyed the fact she made him think. He would far more enjoy a brief conversation with her than endure any talk with this overly forward, simpering young miss.

His mind flicked back to what he'd mentioned to Sarah, putting foolish words into his mouth. "Perhaps you may prefer to come to Langley. We have hopes of a small dinner in the near future, as soon as Sarah is recovered, to welcome my wife to the family, now that I am returned from abroad."

"Your marriage was rather a rushed affair, wasn't it?" Barnstaple eyed him speculatively.

"That can tend to be the case when one is due to leave for war," James agreed, pleased at his nonchalant tone, pleased too at the way the older man's face fell.

"Well, we would still be *very* happy to have you come to us," Miss Barnstaple reiterated. "It is a season of goodwill, after all." She smiled. "And it will be good to have you join with us."

"I'm afraid I will have to decline until my wife can accompany me, which won't be for quite some time, I'm sure. But we shall look forward to welcoming you to Langley soon. Now, if you'll excuse me." He hastened away, down a narrow path betwixt two buildings through which the gig could not follow. A moment later, his twisting route took him to the church cemetery, where he wandered through the headstones until he found the Langley plot and his mother's grave.

He stared at the headstone as memories flooded of that awful day.

Mama had pleaded with him not to go to London, had begged him to stay and forgo attending the gambling hells with his university chums. So he had stayed reluctantly, resentfully.

And without thought or much care, had given his mother the last of her medicine, only to watch her pupils contract and her drowsy state lead to a permanent sleep.

His throat, his chest, grew tight. He had killed her. Her death had shattered him. He might know God's forgiveness, but nothing could erase the magnitude of the consequences of his mistake.

A crunch of gravel brought his head up to encounter the placid features of the vicar.

"Good day, Mr. Langley."

James dipped his chin. "Mr. Edwards."

"It is a pleasant day to be out."

"A cemetery is not the place I would choose to spend my leisure."

"And yet here you are, which begs a question."

A question which James had no desire to answer. He barely knew why his steps had led him here, save that melancholy seemed to follow him these days.

There came a chuckle. "I see you are content with your own thoughts, and I am not needed. I shall leave you, then. Please pass my greeting to your wife." The vicar moved away.

James nodded, unsettling memories rushing back from the earlier conversations. Was Father right in thinking this Edwards fellow could have made Sarah happy? How much did his wife think she needed him? How much influence did Edwards hold over his wife?

"Mr. Edwards," he called, halting the vicar's passage, "do you have a moment? There . . . there is something I wished to enquire about."

"Why, certainly."

James followed him near where a gate in a moss-covered stonewall marked the entry to a field. He glanced around. Nobody was here, nobody would overhear. "I was speaking with old Mr. Collins earlier, who gave me to understand that you encouraged my wife to take on the care of the baby."

"Ah, yes, I did, in fact, encourage Mrs. Langley to care for the child. She was quite lost when you went away."

His heart thumped. Had she missed him? But no. She would not have been sad, but far more likely been relieved at his absence, given his drunken actions on their wedding night. Regrets at his deluded pride and self-interest flooded through him again, burning his skin in shame.

"Caring for the poor child filled her with new purpose."

"Until the baby died," James stated bluntly. "Are you surprised at how deeply grieved she was?"

"I did not know she was so deeply attached. But it was extremely sudden, and coming on the heels of your return and your sickness, well, so unexpected. I assure you that the child had been in good health, and nobody expected poor little Elizabeth to leave this earth so soon."

"No." Remorse panged again. How could he fling vague accusations at this man when he himself had been the one to bring the sickness that had led to the child's death? Guilt prickled inside, barbing his tongue to say, "It surprises me the degree to which you seem to influence my wife."

The vicar's blue eyes widened. "I'm afraid I don't take your meaning."

"It is my understanding that you persuaded my wife to marry me, then it seems you encouraged her to take on this child. It makes me wonder what next you will induce her to do."

The other man's jaw sank. "Sir, you quite mistake the matter. I assure you there has been no undue influence."

"Hmm." James pretended interest in a nearby grave. One for a Miss Fanny Caflin.

"Mr. Langley," the vicar spoke quickly, "if I have done anything to give offense, I ask your pardon. Regarding the marriage, it was your father who asked me to do that. I'm afraid he is not an easy man to refuse, especially when—"

At the man's sudden silence, James turned to look at him. "Especially when what?"

"Especially when . . ." Edwards licked his lip nervously. "When he holds my future at the parish over my head."

"I beg your pardon? Are you saying my father blackmailed you into arranging the marriage?"

"Y-yes," he stuttered. "To my eternal shame, yes, he did."

James's eyes narrowed. "You are saying Sarah had no desire to marry me?"

"I, er, don't believe so, no."

"So this was arranged by my father, and we were all scapegoats?"

"It would, er, appear so, yes."

James ground his teeth, keeping a most unholy exclamation behind his lips. Eventually he calmed enough to say, "You are a man of God. You are supposed to follow His will, not another's."

The minister stared at him. "But who is to say this marriage is *not* purposed by God?"

James stepped back, heart rearing at such words. Could he regard this marriage as not a mistake, but part of God's plan? Could his moment of weakness actually be used by God?

"God is a Redeemer, One who turns the weak into the brave, who can use the broken ones to save. King David was a murderer, an adulterer, a sinner by anyone's standards. Yet God redeemed even David's story to include him in Jesus Christ's forebears, and even described him as a man after God's own heart. If God can redeem a murderer, then he can surely redeem a marriage forged in such a way."

The words resounded deep in his heart. "Perhaps He can."

"I know He can." The vicar nodded vigorously. "I know Mrs. Langley's faith has struggled of late—"

Another bolt of envy streaked through him. How did he know what James did not?

"—but I believe she still wishes to follow God's ways. And I am hopeful the same can be said of you, sir." The vicar cleared his throat. "I observed you yesterday during services when you prayed."

The thought that someone had spied on him during his sacred moments with the Lord renewed his anger before the ridiculousness of that thought made his heart settle. How absurd to be upset by the minister's observations, especially when they were true. "I have, er, found myself challenged to forge a deeper relationship with God, that is true."

Mr. Edwards's features lit. "I am glad."

And James was too. It helped to know Someone cared for him, Someone loved him, even when others may not. James's future could be trusted to Creator God, who could work all situations out for good. Even this situation with Sarah.

For if God could work all things for good, then He could help heal this mess of a marriage. And perhaps even help James with his father.

Chapter 19

Hurt at her father-in-law's contempt crawled across her chest, stealing away her strength so all she could do was to lie there, listening to the sea, wishing herself away. Sometimes she despised herself for feeling so easily overcome, but each day was a battle to put on cheer and pretend the arrows of criticism bounced off her soul, when really it seemed they had pierced her, their poison seeping in, weakening her resolve, softening her bones.

She had wanted to believe James cared, but yesterday's scene in the library had only eroded such hope. Her emotions felt so fragile. Why couldn't God let her life slip away, that she not wake up in the morn? Another part of her still held contempt for wanting to give up so easily. Perhaps that was the influence of her aunt and uncle, who had long held that the sad and timid were spineless and simply needed to exert some energy and get on with things. How harsh such an attitude now seemed. She longed to be different, but it seemed an impossible thing. Happiness was a far-off star she could spend her life chasing but never capture. This Herculean effort, along with this ice encasing her heart, was exhausting.

"Mrs. Langley?"

Her gaze drifted to Mrs. Broomhead, her staunch companion through past weeks.

"Ah, you are awake. Is there something I can get you? Some morsel that Cook can make?"

"Thank you, no."

"Are you certain?"

"Yes." The only thing she wanted could never be brought back to life. Emotion cramped her throat, blurring her eyes.

"There, there." Mrs. Broomhead patted her hand. "Now, would you like me to read to you?"

"No, thank you. I am content to rest."

"If you are sure."

Sarah nodded, though she was far from sure. The troubled look Mrs. Broomhead gave her suggested she had her doubts as well. She closed her eyes, listened to the call of the sea, as the creak of the floor suggested Mrs. Broomhead had moved to the door.

Heaviness drifted over her, as if the burdens in her heart had spread to weight her limbs. So tired. So tired . . .

". . . said he would have been better off marrying Miss Georgiana!"

What? She opened an eye.

"Then he said he'd never had any liking for this one," a deeper voice said, one that sounded like Mr. Dawson, before the door closed with a sharp thud.

Her chest panged. Such contempt could only belong to Mrs. Copley, but try as she might, she could not deny the truth. James had never liked her. Yes, he had shown some surprising moments of thoughtfulness, but likely that was born of guilt. His father had erred in insisting James marry Sarah. His father had obviously forgotten whatever it was he'd thought in her character might benefit his son. James probably should have married someone else, like Georgiana. He could, if she was not here anymore . . .

She blinked and deliberately pushed such thoughts away. The dark thoughts had swooped in too oft of late, the whisper of failure murmuring through her soul in the darkest watches of the night. She needed to think on good things, so her Bible told her. Things that were good and true. But oh, this fight felt hopeless, as if she were attempting to traverse a mountain while walking in quicksand.

When she woke, it was to Mrs. Broomhead's gentle shake. "Madam?"

"What is it?"

"Your husband is here."

The husband who wanted another woman. Oh, if only he had a measure of affection for her!

"He wishes to speak with you downstairs."

To tell her he wished for a divorce?

"Madam? Here, let me help you dress. I believe his father has something to say also."

The old gentleman who loathed her. How could he have spoken so harshly to her in the library—to her, when she had hoped he was beginning to see her as another daughter?

How could he think her capable of stealing? And to say so in front of Mrs. Copley . . .

Perhaps this was a moment to forgive and not let injustice stain her soul.

She succumbed to Mrs. Broomhead's dressing her, and slowly made her way down the stairs.

James hurried to meet her, hands outstretched. "Sarah. I expected you to let me know so I could have escorted you."

Pain stabbed at her chest. She had done wrong again. She was so often in the wrong. Would she ever learn the proper way to do things, ever learn these unspoken expectations? "I'm sorry, I didn't know better."

"No, I am." He drew closer, tipped up her chin so she was forced to meet his eyes. "I am the one who is sorry. I should never have let Father speak to you that way before."

She blinked, trying to withhold the sudden moisture lining her eyes. "You cannot control how another person feels."

"I wish I could," he muttered.

Yes. For maybe he would have found a favorable response from Miss Georgiana.

He crooked his arm. "My father wishes to speak to you."

She stilled.

Forgive him, a quiet voice bade.

But she didn't want to. She made her steps accord with James's as he led her back to the library.

For once the old gentleman was not reading his paper, but was instead seated on the faded sofa near the fireplace, his expression a perfect match for the tension in her heart.

She willed her lips to curve to friendliness, though she felt none inside.

"Father has something to say." The weight of James's gaze shifted from her to his father.

"It, er, appears that I owe you an apology for what I said," Mr. Langley senior grumbled. "I am assured by my son here, and the maids he summoned who carried out the work, that your request was simply to clean."

An apology. The first she'd ever heard him utter! She met his faded gaze. "Thank you for believing me."

"Hmph." He glanced away, and for a moment it seemed as if his ears had pinked. "That Copley woman doesn't know everything, it appears."

"Indeed she does not." James grimaced. "I think she has made her antagonism toward Sarah very plain."

"Still, I would not wish her to leave," his father protested, to her great disappointment. "She has served this family well over the years." He looked at Sarah. "You would not let such a silly matter become bigger than it need be?"

"Of course not, sir," she felt obliged to say.

Again she met James's eyes, and felt a flash of sympathetic understanding.

"What was the other thing you wished to say to Sarah?" James prompted his father.

"Oh! It was just that I do not mind if you use Mariah's rooms."

Her heart lifted in stunned surprise. "Truly?"

"I suppose it is only right that they get some use."

"To be clear, you don't mind if I spend time there?"

"No."

"And if I change a few things?"

His lips pressed together, then he sighed. "Very well. Do what you must. You are James's wife, after all."

She bowed her head, politely thanked him for his largesse, and expressed her wish to get started immediately, to which the older gentleman acquiesced, dismissing her. She mouthed a *thank you* to James and exited the room, her steps a little tottery. What kind of mischief was this? Had she tumbled into a strange fairyland where wrongs were made right?

"There. That went much better than I expected."

She turned to see James's broad smile of satisfaction. Had he effected this change? "Was that your doing? I don't understand what just happened."

"Father was brought to realize the error of his ways."

"I did not think he ever knew he had any." She clapped a hand to her lips. "Forgive me, I did not mean to say that."

But instead of recrimination, she met an answering gleam of amusement. "No, you are quite right. I am fairly certain up until an hour or so ago my father was in complete ignorance of his shortcomings."

What exactly had transpired between father and son? "I don't know if I should enquire, but I am thankful for your intervention."

His head tilted and he studied her. "Our family has not made things very easy for you, have they?"

"I do not mean to complain—"

Her words faltered as he lifted up a hand. "You are a kindhearted creature. I see that now. And it is not unkind to speak the truth, and we both know my father is prone to fits of mercurial impetuosity." His lips pulled sideways. "Not unlike his son."

She studied him, the wryness of his tone adding yet another layer of complexity to this man. She had seen his earlier anger and chagrin, had known it could not be easy for him to speak to his father, and the fact that he had done so engendered a surprising warmth toward him. "Thank you." She offered a tentative smile.

"You are most welcome. Now . . ." He crooked his arm again. "May I escort you to your new rooms? Best to make the most of it before someone is persuaded to think otherwise."

"Of course."

He laughed and they moved as one to the room that had proved so problematic.

A few minutes later she was ensconced on a sofa in the yellow drawing room, gazing around with appreciative eyes at the hard work the maids had done. Now dusted, carpets freshly beaten, and the furniture waxed to polished perfection, the room shone. Sarah could appreciate anew why her predecessor had enjoyed this room so much. The chamber seemed to hold a peace she could find nowhere else, a warmth that was not evident in the cold December winds outside.

"They have done a wonderful job," James said admiringly. "I do not think I have seen it looking so well, even in Mama's time." He glanced at her. "Have you plans for what you will change?"

"Truly, there is so little that needs doing, save for perhaps some new cushions to be embroidered."

"Would one of the maids be skilled enough?"

"Perhaps, but I should much prefer to do it myself." She met his gaze shyly. "I cannot pretend to be a fine lady, but I have always prided myself on my needlework."

"Then make it so. Do as you wish. I could send Robert to collect you what fresh flowers there are. I'm afraid this time of the year there may not be that many."

"Really? That would be lovely. I do love beautiful flowers, whatever they may be."

"My mother did too."

His perusal of her deepened, until she wondered just what he saw.

"I, uh, spoke to the blacksmith about a pup for you."

He had? What other wonders could this day bring?

"He said he would bring one soon."

Happiness bloomed across her chest. "Oh, thank you. I'm very touched."

He dipped his chin, his study of her seeming to hold a kind of tender regard.

Such regard was confusing, especially given his reluctance to show her any real affection, and rushed words to her mouth. "How is the blacksmith's son? Has his health improved at all?"

His brow creased. "I was not aware his son has been unwell."

"Well, perhaps he is better now." Her cheeks heated. "It has been a while since I called upon them."

"Someone mentioned that you used to take baskets to the village."

She bit her lip. Did he disapprove? "I didn't mean to presume—"

"It's what my mother used to do, many years ago, when she was well." His look grew deep and serious. "Thank you."

For some reason, his approbation drew her near to tears. She blinked rapidly, glanced away, then fingered a small portrait on the table nearby, aware he remained standing, his gaze still heavy on her skin.

When next she dared look up, his eyes dipped to her lips then rose to meet her gaze. The moment stretched, accord swirling around them, leading her to fancy if something especially wondrous existed in this room of gold. And leading her to fill the awkward silence with words.

"I . . . I appreciate your support."

"You will always have my support," he said hoarsely.

For a moment she thought emotion had clogged his throat, and her fickle heart dared wonder if it had something to do with her. Perhaps she had been wrong to feel so low about the future, and this marriage might succeed.

He paced back, as if he was about to leave.

Strange disappointment pinched her chest, along with the desire to make him stay.

A moment later he bowed, wished her joy in her room, and left.

She exhaled. How strange an encounter. She'd scarcely dared hope things might improve, but what miracles had been wrought this day.

What miracles might still remain.

The next day, having completed her list of instructions and consulted with the cook about the day's meals, she was again seated in the room of gold, her fingers busy with mending chair cushions.

A knock drew her attention to the door.

"Enter."

James came into the room with a look of satisfaction. "I thought I might find you here."

"You do not need to knock."

"Would you prefer me to simply enter without a by-your-leave?"

She thought about the measure of safety she felt here, then answered honestly, "No."

He chuckled. "Then a knock will have to do." He glanced at the embroidery work in her hands. "I can see that you are very busy, and I have no desire to delay you, so perhaps I can come back another time."

She laid the cushion aside, fixed her attention on him. "What is it?"

"Well, I may need you to accompany me to the boot room."

"I beg your pardon?"

"The boot room."

She rose hesitantly. "I thought that was what you said."

"I'm glad to know you are not hard of hearing," he said with gentle tease.

She smiled and followed him along the passageway, out to the servants' quarters, and to the room where boots were cleaned.

A whine came from within.

"After you," James said, opening the door.

She entered, only to see Evan clutching a tan-and-white ball of fluff. "Oh!"

"Good morning, ma'am." Evan held up the pup for her inspection.

"Who is this?"

"This is your new friend," James said from behind her.

Evan extended the puppy and she gently stroked the soft fur, feeling the bumpy ridges of the pup's spine.

"Do you like her?"

The puppy's dark soulful eyes looked up at her trustingly.

"She's beautiful."

"She is still young," Evan warned, "and is likely to whine a little."

"No doubt the poor thing must miss her family so."

As if taking the cue, the dog uttered a whimpering cry, and Sarah's heart contracted at the sound.

For a moment the pup had sounded like poor Bethy . . .

"She'll soon settle," James said.

"Aye. She's like a wee bairn and will soon learn." Evan quickly looked at her with a flash of contrition. "Oh, I'm sorry ma'am. I did not mean to remind you—"

"It's quite all right," she said, willing her heart to be so.

"My dear, I'm so sorry," James, all remorse, with a degree of sensitivity she had never expected, expressed more regret. "I do hope I haven't reinjured you with my thoughtlessness."

But Sarah's heart had seized on her husband's first words.

My dear.

Was it possible he might hold a shred of affection for her? His words, his actions today, his consideration and remonstrations with his father on her behalf, certainly seemed to suggest so. He might never love her, but perhaps they could learn to live as husband and wife with a degree of liking.

She glanced up at him now, saw his gaze shift upward once again. Her breath stalled.

At James's bidding, Evan collected the pup and placed her gently on the ground.

Sarah held out her hands for the tiny terrier to run toward her. The dog moved hesitantly at first, before the puppy sniffed at her hands and licked them. The tiny mark of affection drew her laughter, and she exchanged smiles with Evan.

"She seems to be quite partial to baked ham, ma'am."

"That would make two of us," she said. "Thank you for looking after her."

"Oh, that was the master, ma'am. I have just watched her while the master fetched you."

She glanced up at her husband. "Thank you."

James inclined his head. "Consider her an early Christmas gift."

Emotion clogged her throat. Oh, how kind he was to her. She could barely recall the last time she had received a gift. Certainly there had been no gift-giving last year, the old gentleman in shock about his daughter's disappearance and Sarah unsure about her role here. Wryness tweaked her lips. As if she was any surer now.

"I hope she brings you many hours of happiness." James's tone, his gaze, held surprising warmth.

She would have to organize a gift for him. Perhaps she should make some effort with decorating the castle, arrange for gifts for the servants. That's what people in her situation did, wasn't it? Should they have a small dinner to entertain people? What would he like, what would he approve? What would prove a blessing?

"Sarah?" Her husband's brows drew together.

"Oh." She uttered a small embarrassed laugh. "Forgive me. My mind was wandering, thinking about Christmas and all there is to do. It is only a few weeks away."

"I thought we would entertain quietly this year," James said in a soft voice.

Is that what he'd prefer? She glanced at Evan, still playing with the puppy. This was no place to have that conversation. She pushed to her feet, grateful for James's hand as he helped her rise. "Thank you again. And thank you for securing a lovely little companion. She is very sweet."

"Then she is apropos for you."

A compliment? No. She should not set stock in such things. He was a known flirt, his charm as easy to put on as a new neckcloth.

"She'll be a good girl, I be thinking." Evan stroked the little dog's head.

"I suspect Evan is correct." James laughed.

"I beg pardon, sir?"

James's smile grew crooked as he glanced between Sarah and the gangling footman. "My wife may wish to have full charge of this young beast, but on those occasions when she does not, I believe it shall be your good fortune to help train this creature into the goodness Mrs. Langley will prefer to see."

"I like dogs, sir, so that will be a pleasure."

Sarah studied her husband. Had he truly thought of everything?

"Thank you, Evan. Your kindness is greatly appreciated."

"Of course, ma'am," Evan said, as if surprised. "If ever I can be of service, you need only ask."

She was so moved by his kind words she had to duck her head to hide the moisture in her eyes. She murmured something again of her appreciation to both him and James and carried the pup from the room.

Chapter 20

Rain pattered against the diamond panes of the library window, the season's cold alleviated somewhat by the crackle of the fire. James glanced over at his wife as she pored over his father's books at the desk in the corner, a tiny furrow in her brow. At her feet, in a basket, lay the pup, snoozing as seemed to be its preference. The change in his wife in recent days was remarkable, her engagement with the world apparently more like what she had done before, or so his father and the servants said. Sarah was slipping back into her former role as mistress of the house and chatelaine, while James was gradually forging a future, albeit one where he seemed to be stepping blindly into the unknown.

He'd been a soldier, but those days seemed to be done. And while working with his father in studying the estate books might give him a headache, it seemed to be well within his wife's skills, this talented, hardworking wife of his.

As if she felt his gaze, Sarah glanced up and her lips lifted. His chest found a corresponding throb. She seemed to be warming to him, her smiles, her conversation more frequent, and while he was yet to show her any more signs of physical affection, he sensed she would be less inclined to run away.

As for himself, the affection for his wife was growing, as each new day revealed more of whom she was. Clever, capable, conscientious, kind. His esteem extended further than mere appreciation of her character and talents. That brief embrace after her late afternoon walk had fostered both increased tenderness and awareness of her womanliness, a quality he remained hesitant to pursue. But the softness of her hair and skin had increased his desire to taste her lips, to see if they were as pliant as what lingered in his memories from more than a year ago. He could only hope and pray he would keep this desire leashed, and not do anything that might scare her. He needed to prove she could trust him, that his care was deepening into affection, into fondness, his regard for her more rooted than anything he recalled for any woman before.

She broke the connection and returned to her perusal of the ledgers Father had given her, some kind of relic of the castle's records from long ago.

"Are you paying attention, boy?"

James shifted his focus to his father, who seemed determined to familiarize him with the accounts, almost as if he thought that it was time for James to be made accountable for his decision to marry Sarah and gain his father's funds. Guilt writhed within. How much did Sarah know about his reasons for marrying her? If she knew about the gambling debts, hopefully she'd put it behind her, or who would blame her for holding reservations about any proclamations of affection? Would she ever learn to trust him?

"James!"

He ducked his head, tried to focus on the numbers, but they merely swam before him. His wife was good with numbers, not he.

A knock came at the door. He thanked heaven for the interruption, until Dawson entered.

James's lip curled. Studying the estate's accounts in recent days had shown just how deficient Dawson had proved in his duties, although Father had not appreciated his pointing this out.

"Mr. Langley, I came to tell you the roof is leaking in the west wing again."

His father muttered an oath similar to the one crossing James's heart.

"What is being done about it?" Sarah asked.

"Robert and Evan have found a number of receptacles to protect the carpets."

"Yes, but what about higher up, in the attics? Is nothing being done about that?"

Dawson gazed at her as if uncomprehending.

She sighed and stood. "I shall come and see to it."

"My dear," James interrupted, "you must look to your health, and be careful not to overtire yourself."

"You could come with me, if you wish," she said hesitantly.

Indeed he could. He pushed to his feet.

"In a moment, James," Father said. "These matters need to be sorted first."

"Excuse me, sir," Dawson huffed. "I also must announce Sir John is here and wishes to speak with you."

Even more reason to exit. The magistrate had little time for James, and served as one of Father's allies in blaming him for his mother's death. He exchanged a glance with Sarah who nodded, wryness bending her lips, as if she recognized that Sir John had little liking for her either. "I will be with you as soon as I can."

"Send him in," Father said. "Then go help Mrs. Langley."

Dawson showed Sarah a measure of deference at least as he held the door open for her to exit.

"I suppose we'll need a new roof," Father muttered when the door had closed. "What will it be next? How can we tighten our belts any further?"

Guilt trammeled his stomach for his profligate ways. "I have some earnings from the army—"

"Hardly enough for a new roof, though, are they?" Father snapped, eyeing James with that expression that always spoke his disappointment.

Well, no. He strongly suspected his earnings would prove hardly enough to repoint one of the fifteen chimneys. Somehow he was going to have to find a way to increase the family's income. Perhaps he could visit the farms and see if they could be encouraged to produce.

Dawson would not approve of James's being so involved.

Perhaps that was a way to save money. Lose Dawson, and Copley as well?

Further opportunity for conversation was lost as the door opened and Dawson announced Sir John.

"Don't get up," Sir John insisted, waving off Father's attempt to stand.

He refused Father's offer of refreshment, but accepted his offer to be seated, expression sober as he glanced between them.

James's stomach tightened and he pushed to his feet. Whatever the magistrate had to say, he had little wish to be present. "If you'll excuse me, Sir John, I have matters requiring attention elsewhere."

"I'm sure you do," Sir John said, in a manner that suggested doubt instead. "It must be hard settling back into life here, after your many years away."

"There has been some adjusting," James admitted.

"Adjusting to a quiet life, and adjusting to marriage. How is Mrs. Langley?"

Sarah? Was this the first time the supercilious man had ever enquired about his wife? From the way Sir John spoke about her, James had always gained the impression Sir John thought her little more than a trumped up servant. "She is well."

Sir John's lips pressed together, and he glanced at Father.

"You must have just missed her," Father said. "She has been helping me here with my correspondence."

"Working. I see."

Clearly he saw something James did not. "What is it, sir?"

"Spit it out, man," Father said.

Sir John sighed and shook his head. "I cannot but help feel your pain," he said to Father. "It must be hard to see Mariah's place usurped by another."

Usurped? Mother had been gone nearly twenty years. And besides, Father had been the one to make all the arrangements concerning their wedding. Would his father own that now?

"Sarah does her best," Father said.

"She is remarkable," James insisted.

"Indeed?" Sir John's eyebrows lowered. "She has certainly caused remarks among some of the locals."

James knew if he didn't ask the comment would worry him. "I don't know what you mean. What kind of remarks?"

Sir John's gaze lifted to the mantelpiece, avoiding his. "Some people are inclined to gossip. All that fuss concerning the Caflin brat, for example."

James clenched his hands. "I do not see how that is of anyone's business but ours."

"You should hear Barnstaple go on about it. Bringing a lowborn whelp into a place such as this." He shook his head.

"Demonstrates my wife's compassion," James said, his voice edged with growl.

"It is certainly not what your dear mother would have ever countenanced."

No. James's hand stole inadvertently to his chain. Mother's compassion, such as it was, had never extended far beyond these walls. She might have once taken baskets to the poor, but he wondered now if that was from duty, rather than the true care he sensed motivated Sarah, as evidenced by her concern for the blacksmith's son.

Such a thought seemed disloyal, but for the last ten years of his mother's life, she'd had no interest in much beyond the castle walls. Her sickness meant she'd had little interest in anything beyond her health, hence the frequent visits from Dr. Watkins.

Disquiet pushed James to his feet. "Excuse me. I just remembered an urgent task." Then, without waiting for acquiescence, he bolted from the room.

A harsh wind cluttered around the eaves drawing Sarah to pull her shawl more tightly around her shoulders. The sound of rain was almost deafening up here, and she shivered. The roof leak was far more obvious at this level, and she could only regret that she hadn't demanded Dawson see to more substantial repairs than those he had carried out before.

Of course, the nature of the Langley finances meant that a new roof would need to be put off for some time still, so they had done what they could afford. But nothing showed the need to avoid patched-up repairs as when one faced the consequences of disrepairs needing to be fixed properly. Especially when it appeared that rain the equivalent of the North Sea was rushing through the ceiling.

The scent of tar and pitch crawled up her nose, eliciting a sneeze.

"Madam?" Evan hurried to her.

She waved him off. "I am well. It is just a little dusty up here, is it not?"

The room, tucked up against the roof, was a kind of garret, and filled with a conglomeration of furniture castoffs and the like. It was strange but despite living here as long as she had now, even holding the post of chatelaine, she had never ventured into the attic before.

A steady *ping ping* of water dripping from the substantial crack had filled one pail, and Robert was waiting with another empty one to exchange.

Dawson had yet to make an appearance, but there was little anyone else could do. The erection of thick blankets to stop the rain might stop some of the water, but this was a repair job that Dawson should have seen to years ago. It would require far more than buckets and Evan's ingenious manner of trying to fill the holes with heavy material, tar, and hope.

"It seems we shall have to wait until the deluge passes before we can see the extent of the damage," she called.

"Aye," the men responded, as Robert effected a swift exchange of buckets.

Meeks's outdoor skills were being tested as he smeared more of the sticky concoction onto the crack. But already it was sliding in small black rivulets along the walls. Clearly the only remedy would be new slate.

New slate that they could hardly afford, unless a miracle occurred. She bit her lip.

"Sarah?"

She turned at her husband's voice. "James." Relief filled her heart How good it was to see someone who might help by offering a different perspective about what to do, other than waiting out the storm.

"My dear, I'm sorry I was delayed from such joys. Father's visitor proved hard to escape."

Ever since Beatrice's departure, the castle had seen Sir John far less. At least the older gentleman was being paid the courtesy of a call. She could count on one hand the number of visitors she had personally received. One finger, even. And a visit from the local vicar probably didn't count as a genuine visitor, even if she did categorize him a friend.

James glanced around, hands on hips. "I haven't been up here in years."

"I believe there are some treasures you may wish preserved." She motioned to some large trunks, which she'd hastily covered with cloth.

"I remember these from when I used to play up here as a lad. Ah, look." He pointed to a small brown wooden rocking horse, complete with mane and tail of real horsehair. "Even when I'd grown far too big to ride him, I'd fight Beatrice to keep her off. We used to call him Tony the Pony."

How very sweet. She loved these little glimpses into his life, even if they were often shadowed with regrets. Such as the fact that the little wooden horse would never see another child ride it again, unless he gave it to Beatrice. Or a miracle occurred to mend the chasm within their own marriage.

She drew in a sharp breath and changed the subject. "It appears some of the slates are missing or need mending." She pointed to the roof.

"And will likely cost a pretty penny." He offered her a rueful smile.

"Indeed."

"What is being done to attend to things?"

She pointed out the various attempts to address matters, conscious of his nearness, the tug within at his scent, the warmth he added to the room, which only sparkled into strange energy when he brushed against her.

No. She exhaled. She was imagining things. Her skin obviously craved another's touch, especially since she no longer had little Bethy to snuggle into and love.

Her eyes blurred as she fought the emotion.

James drew to her side. "Are you all right, my dear?" he murmured, under the guise of rearranging her shawl.

His solicitude, the tender way he adjusted her shawl, drew her gaze up to meet his, the lashes of dark-green eyes seeming even longer in the attic's dark shadows. And his continued referral to her as *my dear*. Her heart fluttered. Could they make a go of this? James seemed intent on proving his care. Perhaps it was time to dare risk her heart and invest in this relationship too.

Only recently had Sarah said she had forgiven him, so she should act like it now. "I appreciate your asking," she said shyly, "and yes, I'm feeling better every day."

He smiled, and her chest fluttered again.

"Then let's depart from here. It seems to me that everything that can be done has been, and we are simply getting colder the longer we stand here."

She nodded, even though her heart rebelled. Standing here, in this place of darkness, even though others worked in the far corner, she felt quite warm with him nearby.

He drew her from the room, holding her elbow as they carefully descended the steps. It was easier to talk here, now they were away from the pounding of the rain.

"What shall be done about a new roof?" she asked.

He sighed. "I wish there was a simple answer."

His look of discouragement stole inside, and she dared to place a hand on his sleeve, unable to ignore the hard muscle cording his arm. "Perhaps God has an answer."

He exhaled, gaze meeting hers for a long moment before flickering to her lips for the briefest of moments. "You are good to remind me. I will keep praying."

"As will I."

His eyes crinkled. "You truly are a treasure, aren't you?"

Her mouth fell open. He didn't mean that, surely.

His smile grew, and he placed a finger under her chin to draw her jaw closed. "No matter what some may say, I am glad that Father found you, and despite his mendacious ways, that things have happened as they did. Not all things," he hastened to add, as the name *Bethy* floated between them, "but this, you and me. There is some promise here, is there not?"

"Yes," she whispered, as her heart swelled.

Mrs. Copley, down a side corridor, eyed them speculatively, her brows rising as James tucked Sarah under his arm.

Maybe this marriage had a chance to succeed. Maybe God would help them, would help her learn to trust he'd changed. Regardless, she determined to do all she could to prove her value here, to find a way to economize even more. And to show James that the mistakes of the past that had brought them together need not reflect their future.

Chapter 21

The question of what to do about the Langley finances plagued James. The extent of damage to the roof wove concern through Christmas and New Year's, and propelled him to visit the castle's farms in order to see what could be done to improve productivity, and thus improve their rents. But everything he'd seen led to questions about the management of such things, which had dug further incentive to do what he could. He had so much to learn.

"And the lands be near exhausted," Mr. Giles, the home farmer, said, sighing as he gazed around the frosted fields. "I planted a winter crop of wheat, and it's struggling away, as you can see."

James could indeed see. It seemed the estate's home farm's fields were, if not exactly barren, then producing nowhere near the yield he remembered from younger days, when his father used to force a reluctant James to accompany him with the threat of no dinner if he followed his inclination and played with the village boys instead.

"What improvements can be made?"

Giles began to speak of fertilizer and disease prevention and crop rotation, things so foreign to James, but things he would likely have to understand now he was here trying to adjust to his role as his father's successor. There was so much to learn, both with his relationships and his place in this part of the world in which he'd never felt truly comfortable.

"It be good you are here, sir." Giles shot a sideways look at James that made him wonder how long it had been since his father's routine inspections. Or those conducted by Dawson.

"Has Dawson not been around?"

"We seen nowt of that man for many a month."

Then what was the man doing with his time? "I was under the impression that he made regular inspections."

"Regular inspections of the alehouse to my way of thinking, but then I might be speaking out of turn."

Tightness grew across his neck. Another thing to add to the growing list of his responsibilities.

"That's why it be good to see you at last, sir."

"I should have come much sooner, but matters at the house have demanded attention."

"Aye. I have heard about the transformation."

"Transformation?"

Giles's grey brows lowered. "The new Mrs. Langley. I heard you have a fine one there. They say it was she who finally made the grounds look as they ought."

And the house. "She is certainly a hard worker."

"Aye. And a smart one. Joseph, my youngest, works in the gardens as you know—"

He knew that now.

"—and says she was most direct with that Meeks creature about how to get the kitchen garden to grow. Did you not hear of this, sir?"

James gave an embarrassed shrug. "It appears I have still much to learn about my wife."

"Most impressed, was our Joe. Said she knew exactly what she was about, and would tolerate no nonsense from Meeks. I swear that man thinks he knows it all, but he is as lazy as a maggot in an apple. Aye, a fine worker be your wife, and verra sorry we were to hear about her sadness after the passing of the little girl."

"Thank you." His heart prickled. It was funny the numbers of villagers who had shown an interest in his wife's welfare and that of little Elizabeth. Perhaps his wife's kindness to others was not the very great abomination certain people had declared after all.

The farmer continued to share, and James did his best to listen and try to understand, but during his return to the castle, his focus drew more fully on his wife.

She was an interesting thing, equal parts boldness and timidity, courage and distrust and fear. Her gratitude at the pup had suffused her face into something like beauty, and he'd marveled at the alteration. Perhaps it was sadness that had stolen her bloom and made her appear older than her years. He'd seen a similar alteration recently on Christmas morn, when, with his father's permission, he had given Sarah his mother's brooch of fine pearls, and she'd protested the fineness of the gift as too extravagant. He'd countered that she was worth every penny and more. Her look of surprised gratitude, as though she wasn't sure whether to believe him, had drawn new warmth inside his heart, and heated desire to kiss her.

His heart quickened. Not yet. She needed to trust him more.

Hmm, when exactly was his wife's birthday? A good husband would know. He should probably learn this soon, and ensure she received due acknowledgment on her special day.

He drew his horse onto the road, memories flicking back to her delight, to the moment when he'd wondered about kissing her. How long would this physical estrangement between them last? He hoped—he would continue to pray—that she might find it in her heart to love him at last and return his affection.

"Mr. Langley!"

He drew his horse to a halt as the Barnstaple curricle drew near. "Good day." He nodded to young Mr. Barnstaple and his sister, rugged up warmly in the frosty air.

Georgiana smiled. "We trust you had a good Christmas, sir."

"Thank you. It was quiet, but pleasant nonetheless."

And surprisingly relaxing. With no plans or grand entertainments save for a church service, the day at home had been a chance to enjoy getting to know his wife a little more, as they played chess while the dog scampered about and his father snored. James had been glad to see his wife had not forsaken the old way of giving gifts to the servants, though how she had arranged it when their funds were so tight was a surprise. As had been her gift to him—embroidered slippers, which she'd handed him, saying, "I'm sure they shan't be to your taste, and if so, please feel free to not wear them and just not tell me."

He'd smiled at this, liking her adoption of playful tease. She was intriguing, this wife of his. A slow-developing but deep fascination was growing in his heart.

"I have not forgotten your promise to dine with us soon, sir." Miss Barnstaple's words intruded into his thoughts. "But it seems as though you have neglected our invitation."

"I beg your pardon, but I was not aware one had been sent."

"I don't understand how that could be. Your wife did not tell you?"

Why did her question seem so barbed? "Perhaps it has slipped her mind. She has been busy of late."

"Well, if you don't have plans for this Thursday, then I hope you shall attend."

"This Thursday?"

"At seven. A small gathering, really, just some of the neighbors. But now you are back, it would be good to welcome you properly."

And it would be good to finally introduce his wife in her new role. "You can count on us both being there."

"Wonderful! I haven't seen your father in an age. He is rarely at services these days."

James cleared his throat. "I meant my wife."

"Oh!" Her blue eyes widened. "Oh, forgive me. Of course. Yes, she is welcome too." Her smile seemed laced with honey. "Just an informal affair, remember. No need to dress up when it is old friends."

He inclined his head, bid them adieu, and hastened back to the castle. Why had his wife not passed on any invitation?

The Christmas season had passed, and the new year had begun with the hope that things might finally improve. Her husband had seemed so pleased with her meagre attempts to make things festive, new warmth toward him had risen in her chest. Of course, Mrs. Copley had been less than impressed, denouncing Sarah's efforts as "rather less than what the previous Mrs. Langley would have done, God rest her soul, but one couldn't have expected much more, I suppose."

How surprising that Mrs. Copley expected anything from her at all. But such matters didn't need to carry weight. As long as her husband and the old gentleman were happy, her contributions had been worth it.

As for herself, her husband's gifts had proved so wonderful. His mother's brooch, on which he'd obviously sought and won his father's approval before giving it to her, seemed to suggest he truly accepted her as his wife. His gift of the puppy, which she had named Esther, as a reference to another female once considered as an outsider in a foreign land, had, after a few sleepless nights, soon shown her warmth and affection. Between the joy of the pup and the various household duties that she had resumed, Sarah was slowly believing hope might fill her future. Essie's scamperings and teasing of wool even seemed to draw Mrs. Broomhead's smiles, despite the little puddles and deposits of a less pleasant nature. It seemed most of the staff enjoyed the little dog's company, save for Mrs. Copley, who complained about the messes. Which was ironic, as she never had to clean them up.

And with the gift of the brooch—how Mrs. Copley's eyes had widened when she'd first sighted that pinned to Sarah's bodice—and the former Mrs. Langley's rooms, it seemed Sarah's position was slowly being woven into the fabric of the castle. Perhaps this new accord with her husband might lead to warmer affections one day soon.

She placed Essie in her basket by the escritoire and sat to compose her letter to Beatrice. It was strange, but the only correspondence she had had in all her months was that which was still smuggled by Mr. Edwards. Perhaps her aunt and uncle had maintained their offense at her new role and felt no need to enquire after her, even though she had sent them several letters. Ah well. At least Beatrice was constant in her communication.

She had just prepared the nib to an elegant smoothness when a knock came at the door. "Enter."

Her husband passed into the room.

Her heart gave a little leap.

"Ah, I thought I might find you in here."

"Good afternoon."

He glanced at her stationery. "You are busy?"

"Nothing that cannot wait a few moments," she assured. She was still not entirely sure if writing to his sister would meet with his approval.

"I wanted to ask why you had not informed me of the invitation to the Barnstaples."

"Because we've received no such invitation."

"Are you sure? Miss Barnstaple was most insistent she had sent one to us."

Envy tugged. Miss Barnstaple. She whom others thought should have married him. Was she the one who'd given him the chain? "I have received nothing from her." Should she mention no invitation had ever been sent to her from anyone, or would that embarrass him?

"Why do you look at me like that? What is it, Sarah?"

"Perhaps people have been busy, or they have known there was recent illness in the house, but there has been very little correspondence from anyone by way of invitations." Or other mail, she could add, but didn't.

"What? That cannot be."

Was he calling her a liar? She knew a puff of indignation and was tempted to say it most certainly *could* be.

"Well, never mind. Perhaps it went astray. I thought you might like to know that they have invited us to dine there this Thursday night."

"The Barnstaples? Are you sure?"

"Yes." He laughed. "Stop looking at me like that. I just saw Miss Barnstaple. She has invited us."

"And you are sure she wants me to come?"

"Why do you doubt me?"

"She never speaks to me at services, and so has certainly never mentioned anything of the like. And this is the first invitation anyone in the district has extended to me." It hurt a little to say that, and hurt even more to see the confusion on his face.

"How can this be?"

She ducked her head. *Easily*, she longed to say, *when your friends and neighbors have no respect for the hasty wedding between those considered a servant and a knave.*

"Well, it is high time they gave you your dues as my wife, and for you to meet some of the other important personages in the area. I believe Mrs. Jordan will be there, an acquaintance of my mother who has long been considered one of the most stylish women of our acquaintance. She lives further north of Sir John, which is why you likely haven't met her yet. So, I hope you can find it in your heart to forgive them and do them the honor of appearing on Thursday night. I have made our acceptances already."

"I . . ." She swallowed. "I have nothing very fine to wear."

"I know I said something about a clothing allowance, but with finances as they are . . ."

"It does not matter."

"I'm sure it won't. Miss Barnstaple assures me it is to be a relaxed affair with no need to dress up."

Maybe instead of looking to see offense, she should shake off this cynicism and regard the invitation for what it was. A chance to get to know James's friends and neighbors, even if she still felt a fraud to go there as his wife. How she hoped she would not embarrass him.

But when the night of the dinner came, she found herself feeling far too wretched to attend. Whether it was nerves or some other malady, this headache, shivering, and unease across her midsection had garnered Mrs. Broomhead's sympathy, yet not her agreement that Sarah should remain at home.

"It would do you good," Mrs. Broomhead insisted. "You should go out and enjoy yourself for a change. You've been ever so busy, staying up until all hours mending the cushions, working in the library, organizing records and the like."

"I prefer to feel useful."

"One only needs to look at you to know that is true. You are certainly far more industrious than most of the ladies who have lived here, so I'm told."

For some reason that did not sound like a compliment, even though she was sure Mrs. Broomhead intended it as so. Instead, it tugged at her doubts, yet more proof that she did not belong, she did not fit in, that she was odd and peculiar and would never be accepted.

"Come now, madam. Let me help you. You are sure to enjoy yourself once you are there."

"I do not think it would be so enjoyable, not when I feel I have a hundred knots inside."

"That is just nerves," Mrs. Broomhead assured.

But a wave of dizziness made Sarah stagger, and a hand on her forehead transformed pleas to attend to concern and the hasty admonition to get into bed.

"My dear, why ever did you not say something? You are burning up."

"I'll likely be fine in the morning." It couldn't be anything more. It most certainly was not the return of the sickness that had stolen Bethy's life away. She blinked against the emotion. "I . . . I thought it might improve by tonight." And she had not wanted to disappoint her husband, not when this accord between them still felt tenuous. Wouldn't he merely think her hesitant and cowardly?

"I don't suppose that Copley woman's brangling today helped matters any." Mrs. Broomhead tucked in the bedclothes around Sarah's shivering frame.

No. It had not. Nothing about that woman helped matters. Her quibble today had been about something so minor Sarah had barely energy to deal with her. Never mind.

A knock came at Sarah's bedchamber door, and Mrs. Broomhead opened it.

"Ah, is my wife ready? I have no wish to be late."

"I'm sorry, sir, but Madam is not feeling well."

"I beg your pardon?"

"She has something of a fever."

A beat passed. Two. Then he said, "I am very sorry she is not well. May I be permitted to see her?"

Mrs. Broomhead glanced at her from her position at the door with questioning eyebrows.

Sarah gave a nod.

"Of course."

He moved into the room and turned her direction. The shadows of the room made it hard to discern his expression. "I am sorry you do not feel well, Sarah."

"I am, also."

"Are you? Or are you wishing to stay home?" he asked softly.

Her skin prickled with new heat. Did he think she was feigning sickness? She forced herself to speak. "I am sorry to disappoint you. Please extend my apologies to the Barnstaples."

"Of course." He eyed her with a blanked face that failed to reveal whether he believed her. "I trust you will feel better on the morrow."

She had upset him, but the upset was inevitable even if she had attended. She did not fit. She was not the same as James, or any of those other fine ladies and gentlemen he counted as friends and neighbors. Attending any such function would only reveal that all the more. Such a thought provided little comfort as she struggled to find sleep.

The next morning she felt more the thing, her headache having cleared sufficiently so she could attend to her letters again. She was writing to Beatrice when a knock preceded her husband's entry.

"I see you are feeling better today."

"Yes, thank you."

"Doubtless the malady cleared soon after the carriage departed."

"I beg your pardon?" Just as she feared—he was suggesting she had pretended to be sick to avoid the meal last night.

"You may be reassured to know that several people enquired after you last night. Miss Barnstaple was saddened to learn of your sudden illness, and Mrs. Jordan said how very sorry she was not to have met you at long last. I assured her that you were in no way invalidish and promised you would prove it by hosting a dinner of our own soon here at Langley."

Her heart sank. A dinner? With no funds? However would she manage? "If you wish."

"My wife is always so obliging."

A compliment? That sardonic tone suggested otherwise. "What . . . would you like me to do?"

"I'll give you a list of names, and you will send cards of invitation. The next full moon is the Saturday next week, which would be manageable, I believe."

She swallowed. "Quite manageable."

He issued a short list of various local notables, and her shoulders relaxed at the mention of one guest whom she regarded as a friend.

"You are pleased to have Mr. Edwards attend, then?"

"Oh yes. He's most amiable and has proved to be sympathetic in recent times."

His eyes flashed.

She did not know her husband overly well, but ascribed it to his self confessed mercurial moods and impetuosity.

"Do . . . do you think your father might be amenable to having a visit from Beatrice? Perhaps that might prove a good reason for the gathering."

"I don't think we need to provoke Father too much at this time. Besides, do we not already have a good enough reason to want to celebrate with our neighbors?"

"What is that?"

He studied her for a long moment, with something that could be entreaty softening his eyes. "We can celebrate our marriage."

Hope lit her heart. "You wish to celebrate that?"

"I do. I wish for all of our acquaintances to know how happy I am with my clever wife."

Sarah stared at him in amazement as he bowed and made his adieu. She wasn't sure if she believed him, but no matter. She would do her best to ensure she saved him from any more embarrassment.

She wrote the list of names lest she forget, and then moved to the Great Hall, where a request to Evan soon gathered all the servants. She straightened her spine. And hoped she didn't appear too incongruous with the painting of the estimable sainted former Mrs. Langley hanging above her.

"Mr. James Langley has invited a number of friends and neighbors to a special dinner next Saturday, and instructed that the house and grounds should be prepared appropriately."

The ripple of excitement across the servants drew her own.

"I understand it has been some time since a party of this nature has occurred, and I'm sure that you, like myself, will be keen to do our utmost to make the castle shine and preserve the honor of the Langley legacy."

She answered a few questions then spoke with a most excited Cook.

"I'm ever so pleased to finally put my skills to use again, madam. It's been that long since we entertained."

"I understand." Sarah said, inwardly wincing at how much this would cost. "And I shall trust you to guide me."

"P'raps we can find a copy of the menu when the last dinner of this nature be, twenty years or so ago, when the master and the prior Mrs. Langley celebrated their wedding anniversary."

"And see if his stomach serves his memory in that way?"

Cook laughed, and Sarah smiled. Might she finally be winning the woman over?

Outside, Meeks was encouraged to see what greenery and the like could be obtained for floral arrangements within the house. Mrs. Copley's arguments Sarah ignored as she instructed Robert to finally oversee the removal and hanging of the paper within the library.

"But miss—"

"Mrs. Copley, I find your extreme reluctance to follow simple requests most undesirable, and unless you would like your title and wages to reflect my faith in your abilities, then you shall not interfere. Do I make myself clear?"

"You cannot do that."

"I can. I will." Sarah felt her strength for yet another battle waning and grasped the newel at the bottom of the stairs to stay upright.

"But Dawson pays the wages, miss."

"My father pays the wages, Copley," James said from behind her, "and Dawson is obliged to carry out his instructions. Additionally, I am in full agreement with my wife that your inability to carry out simple tasks should be reflected in a drop in your wages and station. It leads me to wonder, especially given your reluctance to address my wife appropriately and with respect, whether you would be best suited as an underling for Cook, or perhaps a parlor maid." He moved to stand beside Sarah, his very presence lending strength to her. "Would you agree, my dear?"

Sarah swallowed, surprised he spoke the endearment in front of others, something she endeavored to hide as she eyed the recalcitrant servant. "I agree entirely."

Sourness flashed across Mrs. Copley's face as she stood before them. "Beg pardon. What is it you would have me do?"

Sarah studied her. This contention between them had gone on long enough, and with everything else that remained to be done before the castle was at the standard Sarah considered acceptable for such an important dinner, she could not afford to waste time chasing whether Mrs. Copley had followed instructions.

Perhaps it was time to do something different.

"I would ask for your assistance. As Cook says, there have been few occasions for entertaining, and as someone who has served the family for many years, I am sure you remember how things were done in the former days. I know you do not like me, but I hope you respect Mr. Langley and Mr. James enough to overlook such dislike and help me to plan an evening that will be enjoyable and memorable for all the right reasons."

James inhaled as surprise lit Mrs. Copley's face.

"Are you sure you wish to do this?" James probed, once the housekeeper had stuttered her acquiescence, and departed with the assurance that the torn paper would be attended to at once.

She nodded. "I will listen to her suggestions, but may need to check things with you, if that would be acceptable."

"I don't know how much use I shall be. I'm afraid whatever ideas I have will be sadly outmoded."

Oh. Her heart dipped. She'd got it wrong again.

"But I am, as ever, happy to do whatever pleases you." His smile seemed to hold a plea, and it nudged out her own.

He wished to please her? One might think he truly cared. And if that was so, then perhaps, in this new year, she might finally throw off the garbs of caution and allow herself to trust him with her heart.

Chapter 22

"Good morning, Sarah," James said the next morning when he attained the library.

Her gaze lifted to his as she murmured a greeting that left him unsatisfied. Would they ever reach a stage when he might expect a kiss good morning, or any sign of warmth from her?

James settled in at the long table, his position one where he could see both Sarah and his father's preferred seat beside the fire, and picked up the pile of papers. This, a collection of leases that listed rents, was his latest avenue to finding ways to boost their coffers. But it didn't seem fair to raise rents, not when it was plain that little expenditure had been outlaid on the properties owned by the Langley estate. And to sell off more land seemed the height of shortsightedness, though from every conversation he'd been privy to between Father and Dawson, that seemed to be the preferred option.

Father grunted, drawing James's attention. "The estimate for the slate has arrived."

He passed the paper to James, who looked at it and withheld a groan. There was no way they could afford that. It looked as though at least ten more years of buckets and pitch and tar would have to do. Or perhaps they could give up food.

Really, he should cancel the dinner arranged for this Saturday night. But how could he do that, when he knew how his wife had worked so hard? And canceling would surely send the wrong message—that their marriage was not worth celebrating—when everything within him wanted it to be worthy of delight.

A glance up and he caught the turn of Sarah's head as she returned her attention to her books.

He studied her, waiting, waiting . . .

"Any joy there, James?"

"No." He knew Father referred to his finding ways to scrape together more savings, but it might as well be the same in regards to his wife. Sarah spoke little, but she certainly had a way of telling him what she thought. Oh, how he longed for her affection.

"I don't know what we're going to do." Fear laced Father's voice.

Again James felt the throb of guilt. If he hadn't spent such a wild youth, if he'd gambled not and enjoyed fewer misdeeds, then his family wouldn't be in this financial predicament. It was up to him to find a way. But how? *Lord, please help us.*

A knock came at the door, and Dawson entered holding the day's post on a silver salver.

Sarah did not look up, as if she did not expect to receive any mail.

Puzzling. "Nothing for Mrs. Langley?" he asked Dawson.

"I, er, I'm afraid not, sir," Dawson said, less than smoothly, which only fueled further speculation, as the man exited.

"Were you expecting something, my dear?" Father asked her.

"No," she said blandly, offering Father a brief smile before bending her head to her task again.

James pushed to his feet, determining to break this stalemate. "Sarah?"

She stilled, but did not look his way, not even when he drew close, so their conversation need not be overheard by Father.

"Do you receive much in the way of correspondence?"

After a moment she offered a negative with a shake of her head.

"My sister?" he asked in a lowered voice.

Her gaze lifted to connect with his. She bit her lip, and glanced past him. "I had no wish to upset your father. Mr. Edwards passes her letters to Evan for me."

Mr. Edwards. That stupid envy spurted. If only she could be so quick to turn to James instead. "Would you care to take the air with me?"

She shook her head. "I am sorry. Between all I've been doing for Saturday night and the work your father has asked me to do, I cannot spare the time."

He stifled a swell of frustration. "What is it you are doing here anyway?"

Her gaze slid to him again. "Your father has asked me to write down the history of the castle, adding in such notes as he has made along the years."

"That's right. You are something of a historical expert, are you not?" he gently teased.

"I make no claims for expertise," she countered softly.

"Enthusiast, then," he offered instead, wishing her to receive the compliment, clumsy as it may be.

Her grey eyes held no amusement. What must he do to convince her that they could be friends? "Where events or time are you up to?"

He leaned down and couldn't help but notice her easing away. "I am not through as far as I had hoped, so I am still recording the various details of the Roman age."

"Ah, when the little pot was found."

"That is so." She tipped her head, as if thinking.

"What is it?"

She shook her head.

"Please," he persisted.

"Beatrice told me about the tunnels, and how a relative of the Langleys went missing below long ago. I just wondered . . ."

"Wondered what?"

"You'll probably think me foolish, but I wondered if there might be more artefacts yet to be discovered."

"You truly think so?"

"I merely wonder, that is all."

"Well, what is to stop us looking for them?"

"Us?" Her features lit with surprise.

"Why not?"

"But I am so busy."

"You can take a little break, can you not?" he pleaded. At her hesitation, he asked, "Do you have an idea where you might look?"

"From the various journals I have read here, it seems the tunnels underneath the chapel are the most likely places for something to be found."

"Then we shall search there directly."

"Search where?" Father called.

"I have need to borrow Sarah for some time." James held his hand out to help her rise.

She glanced at his hand, then him, then placed her fingers in his palm. Sparks rippled up his skin.

Judging from her pink cheeks, perhaps she was similarly affected too.

Within the hour, changed to clothes more appropriate for traipsing through muddy depths, he held a lantern as they traversed the stone steps that led from the kitchen to the cellars and beyond. Evan and Robert walked with them, carrying lanterns of their own, plus tools that might prove useful should they come across any object that might be deemed worthy of more investigation.

Sarah held his other hand, forcing his steps to be slower than he would have chosen if she weren't with him. But because she had deigned to accompany him on this quest, he was determined to do all he could to make her feel safe.

He squeezed her hand. "Thank you for coming."

"I didn't know I had a choice."

He paused. "Of course you did. You still do, if you would prefer to return upstairs." He held the lantern higher, so he could see her face. "I simply thought your experience in knowing where such things might be located would be helpful."

She shook her head quickly. "I make no claims to knowing where things might be."

"Underneath the chapel, you said."

"The journal entries seemed to suggest," she corrected.

Just then a grey-furred creature slithered past.

Sarah shrieked and jumped nearer to James.

He fought the smile of pleasure at her proximity as he sought to soothe her fears. "You need not worry. I think you scared him more than he scared you." He dared to gently stroke her back.

Evan backtracked a few feet. "Is everything all right back here, sir?"

"Mrs. Langley took exception to some of the wildlife," James explained. "Which is completely understandable."

"I have never liked rodents," she confessed.

"I think your little dog will prove most persistent in dealing with such things, so you need not worry."

"Aye," Robert said. "Terriers be good hunters."

"But it's a good thing she's not with us now," Evan said. "Otherwise we might not see her for days, these tunnels be so long."

Sarah stepped even closer to James, and he used the opportunity to place his arm around her, knowing relief when she did not shrug off his arm. "You are a valiant soul, my dear Sarah, so you need not fear. Now men, how much farther do you think?"

How strange her life could be. One moment ruing that she had no fine gown to wear for Saturday's dinner, thus confirming to the neighborhood she was not the fine lady they'd prefer her to be, the next having adventures the like of which she never would have dreamed. And now, to have James's arm around her, calling her valiant and his dear, all while taking her at her word that there might be undiscovered treasures out here.

This close proximity to him fueled a greediness within. His touch, innocent as it was, seemed to ignite fire in her blood, making her long to step closer still, though her skirts would simply trip him up. Still, to have him so near, to witness his caring attention even as they walked across goodness knew what in this stale musty air, mitigated the pain of knowing she had nothing grand to wear for the dinner on Saturday night. Surely he could overlook such things if he wished to tuck her by his side.

The brickwork changed, the stones holding a reddish color more like what she recalled from the chapel. "I think it must be near here."

Robert lifted a lamp which illuminated a carved stone cross. "The chapel must be above."

"Then we should spread out and search," James commanded.

For a moment she was left alone, as the men diverged to various corners. Then James, with an apologetic smile, drew to her side again. "Forgive me. I did not mean to desert you. Which corner do you think the best to start?"

She pivoted, working to remember exactly what the journal entries had said. "Are there any signs of a well?"

Lamps lowered closer to the ground, as they looked for depressions in the earth, or other signs that might signify a shaft.

"Mrs. Langley?" Robert pointed to a dip that might be a filled-in pit. They moved closer.

There were signs of scratching, little nicks on the stones around. Excitement throbbed. How glad was she not to be such a proper lady that she did not participate in such things. This was all too thrilling.

"Stay back here, where you'll be safe," James instructed, with a smile. "I should not like you to be hurt by a flying shovel or the like."

The men began their excavations, and she watched, anticipation building. Perhaps they'd find some coins or some other treasure, artefacts which would help the Langley estate.

Dirt flew in brown clods and clouds, as amidst the men's grunts and groans dust tickled her nose.

She shivered and stepped closer, peering around James's broad shoulders. Really, he seemed to be viewing this as a boys' adventure, digging deep, hurling dirt back faster than Robert or Evan. She shouldn't be surprised. He seemed desperate to prove himself to his father, to make up for the failings of his past.

Which she couldn't blame him. It was what they all did, wasn't it?

A different clanking *thud* echoed around the room, fueling greater impatience.

"I think there's something down there!" Evan cried.

"Aye, it seems to be a box, sir," Robert confirmed.

She inched nearer, trying to see what the men could, when another streak of fur flew between them, and she gasped.

"Sarah?" James clasped her in his arms, and she suddenly knew another reason for her breathlessness.

How strong he seemed.

"Are you all right?"

She nodded. "Just another rodent." His smile caused another twinge in her chest.

"Shall we continue?" He released her gently.

The men moved to the hole, where the box lay undisturbed, and James instructed for the menservants to clear the remaining dirt, before beckoning Sarah near. "Do you not think we should open this together?"

Together. "Very well." She joined him in crouching down—ladylikeness was sometimes overrated—and with gloved hands, together they lifted the rusted metal lid.

Nothing.

Her heart dropped.

Nothing save for some fragments of wood.

She glanced up at James, saw the disappointment on his face. "Oh. I'm so sorry."

He reached into the box, drew out one of the fragments. "Why would this box be buried here if it holds nothing but wood?"

"You mean there's nothing, sir?" Evan asked.

"Nothing valuable, anyway." James sighed.

The disappointment was palpable, perhaps made more so by the great hopes they had entertained before.

Again, she peered inside the box, the light making it hard to see.

Again, nothing.

Despite her best efforts, her prayers, her research, they'd found naught of value.

As the men debated how best to remove the box, she moved to James's side. "I am sorry," she whispered.

"You cannot blame yourself," he said tiredly.

But she knew this wasn't true. He would never have had his hopes raised then dashed if it wasn't for her. This whole exercise had been one of frustration. She should never have left her duties for such a fruitless expedition. She had failed. Yet again.

Chapter 23

"Evan, has any mail been delivered today?"

"I believe there has been some correspondence addressed to Mrs. Langley. She is in the yellow drawing room if you wish to speak with her."

"Thank you." James hesitated, gaze drifting to the table beside the large carved fireplace, where the post for delivery or collection usually lay.

"Was there something else, sir?"

"I wish to know if you have noticed anything at all unusual about the post."

"You mean apart from the fact that there has been more correspondence for Mrs. Langley?"

"She did not receive letters?"

Evan glanced around the room, as if watchful for those who might overhear.

"What is it?" James pressed. "You may tell me."

"It's just that, until this week, I have not known Mrs. Langley to receive any letters. It is strange, because I have seen her write a few. I've noticed the letters when they were laid out, ready to be posted."

"That is Dawson's responsibility, is it not?"

"Aye, sir." Evan looked uncomfortable. "P'raps I'm speaking out of turn, but I have always wondered why she receives nothing back."

Something that a conversation with Dawson might best clear up.

"Can you cast your mind back a few weeks ago and tell me whether you recall if Mrs. Langley received a letter from the Barnstaples?"

Evan's brow furrowed. "I'm afraid I couldn't say."

"No matter. But perhaps in future if you do see correspondence for Mrs. Langley, you could be so kind as to hand it to her directly. I think she will appreciate knowing it has not gone astray."

"Of course, sir."

James dismissed the footman and glanced around the hall, which had been freshly dusted and polished in preparation for tomorrow night's dinner. The levels of industry which his wife's efforts had induced were truly remarkable. But then, Sarah, this woman he had married against his wishes, was truly remarkable, even if she'd been disappointed that her hunch about the Roman artefacts had led them astray. Still, the box had been dug up and shown to Father, who had dismissed it with a cursory look, then demanded it be removed from his sight. James had obeyed, and since then, matters for the dinner had consumed every minute, his wife's near panicked efforts twisting guilt that he'd stolen her attention for what proved to be a fool's errand. Poor Sarah.

He walked down the passage to her rooms, contemplating what Evan had just shared. Had some of the servants deliberately withheld her mail? It would explain the lack of invitations, and doubtlessly would have contributed to her feeling isolated. Of course, he knew some of the locals with toplofty notions would scorn her, but from the conversation at the Barnstaples last Thursday, there were none who had made such sentiment plain. And if they had, well, he had no desire to continue bonds of friendship with people so unwilling to recognize her uncomplaining spirit and loyalty to this family, which had at times done her wrong.

He paused, then switched direction, moving to search out Dawson in his father's preferred room. A knock, he entered, and discovered the steward-butler talking to his father in front of the library's roaring fire.

"Ah, Father. And Dawson. I had hoped to find you here."

"How are preparations going for tomorrow night?" Father asked.

"Sarah seems to have things well in hand," he said, noting the slight souring of Dawson's expression. He pressed a little harder. "She really has worked tirelessly, wouldn't you agree, Dawson?"

The man gave a noncommittal grunt of an answer, which deepened James's ire.

"I think you will be very pleased, Father. Sarah has achieved quite wonderful things."

There it was again. A flash of impatience.

"I beg your pardon, Dawson? Was there something you wished to say?"

"No, sir," he muttered.

"That puts me in mind of something else. I was speaking with Giles recently at the home farm, and he mentioned you had not been to see him or the farm for quite some time."

"He be forgetting, sir."

"Forgetting?" James put up his brows. "When was the last time you were there, Dawson?"

"I, er, cannot quite recall."

"Seems Giles might not be the only one with a poor memory. Ah, well. Perhaps you forgot because it was so long ago," James said smoothly, before turning to his father. "It appears the home farm needs more attention than it has been receiving. I would suggest the farm is not the only area where things are amiss."

"What do you mean?"

"It's also come to my attention that Mrs. Langley's correspondence has also gone missing over the past few months. It is strange, for Evan declares he has seen Mrs. Langley's letters awaiting postage, but incoming mail has, up until recently, been nonexistent."

"That is strange," his father agreed, glancing at Dawson with a frown.

"Perhaps it is simply that she does not receive letters," Dawson said.

"I don't think so." James switched his attention to Dawson. "Instead, I worry someone has been suppressing her letters."

"Why would anyone do that?" his father said.

James cocked his head. "Dawson?"

"I do not know," Dawson muttered.

"Do you not?" James asked. "I hope that, as the person responsible for such things, you will take extra care to ensure any such thing does not happen again, else I would take it as a personal affront, as it can appear to be vindictive against my wife."

Dawson blinked, his feet shuffling on the dark carpet.

"Indeed, it almost seems as if your duties are getting away from you,"

James persisted. "Perhaps it's time you considered what role might be more suited for you should you no longer work here."

The servant hastily assured that he would do his best.

"Your best had better be good enough," James warned, "else it might be time to be asking someone else to take charge of such an important household responsibility."

"Yes, sir." Dawson shot James a sullen look.

James exited, praying his father had read between enough lines to understand Dawson's antipathy toward Sarah, as he moved back through the hall and along to her rooms.

Undoubtedly she was nervous about events tomorrow night, but her ability to extend herself in efforts with cleaning, preparing, and planning had put his own meagre exertions to shame. He'd barely seen her, given her early rising and apologies at missed dinners due to her exhaustion. Such efforts were enough to make him wonder if perhaps her declining of the Barnstaples' invitation was not a sham but really because of illness, and he'd cautioned Mrs. Broomhead to do her best to ensure Sarah would be rested and ready for tomorrow night.

For he wanted her to shine brighter than the castle, this woman who was fast becoming entwined around his heart.

Sarah glanced through the pile of correspondence awaiting attention. After months of wondering whether she would ever receive responses to her letters, she'd finally begun to receive some mail.

Beatrice's writing. Her pulse accelerated. She read it eagerly.

My dearest Sarah,

Thank you for your kind wishes. I do hope Papa and James are well and in good spirits. Perhaps they will be when they learn our news: we are to be parents! The doctor has confirmed it is to be a midsummer child, and I cannot wait to have you as her godmother . . .

How wonderful! How marvelous. Beatrice would be a wonderful mother. A wonderful—

Oh. Her initial joy plummeted, the words stirring dormant pain in her heart. How she hated herself for not rejoicing in her friend's good news. *God, forgive me.* But the script seemed to have burned in her brain. Bea would make a wonderful mother, but Sarah had proved a failure, a disappointment, and lacked any hope that she could also one day share such news. Emotions weighed so heavily on her soul. Perhaps the other letter might bring better news.

Arms leaden, she slit the seal—it was blurred, so she could not read it clearly—and scanned the bottom of the page to see it was from Sir John Willoughby.

She read the words penned in a strong hand:

I find I must decline the invitation. I have no desire to dine with an elevated servant . . .

The letter slipped from her hand, the harsh words seared across her soul. *An elevated servant.* She was nothing more.

Oh, how she would bring shame on this family. How could Mr. Langley—either of them—have thought she could be suitable as James's wife?

Tears burned in her eyes. What would she say when the old gentleman asked why his friend was not attending? She'd been rejected, had brought embarrassment. She was not fit to take the place of James's sainted mother.

A *thump* began in her head, even as a *thump* sounded without.

She glanced down at the sleeping pup. She had no wish to disturb Essie. Emotion balled in her throat. The door handle turned, and she called out, "Who is   oh!" as the door opened.

Her husband appeared, sheepishness on his face. "I wasn't sure if you were in, but Evan mentioned you had received some post. Was it an acceptance to your dinner?"

The boyish hope lighting his features dulled her heart anew. She licked her lips. "I . . . I am afraid not."

James approached her escritoire. "But there's the Willoughby seal, and I cannot understand why else Sir John would be writing to you."

She released a silent sigh of exasperation. Were there no secrets to be had at Langley House? "It was in reply to my invitation," she said slowly.

"He refused?" His eyes rounded.

Should she? Oh, why not. James already knew what a poor bargain he had married. She handed the letter to him, watching his expression closely as he read the short note.

He gritted his teeth, and handed it back to her, eyes dark with anger. "Sir John has a rather too high opinion of himself," he said, his calm tone most unlike the tight fury in his expression. "I should not regard it. Let us be thankful, instead, that our party will not be attended by those who do not wish us well."

Did the other attendees truly wish to celebrate their union? How many of the other acceptances had been but excuses to see the new Mrs. Langley fail? Dread filled her heart.

"Now, are you sure you are happy with the gown?"

"Thank you, Mrs. Broomhead. It looks well enough."

The gown was the only one she deemed appropriate, the muslin she had worn at the assembly with Beatrice nearly a year and a half ago. James had requested she wear something new, and this was the newest gown she owned, even if it was several years old. Hopefully his unexpected gift of a silk shawl would hide her gown's deficiencies, such as they were.

She studied her reflection as Mrs. Broomhead finished tonging her hair and stepped back with a grimace.

Why that expression? She wasn't the one with the headache from such tightly pulled back hair.

"I wish I was more talented with styling hair. But then, I have always been more capable with managing children than arranging tresses."

"It looks very nice. Thank you," Sarah acknowledged.

"And are you looking forward to tonight?"

"Of course." That was an exaggeration. She was exhausted, and the ache thumping in her head meant she would be hard-pressed to enjoy tonight's proceedings. The servants had labored for days now, to ensure the rooms the guests would visit were especially clean and bright. No one would have any reason to judge Sarah as wanting in that regard, at least. Even if they might judge her appearance.

"I'm sorry, Mrs. Langley, it simply doesn't want to curl."

"It is no matter. I'm sure it is my heavy hair that has a mind of its own rather than any fault of technique of yours."

"You still look quite pretty."

Quite pretty. Sarah swallowed and concentrated on the kind intent. "I hope Mr. Langley is pleased."

"Oh, how could he not be? Especially with that lovely necklace around your pretty throat."

Sarah touched the former Mrs. Langley's strand of pearls, another gift from James earlier.

When he'd presented it, she immediately had asked, "Should this not belong to Beatrice?"

He demurred. "Yes, if she had not chosen to run away."

If she had not run away as Sarah had advised. Sarah cringed.

"They'll look very well on you," he'd insisted, and she did think it was not too prideful to agree. She'd never owned much height, but the way the necklace draped, it seemed to elongate her neck and confer a demure attractiveness.

As Mrs. Broomhead chattered on, Sarah wondered at herself. She did want James to take pride in her. And she wished to not disgrace him or the Langley name. *Dear Lord, may tonight go as it ought.*

She pushed to her feet, grasping the corners of the dressing table, hoping to hide her weakness from the woman who was too inclined to fuss.

Essie whined from her basket near the fire, drawing Mrs. Broomhead's attention, which likely swayed her focus from honing in on why Sarah needed assistance to remain upright. The busyness of the day had meant scant opportunity or appetite for food. She hoped that would not prove a folly.

After pasting a smile on her face, she pinned the brooch on the silk shawl, adjusted its fold, and eyed herself critically in the looking glass. She thanked Mrs. Broomhead for her endeavors and moved out to the top of the stairs, clutching the bannister as her head's ache suddenly sharpened. She paused, closing her eyes, summoning her strength, willing herself not to fall.

"Sarah?"

Her husband. She opened her eyes, affixing her features in an expression she trusted counted as pleasant.

He drew nearer, nodding as if in approval. "You look quite well."

At least she *looked* quite well. She summoned a smile. "As do you." Actually, he looked extremely well. His coat and breeches appeared molded to his form. His snowy cravat highlighted his dark good looks. He, at least, would not bring shame tonight.

He offered his arm, which she gingerly accepted. Despite his many kindnesses in recent days, she was still not completely certain if they were not some part of a grander plot to lull her into a false state of assurance, before he whisked the mask away to reveal the colors of his drunken wedding night.

She shuddered.

He folded his hand over hers. "Are you cold?"

"No." She still felt an odd lurching in her midsection, though. A seat would be nice to attain soon. She licked dry lips, and confessed, "I do not feel especially well."

"I expect it's just nerves."

"Are you not nervous?"

"Once upon a time I might have resorted to drink to get through a night like this, but those days are gone, I promise you." He patted her arm in a reassuring manner. "Come, let's go greet our guests."

She paused at the bottom of the stairs, steadying herself, whilst pretending to flick away a speck of dust from her gown. Oh, how she hoped to do him proud tonight. If only her head would let her.

She followed him to the Great Hall, where they would stand with his father and receive their guests. Under the watchful eye of his beautiful saintly mother from the large picture hanging directly above.

Chapter 24

James glanced around the dining room, glad that things were going so well. Their guests consisted of the notables of the district, and, save for Sir John Willoughby, he was gratified to see so many acceptances tonight. Not that they were a large party. He hadn't wanted to overwhelm Sarah. But she seemed to be holding up satisfactorily.

He glanced at the opposite end of the table, where she sat between Mr. Edwards and young Mr. Barnstaple. The vicar had proved most assiduous in his attentions, even as the other younger man had not. James frowned.

"Mr. Langley?" Miss Barnstaple placed a gloved hand on his arm. "Is something not to your liking?"

He carefully withdrew his arm, leaning back in his chair to avoid any further overly familiar gestures. "Forgive me, I was not attending. You were saying?"

Her catlike green eyes shifted from him to the table end. "Mrs. Langley looks well tonight."

"Yes." He took a sip of wine. He'd scarcely touched a drop since his return, but perhaps that would help ease his tension. He relished the flavor slipping down his throat to heat his body. Why had he forsaken its delight for so long?

"That pretty necklace was your mother's, was it not?" Mrs. Jordan said, from his other side. "I seem to remember she had a particular fondness for it?"

"Yes." *To both questions.*

"When I saw her wearing those pearls under your mother's portrait, I couldn't help but wonder at the contrast." Mrs. Jordan smiled softly. "Your mother was such a beautiful woman, wasn't she?"

He frowned. Surely she did not mean her words to hold that insinuation?

She widened her eyes. "I meant no offense, I assure you! Your wife looks quite charming, I'm sure. She was your sister's companion, I believe?"

He stiffened. "Sarah was my sister's dearest friend."

"How is dear Beatrice?" Miss Barnstaple asked.

"She is well." He hoped. He really should write to find out. Perhaps he should even risk his father's displeasure by inviting Beatrice to stay.

"I hope we can see her again soon. It was such a shock when she departed so quickly, before we even had time to say goodbye."

"Indeed." His gaze returned to Sarah. She seemed pale, and the food on her plate lay untouched.

"It is truly wonderful how enamored you are by your wife," Mrs. Jordan said. "A love match, I suppose?"

He permitted a thin smile before shoving a large piece of meat into his mouth and making a show of chewing it for a time. Let her suppose all she liked. He glanced back over at his other neighbor, who smiled prettily at him.

"That is a lovely shawl Sarah wears," she said. "Is it silk?"

"I believe so, yes." Another item of his mother's, all he could afford.

"A shawl like that does much to hide the, er, disadvantages of one's gown." Miss Barnstaple looked across the table at the woman seated beside him. "Would you not agree, Mrs. Jordan?"

"Oh, yes. A shawl can do wonders for one if the color of the gown is not quite right for one's complexion, or perhaps is a *teensy* bit outmoded in style."

He glanced at the well-dressed ladies beside him, recognized the contrast in their bared shoulders and lower necklines and his wife's unadorned gown that seemed to reach her chin. Frustration spurted. Had he not requested for Sarah to wear something new?

Of course, with no funds to secure such a thing, and no one but himself to blame . . .

He took a larger sip of wine, and drew the geniality expected of a host around him with an effort. "Something neither of you ladies would know anything about, I'm sure."

They tinkled laughter at him, drawing the attention of Sarah. He ducked his head, ashamed to look at her. He should never have suggested this, not until he could afford to buy her a new gown. Anger stirred within at himself. Would he ever be the husband who could provide?

"Perhaps a word from a friend might help," Mrs. Jordan said, giving Miss Barnstaple a significant look.

Miss Barnstaple dipped her chin. "If you like, I would be most happy to talk with her. I have always had a particular interest in looking my best."

"Something you have achieved most admirably," he said, with another stab at gallantry. Of course, the Barnstaple fortune allowed for such indulgences.

"Well, if you're sure it would be received well, I could perhaps drop a word of advice in her ear. Provided you don't think it would be seen as presumptuous, of course, sir."

"I think she would be glad for your advice."

Well, he would be glad for Sarah to learn something more about dressing to advantage. She really did look pale.

Their gazes met, hers unsmiling, and he felt his own attempt to project good humor fade, as his emotions slid and tipped like a slippery pebble at the shore. She shifted to talk with Mr. Edwards, and James experienced another moment's stupid envy. How he wished she could be so quick to talk to him.

The meal progressed, and thankfully, his father refrained from impolitic observations. Who knew just what might spring from his lips these days?

Conversation moved to other matters, other people, before circling around to his family again.

"Your father is looking well," Mrs. Jordan observed.

"His gout has been troubling him some," James admitted.

"Ah, gout." She nodded sympathetically. "My Henry suffered from it, God rest his soul. I wonder what the doctor recommends as treatment now."

"My father does not consult Dr. Watkins often."

"Of course. I always thought Watkins quite a charming man, but then he changed after the sad loss of your poor mother. He seemed to take her death very hard."

As she went on to talk about the various treatments and remedies her husband—and by extension, herself—had been forced to endure, James suddenly wished the evening at a close. He wanted to talk to Sarah, not listen to insipid conversation about people he barely knew. He wanted to know what made her sad, for it seemed he suddenly recognized that she wore sadness around her neck as much as any pearl necklace. He wanted to know what it was that Mr. Edwards said that made her smile. He wanted to know *her*, fully, in every sense of the word.

He exhaled, forcing his thoughts away. He would not demand such things of her. Not until she held him in some form of affection.

He eyed the glass of wine, temptation strong. But he'd promised God—and Sarah—that he'd not get drunk, and after abstaining for so long he could already feel the loosing of inhibitions. *God, help me.* He pushed the glass aside.

"So, Langley." The elder Mr. Barnstaple leaned back in his seat. "We've barely seen you since your return. Tell us how things went on the Peninsular."

Finally, the opportunity to talk about a topic that made him feel alive and like a man. No more the silly speculation over women's clothes, and trying to impress his wife, who now seemed determined to avoid his gaze.

His stories became more garrulous, the laughter as he shared about his funny escapades louder, and he reverted to the role he'd played in London, the voluble man of the town his friends had laughed and drunk with. A quick glance at the table revealed his father looking at him askance, and his wife blushing as Mr. Edwards leaned close. She was not looking at James, and he suddenly wanted her to pay him attention.

He heaved to his feet, glass in hand. "A toast."

The guests lifted their glasses obediently, expectantly.

What were they waiting for?

Oh. For him to speak.

"To my most wonderful wife." He studied her, her dark-grey eyes filling her face. Such pretty eyes . . .

But she did not love him. She'd never love him. She'd always prefer that milksop of a vicar to him.

Hurt creased James's chest. He wanted her to want *him*. "Join me in drinking a toast to my clever and so capable wife. My father couldn't have contrived to foist a better bride on me."

A gasp rimmed the room, forging awareness he had said something out of place. But he couldn't think, his brain hazy with disappointment. He lifted his nearly full glass and downed the contents, avoiding the eyes of the woman seated at the other end, and the betrayal on her face.

She was a failure. A failure as a wife. A failure as a mother. She had failed to be accepted. That was only brought home all the more when she'd sat with the other ladies in the drawing room while the men drank their port, and she'd tried to avoid their clumsy efforts to smooth over James's earlier appalling lack of manners. How could she pretend it was of little consequence, when this, the evening supposed to celebrate their marriage, had dissolved into such a farce? In admitting his father's machinations, James might as well have shouted he did not love her, would never love her. That their marriage was merely a way for him to pay off his debts, and she was the chaff left of his poor choices. Her eyes burned with unshed tears.

Miss Barnstaple now sidled up to her. "I'm so sorry. I can't imagine how he could say such a thing." She giggled, as if nervously, yet with a look in her eyes not unlike that Sarah had witnessed in Mrs. Copley's more triumphant turns. "I expect it was the effect of drink."

Sarah suspected that also. And yet he'd promised! But not a word of this would she admit.

"He always had rather a propensity to drink and to be regarded as quite the scapegrace of the community. And yet, somehow, he still manages to charm us all." Miss Barnstaple giggled again in her annoying high-pitched manner. "Now, this could also be from the influence of wine, but Mr. Langley felt it only right for me to drop a hint."

Another neighbor, a handsome woman called Mrs. Jordan who had sat at James's right hand and been introduced as Miss Barnstaple's godmother, drew close. "Are you finally telling poor Mrs. Langley about her gown?"

Sarah looked between the two. Is this what they and her husband had been laughing about? They had been laughing at her? Mortification scorched her cheeks, she felt once more light headed. "You must excuse me," she faltered, "the other guests—"

"But before you go"—Miss Barnstaple plucked Sarah's sleeve—"please forgive my impertinence, as you are so much older than I"—another giggle, one that made Sarah feel as old as Methuselah—"but your husband wanted me to offer you some hints about your dress. That color truly does nothing for you, only washes you out, I'm afraid. I would like the opportunity to assist, if I may. I consider us as friends—"

Was she serious? Or was Sarah suffering delusions?

"One day soon I hope you may permit me to visit with my dressmaker— she's French, you know, and has quite the best taste—and we could find what colors and styles suit you best. However, that *is* a pretty shawl." She nodded encouragingly, as a sop to Sarah's pride.

"You are all consideration." Sarah struggled to find her next breath.

"I do like pretty clothes," Miss Barnstaple exclaimed. "Truly, nothing pleases me more. You could be like one of my paper dolls. I would enjoy it so."

Her pleading blue eyes, the hand clasp, it couldn't be all contrived. Could it?

But Sarah had been wrong before. Wrong that her husband would spare her this embarrassment even if only for his own pride. "Thank you. I will consider it."

"I hope you do." Mrs. Jordan gave Sarah's ensemble a somewhat critical stare. "You are not in the first blush of youth, but that is no reason to appear dowdy, especially as you are a new bride."

A new bride. Sarah dredged up a ghastly smile. This evening's attempt to convince the neighborhood of the strength of her marriage had instead proved its falseness and frailty.

Her head swam, and she once more thanked the ladies, before moving to some of the other guests she had barely spoken to. She glanced at the ormolu clock, willing the minutes to tick by, willing the gentlemen to appear so she could swiftly bring this evening to the close she so desperately craved.

When they finally arrived, her head swam with pain, her heart ached desperately, and her conversation had exhausted. She had nothing in common with these people, with their pride, with their fixation on appearance, with their jests and laughter at the expense of others. Such cruel joking only appalled. She had worked so hard to make her husband's family proud and make Langley House appear to advantage, but it had always been in keeping with what they could afford, not at the expense of mortgaging the future. The purchase of new clothes she would rarely wear seemed a profligate waste of money.

But is that what James wanted? For her to look similar, be similar, to these vain, peacocking people? She could never be, would never be. She was too plain, too ordinary, for that.

Her husband glanced at her briefly, then looked away, leaving her aching with fresh shame. He had no use for her. He regretted marriage to her. He'd only married her for his father's money and at his father's instigation, as he'd earlier made so very plain.

Humiliation crumpled her chest, and she moved to shift glasses, then realized this might be construed as an action too much like a servant for some here. A move past some of the men and she heard her husband's voice again as he talked in barely hushed tones with Mr. Edwards.

" . . . Barnstaple would never have brought a lowborn whelp into the castle."

What? Sarah shrank, her heart bleeding. This was his opinion of Bethy? How could he have pretended to have cared? She staggered slightly.

"Mrs. Langley?"

She blinked, tried to focus on what had just been said. "Forgive me, Mrs. Barnstaple."

"Mrs. Langley, are you quite well? You seem a little pale."

Because her gown was wrong. Or was it because her heart ached as terribly as her head, and she was suffering a distressing sickness in her stomach? "You must forgive me. I am not feeling quite the thing."

"Ah, that is a condition not unexpected from a new bride, is it not, my dear?" Mrs. Barnstaple said with a knowing nod.

Sarah offered a weak smile. That particular condition could hardly be expected from a situation where the bride and groom did not share a bed.

Before she knew it, the other ladies began clucking about the new Langley arrival, and nausea take hold. How could she explain she was in fact not pregnant? What book of etiquette ever explained that scenario?

"I had wondered," Mrs. Jordan said, with a none-too-subtle glance at Sarah's midsection.

Oh, her humiliation was complete!

"Ah, well. This will no doubt help overcome the sadness of that poor mite's loss." Mrs. Jordan's tone was colored with what appeared to be faux sympathy. "Such an odd thing as it was. You set all the district talking."

Sarah's heart reared in pain, as a rushing sound filled her ears. How could they speak so about poor little Bethy? Such dismissiveness, such contempt, the way no one here had spoken of her save with sneers . . .

Beatrice's news, their words, their misconceptions, swirled inside and sharpened her pain. She was a failure. She didn't fit in. She'd never belong.

Ice laced her skin. Nausea cramped within. She couldn't do this anymore.

She rose, the action prompting the men to stand. At least they accorded her that much respect.

"Sarah?" James frowned at her.

But she had no use for his frowns. "Please forgive me. I do not feel well."

"My dear—"

"Oh, James, why did you not tell us the happy news?"

"What happy news?"

Dear heavens. She hurried on, addressing the guests. "I'm sure my husband will entertain you all sufficiently. Please forgive me for not being able to stay longer." She curtsied, eyes seeking no one's, and left the room with her head held high.

See? The new Mrs. Langley could behave with dignity.

A moment later her husband rushed to grasp her arm. "Sarah, please—"

"Please release me." She could not look at him.

"You are truly unwell?"

She did glance at him then. "You doubt my word? Would you prefer me to splash your shoes with my sick?"

He flinched. "I'm sorry."

"Yes." She shook free his arm, moving away. "I've heard it all before."

"Sarah, why is Mrs. Jordan talking of Langley's new arrival?"

"It was a misunderst—"

"You are not expecting, are you? You can't be pregnant. Not unless—" His eyes widened, then grew hard. "It's Edwards, isn't it? You have always preferred him to me, and that's why you can never love me."

"What?"

"You and him." He gripped her arm, shook her. "I should have known. Did you entertain him when I was away? Is that it?"

"You must be mad with drink. Let me go."

"Alas, I am quite sober." His eyes narrowed. "Am I a cuckold, then?"

"No! How can you be so stupid? I am unwell, that is all, and I desperately want my bed." A sob erupted. "Please let me go."

His face grew stricken. "Sarah, I'm sorry."

"Of course you are. You're always sorry. Whereas me? I'm sorry I ever came here." She jerked her arm away and stumbled up the steps. Away, away, she had to get away.

"Go and rest. I'll send for Mrs. Broomhead—"

"I want to be left alone."

"Sarah—"

"No!" Her head whirled, her heart was sick, her soul was heavy and oppressed.

Somehow she made it up the stairs, dismissing Evan's concern.

Somehow she made it to her room and, shaking off Mrs. Broomhead's attempts to help her, locked the doors.

The puppy woke, stared at her with bleary eyes, then settled back to sleep.

Her heart knew a craven tug. Oh, if only she could be wanted by someone, could be esteemed by someone, even a pup! But she was not wanted. She was a mistake. She had tried so hard to fit in, only to know herself forsaken. Abandoned. Deemed as hopeless, helpless, friendless.

Sarah moved to her dressing table, slowly taking out the pins that held her hair, slowly removing the pearl necklace that had once belonged to James's mother. She did not want the thing. She wanted nothing he had given her to touch her anymore. How could he accuse her of such a vile thing?

She dropped the shawl. It pooled on the floor, a gleam of light green. She unhooked her gown, thankful for such ease of use, slipped into her nightdress, and removed her stockings and shoes, then sank onto the seat where only hours before she had dared pray for a miracle. None had come. None ever would. God had turned His back on her.

Heaviness weighed upon her. She leaned her elbows on the table and placed her head in her hands, her eyes straining through the darkness to where the sea rolled relentless under a midnight moon. Flashes of white dissolved in deepest dark, surge after surge of waves.

The sea at once lulled and beckoned. Beckoned and lulled. Was respite to be found in its waves? She'd never tried sea bathing. Perhaps she ought. It might help her escape this wretched, weighty oppression. It might make her feel better. Perhaps she'd float.

To float. Drift away. Feel at peace. Oh, how she *longed* to escape this pain. To be freed from this constant sense of failure. This world of utter loneliness. Words swam around her head. Recriminations etched her heart. She was so tired of it all. So very, very tired.

A knock came at the door.

"Sarah?" James's voice.

She blew out the candle and sat still, willing him to go away.

There came another sound, a scrabbling of keys, which hastened her movements into bed. She had no wish to speak to him, no wish to continue this pretense.

She lay still, facing away from the door, breath suspended as light finally spilled through the opening door.

"Sarah? Are you asleep?"

She closed her eyes, listening to the soft pad of footsteps as he drew near. Oh, she'd pretend to be asleep. Anything, *anything* to not have to speak to him ever again.

"Sarah?" A touch on her shoulder. "Mrs. Broomhead was worried about you, otherwise I never would intrude."

She maintained her pretense.

"I'm so utterly sorry."

Yes, he was. Anger burned. He was so utterly pathetic. As was she.

"I'll talk to you tomorrow."

No, he wouldn't. Not if she had anything to do with it.

His lips brushed her brow, and her heart spasmed at the touch, before she smelled the alcohol. She nearly gagged, but maintained her illusion, waiting until the door closed, and she could finally heave a breath of relief.

Indignation burned anew. He'd promised to not get drunk. She'd thought he'd changed, but tonight proved otherwise. How dare he pretend to care, after making such a mockery of her before? After mocking *Bethy*? For that she could never forgive him.

Anger soon subsided, replaced by grief, guilt, and the renewed certainty she had failed. There was no point to this mockery of a marriage. Was there any point to her existence at all?

She started as the connecting door opened. *Dear God, no.* He was back? *Please, let him simply sleep.* She could not fathom anything more.

He moved to where she lay, and she once more felt his hot breath. She pretended sleep, and relief cascaded through her as he shifted away, before a dip of the bed suggested he'd lain down beside her, that infernal gold chain clinking against itself, his sleep soon punctuated by quiet snores.

She hated him. Hated his insistence on moving into her space that might well impair her escape. And she had to escape. *Had* to. There was nothing left for her here.

Through the night, she listened to his snores, smelled his stale sweat, and stayed relentlessly still in case her movement arrested his sleep. At some point in the night watches, the door opened a hand width, and a servant—probably Evan—clicked for Essie's attention, the dog obeying for her nighttime toilet. Still James did not wake. Her eyes burned, but she refused to let a single tear fall. She would not cry; that would be weak. And she had to be strong to carry out what remained to be done.

At the first streaks of dawn's light, she carefully pushed upright, then eased from the bed to look out the window.

The sea's tug and tow called to her.

She silently pulled on her wrapper. Glanced at the sleeping pup. Gazed at her husband as he still blissfully snored. Took a final look around the room that should never have been hers. Then she stole from the room, silent step by silent step, down the stairs, past the distant sounds of servants, and outside. Through the Egyncleugh gate, down the track to the cold churchyard.

Bethy. Poor Bethy. Sweet, perfect Bethy. Her knees crumpled and she collapsed to clasp the mound of dirt. How she longed to hold her one more time, yearned to feel her sweet, soft skin. Bethy would be so cold now. So cold. Even colder than Sarah was, trembling as frost-laced grass poked at her skin.

Filtered light stole past clouds, as a breeze shivered coolness down her spine, around her face. There was no peace here. Mr. Edwards said Bethy wasn't there anymore. Not really. Perhaps peace might be found along the shore.

She pushed to her feet, glanced at the mud smearing her nightdress. Oh well. That would not matter soon. She stole through the gate. If anyone saw her, they'd think her an apparition in her white nightdress and loose hair. She moved past the marshy ground to the sand.

At this time of day there were few sounds, just the cawing of gulls, the whisper of the waves. She closed her eyes, drew in the mesmerizing scent of salt and brine. Peace. The sea held peace. She could finally find peace.

The sound never stopped. Never ceased. Never . . .

Ceased.

Desolation swept over her, the loneliness pressing down, deep into her heart. No one cared. No one understood. And here she stood, at the edge of promised peace.

She opened her eyes, examined the far cresting wave. How distant was that? Twenty yards? Fifty? How long would it take before she reached it—could reach the oblivion that wave might bring?

She took a step. Another. Her foot pressed hard against sharp stones. She picked them up. Slipped them in her wrapper's pocket. Wave-washed rocks bit her tender soles until cool sand thrust between her toes. She ignored it. Took another step as water surged. Finally, she would learn what peace the sea held.

Cold wetness shrieked up her skin, dampening her nightdress around her feet. She withheld a cry as she nearly slipped, so bent to pick up two more stones from their sandy clasp, and moved further into the sea.

Nothing mattered. No one would remark on her absence. She was nothing. Nobody. Of no value. Of no importance. She was a failure. A failure as a wife. A failure as a mother. She had failed to be accepted.

Water reached her calves, her knees, her thighs.

God didn't see her. He didn't care. He hadn't cared before, so why would He pay attention now?

A large wave approached. Her chest hitched with fear as water surged over her. A whimper escaped. Cold. So cold. But one needed to endure such things to finally find that peace.

Her clutch on the stones strengthened. She had to succeed—had to succeed at something, at least. Then she might finally know a sense of peace, of rest and release.

Another wave, much larger than the previous, rushed toward her. Her grip on the stones released. This wave was too big. She didn't really want to drown.

But her skirts were sodden, her foothold unsure. The wave rose to meet her.

And she screamed.

And fell.

Chapter 25

James woke, skin prickling. It took a moment for his thumping head to alert him to his surrounds. No, not a crowded room in London. The sound and scent of sea . . .

He was in his bedchamber. No, not his bedchamber. Another's. Whose—?

His heart thumped. His wife's. She'd relented, after all?

No. He'd come because Mrs. Broomhead had spoken last night of her apprehension, unease he'd shared that had trumped earlier sensibilities about waiting for Sarah's permission before entering her bedchamber. Not that he'd intended to sleep on the bed. A chair had seemed fine until his own exhaustion begged for more, and the knowledge Sarah was his wife made sleeping elsewhere seem suddenly ridiculous.

He rolled over to see her. Pressed a hand over the rumpled bedclothes, the cooling sheets. She had been here recently. Where was she?

The long white curtains gently moved, and he shivered from the cold dawn air. She'd left the window open, as she often did. He should close it. She'd be back soon, and he didn't want her catching a cold. He didn't want anything to get in the way of the conversation they needed to have. His apologies for his imbibing too much the night before. His wish to finally put estrangement to an end.

Where was she? A prickle of dread made him push off the bed. The room was silent. No sound came from without. He moved to the window. Spied the shawl on the floor, and picked it up. He should have told Sarah—told everyone—how thankful he was for her, how proud he was of her. He should have kept a tighter rein on his tongue. And he should never have permitted himself that first glass of wine, that had soon become several glasses' worth.

He pushed a hand through his hair, rubbed the sleep from his bleary eyes, felt the bristles on his chin. What time was it? Far too early to be up after a big night. A sad night. A night he suspected might have broken her faith in him once and for all.

He glanced around the room, saw nothing to give concern, save the littered detritus of last night's attire. Poor thing. He clutched the shawl, lifted it to smell her sweet perfume. He should tell her that he loved her scent. He would, as soon as he found her.

He took a step to the door. He should really have a shave. But then something caused him to hesitate, to turn, to move toward the view, to glance out the window and see the first pink streaks of dawn. To see a tiny white figure struggling in the sea.

Fear trammeled his heart as he peered more closely. Was that—?

Good God, no.

He fastened yesterday's breeches and raced from the room, down the stairs, yelling at the startled footman, "Get help! Send for a doctor!"

He sped outside where the shock of cool air met him anew, around and down the stone-lined garden path to where the Egyncleugh tower presided. Through the door and outside, he then vaulted the gate, eschewing the path for a rough track he'd used as a boy.

He could see her more clearly now, the white form bobbing in the waves, her arms flailing. "Sarah!"

He quickened his pace, feet sliding on slippery stones, threatening to roll his ankles. Why—? Merciful heavens!

She slipped beneath a huge wave.

"No!" He rushed into the sea, ignoring the pain of stones eating into his feet, the water reaching his knees, his thighs before he took off swimming.

The sea was rough, too rough. How long had she been out here? Her nightgowned figure struggled just a few more feet away, her head going under the water, once, twice.

"Sarah!"

She turned, met his gaze, eyes dark in a stare of horror. Then another wave crashed over her head and she was lost from sight.

"Sarah!" He ducked down, caught a glimpse of white fabric being sucked away in the churning dark-grey sea. He reached out a hand. Missed. Stretched out again. Just managed to snag her. Drew her upwards.

She was still. Eyes closed. Face paler than he'd ever known.

"Sarah!"

She didn't stir.

He lifted her higher, her nose and mouth now out of the water. He dragged her back to shore, struggling until his feet found purchase on the rocky sand. He drew her into his arms, staggering as the waves pummeled and pulled, threatening to tug free his precious cargo.

She remained motionless.

From the shore came a scurrying figure, then another.

"Get the doctor!" he yelled, his words snatched by the wind.

Heaven help them! By his reckoning, Sarah needed more than a doctor. "Sarah, wake up. Please."

Her head tipped, and he held her more securely in his arms, sodden clothes gripped tightly to his chest. "Sweetheart." Where had that word come from? "Wake up, please."

He stumbled to the shore, where willing arms were eager to take his burden. Finally he could catch his breath, and he collapsed to all fours on the sand, next to where they laid his wife. "Is she breathing?"

"Not yet." Evan knelt beside her.

James shifted closer, pressed his ear to her chest. He could hear a thundering, but was that fear rushing through his pulse and filling his ears?

Lord, what do we do? An idea sparked, a memory from years ago, when a doctor attended a young corporal caught in a swift river. He gently pushed her onto her side and turned her head, lightly slapping her back until water gushed out and she choked and startled.

She coughed and retched, exhaustion writ heavy in her slow movements and slumped shoulders. But she was alive. Thank God, she was alive.

"It's all right," he assured her, leaning closer to cradle her head as she eased back and gazed up at him with frightened eyes. "You're safe now."

She coughed again, and turned her head, as if she didn't want to see him. The elation he'd felt dipped, his breath snagged, hurt swelled across his chest.

"Sir?"

He accepted Robert's proffered hand to stand as he fought the fear-induced cold and fatigue. He would not let her down. Not now. Not again.

"Give her your coat," James ordered. Her gown was near diaphanous.

"What happened, sir?"

James could not respond, his thoughts too dark to utter.

Had she really tried to drown herself because of his evil accusations from last night?

By the time the sun had risen above the water, James was carrying Sarah back inside the castle, and calling for assistance.

"Get hot water!" he snapped at Mrs. Copley, who hovered wide-eyed near the stairs.

"What has happened?"

"A swimming accident." He brushed past her. "Mrs. Broomhead!" he called. Then, seeing Copley hadn't moved, said more sharply, "She needs a hot bath. Get to it, woman."

She jumped as if frightened, and he hastened up the stairs, Sarah still firmly clasped in his arms. "Mrs. Broomhead!" he called again, as he rounded the hall to the family rooms.

The door opposite Sarah's opened, Mrs. Broomhead's greying hair in loose strands around her face. "Oh, my goodness! Sir, what has happened?"

"She had an accident. She needs to be warmed immediately."

"Of course, bring her in here."

She flung open the door to Sarah's room. "Put her there," she motioned to the bed, eyes lifting to his as she noticed the covers on the bed's other side were thrust back at an angle.

"I slept here."

She nodded, a rare pleased expression on her face, before her attention returned to his wife. "She's shivering. Oh, the poor dear! Evan." She turned to the footman hovering in the doorway. "Shut the window and stoke the fire."

James drew closer, rubbing Sarah's chilled limbs with rough movements.

Sarah's heavy eyelids opened, but she made little protest save a small groan.

"Don't be rough with her, sir!" Mrs. Broomhead pleaded.

"She needs the blood to circulate," he said, as the first maid entered carrying two cans of steaming water, which would be added to a can of cool. "I saw men in France lose toes because they lost blood to their feet due to poor circulation."

He continued his ministrations as Mrs. Broomhead instructed Evan to fill the hip bath screened in the corner, checking the temperature with her hand. Another maid came in with more heated water, and James helped Sarah shift upright.

She protested through chattering teeth. "Don't. Too tired."

"We'll soon get you warmer," he promised. "Then the doctor will come." How much longer would the man take? He stifled his impatience, focused on gentling his movements with his wife. What would deal with this chill?

"Send for tea," he directed Evan, who at once got up and obeyed. "You'd like some tea, would you not, Sarah?"

Her eyelids flickered up, her gaze met his, then strayed away. The pain in her expression echoed that which rimmed his chest.

By now the bath was half full, and Mrs. Broomhead was encouraging Sarah to the bath. But she barely moved, her eyes now closed, which left one thing to do.

He lifted her and carried her over.

"Place her in, sir, gently. That's it. Never mind about her clothes."

Sarah wore only the night rail and wrapper, the thin material making him glad the others had by now left the room. He swallowed, concentrating on his movements, as Mrs. Broomhead fussed and fretted over her.

He withdrew from the warmth reluctantly—he'd enjoy a bath soon too—when his hands snagged on something hard and round. He withdrew it from the pocket of Sarah's wrapper.

A stone.

What? Why? His heart sank. No.

"Oh, Mr. Langley, sir, whatever happened? I did not think Madam ever swam."

He tucked the stone into his own pocket. Offered the only explanation he could think of. "Perhaps she wanted to clear her head and was surprised by a wave."

"She hasn't been well for some time, so mayhap that's it," she agreed.

Fresh remorse twisted within. Of course. Sarah had admitted as much last night. Had that, compounded with his foolish actions and comments, driven her from her right mind?

"Come now, Mrs. Langley," Mrs. Broomhead said, helping Sarah sit forward. "That's it." She glanced up at him. "I can look after her now, if you like, sir."

He ignored the polite dismissal. "I'd prefer to stay here. She is my wife, after all."

"I, er . . ." Her cheeks pinked. "I just wondered if perhaps you might wish for your own bath. You must be cool yourself."

He glanced down at his bedraggled attire. "I will slip on a robe, but there's no point changing until I have my own bath, and that I will not do until the doctor has seen her," he added firmly.

His movements to the connecting door were cut short by her startled exclamation.

"What is this?" She held up a stone, her brow pleated. "I found it in her pocket."

Her eyes met his, and she gasped.

"She has not been well," he said deliberately.

"Oh, the poor child!"

His heart wrenched as he bent to search for more stones, removing them swiftly. "I think it best we keep this between ourselves, would you not agree?"

She nodded. "She would not survive being sent to Bedlam or some such place."

"There is no need to contemplate such things," he said sternly. "She is unwell, and she needs those of us who love her to be the ones who care for her now."

"Love her?"

He nodded, heart twisting once again, this time in recognition of this truth. "That's what I said." Noise came from without, reminding him to extract a promise. "Now, not a word, remember?"

"I'll be silent as the grave."

He winced at the unfortunate expression and hurried to the door to twist it open. But it was only Maggie with the tea. "Set it down there," he instructed.

The maid bobbed a curtsy, and after giving him one quick, scared glance, scurried out.

"Sarah," he knelt beside her, the bath's metal rim digging into his chest. "Dearest, would you like some tea?"

Sarah slumped against the side of the tub, and he glanced back at Mrs. Broomhead.

She nodded. "Now, now, Mrs. Langley. A nice hot cup of tea will be just the thing. The water is getting a little cooler, isn't it? How about Mr. Langley and I help you out now?"

He followed her soft-spoken directions, and they soon had a dripping Sarah being toweled vigorously by Mrs. Broomhead in front of the fire.

"There, I'm sure that's feeling better. Now, how about I help you get changed before the doctor comes? Then you can have your tea and be tucked up in bed all nice and cozy." She gestured with an inclination of her head, and James obeyed her silent directive to exit to his room.

Really, the woman was proving herself a wonder, and well worth the salary increase he'd give her as soon as they could afford it. Evan, too, had proved his faithfulness, and was also most deserving of a raise. But was it truly any surprise when Sarah already knew that she could trust them?

That same trust that Sarah should have in her husband.

His eyes blurred. If only he'd handled things differently. If he could only prove to her just how much he cared.

He wearily dragged on his thick robe, tied the sash slowly, aware of his great fatigue from the actions of the morning. Regrets continued to murmur, but he could not afford to indulge, not when Sarah's door was being knocked on again.

This time he heard the doctor's voice, so he hurried through the connecting door. As promised, Sarah was in bed, covers pulled up to her chin, eyes closed, with a steaming cup of tea evidently freshly poured. The doctor stood at her bedside, holding her wrist and frowning. His heart constricted. No, she hadn't—?

"She's just resting, sir," Mrs. Broomhead assured.

Thank God. "Doctor. Here at last." James heard the irritation in his tone and tried to soften it with, "Thank you for coming."

"I understand she nearly drowned."

"Yes."

The doctor's brows rose. "May I ask how this happened?"

James exchanged a look with Mrs. Broomhead. "We, er, decided to have an early swim. It's a practice I grew used to as a younger man."

"In this cold?"

"A swim can be most refreshing when one has had a late night before."

"I see." And from the doubt in the doctor's voice and eyes, James was fearful he actually did.

"We brought her here as soon as possible," James assured.

"Yes, and gave her a nice warm bath and warm drink besides," Mrs. Broomhead added.

"So I gather." The doctor peered at Sarah again. "Mrs. Langley. Mrs. Langley, can you hear me?"

She did not stir.

"Mrs. Langley, if you can hear me, please open your eyes."

Her eyelids slowly opened, but her eyes still held blankness.

"How long was she in the water?" The doctor's voice had sharpened.

"I could not say."

"But were you not there?"

"Well, yes, but . . ." How to explain without incriminating anyone? "She had gone to the beach before me."

"Did you not go for a swim together?"

He could hardly admit his suspicion about his wife seeking to end her life in the waves. "I did not expect her to go without me, that is true," he hedged. "So, she was in some trouble when I arrived."

"Trouble? Her head was under water? For how long?"

He tried to think, but fatigue was blurring his thoughts. "I really can't remember. Not more than a minute, I'd say."

"A minute?" The doctor looked horrified. "She might now be damaged in her mind!"

Sarah's gaze shifted to meet James, and she visibly flinched.

Her recoil felt like a slap, and he could only hope the doctor hadn't noticed. But the way Dr. Watkins eyed him, James suspected he'd missed nothing.

His throat constricted, forcing him to swallow. "We did all we could," he tried to assure, as Sarah closed her eyes once more.

"I cannot like this," the doctor muttered. "Something isn't right here."

"Mrs. Langley was not well yesterday," Mrs. Broomhead said.

"What's this?" the doctor glanced up and stared hard at James. "Is this true?"

"Yes. We, er, had a dinner for some friends, and when she looked unwell earlier, I thought it was just nerves. But later she had to excuse herself and seemed most out of sorts." All true.

"She has taken quite some time to recover after the baby's death," Mrs. Broomhead added.

"You suspect she was suffering from low spirits, that she was not in her right mind when she went for her swim?"

"No! Not at all," James rushed to say. Heaven forbid the man advise Sarah be sent away! "Sarah has grieved since the death of the child, but such sorrow is understandable after loss, is it not? And lately she has been much happier." *Much* happier might be pushing it. A tad happier might be more accurate. Until last night, at least.

Anyway, what was with all the suspicious-sounding questions? It was time to exert the authority of the oldest name in the area. "I must admit I do not like the tone of your questions, doctor. Do you have any treatment to suggest or advice to offer?"

"Not at this stage, no." He turned to Mrs. Broomhead. "I suggest you keep her warm and comfortable. It may be that she recovers quickly, as it seems like she would have merely taken cold. But if she were out longer than what Mr. Langley says, then it may prove to take longer, especially if her condition was exacerbated by an underlying malaise."

She bristled. "I see no reason to question Mr. Langley's version of events."

"I'm sure you do not." The doctor cast James another look from under his bushy brows and placed a bottle beside the bed. "This is a tincture of laudanum, something that may ease this nervous disorder, should she tend toward melancholy again."

Laudanum. His heart froze. "I really don't feel we need such a thing."

"And I really don't feel we need a woman being taken into the sea against her will, do you?"

What?

Mrs. Broomhead gasped. "She was not pushed."

"So you say. But how would you know? Were you there, ma'am?"

She had to deny it, glancing at James apologetically.

The doctor's brows rose. "So we only have her husband's word she was not forced into the water, the same way the gossip says she was foisted upon you."

James sank into the bedside chair. Had he really claimed that publicly? His own words could be used as a weapon, a reason for getting rid of her. Sorrow clutched his chest. He was such a fool. Such a *fool.*

"We shall have to see what Mrs. Langley says—if she's ever in a condition to say anything at all."

James shook his head, tried to stand again. "Don't be ridiculous. You cannot accuse me of something so heinous."

"Because you're one of the famous Langleys? I hardly need remind you that such a thing does not make you above the law."

His stomach tensed. "I saved her life. I did not try to end it."

"We may have to let the constable determine that."

"How dare you?" Mrs. Broomhead snapped, puffing up like an outraged older hen. "Mr. Langley loves his wife. Why, I heard him say so just before you came in!"

"That's not what others have been saying. Now, if you'll excuse me."

"Gladly." James held his anger behind his teeth. It would not do to stir up this man's animosity any more.

He summoned Evan to escort the doctor out and when they had gone, glanced at a worried Mrs. Broomhead. "Why would he think such an evil thing about me?"

She bit her lip, glanced down at the still-sleeping Sarah. "We shall have to pray she wakes soon and can clear up these matters."

Amen, he muttered under his breath. It would seem he'd done all that he could do.

Chapter 26

He'd never thought himself a weak man. Had never thought he could be laid so low. But nothing had prepared him for the revelations of the past few days. When faced with the greatest loss, he'd known just how much he longed for that loss not to be so.

His words to Mrs. Broomhead three days prior had burned deep. He loved Sarah. *Loved* her. Imperfect his love might be, but it was based on something deeper, something sweeter than the times he'd imagined himself in love before. This was not a feeling based on her looks or charm or pretty ways. This feeling was built on the foundation that now anchored his soul, as recognition of the qualities he esteemed most of all. Kindness. Mercy. Grace. He loved Sarah, he wanted the best for her, and now that her life had been shown to be so fragile, he grieved for her as he'd grieved for none since his mother's passing.

He stole closer to the bed where she still slept, in what seemed a never-ending rest. Mrs. Broomhead was faithful in carrying out the doctor's instructions, spooning a little of the elixir into her mouth regularly as charged. He couldn't help but fear that the laudanum made Sarah less prone to wake, less able to think clearly and fight her way through this terrible lassitude. Just as he'd seen with his mother.

"Sarah?" He possessed her hand, sat in the chair next to her bed placed for this purpose. Negotiations as to who should care for Sarah had become quite tense between himself and Mrs. Broomhead, the faithful servant even saying she would be willing to forgo the proposed new pay raise rather than be forced to abandon her post by her mistress's side. Faithful she had proved, helping Sarah eat and drink, taking care of her personal needs.

"You cannot care for her both day and night," he'd said. "If you take the morning through afternoon shift, I will take the evening and night."

"Then you'll be sleeping here?"

"Yes," he'd responded coolly, refraining from answering *sleeping, nothing else.* What business was it of hers? "After all, she is my wife."

Again he'd seen that flicker of relief in her eyes, as if she approved of him at long last. "Just be careful you do not fall asleep so soundly that you miss her little movements and sighs."

"I learned in battle to respond to such things. You can trust me."

"I hope so." She'd looked at him with worry in her eyes.

Each night he'd been alert, lying near but not too near, his nerves tense at every sound. He couldn't help but wonder if his decision to sleep here that fateful night had precipitated her flight.

He now drew the chair closer, glad for the chance to speak again, after Mrs. Broomhead had been summoned downstairs just now. Maggie hovered near the window, eyes watching his wife most worriedly.

He dismissed her and began to tell his wife something of his day.

"I brought back mail," he said, as if Sarah were awake. "It appears you have a letter from your cousin, Sophia." He examined the address, one in a little village in the Lake District. He put it to one side. She would likely enjoy reading it, or having it read to her when she was awake.

But Beatrice's letter he did not hesitate to open. He slit the seal, opened the page.

My dearest Sarah,

Thank you for the kind words you wrote. I realized after my latest missive that perhaps you may have found such news hard to bear . . .

What news?

. . . especially coming on the heels of your own sadness. I do hope you know how much I look forward to you and James being our child's godparents. I must confess it seems so strange to think of my brother as one who might instruct our child in God's ways, but I trust your judgment, and thank God that His ways are higher than our own . . .

Beatrice was expecting, and Sarah had known? Why hadn't she said something? The shock and hurt of her news gently subsided as he studied his sister's later words. It seemed Sarah had passed on something about his changed ways, which was gratifying. Perhaps he wasn't such a hopeless case after all.

He glanced at his wife, her face pale, her cheeks growing thin, her dark lashes splayed over the shadows under her eyes. "Lord, I do not deserve her. She sees what can be, when I have been so blind. Give her strength and heal her body, soul, and mind."

She stirred, but eased back to repose, leaving him free to read the last piece of correspondence delivered today.

This was from Captain Daniel Balfour, and like the man, was short and to the point.

Langley, I trust you are in good health and spirits, and remember what we talked about in Spain. You have been much in my prayers of late. I have received word that my sister is unwell, and I look to be in your vicinity in the not too distant future. I hope it will be agreeable to you if I come for a brief visit on my journey further north.

Your fellow soldier in Christ,

D. Balfour

He swallowed. Thank God for his friend, for the man who had pushed past James's drunken, arrogant ways to share the truth. Thank God that he stayed in touch still. "Have I told you much about Captain Balfour, Sarah? I think you would like him. He's a mix of soldierly responsibility, determination, wit, and fun. I've known no one like him."

Perhaps it was these qualities that had first drawn him to the man. James's war had consisted more of drinking and pretense until a chance conversation had led to something deeper. He'd sensed this man, who lacked the connections that had led James to an undeserved captaincy, held convictions of far greater worth, and owned a spirit of daring adventure with a deep faith that flowed to touch others.

"You would not mind if he visited, would you?" he asked his sleeping wife.

No answer.

He spent the next few minutes praying, pleading for God to touch his wife, while at the corner of his mind he wondered what was taking so much of Mrs. Broomhead's time.

A knock came at the door, which opened to reveal Dawson.

Dawson? Where was Evan?

"Please excuse the interruption, sir. You are needed downstairs. Sir John has arrived and wishes to speak with you."

His heart tensed. "But Mrs. Langley—"

"Maggie is here to sit with Mrs. Langley again," Dawson said, as the little maid slipped in the door.

James nodded, waited until the man left, then kissed his wife's brow and trudged downstairs.

"The doctor has informed me of his concerns, and I bear this as my solemn duty as presiding magistrate."

If it wasn't so serious, it would be laughable, yet it was hard to care about anything. Hard to think anything more important than the woman lying so still in the upstairs bedchamber. From his seat next to Father in the library, James lifted a heavy head as he eyed the pompous man standing opposite him.

"I'm afraid, sir, that matters concerning near loss of life are of gravest importance, and subject to examination under the fullest extent of the law."

"What nonsense," Father expostulated. "You cannot accuse my son. He is a Langley, and there have been Langleys here for hundreds of years."

"And he is now a Langley under suspicion of attempting to murder his wife."

James's breath suspended. "You are joking. That is ludicrous."

"Is it? That remains to be seen." Sir John Willoughby eyed James with an expression of dislike.

So, no help for him there. He dragged in a breath. *God, help me.* "I do not understand why you are so quick to accuse me when you are yet to speak to my wife."

"And therein lies the problem. How can we speak to her, when it appears she may never wake properly again?"

His heart protested. Sarah still functioned, even under this heavy lethargy. Was that a result of Dr. Watkin's constant sedation?

But how could he argue with the doctor and insist he stop, the man who seemed determined to take every one of James's oppositions and twist its meaning for the worst?

Father struck the armrest of his chair. "I fail to understand what possible motive you might have for making such baseless accusations against my son."

Sir John sniffed. "That was most evident to those who witnessed his remarks at the dinner party."

"What remarks?"

Sir John continued, as if not hearing Father's question. "It would appear that Mr. James Langley resented his wife, resented being married to what amounted to a servant—"

"That is not true!" James cried.

"And intended to humiliate his wife, and certainly not honor her, according to those who witnessed the sad event."

Who had dared slandered him thus? "They are wrong. I was dipping too deep—"

"Yes, yes, so you have said before. But a few glasses of wine hardly makes one drunk, does it?"

"It does if one has forsworn alcohol for many months," James said with gritted teeth.

"And why should you have done so?"

"Because I did not like myself when I was drunk."

"Exactly so." Sir John leaned in, fingers pressed together. "Every one knows you are a hothead. Everyone knows of your involvement in the death of your dear mother. Why should anyone believe you have changed?"

Why should anyone, indeed, a little voice chimed, as guilt twisted in his stomach.

"I was exonerated for my mother's death, as you well know. I loved her, and I love Sarah," James insisted.

"So you say. But it beggars belief that one who loves his wife would treat her so. Plus, the question was raised as to whether you are indeed enamored of another, given the closeness you were seen to share at the dinner table with Miss Barnstaple. That lends strong suggestion of a motive for disposing of a woman regarded as not quite equal to the role of the wife of a Langley."

James pushed to his feet. "How dare you?"

Sir John eyed James as he might a snake.

Oh, he dared all right. *Lord, what do I do? What can I say?*

"In fact, the entire district is aware that the two of you did not get on, that you were ashamed of your wife, and barely spent any time with her. There were witnesses who heard you arguing after the dinner, heard you accuse her of infidelity."

"I was wrong—"

"Why, just two weeks ago you refused to bring her to the Barnstaples dinner."

"Refused to? She was unwell. Mrs. Broomhead will attest to that."

"Will she? Or has she been paid to agree with what you wish her to say? I have been reliably informed by guests who were here that your wife is expecting—"

Father turned wide eyes on James. "What?"

"—so it isn't any wonder that you felt the need to take matters into your own hands, so to speak."

James sucked in a breath. "She was simply unwell. There was a misunderstanding."

"But there was no misunderstanding concerning your dislike of the child your wife adopted and was raising here. Dr. Watkins was very clear about the circumstances pertaining to that unfortunate situation, and the reason for the child's demise."

Dear God. How much did he know? God protect Sarah from learning all of that truth.

"She is not expecting?" his father asked, patently disappointed.

"No."

His father huffed. "You need to share a bed for that to occur."

Sir John studied James as if questioning why that was not the case.

James clenched his fingers as the panic rose. He was trapped in a sticky web of circumstances, with Sir John as the menacing spider.

"Well?" Sir John asked. "Anything to say for yourself?"

Dear God, help me. He sucked in a breath. Exhaled. "I am the first to admit that my actions have, in both the past and more recent times, been less than honorable," James said quietly. "But I cannot allow you to impugn my wife's character. She is a pearl amongst women, and should not be maligned because of the prejudice and bigotry of people whose ancestry does not extend nearly as long as that of the Langley family."

"Well said," Father agreed.

James drew in a deep breath, prayed for patience. "Regardless of whether you believe, my love for my wife is true. Surely you would need witnesses for the event in the water. You have none, I believe."

"Well, that was rather astute of you, wasn't it, to deal with matters in the early morning as you did?"

"What?"

"You waited until no servants were around before carrying out your plans."

"That isn't so. Speak to Evan and Robert. They were there when I called out for their help."

"Yes, but it's become hard to accept whatever they say."

"What do you mean? Evan is as honest as the day."

"Yes, so honest that he admitted earlier that you recently promised to increase his wages. One can only wonder as to the timing, and whether that was done to hide certain things."

God bless Evan, but he need not be quite so accommodating in sharing everything. "You are mistaken. Evan has worked well and was due a raise."

The magistrate raised his brows. "And young Evan is not the only one. Your wife's servant, Mrs. Broomhead, also made similar allegations."

How could this woman Sarah considered as a friend state such baseless lies? "No." James shook his head. "You are mistaken."

"Then why would she also admit that she was recently promised a raise? The implication is clear."

"Yes, that she has served my wife commendably—"

"That she is being paid to keep her mouth shut." Sir John pulled at his ear. "Why? What is it you are hiding, James?"

He swallowed. "She cared for my wife with such tenderness when—"
He could not admit to Sarah's moment of mental weakness. The act of
self-murder was considered *non compos mentis*, and if he admitted such
a thing, Sir John might well recommend she be locked up in Bedlam or
some other such institution for those considered insane. James wouldn't
let that happen.

"When what?" Sir John's eyes gleamed. "I must say I do not like this
dissembling I sense in you, James."

He would not expose her. "You have this all wrong."

"So you keep say—"

"Sir John, I ask that you wait until Sarah awakens, and in the mean-
time, I beg you to speak with Captain Daniel Balfour."

"An army friend of yours?"

"A honorable man who truly knows me, and will gladly bear witness
to certain changes I've undergone in the past year."

"And where might this Captain Balfour be?"

James thought desperately. What had his last letter said? "I believe he
has recently arrived in London and plans to visit this way soon."

"London! I don't have time to go to London."

"You do if it will take some time for Sarah to be restored." James studied him. "Unless you have another reason to see an innocent man tried."

Sir John's eyes narrowed. "You can still be tried for slander."

"As can you, if you make these allegations any more public than what
you've done."

"John," Father said, "you know my boy would never stoop so low."

"I know your son was remiss in matters pertaining to dear Mariah
before."

"How dare you?" James said, fresh anger boiling inside. "That was
an accident—"

"That was a precedent," Sir John said, his expression like steel.

Who could be so evil to make up these baseless accusations? Surely
not even Copley and Dawson would stoop to such depths of depravity.
Despair balled within.

"Well, I have said my piece." Sir John retrieved his hat, donned it, and
glanced at Father. "I will need to question your servants again." His gaze

shifted to James. "You must remain on the castle grounds, and should you leave or anything further happen to your wife, I will ensure that the full measure of the law is brought against you. Given your history, I dare say the gallows would be in your future. Do you understand?"

Gallows? Heaven help him. "Yes," he gritted out.

"I will leave you both now. Good day."

James inclined his head, but the words of polite rejoinder could not be said.

Accusations of murder were secondary to poor Sarah, lying weak upstairs and misbelieving that James did not care. No, it was most certainly not a good day at all.

Chapter 27

Sarah lifted heavy eyelids and studied her surrounds. Her head felt very thick, as if it were stuffed with balls of wool, and thoughts seemed to slip and slide off without ever cohering enough to make sense.

Her heart lifted at a sweet fragrance. A peek revealed a vase filled with snowdrops, ivy, and dried roses. Didn't such flowers symbolize something? Snowdrops meant purity and hope, ivy meant fidelity. Roses meant . . . what? Oh, her brain was too tired to think.

Her ears sharpened, discerning the faint *hush hush* from beyond. A tap of ivy blowing against the window. A crackle from the fire, a sizzle and pop. Wind moaned around the eaves. And a soothing sound, a voice, deep, and sure. She listened, gradually discerning the words, the fog of sadness beginning to lift.

"Bless the Lord, O my soul, and forget not all His benefits. Who forgiveth all thine iniquities . . ."

There came a catch of breath, which did strange things to her heart.

"Who healeth all thy diseases; who redeemeth thy life from destruction; who crowneth thee with lovingkindness . . ."

Lovingkindness. The word pricked, like a distant star's first twinkle in a midnight sky. How she longed to know she was loved. To know she was wanted. To know she belonged.

"Lord, heal Sarah. Set her free from this dark oppression, and help her see Your light. Make her strong in body, soul, and mind, and help her know she's loved. And Lord . . ." The voice took on a ragged edge. "Soften her heart to forgive me. Assure her that I care."

The man's voice broke, and she slowly lifted weighted eyelids to see James sitting in a chair, leaning over a book. His head was bowed as he wiped a hand across his cheeks, his tears deepening the ache within her chest.

"God, forgive me for praying such self-centered prayers," he rasped. "But You know that I'm weak, and need Your help to be the man You desire me to be, the husband Sarah needs. Let Your righteousness prevail. But most of all, help Sarah know she's deeply loved by You, and by me."

She closed her eyes, his words echoing within, as her heart toyed with these words of love, of deep assurance. She was deeply loved?

No. She was a mistake, friendless, a failure. How could she be loved deeply?

And yet, the man's words, his emotions, suggested this was true. Memories flickered. His kindnesses, his forbearance, his gifts to ease her pain. Was that borne from affection, after all? Affection she had craved?

Deeply loved? By God and by this man?

Deeply loved.

The words settled softly. Could she dare believe it was true?

In all her years of growing up in a manse, she had heard many, many sermons about God but had never really considered Him as the God of love. The God who loved *her*.

But now, like fog had lifted, she could see that it could indeed be true. She might have felt abandoned, but God had placed her within a family, first with her aunt and uncle, then here with the Langleys. She had never truly been forsaken.

And yes, she might have felt weak and broken, her soul as frayed as those cushions downstairs. But she'd seen a stitching together here, where her talent for practical helps that others dismissed had proved valuable and needed. As though this was where she belonged and was meant to be.

How long had she focused on the tattered threads, on the tapestry's dirt and dark strands, instead of seeing the picture twined with gold on the other side? The knots she had sometimes thought lashed too hard had instead secured her in place, in this place, in this home, in this life.

Deeply loved. The words roiled inside her, gathering weight and form and substance and truth.

I am deeply loved. Her lips soundlessly formed the words. *I am deeply . . .* Loved.

It was as if the dust of years settling into a tapestry had finally been beaten out, and she could finally see the bright and glorious colors as they were designed to be. She *was* loved, by God and by this man. Hadn't they both proved it, time and again? God had provided for her, protected her, saved and helped her in so many ways. And James, too, had done the same. He was kind. So much kinder to her than she had been to him.

She was loved by God.

She was loved by this man.

Her eyelids lifted, enabling her to peek again at James, his face still cradled in his hands.

Why did he despair?

She slipped her hand from under the prison of blankets, but the effort was too great. "James," she whispered.

He glanced up, features moving into shock. "Sarah?" He pushed from his chair to kneel beside her bed. "My dear, you're awake. I knew stopping the laudanum would help. Can you hear me? Oh, say something, please."

She tried to speak, but her words were mere air.

He grasped her hand, pressed it to his lips. "Sarah, please, just tell me you forgive me. I know I've begged you to forgive me a thousand times, and it must seem so very hard to hear it once again. But I wish you would. I pray you will."

God, who loved her, who had forgiven all her iniquity, would surely want her to forgive.

"I should never have accused you of holding a tendre for Mr. Edwards." He shook his head. "I was jealous, I suppose. I wanted you to delight in time spent with me the way you seem to enjoy Mr. Edwards's company."

But I do, her heart whispered.

He grazed her knuckles with his lips. "I know you are faithful. I know you are good. Why, I was telling people at the dinner just how wonderful you were to care for little Bethy."

The memory stung. "The lowborn whelp," she whispered.

"Did you hear me say that? I was simply repeating what the Barnstaples had said before. You must know I didn't think of Bethy that way. Miss Barnstaple would never have thought to care about poor Bethy's situation. You did, however. My wonderful, wonderful wife."

The sincerity in his eyes, his voice, stole inside. Yes, this more accorded with the man she thought she knew. Shame at misjudging him chafed inside.

His grip on her hand tightened. "You will never know how much I regret having brought home that fever that took her. I am eternally sorry." He wiped underneath his eyes.

How could she hold this unfortunate happenstance against him? Not when she had deliberately sought to end her own life. "I forgive you." She swallowed. "I . . . I hope you will forgive me for my despair, and . . ." She shrugged helplessly, unable to find words to explain her actions in the sea.

He slid a hand down her cheek. "There is nothing to forgive. God's forgiveness means I'm forever in His debt, and yours."

She moved to sit up, and he rushed to help her, checking she was comfortable and warm, offering her some water to drink, fussing over her so tenderly she knew his words before were true. *Deeply loved.*

He pulled the chair closer and leaned forward, threading his fingers through hers, waiting until her gaze sunk into his. "Sarah, you are so very good. Everything I'm not."

"You are changed," she averred.

"I thought I was, but that night at the dinner . . ." He shook his head. "That night proved how far I still have to go."

"None of us are perfect." She squeezed his hand. "Least of all me. I . . . I've been such a failure. Failing as a wife, failing as a mother, and so envious of the easy rapport you seemed to share with Miss Barnstaple and Mrs. Jordan. I always get things wrong, and never fit in." Her eyes welled.

Pain crossed his features. "There was never any reason to be jealous."

She swallowed and gathered the courage to finally ask. "But your chain?"

"This?" He touched the golden chain around his neck. "This was my mother's."

A rush of gladness filled her chest. "I thought someone special had given it to you, someone you loved."

His lips lifted on one side. "I loved my mother very much."

Still, she had to be sure. "People say you would've been better off marrying Georgiana, someone who was a proper lady," she confessed.

He paused, then said quietly, "Did I make you feel that way by what I said on our wedding night?"

She might have forgiven him, but his words had struck so deep. "You said I could never be equal to your mother," she whispered, looking down at the bedclothes.

"I was wrong. You are so much more, my dear."

Her gaze touched his again. "Am I really 'your dear'?"

He smiled, and the sight fluttered sensations deep within. "You are. Dearer to me than any other. Faithful, honest, and true. You are kind, and your compassion like a well others draw from. You belong here. This house is now a home because of you."

Her heart felt as though it might crumple under the weight of glorious sensation. How she had *longed* to hear such things.

"My parents' marriage was never easy, and what happened with my mother made my father hate me and reiterated what a failure I felt myself to be." His voice now held a rasping burr of pain. "That's why I ran away to join the army. That's why I ran away after our wedding. I hate feeling like people despise me, that you despise me. I want you to like me, to want me, at least a little bit, broken though I am."

"Broken, but being healed by God. Isn't that what you were reading before?"

He nodded, a small smile tweaking his lips. "How good you are to remind me. Yes, God has redeemed my life from destruction."

"And mine too." From her quest to sink into the sea.

He kissed her hand again. "I wish you could know how much I care. I suppose I didn't realize it until you tried to swim out into the deep. We may not have started the best way, but that is no reason to give up. I wish we could start afresh. I . . . I love you, Sarah. I want you in my life. Please," he added hoarsely, "say you want to be in my life too."

She had the strangest sense of standing on the edge of one of life's precipices, where what she said next would forever determine her future. *Their* future. James wanted her? He loved her? "I . . . I want that too."

Joy lit his features, but still he held back. "Truly?"

"Yes," she whispered.

Then he inched closer still, his hands sliding up her arms, leaving delightful tingles in their wake, before they slid to her shoulders, and up to capture her face. "Sarah, I will strive to be the husband you deserve. God knows I need His help, but I will love you fiercely all the rest of my days. I will honor you, I will protect you, I will show you—and all the world—just how much you mean to me. I want you to know, without a shadow of a doubt, that you are loved and that you belong here with me." He brushed her cheeks with his thumbs. "You are lovely to me."

She inched back. He couldn't mean it.

"Do you doubt me? Do I need to prove to you how lovely and appealing I find you, Sarah?" He raised his brows.

Her cheeks flamed. "Not right at this moment."

He smiled. "How about now then?" Once again he gathered her close and bent his head, lower, lower, until he paused. Then he pressed his lips softly to hers in a kiss so unlike the one they'd shared so long ago.

This embrace held respect and honor, sparked joy and awe. This kiss slid her hands behind his neck, as his hands stroked her back, and tilted her head back to receive more. As if he recognised the invitation, his kiss deepened, and the hunger there met an answering flame within her as they exchanged silent vows of trust and devotion. This . . . this swirl of sensation, of affection, of promise, this was what she'd yearned for, his embrace and assurance all she'd ever wanted.

Finally she drew back for breath, the dizzied expression he wore sure to be on her face too.

"Well." He exhaled. "For someone who has worried over ever being loved, you certainly know how to kiss, my dearest one."

Was this a dream? "I am glad you think so."

"Does this mean you return my affections?" he murmured. "You know I love you."

She knew that now as certain as she breathed. "I love you too," she whispered, tracing a hand down the stubble of his cheek.

"Truly?"

At her nod, he captured her lips with his again, convincing her quite thoroughly of his ardor, as he shifted to sit beside her and fold her more deeply in his embrace.

The door opened, admitting Mrs. Broomhead, who startled at the sight of his position on Sarah's bed.

"Dear Mrs. Broomhead, you may find it might be wise to knock in the future," James advised with his old drawl.

"Sir! Goodness. Forgive me. I shall just leave this here, shall I?" She placed the tray on the table nearby, her cheeks pink, gaze averted. "I'm so pleased to see you are feeling better, Mrs. Langley. Well, if there is nothing more . . ." Mrs. Broomhead exited and shut the door firmly.

"Poor lady," Sarah laughed softly. "She didn't know what to think."

"I believe she knew exactly what to think," James said with a roguish gleam in his eyes.

"James!"

"Sarah." He kissed the curve of her neck. "My wife. My dear. My love."

Her heart danced. *Deeply loved.* She offered him a smile that held a promise. One day. Very soon.

Today was his day of reckoning. It had been five days since that terrible farce of an interview had been conducted by Sir John in the library. Five days that had seen more letters sent, and more interviews conducted amid increasing village speculation. The one bright spot in this weight of days had been getting to know his wife. Their mutual confessions and explanations had brought a new ease and affection between them, the sorrow and guilt of the past ebbing away. So far the servants seemed to have kept Sarah's secret, but that might change soon. For the next step in this awful affair was to take the allegations public, a step that now seemed likely to occur this day, as the magistrate was expected to come within the hour.

James held Sarah's hand, squeezing tight, as Dr. Watkins made his final examination before he would advise Sir John as to Sarah's fitness to speak.

His attention returned as the doctor leaned over her, his expression—as usual—one of a worried frown. "I cannot like it." The doctor straightened, gaze shifting to the table. "Where is the laudanum I prescribed?"

"She did not need it," James asserted from his chair next to her bed.

"So you're the practitioner of medicine now? What gives you the right to change my prescription?"

"I am her husband."

"I fear such an action leaves me with little course than to inform Sir John about your conduct."

James gave an incredulous laugh. "You would have me chastised because I wish my wife to be of unclouded mind so she can refute your baseless claims? You are the one who seems impaired of judgment."

The doctor's eyes narrowed, and he huffed from the room, pausing in the doorway to say, "This is the last time I shall set foot in this house. You have made your contempt for me very clear."

"As you have made yours toward me abundantly clear over the years." James rose and moved toward him. "Is that what this is about? You have sought some form of revenge for my foolish actions when I was a stripling?"

The doctor's eyes flashed as his face tightened.

Shock rippled through his soul as he continued slowly, softly. "That *is* what this is about. You are taking your revenge upon my wife because she is not like my mother. Are you in league with Sir John too? He seems to have a similar view of my mother's sainted standing in society."

"Do not speak about her so." Dr. Watkins stepped back into the hall. "Your mother was a truly great lady. No one can ever hope to take her place. No one."

"I remember the way you were always over here, fussing over her with every kind of tonic and medicine. You used to insist on coming here, against my father's wishes. But you had my mother wrapped around your little finger, didn't you?"

"Don't be ridiculous, boy."

Mama's dulled eyes and lethargy near the end of her life were such contrast to the merry mother of his boyhood. She seemed to fade a little more after each doctor visit instead of getting better, yet she had persisted in a kind of desperate longing to see the man she seemed to regard more highly than her own family, her own husband. The same regard he'd mistakenly thought Sarah had for the vicar. *Forgive me, Lord.*

James drew closer, forcing the doctor's further retreat. "Did you sedate her with such poison as your laudanum too? Mother always wanted your special tonic—or was it *you* she was so keen on?"

"How dare you say such things? I could never poison her. I loved—" He stopped, eyes round with shock, as if he'd realized what he'd admitted.

"You loved my mother?" James's chest tightened. His mother, poor love, a fragile beautiful flower, little regarded by the man she married, sought by a man who had an unholy reverence for her. "You say you loved her, yet you killed her."

"Don't be ridiculous. You were the one who gave her the fatal dose."

"An *accident*, the inquest said." An accident that had precipitated his flight to London and his pledge to go to war, after his father had spoken words James always remembered. He'd never forgotten the words spoken at the inquest either. "An *accident* caused by the settling of the mixture at the bottom of the glass container. Which would not have happened if you had not constantly prescribed her with laudanum she did not need."

Suddenly the shame of that time fell away.

He stabbed a finger at the man's chest. "You were responsible for my mother's death, not I."

The doctor drew back, one step, two, nearing the stairs as if readying to flee. "It was your fault. Yours, not mine. She needed to be sedated because of all your wild and stupid pranks."

"She needed to be alert to be the mother my sister and I needed. How dare you have made such a decision?"

"I dared because someone had to be concerned for her. Your father certainly never cared for her one whit."

"Enough!" The voice roared from the bottom of the stairs.

James glanced down to see his father, an expression of outrage filling his features like he'd never witnessed before.

"You took advantage of my wife when she was most vulnerable. I should have seen it. I half suspected it, but now I know. I shall ensure you are fully convicted by the law, and my son, my poor falsely accused son, is exonerated from all."

James blinked back sudden tears—how unmanly he was becoming—and took swift steps to the doctor.

Watkins scuttled back, but lost his footing on the top stair and fell.

James reached to steady him, but he snatched at thin air.

The man screamed, arms flailing as his body bumped down the stairs, before coming to a halt on the floor with his leg and arm at an unnatural bend. He was still breathing, though, as James raced down to meet him. The doctor's eyes glittered like poison as he glanced up at Father, who had drawn near. "She was never yours, you know."

"Mariah was *always* mine," Father said hoarsely.

Watkins's mouth twisted into a cruel smile. "Then why does your daughter have blue eyes?" he uttered faintly. And with that, he exhaled, his own blue eyes fixed in a rigid stare.

No. *No.* "Doctor?" James dropped to his knees and shook his shoulder. "Wake up."

"Leave him," his father muttered wearily.

"Doctor?" James shook him again, as blood pooled around the back of his head.

No response.

Ice clutched his chest, chased by a rush of nerves. Mouth drying, he swallowed, his gaze lifting to his father. "I think he's dead." He grew vaguely aware of exclamations and movement, but his gaze remained on his father as he pushed to his feet. "Why didn't you deny it, Father? That Mother would—"

"Sir!" Evan hurried to his side, mouth slack with alarm. "I saw it all from the doorway. I was giving entrance to this gentleman." He gestured behind him.

It took a moment for the dots clouding James's vision to finally clear and focus on the figure behind Evan. "Balfour!"

"I came as soon as I got the magistrate's note." Captain Daniel Balfour crouched beside the doctor's body. "I saw him fall too. What calamity has led to this?"

"What calamity has not?" James stood, swaying, blood rushing from his head. Beatrice. His sister, Beatrice. Was she not truly his sister after all?

"Come, sit." Balfour glanced at James's father. "Sir, I believe I address Mr. Langley?"

Father looked up, his face grey, and holding a dangerous sheen.

Dear God, no. "Robert, help Father to the library." His favorite place. His safe place. "Balfour . . ."

The captain looked up from where he was examining Watkins's body. "I'm afraid he hasn't made it."

There went his chance at freedom. Sir John would arrive and James's word would never be believed. His chest constricted as his throat closed.

Run, screamed a tiny little voice. *Run,* just as he had years ago. *Run!*

But . . . no. Sarah needed him to stay. Father needed him to stay. The castle, the village, his honor, God, needed him to stay.

James planted his feet firmly, his glance around the fast-gathering servants putting steel into his spine, his voice. "Quickly, Dawson, get something to cover Dr. Watkins, then Robert, help Father please. I shall need to speak with the magistrate when he arrives."

"You can speak to him now," Sir John growled from the entry. "Good heavens, is that Watkins?" He hurried over to where Balfour now rose from Watkins's side and inspected the body, releasing a mild oath. "Dead, indeed."

Dawson approached hesitantly, holding a large sheet of fabric James recognized as a dustcover. "Sir?"

"Good. Cover him, then stand guard until I have need for you." Sir John's mouth pursed. "How ever did this happen?"

"He fell down the stairs, sir," Balfour said. "I saw it all from the door."

"And you are?" Sir John peered at him.

"Captain Daniel Balfour, sir. And you?"

James marveled at the way his friend could ask a question that could be considered impertinent, yet the crusty man didn't seem to take offense, Balfour's polite good humor edged with soldierly forthrightness.

"I am Sir John Willoughby, the magistrate." He scrutinized the captain. "Are you the man I sent for?"

"Yes, sir. You requested information about Major Langley here. I came as quickly as I could."

"Are there other witnesses to this recent tragedy?"

Balfour nodded, gesturing to Evan. "This man and I were together. The doctor fell backward from the stairs."

"Backward? Was he pushed?"

"Of course not!" James said, as the library door closed behind Robert and his father with a *click*.

"No." Balfour's grey eyes remained cool, his voice calm. "Mr. Langley was several feet from him when this occurred."

Evan nodded quickly. "Several feet. Three, four, possibly five."

"That be so," a female voice called from above. Mrs. Broomhead hurried down the stairs. "I saw and heard it too." She stared pleadingly at James. "Sir, you best tell him."

"Tell me what?" Sir John demanded, face like granite.

James released a long sigh. The time for keeping secrets was done. The day of telling truth had finally arrived.

Chapter 28

". . . And that is what happened." As he finished his rendition of—most of—the events leading up to Watkins's fall, James searched Sir John's expression. Did he believe the truth?

"Aye, that is what I saw," confirmed Mrs. Broomhead.

"And I," said Evan. "The doctor spoke something I could not hear, then just . . . died."

"I saw Langley at least four feet from the other man when he misplaced his step and fell." Balfour's words, his countenance, held the ring of truth.

The magistrate looked hard at James, then scribbled in his journal.

Minutes ticked by, the library's silence punctuated only by the snapping of the fire.

Sir John glanced up, met James's eye. "And you say you were arguing about Mrs. Langley's treatment."

"Yes. I did not feel that his constant use of laudanum was helping assist her recovery, and now she is awake—"

"She speaks?"

"Yes. And is of sound mind." Thank God for His great mercy.

"I will speak to her soon." Sir John gestured impatiently. "Go on."

"When I mentioned she'd woken, Dr. Watkins took exception to the fact that I'd requested Mrs. Broomhead to refrain from administering further doses of laudanum."

Mrs. Broomhead nodded. "That he did, sir."

Sir John glanced at her, gaze hard, his expression inscrutable. "And may I enquire as to what happened next?"

James glanced at his father, bitterness rising at the memories from so long ago. He swallowed. *Lord, help me protect him, yet still speak the truth.* "I realized certain similarities between the doctor's treatment of my wife and that of . . . that of my mother."

Balfour glanced at him with surprise.

James had only ever admitted part of his history to his friend. This next part would be a shock.

"Go on."

"Dr. Watkins treated my mother for a number of years. He was here so often, he was almost considered our resident physician." He glanced again at his father, careful to tiptoe through the past and only share the most necessary details. "My mother was never very strong, but the woman of my youth was a different woman from the one I recalled from younger days. When I was a lad, she was bright and interested in me. She changed in the year preceding the birth of my sister." He almost gagged, thinking of it now, but forced himself to continue. "Which is when Dr. Watkins first started treating her."

"Can you account for what might have caused this change?"

Oh, he could. But there was no way he'd speak of such matters in front of the servants. "I believe my mother became dependent on laudanum. She was always frail, never complaining." Hence the saintlike status she'd taken on. "But she never seemed to get stronger. I was afraid my wife would end up the same."

"And you believe that Watkins took exception to this?"

"Oh, yes, sir," Mrs. Broomhead broke in. "You should have heard him, the doctor that is. He was most upset."

"Thank you, my good woman, that will be all."

"Sir John, if you no longer require Mrs. Broomhead's services, may I request she return upstairs to check on my wife?"

"Of course."

Mrs. Broomhead curtsied and exited, her leave-taking prompting Evan's too, at Sir John's nod.

With the departure of the servants Sir John relaxed and slumped into his seat. "I don't suppose a glass of wine could be had now, could it?"

Perhaps today's interview held a measure of hope after all. James poured the magistrate a glass, and checked if Balfour wished for refreshment, but he waved it off. James moved to his father, who had barely spoken from his slumped position in his armchair, his only sign of life the occasional blink of his eyes. "Father? Is there something I can get you?"

A barely discernible shake of head was his only reply.

James placed a hand on his arm, felt the withered muscle of the once-proud man. "Father, you know I must speak of it."

His father's gaze lifted and met James's with a look of such weariness, then he dipped his head.

"Langley, I am sorry if such questions seem intrusive, but they must be asked." Sir John drank his wine in two swift swallows, then glanced at Balfour. "Is there anything else you wish to testify to, Captain Balfour?"

Grey eyes shifted from the magistrate to James then back again. "You wished to know what I saw, and I have told you. But what I haven't yet spoken of to you concerns the matter of James Langley's transformation. I did not know him when he was a boy, but he shared enough of his story for me to gain an impression of a boy who enjoyed mischief. Not unlike myself, I'll admit." He gave a wry grin. "Perhaps such need for excitement compels us to seek adventure in the army, I don't know. But I do know that when I first met James a number of years ago, he was a wreck, drinking all hours, raking his way through France, actions not unlike many others partook of, especially those who have tried to run from their pasts. I did not know about the sad circumstances of his mother, but his testimony today accords with what he told me when we met again after a particularly horrific battle that left scores of our men dead and injured. He was frightened of death, of what the future beyond held, and knew himself to have sinned. Like the prodigal son, he'd broken his connections back home." Balfour turned to James's father. "He knew he had hurt you, sir, and was so very sorry."

Father glanced at James, his dark eyes as penetrating as ever, holding now a new measure of sadness.

"During the course of that conversation, and several others after it, we discussed matters of life and death, faith and damnation, and Langley made a decision to follow Christ. The change in him was immediate. Gone was the sullen, careless, lewd drunk of a man. In his place was a gentleman whose first thought was of others and how he could help them. He no longer feared death for himself, but instead sought to assist and to save those he could, all the while sharing his new faith as one of the apostles might have done. This transformation was such that the soldiers noticed, and his selfless actions I believe were of great benefit in helping him win his majority. You did hear of the reasons behind that, did you not, sir?"

Sir John inclined his head.

"How any man who risked his neck to save that company of soldiers could then be accused of wanting to murder his wife is beyond me, and I simply cannot understand that anyone could be such a ninnyhammer as to believe it."

Sir John's brows gathered in what looked like indignation.

Balfour's mouth tweaked infinitesimally, then he continued. "His greatest regret was that of how he'd misused his new wife. I have not yet had the pleasure of meeting Mrs. Sarah Langley, but he said he'd mistreated her, that he had resented the fact that it was an arranged marriage and become drunk from his frustration and behaved in a manner in which he was most deeply ashamed. He wished to make amends and I am convinced that, observing his soul sickness over his prior behavior, he would never do anything to hurt her again."

This last was said with such conviction that James was inclined to believe his friend too. If only he had been proved right.

Still, Sir John appeared more convinced. He nodded, and jotted another note in his book, then glanced up, his gaze shifting between James and Balfour once again. "Is that all?"

"I trust that is enough," Balfour said quietly. "I know he is an imperfect man—who amongst us is not?—but he would never willfully threaten his wife's person. He is not that type of man at all."

"That is true," James's father rasped, the words striking James in the heart. Might this tragedy somehow bring reconciliation between them at last?

Sir John shot him a quick look, and scribbled more notes in his black book.

Balfour stood and stretched to his full height. "James, I hope it will not inconvenience you overly if I should request an invitation to stay." His lips curved. "I can understand you may not wish it, especially given as this place is rather small." His brow lifted ironically.

"Of course you must stay. I will speak to Evan——"

"Thank you. No, don't get up. Stay and finish your business here. I am well able to speak to Evan and take care of arrangements. Good day, Mr. Langley, Sir John." He offered a short bow and was gone.

"Well." The magistrate shifted to look at James again. "He seems an impressive young man, and very willing to vouch for you. But I gather he hasn't known you since your return."

"I haven't seen him, no."

"Hmm." He glanced at his notes. "It seems most convenient that he was here just at the precise time."

"He came at the time you requested, sir. It was also the time the doctor had arranged to meet us. You were not far behind to arrive."

"Yes, well, I admit I did see Captain Balfour's carriage arrive." He peered at his book again, his frown reappearing. "Now, Evan said he did not hear the doctor's final words."

"He was standing farther away."

Sir John looked at him expectantly. "I gather they were not ones you wished repeated in front of others?"

James's father twitched his hand in what seemed a signal for James to carry on.

He swallowed and repeated Watkins's claim to have fathered Beatrice.

Sir John blinked. "You are not serious."

"I have barely had time to consider it," James admitted.

"But—" Sir John glanced at James's father. "Forgive me, sir, for asking such a personal question, but did you know?"

The room filled with the deepest silence James had ever known, his nerves straining like the skin on a drum. Had his father known?

"Suspected," he said, in a low voice.

James's heart hitched.

"Mariah became different after Watkins came. She couldn't stand me. I knew I couldn't have fathered the girl."

Just like James had known that Bethy could never have been his. Regret kneaded his stomach.

"So Beatrice is truly not your own child?" Sir John's expression appeared pained.

"No."

James pushed his hand through his hair. "This is not news I wish anyone to know, not even Beatrice."

"Of course not," Sir John said hurriedly. "We shall say nothing. You have my word."

Amid James's appreciation for the magistrate's silence, his cynical side saw another reason for the magistrate's wish to keep things hushed. It would not look good for him to be thought to have spent so many years hankering after a woman whose birth was now shrouded in depraved deceit.

As illegitimate as poor Bethy's own circumstance had been.

"This new development obviously puts a different construction on matters." Sir John snapped his book closed. "I would like to be assured that Mrs. Langley does feel safe, but it appears from all that's occurred that Watkins made such an allegation for his own nefarious reasons."

"Does it follow that I am cleared?"

"As I said, I will speak to Mrs. Langley shortly to be reassured of these things, but if all is satisfactory, then yes, I see no reason to pursue this matter."

Thank You, God. "And Dr. Watkins?"

"I see no need to take this matter further. His death was accidental. And as far as your mother is concerned, I believe it best left in the past, would you not agree?"

"Yes," James said.

"Indeed," his father muttered.

"Then we shall say no more of it. Poor Beatrice," Sir John added, as an aside.

James cleared his throat. "And the body?"

"Watkins?" Sir John sighed. "It's probably easiest for him to remain here until he's ready for burial. I will inform Edwards and instruct the men to take the body to the cellars."

"Thank you, sir."

"I suppose I should go and check through his effects. What a sad business this is. A sad, sad business."

"If you happen to come across any personal items that may have belonged to my mother, letters or the like, I would be obliged—"

"Of course, my boy. Of course." He met James's eyes. "Your mother may not have been the saint we all thought she was, but there is no reason to see her name maligned."

"Thank you."

Sir John nodded. "And as for you?" He tugged on his ear as a wheezy sigh escaped. "Well, I suppose I should offer my regrets for all this has put you through, both today and for all that transpired in the past."

Throat tight, James nodded.

"Take care of your father." He clapped a hand on James's shoulder, and lowered his voice. "He does not look at all well, and it seems we're rather short of doctors around here."

James inclined his head, but amusement at the magistrate's unexpected raillery dissipated at his father's lack of color.

"And now, I shall go to speak to your wife, if that is convenient."

"Of course." James pulled the bell rope and instructed Evan to see if Mrs. Langley could receive visitors.

Sir John's expression held embarrassment. "If she's willing to see me. I sent her a note that was rather less than kind. I hope she will find it in her heart to forgive me in time."

"My wife is very kindhearted."

"I see that now." He bowed. "You have married well."

Sarah stirred, conscious of warmth at her back, a heaviness across her side. She blinked in the midnight shadows, the flicker of light from dying embers of the fire revealing a muscled arm. She stiffened, then relaxed. James. Here. Slumbering beside her again.

She snuggled deeper in the bedclothes, threaded her fingers between his own, marveling at the wonder of what had happened in past days. How miraculous God was. How redemptive His awesome power.

Her interview today with Sir John had proved so much easier than she'd anticipated. Far from feeling judged and shamed, she sensed the magistrate wished to put her at her ease. She'd answered all his questions honestly, admitting to the long months of acrimony she'd sensed from Dr. Watkins, tension she now regretted since his unfortunate end.

She shivered, remembering the awful scream, the panicked shouts. Poor Mrs. Broomhead had been very pale when she'd returned to Sarah's room, admitting there had been an accident and the doctor was badly hurt. Somehow Sarah had found herself praying for him, proof that God had indeed changed her heart, and between that, and all the support and tenderness James had shown, she knew herself very different from the woman who had entered the sea not too long ago.

Sir John had pronounced himself satisfied, had even said that James was blessed to have her as a wife. She'd been so shocked at his approbation that she had even dared ask if he might stay for dinner. He'd refused, saying he had more to do to close the investigation, but promised he would appreciate an invitation soon.

Perhaps she might one day be accepted by the more prominent families in the neighborhood.

Not that their approval really mattered anymore. God's love buoyed her heart. Such love meant He approved of her, and once more she sensed He would use her. She would not forget His redeeming power, nor His lovingkindness. God had bestowed upon her many blessings, blessings that were almost too numerous to count. Not least of all, this man who lay beside her.

James. Her husband, her friend, her love. She knew a little more now what it meant to be deeply loved by him. He had proved so tender, so kind, she had relaxed into his arms and kisses. Her cheeks grew hot thinking of how his passion had provoked hers, flame igniting flame, the weaving of emotions encasing them in a cocoon of togetherness. And afterward, when he'd fallen asleep, she enjoyed this new feeling of delirious comfort, her emotions still dancing while her limbs lay sated.

She knew he loved her now, knew it in every sense of the word. And she loved him, and enjoyed telling him, seeing the effect it had each time she spoke the words. He seemed hardly to believe it. Whatever had caused that initial doubt that he could be loved had been a wound that had struck to his core. It would be her role now, hers and God's, to remind him that he was loved deeply, and she would remain faithful to him.

She nestled closer, drew his arm across her chest. It was truly remarkable how God had worked such tender affection into her heart. It had to be His grace that had helped her finally see that this man was worth holding dear. For so long she had focused on his shortcomings, on his failures, on his sins, rather than see the times he'd tried, the times he'd shown compassion.

Now she could recognize her own failings. If she was capable of contemplating thoughts of self-destruction, of wishing to destroy the very gift of life God gave, then there was very little that James had ever done that could compare to such massive self-delusion. She shivered again, felt him nudge closer.

"Oh Lord," she whispered, her heart too full to close her eyes, "Thank You for Your goodness. I can barely count the ways You have blessed me. Thank You for saving me, for showing James that I needed help. Thank You so much for his forgiveness, for his humility, that he did not treat me as I deserved. Help me to cherish him and be the wife he needs. Help him find his purpose and assurance in You, and heal his relationship with his father. Lord, bless him, and help me be a blessing to him, also. Amen."

"Amen," a deep voice, raspy with sleep, murmured from behind her.

She froze, then joined in his soft laughter. "You, my dear sir, are incorrigible."

"And you, my dearest dear, are simply wonderful."

"Then go to sleep."

"Yes, Mrs. Langley," he mumbled.

She smiled and finally drifted into most blissful rest.

Chapter 29

The next day James watched his two dearest friends as they met in the green drawing room.

His wife curtsied. "It's a pleasure to make your acquaintance, Captain Balfour."

"Please call me Daniel, Mrs. Langley."

"In that case, you must call me Sarah." She smiled. "I have a feeling we shall be good friends." She gestured for him to be seated, then gave James a coquettish glance he never would have guessed she possessed.

He'd enjoy getting to know this wife of his, with her intriguing cheeky qualities and charming quirks.

"I trust you have been well looked after since your arrival?"

"Your staff do you credit," Balfour acknowledged. "For my part, I am very glad that you're feeling so much better. I would not have you extend beyond your strength on my account."

"Thank you." She enquired whether he'd like tea, which Balfour accepted. Sarah rang the bell and instructed Dawson to bring the tea-things soon. When he'd gone, she turned back to Balfour. "I have invited Sir John to join us for our midday meal, but before he arrives, I have told James I am keen to hear your version of his time away."

Balfour tossed James a sly grin. "I'm sure that made him tremble in his boots."

"Indeed it did." She nodded, eyes sparkling at Balfour's laughter and his own snort of amusement.

Who was this saucy creature with her mischievous words and looks? "I will admit that Sarah has me trembling in all situations, as I never quite know what to expect." James gazed at her fondly and reached for her hand.

She stretched out her fingers to meet his and squeezed. "I look forward to surprising you on a regular basis."

Balfour laughed. "I see you have found exactly the right kind of woman you need, Langley. You are blessed indeed."

"I am, that is most certainly true." James stretched out his legs. "Your turn will come soon enough."

"I confess I am in no particular hurry to get leg-shackled."

Sarah leaned forward. "There are no young ladies who have caught your eye?"

"I have scarcely had time to think on such things," Balfour admitted. "I have been in London, and now have business further north. Apart from seeing my sister and niece, I have no further plans."

"But when the right lady comes along . . ." Sarah's lips curved to a quarter moon.

James pointed to Sarah with his free hand. "Then you best be quick to snap her up."

Balfour inclined his head. "I bow to your superior expertise."

"About the first time he's ever done that," James murmured as an aside to Sarah.

She chuckled, the door opened, and Dawson appeared with the tea. The next minutes passed in her pouring and serving the tiny cakes Cook evidently thought worthy for such an agreeable guest as Captain Daniel Balfour, who had made no bones about his appreciation of last night's meal.

"Daniel, I trust that you will consider yourself invited to stay any time you are this way again."

How much the lady of the house she seemed. And how wonderful to see the two get on so well.

"Thank you. I will certainly take you up on that offer."

She glanced at James, then back at Balfour. "Now, I would dearly enjoy hearing about your time away."

Balfour shared about how he and James had first connected. It was fascinating to watch his wife's expressions as she learned more of his history and his efforts during the war.

She stared at him, eyes wide. "I did not realize the extent of your exploits."

"Ah, there is more you still need to learn." James glanced at Balfour. "I am not sure how much you heard yesterday, so forgive me if my story repeats what you've heard."

Balfour leaned back in his seat and gestured for him to continue. "Please, I'm all ears."

Very well, then. "Nineteen years ago, when I was a lad of seventeen, my exploits were the talk of the village. My father despaired of me, as I had little interest in the castle or estate, and my mother had long succumbed to a malaise."

He glanced apologetically at Balfour, then shared yesterday's revelations with his wife.

"That is why you think Dr. Watkins did not like me?" Her eyes grew troubled. "Because he thought I was a poor replacement for your mother?"

"To him, anyone would have been," James admitted, before sipping his tea. "Of course, he is the only one who thought such things, and that because of an unnatural obsession. You must know that my father and I are so thankful for your presence."

"Your father's appreciation I have seen but rarely," she said wryly.

"Please pardon my intrusion on such a personal family matter, but I fear I must contradict you there," Balfour interrupted. "James's father and I had a very pleasant conversation this morning at breakfast, and in the course of our talk he admitted just how indebted he was to you, not only for the sake of his son's happiness and health, but also for the way you have cared for the house."

"Oh!" She pinked with pleasure. "Forgive me, but he had never been particularly open with his commendation."

"He shall no doubt be remedying that the longer he spends time with you." He lifted his teacup in salute.

"Very suave." James eyed his friend, who laughed. "And true, my dear, very true." He lifted her hand and pressed his lips to her knuckles, and her smile drew his own. Last night had been a revelation in many ways, and he was so glad she was open to his displays of affection. In Sarah, he had found a woman he could trust to be his, and he be hers, with no shadow of uncertainty.

Balfour's smile held satisfaction as he regarded them. "It is most wonderful to see how God can restore the brokenhearted, and free those who have been bound to their pasts."

"Most wonderful," Sarah said, nestling closer to James's side.

Later, they met Father and Sir John in the dining room for a light repast, the tension of past encounters having eased away. Whether in deference to Sarah's presence or not, little mention was made of the doctor's demise, for which James couldn't help but be grateful. He was grateful, too, that Father's color was much improved. Though his conversation rang astringent as ever, at least he had the grace to speak kindly to Sarah and Balfour from his position of head of the table. Both he and Sir John seemed to have taken to his friend, but that was part of Balfour's easygoing appeal. The man could tell stories that had them all in stitches, then have them sobering the next minute to contemplate a truth raw and real.

The conversation flowed easily afterward, when they joined his father in the library.

Balfour gestured to the wooden box sitting in the corner of the room, now cleaned and polished by Evan. "What is that?"

James exchanged a rueful look with Sarah, then moved to retrieve what they had dug up several weeks ago. "We attempted to go treasure hunting in the tunnels below." He placed the box on the table between them.

Balfour cocked his head. "Treasure hunting?"

"Some Roman artefacts have been found here." Sarah smoothed her skirt, sighed. "We thought we'd found more, but . . ."

"May I?" Balfour asked.

James opened the trunk. "Sadly, nothing but wood fragments." James lifted several of the pieces.

"But why would such things be in a box?" Balfour asked.

Why indeed. Buried with such care, as well.

Sir John cleared his throat. "You are sure that is all?"

"Yes," James said patiently.

"Hmm."

James studied the box again. The depth inside did not quite match the exterior dimensions. His chest tightened. Was there a false bottom to it? He removed the remaining remnants and ran his hands over the wood, feeling for something, anything, that might signify a difference, pressing carefully, shaking it gently.

"What is it, Son?"

"Did you hear that rattling noise?" James shook it again. "There's something more inside."

"Here." Sarah passed him a paperknife.

He slid it carefully around the internal bottom layer, doing his best not to damage the wooden sides. Dirt-encrusted crevices demanded the knife be wiped and wiped again. When he judged he'd removed as much as he could, he lifted the box and turned it upside down. Centuries of muck fell to the table, along with another wooden piece that had evidently been dislodged by his cleaning. Then the bottom wooden layer crashed to the table, along with an abundance of other small round wood-like disks.

Sarah picked up the layer of wood which had served as the box's false bottom. Her breath hitched.

"What is it, my dear?"

She showed it to his father who frowned, examining the article carefully.

"It was such a busy time that I did not see it properly before, and I cannot be completely certain, but . . ." She rubbed it with her forefinger, and the faintest of inscriptions appeared. "I think this is a writing tablet."

"A what?"

"Can you bring that lantern nearer so we can see it more clearly?"

James obeyed. By now Balfour and Sir John had drawn closer.

"See this?" Sarah pointed to the marks. "I am sure that my uncle talked about something not dissimilar that had been unearthed from other parts of the Roman Empire."

Sir John nodded. "I have seen an ancient writing tablet before in a London museum."

"Another Roman treasure." Father rubbed his hands with glee. "How fortunate we are, lass, to have you in our midst."

James patted his shoulder. "It may not be worth very much, but it's still fascinating that it was found beneath our home."

Sarah moved back to the box, her small fingers carefully sifting the remnants. She fished out a small circular piece. She held it out to the light, then gently wiped it with her finger. "This might be more to your liking." She passed it to James.

"This?" Eyebrows aloft, as he held it close to the light.

"That." She nodded.

"What is it, ma'am?" Balfour asked.

"It will take some cleaning, but I think you'll find what looks like broken bits of wood are in fact Roman coins."

"Truly?"

She tugged off her glove and gently picked at the rusty dirt with her nail.

Sure enough, the faintest inscription of letters and a bust could be seen. She flipped it over.

Here was a different image, a man holding something in his hand.

She handed it carefully to James. "I cannot be certain, but this could be one of the more important coins my uncle spoke of. A coin of the emperor Hadrian."

"Truly?"

"We shall not know for certain, not until the coins are cleaned, but I would think these are certainly worth something."

"Indeed," Sir John said. "I have collector friends who would pay a pretty penny for such things."

"Enough for a new roof?" Father asked.

"I can write to them and see." Sir John's smile grew wry, as he picked up one of the specimens. "Mind you, the coins I saw were in much better shape when I saw them."

"How does one clean coins like this?" James rubbed it with his thumb.

"Lemon juice, a soft bristled brush," Sarah said. "Really, the person who would know best how to undertake the cleaning is my uncle."

James glanced at his father, and seeing his nod, said, "We should invite him here."

"Yes." Sarah's smile at him caught his heart. "The time for estrangement is done."

It was not too many months later when Sarah waited anxiously at the front door, James at her side, as a carriage trundled up the daffodil-lined drive. She smiled up at him, anticipation filling her pores, as he picked up her hand and kissed it.

"I like seeing this side of you," he murmured in her ear.

"The side where I run around working to get everything polished and clean?"

"I was going to say I like seeing your excitement, but polished and clean works also."

She laughed. Hopefully his father was looking forward to this visit too. He'd said he was but . . .

The carriage drew nearer, the figures inside smiling and waving.

Sarah felt ready to burst from her skin.

It slowed to a stop, Robert opened the door, and a guest made her smiling descent.

"Beatrice!" Sarah wrapped her friend in a hug. "Oh, how I have missed you."

"And I you."

The moment held a myriad of answered prayers. Thank God Beatrice's father had deigned to receive his daughter and son-in-law at last. Thank God matters had improved here at the castle after the past few months of stress and strife.

It had taken time for the village to come to terms with the shocking death of Dr. Watkins, which Sir John upheld was a tragic accident when he'd misjudged the castle's stairs. It had taken time for certain neighbors, like the Barnstaples, to follow Sir John's lead in inviting Sarah and James to their houses for dinners and the like. But she had found a place to belong, here in this grand pile called Langley House. How good God was.

This was proved a short time later when the older gentleman received his daughter at last, holding her in an embrace that had James wipe away a tear. She'd nestled closer to his side, heart full at the welcome to one once deemed a prodigal daughter. How gracious God was, redeeming lives, redeeming families, redeeming hope in this once-crumbling castle.

"I admit that I scarcely recognize the place," Beatrice said later, when they were ensconced in Sarah's yellow drawing room, drinking tea, the sleeping pup in her basket at Sarah's feet. There was something so soothing about listening to a little puppy's snores.

Beatrice gazed around the room. "You have worked wonders."

"We are not quite there yet, but it will help to have the money to afford some more repairs," Sarah admitted.

"See? I told you there was treasure." Beatrice's blue eyes sparkling at her over the rim of her teacup.

Sarah didn't *quite* remember things that way, but no matter.

Aunt Patricia and Uncle Loftus had visited six weeks ago, the promise of Roman artefacts apparently seeing them find enough Christian charity to overlook her independence and marriage and condescend to visit. She smiled, remembering her uncle's exclamations of "Bless my soul!" as the rusty Roman coins were cleaned to reveal their true value, which had soon drawn Sir John's magnanimous offer to write to his collector friends and see if this held interest. It had, and while the sum raised might not have proved enough to pay for a new roof, it certainly was enough to avoid having to sell off any more land.

"It's also helped to finally have the likes of Mrs. Copley and Dawson willing to fulfill my orders."

Beatrice nibbled her slice of cake. "They have neither of them been inclined to go out of their way to help newcomers."

"I am not sure how long one remains a newcomer," Sarah said with a wry smile. "In September I will have been here for two years, but I suspect they will only truly accept one who is born here."

"Which is peculiar, considering neither of them were."

"It's a good thing that people can change."

"How true that is." Beatrice placed her plate on the small mahogany table. "Why, I have never known my brother to be so happy. You have certainly done wonders with him."

"I believe that it is God who has worked wonders with him. And with me." Their two hearts had grown closer over time. Such different people, with such contrasting backgrounds and personalities, could only knit together so well under God's masterful touch.

"Well, regardless, I am grateful for the change, in both James and in my father. As for their kindness to me, well, I have never seen the like."

"Perhaps their thoughtfulness is helped along by your interesting condition." Sarah glanced at her friend's less-than-svelte midsection.

"Perhaps." Beatrice laid a hand on her swollen waist. "Oh, I am glad those first few months are behind me. I remember what it was like to be feeling green and wishing to cast up my accounts every morning."

"You poor thing," Sarah sympathized. Thank heavens that was not the case for her.

"Ah, but not too poor. How can one be when one is rich in love?"

"You are the repository of much wisdom," Sarah said with a teasing smile.

"I am glad you finally recognize such things after all this time. I am, after all, your oldest and dearest and *wisest* friend."

Their weeklong stay boosted her spirits, as had the acceptance she felt she now received in the village and among their neighbors. Sir John Willoughby's approval helped, as did Mr. Edwards's, although he said it was her willingness to help the villagers as much as anything else. "For they remember your kindness to poor Bethy, and recall how devastated you were at that time. They have respect for one who has shown great compassion for their own, so to speak."

The reference to Bethy still ached, and she made regular visits to her little grave. A rosebush of pink blooms now grew there, planted by her husband, so Mr. Edwards said. It was just another way James had shown he loved her.

The pain of losing Bethy would never fully disappear, but it had been tempered with being loved, and as a result of that love she would bear a child of her own before the winter. She hoped to tell James very soon. She would not have him making any more comments about her love of food, as he was getting in the habit of doing.

A knock came at the door of her golden room, and at her call of *enter*, her husband passed across the threshold.

"Ah, my dear, you are here. Busy at your embroidery again, I see."

She held up a cushion she was readying for the dining room. "It heartens me to see how much you appreciate my humble skills."

"I definitely appreciate all your skills. Particularly this one." He placed his hands on either side of her chair and leaning close to give her a slow, deep kiss, much to the puppy's displeasure, as she gave a strong "wuff" of objection.

"James!" she laughed and pushed him away. "You mustn't disturb the baby," she said, stroking the puppy's head.

"I wonder what will you say when we have a child of our own," he commented, before peering at her more closely.

She looked at the threads in her hand to avoid his gaze.

"Sarah? Why do you have that look in your eyes?"

"What look?" Surely he couldn't tell?

"That look. Like you have a secret."

"I cannot help the look I have," she protested, smiling as his lips slipped to her neck.

"I am always the biggest fan of your looks, except the one that makes me fearful you will scold me. But I cannot help but wonder . . . is there something you wish to tell your husband?"

She drew in a breath, put the embroidery aside. "Perhaps you might accompany me on a walk to the garden."

"If it means I can learn the reason behind your enigmatic smile, then I am most certainly in favor of a walk."

They moved outside. It was a fine May day, and the roses in the walled garden were in full bloom. She drew near one of the freshly planted pinks and inhaled its delicate scent. "How lovely."

"How lovely, indeed." He lifted her hand and kissed it.

Delight curled the edges of her heart. How could she have not recognized that James was another soul in need for affection. Now, he seemed to touch her every chance he could, bestowing kisses or offering tokens of his regard, all of which spoke of his love.

He'd surprised her yesterday with this new rose bush, Common Provence, which had numerous light-pink petals and the most wonderful fragrance. "I thought you might like to see a constant reminder of my love," he'd said, adding, "especially as it's your birthday."

"You remembered?"

"How could we not celebrate Mrs. Langley's special day?"

Now James wrapped his arms around her, and she leaned back against his chest, savoring the sunshine and the tinkle of the repaired fountain. How lovely it was to relax and revel in such restoration.

"Oh, pardon me, Mr. James, Mrs. Langley." The gardening boy came from behind some bushes and picked up his cart and shears. "I almost didn't see you there."

"Good afternoon, Joseph," she said.

"Would you like me to pick some roses for you, Mrs. Langley?" he asked. "I was just going to collect some lavender leaves for Mrs. Copley. She wants to make some pillows for—" His eyes rounded. "Sorry, madam. I'm not supposed to say."

"Then we'll pretend we did not hear you, won't we?" she said to James.

"Hear what?" James grinned. "You can collect your lavender now if you like, Joseph. Mrs. Langley and I are going to enjoy the sunshine while we can."

The boy nodded and drew out his shears and snipped at the heads of the purple flowers, chatting all the time. "My da says we're in for some more storms soon. He can feel it in his bones, or so he says. It's why I needed to collect the lavender now, while it's dry, or so Mrs. Copley says."

"It's best to not cross that woman unless absolutely necessary," James murmured.

"Oh, I think she's slowly improving." At least she had seemed so just yesterday, when her wide-eyed glance had bounced between Mrs. Broomhead and Sarah and Sarah's thickening middle, before her congratulations had stuttered out. The housekeeper's delight had been unexpected, and she'd sworn to keep the secret as long as necessary. Perhaps in making James happy, and potentially providing him with an heir, Sarah had finally found the key to being accepted.

"Got all I need now." Joseph dipped his head and gathered his supplies before making his exit.

James looked at the gate where he'd disappeared. "He's a friendly little fellow."

"And such a hard worker. I'm sure he keeps Mr. Meeks and Mr. Derry on their toes."

"Meeks has definitely never worked so hard since Joe came along. But then, many things have changed for the better in the past year or so."

At times happiness had seemed so far beyond hope, beyond her strength. But now, to see what had seemed impossible become real . . . God was good. So very, very good.

She glanced over to see a tiny weed flower growing in the cracks of the stone wall.

"What has you so fixated, my dear?"

"I was merely looking at the tiny flower here, growing against the wall. I suppose I've always thought myself not dissimilar."

He shifted and picked the tiny mauve star-shaped flower and deposited it in her hands. "Small and yet hardy, stouthearted, and sturdy?"

"If by that you mean stubborn enough to exist where I'm not supposed to, then yes."

"If you suppose yourself a weed, that simply will not do. You are infinitely more precious, and I would have you put such foolish notions from your head at once. I do not see you as that, not at all."

"What do you see me as?" she asked shyly.

"Of far greater worth than this rose." He moved to the garden bed protected by the wall and plucked a creamy one. "You are sweet and pure to look at, a restful, reassuring sight, faithful year after year." He stroked the petals. "You possess so few thorns that one can almost forget you are a rose, but when one truly gets to know you"—he drew closer—"one can sense your subtle perfume, the way you fragrance everything around you with your kindness and good works."

Her eyes filled with tears.

"And when one is as privileged as I am . . ." He lifted his hand to gently trace her cheek. "One can know your cheek is as soft and velvety as these petals, and you, like this rose, possess a heart of gold." He offered it to her.

She saw the golden yellow depths of the petals within. Petals yet unfurled, but with time they'd bloom fully and share their welcome scent.

He bent his head and dropped the lightest of kisses on her lips, then wrapped her in a warm embrace.

The dizzying sensations swamping her senses buckled her knees.

He drew her to one of the wooden seats overlooking the pond, brushing it off before encouraging her to sit.

"I fear you are full of flattery, and scarcely know what is true."

"Oh, I know what is true." He sobered, eyes intent on hers. "I see her standing here before me. Someone honest, and faithful, and good. And I thank God that my father had the sense to see what I first could not. You have no idea how grateful I am to him for you."

"I have some idea." She wound her hand through the crook of his arm, drawing closer. "I am thankful for my loyal husband, that he is someone who understands the depths of pain and the heights of love. Not that I am glad that you have suffered, but you found purpose in your pain."

"I understand." He squeezed her hand gently. "When we're in the depths of midnight's pain and darkness, we cannot see that God is still working goodness for tomorrow. But He is, isn't He?"

"Yes." *Thank You, Lord.*

"What we have endured together has forged us closer."

"Forged through fire."

After another delightful moment, he drew back, eyes serious. "Now, Mrs. Langley, I believe you were going to fill me in on a secret?"

"Was I?"

"Yes," he said firmly.

"Very well," she said with a sigh, begging her lips to not tilt up and give her away.

"Is something wrong?"

She captured his face in her hands, gently tracing the scar on his cheek. "I'm afraid . . ." She sighed again.

"Afraid of what? What is it? What can I do?"

"It's what you've already done, James."

His brow creased. "What did I do? Just say the word, and I will undo it."

Another exhalation. "I'm afraid you can't undo this. Not that I'd want it undone."

"I don't understand."

She took pity on him. "How do you feel about a little Langley?"

"A little . . ."

His eyes rounded as she placed his hand on her midsection. "A little Langley," she repeated.

"I'm going to be a father?"

"Yes." She could feel the joy in her heart explode from her smile.

"Truly?"

"Truly."

"Oh my dear. How *glad* you have made me." He stole another kiss.

She felt herself blush. "Stop it. Someone will see."

"So what if they do? I'm not embarrassed to admit I love my wife. And such a sentiment will not exactly come as a surprise to anyone around here."

No. He'd definitely made his affection plain. The servants, the villagers, all knew.

"I love you, my dearest Sarah. My oh-so-clever, oh-so-capable, oh-so-charming wife."

"I know." And she did. It was warm assurance in her bones, as sure as the ancient stones that surrounded them now, that would remain here for hundreds of years to come.

Assurance that was grounded in trust, trust that was borne out of love, love that had first flowed from a most merciful God.

Acknowledgments

This book was an easy book to write, but a *hard* book to see published, and there were many times along the way I was tempted to give up. I'm so grateful to all those who believed with me to see this Gothic-flavored story of redemption finally see the light.

So, thank you God for Jesus Christ, whose death on a cross means forgiveness is possible for anyone who dares to believe. Thank you for the peace, hope, and life-giving purpose this brings.

Huge thanks to my husband, Joshua, for believing in and supporting my writing dream, and the hugs when I was in tears. Thank you Caitlin, Jackson, Asher, and Tim for understanding why your mum talks as if imaginary people and problems are real. Thank you to my extended family and friends, in particular my beta readers, Roslyn Weaver, and fellow Australian author Jenny Glazebrook, and my parents Kay and David for their constant encouragement.

Thanks to my agent Tamela Hancock Murray and the team at Kregel Publications for allowing me to write books that can be considered unapologetically Christian. Thanks to my editors, Janyre and Christina, for helping me to shape this story into what it is today, and the wonderful designers who make such beautiful covers that always get high praise.

Thanks also to the authors and bloggers and influencers who have endorsed, and encouraged, and opened doors along the way. You are truly appreciated.

And thank *you*, wonderful readers, for choosing to read this book (and hopefully others of mine also!). Thank you for buying my books and sharing the love with others through your kind reviews and your encouraging messages and emails.

I hope you enjoyed James and Sarah's story. God bless you.

Author's Note

I don't know about you, but I don't mind reading a bit of Gothic-inspired fiction, and it was fun to turn my hand to a story involving a wallflower, a rogue haunted by his past, and a crumbling castle by the North Sea. I took inspiration for Langley House from the amazing ruins of Dunstanburgh Castle, Northumberland, complete with Rumbling (Rumble) Churn and Egyncleugh Tower, while also "furnishing" my castle with the chapel from Alnwick, and the King's Hall from Bamburgh Castle. (I've always enjoyed architecture!) *The Romance of Northumberland* by Arthur Granville Bradley, published in 1908, proved a fascinating resource for the castle and surrounds.

As with *Dusk's Darkest Shores*, I based the sickness James suffered from on the experiences of English soldiers who fought in Walcheren and the Peninsula. Walcheren fever saw an army of forty thousand men decimated through an unknown (and therefore largely untreatable) disease that seemed to combine the worst of malaria, typhoid, typhus, and dysentery. Many of these sufferers were then shipped to Portugal and Spain, where they continued to fight, even though greatly weakened, and some carried their disease back to England, where it infected family members. Resources included the 1809 *Letters from Flushing* by an anonymous "Officer of the 81st Regiment," with eye-opening details I've referenced in James's account of his time in this part of the Dutch coast.

Laudanum is a cinnamon-flavored opium tincture made with 10% opium and 90% alcohol, and was used as a painkiller in Regency times.

Cheaper than beer or wine, it was affordable for all, usable as a sleeping aid, and able to be prescribed for everything from colds to cardiac disease and women's "hysterias," in both adults and children. In later Victorian times, a potion known as Godfrey's Cordial (also known as Mother's Friend) which contained opium, water, and treacle, was often given to children to keep them quiet! Laudanum was an addictive substance, and overdosing was not uncommon, either by accident or intention.

The mid-1700s establishment of the British Museum and the discovery of a Roman fort and associated remains in Northumberland in the 1790s suggest that there was growing interest in Roman and other antiquities, so I loved incorporating a treasure hunt to help the castle's coffers.

I really enjoyed writing this marriage-of-convenience story about a "bad boy who becomes good" and pray that James and Sarah's redemption touches hearts, and that the message of forgiveness encourages us all to trust God and His ways. Forgiveness and learning to trust others who have wronged us is not always easy, but it is essential if we are to live in relationship with others—especially if we are married. As I said, I know this isn't easy, but asking God's help to forgive others and praying for God to bless them can help soften our hearts to those who have hurt us. If this is something you struggle with, please know that I understand, and you're in my prayers too.

For more behind-the-book details, sneak peeks of forthcoming books, and to sign up for my newsletter, please visit me at www.carolynmiller author.com.

REGENCY BRIDES
A Legacy *of* Grace

Clean and wholesome romance you'll swoon over!

REGENCY BRIDES

A Promise *of* Hope

REGENCY BRIDES
Daughters *of* Aynsley

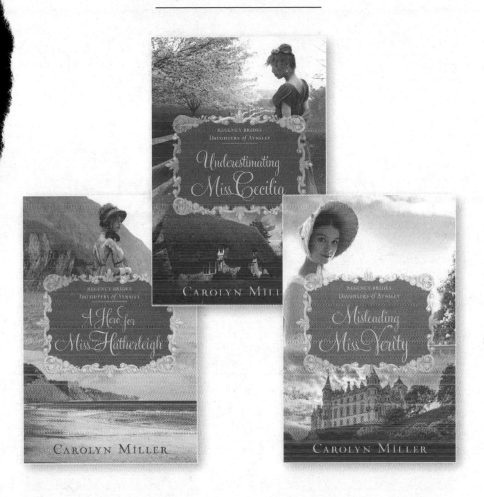

"*[Miller's] inclusion of faith issues with an authentic portrayal of Regency society will continue to delight her fan base.*" —Publishers Weekly

KREGEL
PUBLICATIONS